THE FIRE PEOPLE

'Once more he takes the bare bones of history
and clothes it with the flesh and blood of living,
vibrant people. He conjures up the sight,
sounds and smells of a period which is of
tremendous significance for us all'
                                    South Wales Echo

'The author combines the disciplines of
historian and novelist—to the advantages of
both'   *Sunday Telegraph*

'Mr. Cordell is first and foremost a storyteller,
and his version of these events never lacks in
liveliness, the narrative energy pushing on
from page to page'   *Guardian*

'Colourful'   *Daily Mirror*

'Rousing historical novel . . . the terrible story
springs to life under his pen'   *Daily Telegraph*

'Very well done . . . vigorous, effective and
high-coloured'   *Financial Times*

'Almost too rich in brilliantly realised
characters . . . as a moving record of violent
times, this book must be in the running for
high honours'   *Tribune*

'Compulsive'   *The Observer*

'As a historian of this particular period Mr.
Cordell can have few equals'   *The Times*

The Fire People

Alexander Cordell

CORONET BOOKS
Hodder and Stoughton

Printed and bound in Great Britain for Hodder and Stoughton paperbacks, a division of Hodder and Stoughton Ltd., Mill Road, Dunton Green, Sevenoaks, Kent TN12 2YA (Editorial Office: 47 Bedford Square, London WC18 3DP) by Richard Clay Ltd., Bungay, Suffolk

ISBN 0-340-17403-X

For Richard Lewis,
whom they called Dic Penderyn,
unjustly hanged.

... As to the men I accuse, I do not know them, I have never seen them, I have no resentment or animosity towards them. They are for me merely entities, spirits of social maleficence. And the act which I perform here is only a revolutionary means of hastening the revelation of truth and justice. I have but one passion—that of light. This I crave for the sake of humanity, which has suffered so much ...

Zola

I am indebted to Mr. John Collett, F.L.A., and Mr. Michael Elliott, F.L.A., both of Newport Public Library, for making available to me numerous books of research and rare documents. To Mr. Tom Whitney of Merthyr Tydfil Library I am grateful for nineteenth-century maps and other references, and to Miss M. E. Elsas, the Glamorgan County Archivist, for assistance in historical locations. To these, as to Mr. A. Leslie Evans and other historians, I offer my thanks.

Certain vital papers have come to light during my research which, lost for a hundred and forty years, are valuable evidence concerning the life and times of Dic Penderyn; these new facts have a direct bearing on the Merthyr Rising and are important enough to be included as an appendix to the book.

I wish to acknowledge the assistance given by the Departmental Record Officer of the Home Office in tracing these documents.

1

THERE was more commotion going on than a Tipperary bath night.

Big Bonce was clogging around with Lady Godiva; Curly Hayloft, as bald as an egg, was doing a bull-fight with Tilly; Skin-Crone, the cook, was beating time to the shriek of the fiddle, and the navvy hut was alive with dancers of Kerry and County Mayo.

And as Gideon played he saw in his near-blind stare the twenty beds, the labour-dead sleepers straight off shift and the dark eyes of the Welsh girl who watched him from a seat in the corner. Someone turned up the lamps and he now saw more clearly as he fiddled out the old Irish reel: the coloured waistcoats of the navvies he saw, the violent disorder of the blankets, the mud-stained jerkins and hobnail boots, the soaked dresses of the wives hung up to dry: all this he saw partly by vision and partly by memory, from the days before he was blind. And he knew that in a shadow by the table old Peg Jarrotty, the wake corpse, would be hanging by a rope under his arm-pits, a broom under his chin, and a pint of home-brew slopping in his fist. Hooked on his chest would be the coffin plate—'Peg Jarrotty, Wexford: died June 14th, 1830.'

'There's me wee darling!' cried Tilly, dancing up in a sweeping of skirts. 'Won't you raise us a smile, Peg Jarrotty, for the look on your face makes me miserable to death!' and she tipped him under the chin.

Vaguely, Gideon wondered if it was respectful to the dead, but he played on, smiling: this is what they wanted, he reflected; this was their religion.

Belcher Big Tum came up, all sixteen stones of him. 'Sure, hasn't he drained that pint yet? It's the same stuff he used to sink down the Somerset Arms, isn't it?'

'It is not!' shouted Lady Godiva. 'He never touched that dish-water without a two-inch livener, isn't that right, me lovely dead fella? Shall I lace it up with a drop o' hard stuff?' And she stroked his face.

'Can't you show some respect for the dead?' asked Jobina, the Welsh girl in the corner, and she rose, her dark eyes sweeping around the dancers.

Gideon lowered his fiddle; the noise of the hut faded.

Jobina said: 'I can stand the randies and the heathen language, but I can't abide the wakes. Do you have to act like animals?'

'She's asking for a filling up again,' said Moll Maguire.

'You leave the Irish to the Irish, woman!' shouted Tilly.

'And the Welsh to the Welsh, and remember it!' Jobina put her hands on her hips. 'Irish, you call yourselves? Dancing around a corpse, and him hanging from the ceiling with a broom under his chin? Don't tell me they do that in Kerry.' She strolled the room, looking them up and down. 'You've got him like a pig on hooks. Have him down tonight before I'm back off shift or I'm taking it to Foreman. It's bad enough having to eat with live Irish without sleeping with dead ones.'

'Heavens above!' gasped Tilly. 'Did you hear that? She's asking for a doin' . . .'

'Ach,' said Belcher testily, 'we're not after woman-fighting. If the wee Welsh bitch wants old Jarrotty down, I say let's give it.'

'Why give her anything? She's a foreigner here,' cried Tilly, breasting up.

'You're the foreigners,' replied Jobina, 'or isn't this the county of Glamorgan?'

Big Bonce swung to Gideon, crying, 'What do you say, fiddler—you're Welsh, too, aren't you?'

'The fella's as Irish as me, aren't ye, son?' Moll Maguire now, with her arm around Gideon's waist; she was tall for a woman, yet only inches above his shoulder. Gideon smiled

12

with slow charm, saying:

'It's no odds to me, Irish—I'm only the fiddler, and you pay well.'

'You should be ashamed of yourself!' said Jobina, turning away.

'And why should he?' demanded Skin-Crone, the cook from the other end of the hut: she was sitting astride a chair stirring up a cauldron for the midnight supper, and the steam was going up like a witch's brew. 'When are we putting wee Jarrotty down, then?' she asked.

'He's having a decent Catholic service the moment we find his leg.'

'Haven't ye found it yet, then? Wasn't it buried under the fall?'

'How did it happen?' asked Gideon, and Belcher said:

'He was barrowing the big stuff on the dram-road slope, with the mule wagging along the line as if tomorrow would do, but little Jarrotty slipped, ye see, and the dram came down. The dram came down, then the mule and then the muck, and he was under six tons of the stuff when we dug him out.'

'And he'd only got one leg,' said Moll.

'Where did the other one get to?' asked Lady Godiva, scratching.

'Search me—the mule must have eaten it.'

The talk went on, the drinking was heavy. Gideon leaned against the hut wall and imagined the stars above Taibach, for this was his country. The wind moved over the heath and he smelled the heather and a tang of sulphur from the works, and he raised his face instantly to the salt of the sea-drift, which he loved.

'Here's your pay, fiddler, the dancing's stopped,' said Belcher, and pressed a shilling into his hand; Gideon took it, and did not reply. Instead, he lifted his head higher to taste the sea-drift, and Jobina followed his sightless gaze to the open window, threw her red shawl over her shoulders for the cropping and wandered towards him.

'What's your name?'

He straightened to her. 'Gideon Davies.'

13

Bending, she pulled at a red stocking. 'What the hell are ye doing in a place like this?'

'What are any of us doing?' he asked.

'You local?'

He said evenly: 'I used to be—Taibach.'

'Welsh, eh?'

He smiled at her, and she added: 'It's a pleasure to be civilised, even if ye have to live with the heathen.'

'They're not so bad,' he said. 'Give me Irish in preference to the foreigners.'

Beyond the vision of her unseen face he saw the windows of Aberafon winking at the moon, the square thatch of Rhigos where he stole from the orchard: he smelled again the sulphur of the night wind coming up from Briton Ferry and saw the baying brilliance of the night when the molten iron flashed on the bungs of Dowlais. The white-hot bucketings of Skewen and Swansea were in his bedroom of childhood, and he would lie awake listening to the cries of the mules under the whips in the stack-yards and along the dram-roads of Morriston. There was the black shine of the cassocks in the C. of E. the bearded thunderings of Ianto Nonconform in the little red-brick chapel off the Vernon Arms, and the brown arms in summer of the girl he knew but whose name he had forgotten.

'You play good,' said the Welsh girl, watching him.

'Thanks.'

'Where did you catch it, then?'

'Taibach Copper Works.'

'That bloody place, cauldrons and chopped colliers.'

The navvies had stopped carousing now and were feeding on the bench: the pot Skin-Crone was serving from contained many different foods: vegetables which she had stolen from Taibach market made the slush. The meats were attached by strings, and each portion she pulled out with care and gave it to the owner: half a hare for Belcher, a born poacher; two pig's trotters tied together for Curly Hayloft, a sheep's head between Mercy Merriman and Betsy Paul, Dick of the Iron Hand's woman, who was visiting. Crone and Moll shared an ox-tail they had blackmailed from a butcher with two wives;

14

Blackbird feasted on a pound of ribs of beef, which he had bought, being honest. All had wooden spoons, and these they dipped excitedly into the pot, blowing and gasping at the steam and elbowing each other for room.

'B'ant you eating, fiddler?' asked Belcher.

'No, I'm just off to Mamie Goldie,' replied Gideon.

'Who's Mamie Goldie?' asked Moll. 'She don't sound decent.'

'She is clean,' said Gideon instantly.

'By God, that's a change. You lodge with her?' asked the Welsh girl.

He nodded and she looked again into his face, seeing the telltale tattoo of the furnace grit, yet his eyes appeared untouched by the blast: bright blue, they shone in his brown face.

'How did you collect it?'

He could have gone into the detail, but the wounds were too new to his soul. He could have told her how the copper exploded in a damp mould; that Mike Halloran had just come into the casting-house and stopped for a ladle in front of him, so he took most of it. Also, Popo Hopkin, aged seventy, due to retire in three weeks, took some, too; and screamed and went in circles with his body on fire as the copper bit deep. Halloran died in shrieks they heard as far up as the Brombil dram-road. Strangely, for all his age, Popo did not die, but lived on the black shadows of his forge-sided cottage, nurtured by Company respectability—come in, boys, see what we're doing for Popo Hopkin. Maintained by a devoted wife on four and six a week pension, Popo lived where the children could not see him. And a disability like this do have a bit of compensation—apart from the four and six—he used to say to the Quakers who visited, faces averted—for you can't appear shocking in a two-ale bar and you eat that much less with only half a mouth.

In his two years of blindness Gideon had bred great shafts of hope that wounded despair. The comradeship of ear and nose had constructed a new world in his darkness: and touch, a vital sense left to him, completed the resurrection from self-pity. Now he said lightly:

15

'There is nothing to tell—the mould was wet, and it spat.'

The navvies quarrelled at the table in good-natured banter and oaths, and Betsy Paul shouted: 'You'm a fine fiddle, boy. You tried us up in Pontstorehouse?'

'He do not play in cellars,' said Jobina.

'The money's right in Merthyr, mind—we got fiddlers and organ-grinders, and my Dick Llaw-Haearn is right fond of music. You like to play for silver some time?' She tore at the sheep's head, grinning above it with strong white teeth, and swept back her matted hair with a greasy hand.

'Some time,' said Gideon. 'But it's a Derry fiddle and it sings that much sweeter to the Irish.'

'You Irish?' asked Jobina. 'You said you were Welsh.'

'Welsh parents and born in Galway.'

'It makes no difference, there's still the business of eating. I'm cropping night shift up on Brombil—you going that way?'

Gideon nodded. 'Miners' Row.'

'Bloody good for you—right on top of the mill.'

'I am not there all the time,' he said.

Reaching the door of the hut, he turned and bowed to the room. The navvies, now clustered around the wake of Jarrotty, shouted rough goodbyes.

'The heathen lot of bastards,' said Jobina.

Gideon touched his hair. 'Good night, and thank you.'

'You pay 'em too much respect,' said she.

As she opened the door the night swept in; the wake candles fluttered and the room was alight with the flashing of the Taibach vents. In the sulphurous stink that enveloped them, Gideon said reflectively, 'Once, in a hall in Tredegar, I played first violin in *Judas Maccabaeus*, and I bowed to people then.'

'Who's Judas Maccabaeus?'

He smiled as they went down the steps of the hut. 'It doesn't matter now.'

'You staying on here?' asked Jobina.

'No. I'm on the road in the morning.'

'And you blind . . . ?'

'It makes no difference. Every year I do the round to Merthyr and the Top Towns—on the fiddle with political pamphlets.'

'God! An agitator! You do this all the year?'

'Chiefly in summer—too cold on the mountains in winter.'

'Where you bound tomorrow then?' she asked.

'I won't get far above Mynydd Margam.'

'We'll be at Maesteg this time tomorrow—that's strange.'

'I thought you were cropping at Brombil all summer,' said Gideon.

'Ach, no—there's no bread in it. If I'm bedding with the navvies I might as well work with them, and the Nipper Tandy gang is on the Maesteg dram-road in the morning—might see more of you?'

'I doubt it,' said Gideon.

2

THE Welsh girl left Gideon at the company shop and took the Constant Incline up to Brombil.

'You be all right, fiddler?'

'Of course.'

'I'll hand ye down to Miners' if you want it.'

'I can manage.'

'Good night to ye, then.'

'Good night.'

With his fiddle under his arm Gideon began to tap his way down the dram-road which brought the works coal from The Side, and he knew exactly where he was for the thunder of the drams was behind him, singing on the incline; before him, flashing on his open eyes, the vents of the copper works glowed and flared against dull banks of sulphurous clouds. Here, as a child, he had known this place from Granny's Hole up to The Green where the soldiers paraded. He was at home here, and he knew the blackened trees and the carnage of a burned land. But even in his time he could also remember the clear beauty of the Rhanallt stream where he used to fish for trout with his fingers. Often he had grimly considered the advantages of blindness as row after row of workers' cottages were flung up across the bright fields of his youth. And there still lived in his ears the chinking *tribannau* of the breast-ploughing: the steaming, straining oxen, six abreast and led by a horse was a treasured vision of his past, with his clothes dusted white with the lime-carting from Cornelly quarries. His father, long dead, used to hire himself out at the fairs of Swansea for fifteen sovereigns a year, and by this means came to Taibach and the

Groeswen cottage where Gideon was born. There was home-brewed ale for weddings and cider for harvesting; bread was baked in an earth oven in the garden—and neighbours came for miles for its service—barley bread for weekdays, pure wheat loaves for Sabbaths, all brown and crusty on the top, and his mouth watered now at the thought of the rich yellow-churned butter of the fat wives on the stalls at Taibach market. Then, on *Calan Gaeaf*, the first day of November, a pig would be slaughtered, salted and stored in oatmeal. The girls, he remembered, were gay in poke-bonnets and giggles and mostly dark-haired. But one whose name was Angharad Jones was fair, and it was she whom he had kissed in a lane near Rhigos one Whit Sunday: her lips, he remembered, tasted of bitterness, for they had been picking wild sloes.

He awoke from his reflections as Dai End-On, going to the Somerset Arms, hawked deep and spat at his feet. He did not speak, but Gideon knew him by hop smell.

'Good night, blind man.' A young tramping Welshman with a bundle on a stick passed him at the top of Miners'. He was rolling a little in his gait; there was about him a happy, tipsy charm.

'Good night,' said Gideon.

The red flashes of the casting-house guided Gideon with the accuracy of a lighthouse beam to a ship in an ocean waste, for, by some inexplicable chemistry the vicious light imposed its brilliance on the half-dead retinae of his sight, bringing visions that momentarily exposed panoramas of the blackened landscape. The labouring night shift of Cotton Row and Miners' bellowed his childhood's music with a new ferocity, for a big order had come in from Spain. Dram-wheels grated to a stop on the road behind him and Gideon leaped away with astonishing alacrity.

'You mind your back, Gid!' cried Randy, Mamie's boy. 'You damn near took it that time, remember!'

'You run me down and you will answer to Mamie,' said Gideon, smiling, and waited while the dram went past, pushed by two, for another was there; young Blod Irish, by the sound of her, for he heard the soprano in her gasps.

19

'You fiddlin' at the Jarrotty wake tonight, then?' called Randy over his shoulder: imp-black and in rags was he, and Blod, aged sixteen, with her body as straight as a bar on the dram beside him; hauliers both, and the coal was heaped high, for Randy, to his credit, never pushed easy.

'Yes,' called Gideon back, 'how did you know?'

'Met a friend of yours—get about a bit for a musician, eh?'

A group of men were talking about the benefit clubs as he tapped down Miners'. The copper vents mushroomed with flame then, and he saw his door. Opening it quickly, he entered the room that was shared by Little Randy and Dai End-On. Here flashes of the works did not enter, and he was blind again. Like others in Miners' Row, this was a company cottage, three up, two down; owned by the English Copper Company who owned everything of value in the district, including the population. Yet there existed a paternal benevolence among the masters that allowed them rare acts of generosity, and Nine Miners' Row was one example. In the tenancy rules signed by her husband, deceased six years ago after passing through ten-ton rollers, Mamie Goldie was allowed to continue tenancy on the undertaking that she did not take in lodgers. But there were two lodgers in Nine Miners'. There was Zimmerman, a Pole of doubtful origin, who shared with Gideon in the upstairs front, and it was generally agreed to be one of the best upstairs in Taibach: Mamie herself shared the downstairs back with Dai End-On and Little Randy, her son, who was there to keep it proper, for the neighbours can be buggers where a virgin lady is involved, as Mamie used to say.

'That you, Gid?' she called now.

'Yes, Mamie.'

'You done the navvy?'

'Yes, the wake is nearly over.'

'Pity about him, isn't it?'

'Ay, a good little man was Peg Jarrotty.'

The silence beat about them after a bedlam of snores from the three Irish brothers Tim, Mike and Joe, Mrs. Billa Jam's lodgers next door. Lately come in from Fishguard from yet another Irish famine, they had seen people grazing in the fields like cattle up in County Mayo, though it sounds a tall one to me, said Mamie Goldie, for we don't have the molars for grazin'.

'Astonishin', it is, how Mary's Children always snore in unison,' she said to Gideon once. 'The Welsh, on the other hand, snore in harmony: queer, isn't it?'

It was not queer, it was a fact. Often, when he could not sleep Gideon would wander the deserted streets of Taibach and listen to this phenomenon.

'It's lyin' on their backs that does it,' said Mamie, 'and there's better choral singing done unconscious than swimming the River Jordan in the back pews of Swansea Calfaria up-right, and I do mean Swansea, for this lot don't know a crotchet from tonic sol-fa. You all right, Gid?'

She peered up at him now, clutching at the front of her faded nightgown.

'Fine, Mamie,' he said, moving past her.

'You eaten?'

'I ate with the Nipper Tandy gang,' he lied.

The mill roared obscenely between them, and Gideon sensed the warmth of her humanity. Strangely, although he was nearly twenty-six he had never known a woman's love, nor Mamie the gentleness of a man such as he. He was big, she thought; until now, standing close to him, she had never real-ised the size of him; and he was made even bigger in her eyes by his unusual gentleness. The men Mamie had known were those of fists and ale, with an eye filled up at the very first argument. Their talk was of the copper vats and iron-pudding, with fighting most Saturdays down at the Oddfellows Lodge of loyal brothers, and the lot of them put together as loyal as a bag of biblical serpents, then some, said Mrs. Billa Jam next door. Gideon, for his part, saw in Mamie Goldie the mother he had lost to the Old Cholera when he was ten years old: always in her presence he smelled again the heavy scent of funeral flowers, and saw in a window a candle flickering on polished oak.

'You heard about Merve—Billa's lad next door?'

21

Mamie loved and nurtured Mervyn Jam, aged nine, and his twin, Saul.

'No, what has happened?' Gideon paused at the stairs.

'Collected a backside of buck-shot from that old devil up on Rhigos.'

'Mr. Evans?'

'Mr. Waxey Evans—I'll give him cobbling, shooting at the boys—far too handy with that blunderbuss, he is.' She belched and pardoned. 'All fair to young Merve, he told the truth. Him and Willie Taibach laying night-lines in Rhigos pond and the old beggar comes out and lets fly—got Merve in both cheeks, and one is still in—pellets, I mean. Another two inches and it would 'ave been through his watchercallit. Ain't good enough, I say—might have laid him up for life.'

'Is he really hurt?'

'He was when I was getting 'em out—and Billa nearly fainting off. Daren't tell his da, of course—not that he'd care—oiling his apple down at the Lodge...'

'There are still some pellets left in?'

'Only one, and I'm after that now—just slipped out for a tot of gin to send the little soul off...' She smiled, coming closer, breathing gin all over him. 'Buck-shot in lads is nothing—it's the men's the trouble. If God had a heart for women He'd have let nothing in trousers live beyond the age o' thirteen.' She added: 'You seen my Randy boy?'

Gideon nodded.

Mamie said: 'Were Blod Irish with him?'

'I ... I think so.'

'And Dai ... ?'

'He just passed me, and ...'

'And took his ticket for the Somerset Arms.' She bowed her head. 'I see him; parting his whiskers and pouring in a pewter without so much as a swallow.' Raising her face, she said: 'You see what me life is, Gid? A randy and a drunkard. Did me boy smell clean?'

'Like a pear drop—neither ale nor short on him.'

'Ay, but he's havin' it off with that Blod Irish as soon as I'd take me life. But that don't keep me tossing awake, lad—it's the ale. If he loosens one in her he can always walk her up to God, but it's the drinking that's drowning me—just the same as his father.'

He wanted to go to bed but she retained him with ease, such was her music.

'An' me a Jew-Welsh from London—a fool he is to get mixed up with the Irish.' She turned away. 'God smooth your dream,' said she. 'By the way—Zimmy's in.'

The works flared again as the copper boiled and in its redness she watched him climb the stairs. When he reached the landing and turned from her sight, Mamie leaned against the door of her kitchen, clasped her hands and stared up with clenched eyes through the roof to the stars.

On the first-floor landing Gideon stopped, his hand outstretched for the door, but he did not touch it. There came in a draught beneath it a faint scent of pine and fire; then he heard a step within the room.

'That you, Zimmerman?' He asked this as he entered, but he knew it was not the Pole, for the step was too light for the heavy-footed Zim: also, women breathe in faint sighs when fearful, sounds that only the blind can hear, and he knew that the room window was open for the mill hammers were sharper, the roller-whining keener. Entering swiftly, Gideon shut the door behind him, turned the key and dropped it into his pocket.

Trapped behind the bed the girl glared at him in the flashing of the works, and the smell of her rags, the crushed hay of her rough sleeping came to Gideon's nostrils. Gaining the window, he slammed it shut; the girl made an inarticulate sound when he moved towards her; she backed away.

'No nearer,' she said. 'One move and I'm swipin' ye.'

Gideon knew she was young, and smiled; he preferred this ragged aggressor to a fawning servility; and he was wondering what she could be stealing, unless it was something of Zimmerman's, for he himself owned nothing. Then he realised that he had bought bread and cheese from the Shop that morning. With an agility that amazed him she suddenly leaped across the bed and ran to the door, rattling the handle.

'It is locked,' he said, and approached her, gripping her arm as she slid away, and she beat her fists about his face as he pulled her against him, controlling her, and the door rattled from the fight. Mamie stirred downstairs.

'You all right, Gid?' she called.

The mill was momentarily silent. Panting, they clung to each other; light flared in the window and the girl knew him for blind. Mamie shouted; 'You bumped yourself again, Gid?'

The girl in his arms groaned quietly to the pain of his fingers, Gideon cried at the door: 'Yes, I'm all right, Mamie.'

'Then tell that Zim to stop kicking about.'

Outside in the Row a man was singing drunkenly. Breathing heavily, Gideon and the girl listened automatically, and she no longer struggled. Nor did she move away when he released her.

'What have you taken?'

She hugged the food against her.

'Give it to me,' he commanded.

She made a sweet lamenting noise, and said: 'I'm bloody starving, mister.'

'Give it to me.'

He was impatient of her now. Soon Zimmerman would be back from the Oddfellows, and for all his talk that property was theft, for all his idealistic theories he would hand this one over to the Military because theft was a major crime: property in Taibach was inviolate and the less one possessed the more it was sacrosanct: the child would go to transportation for sure.

Taking the bread from her hands Gideon broke it in half, did the same with the cheese and returned to her a portion of each.

'Blind, aren't ye.' It was a statement, not a question.

Gideon said: 'Now get out before somebody catches you in here.' He opened the door, adding softly, 'Next time don't steal—ask for food.'

'Ach, ye get nothing at all for the asking, for I bloody tried it.'

24

To him it was pleasant that she was so young—perhaps only about fifteen, he thought. His life since blindness had been the blousy, golden-hearted scitterers of the doorsteps, or the bawdy fish-women of the Old Bar. His mind reached back to the kisses of Angharad Jones, and he wanted this girl to stay. Sometimes Zimmerman, for all his talk of morality and social justice, would bring home a woman. And Gideon would be forced to lie in his blindness while Zimmerman denied him the right to other senses.

'Go now,' he said, 'and do not make a noise.'

She did not speak again and he heard her descend the stairs with a burglar quiet, open the street door and softly close it. The night air touched his lips from the window: he knew he had not done with her. Vagrants such as these haunted good-will; they could not afford otherwise. Yes, he thought, she would be back. Men, unlike mules, stand skinning twice.

He listened to the smooth, satin clamour of her bare feet racing down the Row.

Zimmerman, his room-mate, came in hours after midnight: Gideon turned in sleep, opening blind eyes to the light of the candle.

'It is I,' announced Zimmerman, and began to undress.

'It was a good Oddfellows?'

'It was not a meeting of the Oddfellows,' said the Pole. 'Sit up, for I have something to say.'

'It is a damned good time of night.'

'It is not night,' said Zimmerman, 'it is nearly morning. Are you listening?'

Gideon nodded, silently cursing him. This was typical of Zim; everything was dramatic, and if it was not already dramatic, he made it so. Heavy-footed, the big man sat down on the bed.

'I have been speaking with an agent of the Friendly Association.'

Gideon sat up. 'The Lancashire people?'

'Also Doherty of the Cotton Spinners. You hear he has opened an office in London?'

'For the protection of labour?'

'For the drawing together of all trade unions—resistance to wage reductions—even to apply for wage increases . . .'

'*Increases?* That is ridiculous!'

'He is not too ambitious,' said Zimmerman, and lit his pipe, puffing out smoke. 'One day it will come. More, there is to be a meeting of colliers of Staffordshire, Yorkshire, Scotland and Wales—to be held at the Bolton Authority Lodge. Meanwhile, we are to test the pulse—you call it that?—of the Welsh.'

'We aren't ready for full Unionism yet,' said Gideon, sitting up. 'We'd be lucky if we got support for the Benefits.'

Zimmerman said: 'Wales must be got ready, she cannot lag behind. I told the agents—I am always telling the agents—when the trouble comes it will begin in Wales: these people are like mine, of fire. Up in Bolton they all seem half asleep.'

Gideon said: 'Sometimes I wonder if we are working for Unionism or rebellion . . .'

'Are these not one and the same?'

'Of course not.'

'But how can you have Unionism without rebellion? The employers will fight tooth and claw; they will not part with a sovereign unless you eradicate them.'

'It will take time,' said Gideon blankly.

'That is where we differ.' Zimmerman rose and walked about the room. 'You may have the time, but I have not.'

'It can be done,' came the reply. 'There is no need for blood.' The copper works mushroomed flame, the night became white with incandescent fire; immediately in the line of his sight, Gideon saw the Pole quite clearly, then the vision died.

'I am leaving for Merthyr in the morning,' said Zimmerman. 'The population is big—nearly thirty thousand. I am told, too, that unrest is present and that it is likely to grow. You know they have a temporary Union branch there?'

'I did not know.'

'You should read the pamphlets, Gid.'

'I'd be delighted to.'

Zimmerman grunted. 'I apologise to you. Sometimes I am

particularly stupid.'

'You are being particularly stupid if you think you can organise a riot in Wales.'

'You should read your history,' replied the Pole. 'They are an aggressive little people; they have been organising riots since the digging of Offa's Dyke, or must I also teach you history?'

Gideon lay back on the pillow again. Zimmerman possessed the ability to anger him: often he had wondered at the possibility of them continuing to work together, for the clash of their personalities was inhibiting the bond of their common ideals. The Pole's vague antecedents did not particularly worry Gideon; at times Zimmerman talked of Krakow, his birthplace, and the fight of his people for decency in the face of an appalling oppression; and there were occasions when Gideon wondered why Zimmerman was not fighting for them instead of advancing his radical ideas in Britain. But one thing was sure, he had done a lot for Wales; the opening of five benefit clubs and three Union branches, mainly in the north, was no small achievement.

'And I wonder what the Coal-Miners' Union would say about that?' asked Zimmerman, undressing by his bed.

'Say about what?'

'My theory that you cannot have Unionism without rebellion?'

'Little, I expect. It's a theory that's been done to death. Doherty didn't spill any blood forming the Spinners, did he? The same can be said of the Friendly Association.'

'It is you who is speaking of blood, not I,' said Zimmerman.

'I thought riot meant blood, or perhaps I'm mistaken.'

The Pole got into bed and blew out the candle; the mist about Gideon darkened, and the other said; 'Sometimes I think we talk a different language, Gideon Davies. People like Doherty and William Twiss and the Bolton representatives are scratching the surface. When I talk of riot I mean rebellion that leads from riot: if I ever talk of blood I mean a nation in revolt. The natural outcome of such an event would be to

27

decimate this generation in sacrifice for the next; wash the hands clean of it, and start all over again. Often I think that Unionism is stillborn. Its embryo died because it could not exist in a society of thieves.'

'It's an attractive theory,' said Gideon, turning over. 'You should mention it to the Authority Lodge next time you are in Bolton.'

'Perhaps I will do that. By the way—how did you get on with the navigators today?'

'They had their wake, they had the ale and their women, but they were not much concerned with politics.'

'Exactly. Sometimes I think we are wasting our efforts with this generation of workers; this was the point I was trying to make.'

'Let's march on London and have a blood bath,' said Gideon.

'Merthyr first, London later. Good night, my moral force friend,' said Zimmerman.

3

MAVIS SAMUEL, wife of Lemuel Samuel of the Company shop in Taibach, was having her first in that month of June, and I expected she'd have a going-over, said Mamie Goldie, for very big in the head is Lemuel, same as his da.

'Eh dear, love you,' said Lemuel, beloved spouse behind the curtains, while Mervyn Jam hammered the counter in the Shop.

'A ha'porth o' bulls-eyes!' cried Merve. 'Shop, shop, Lemuel Samuel!'

'Who is that?' whispered Mavis, twisting.

'Only one of the kids—that brat Jam by the sounds of him.'

'You there, Lemuel Samuel?' called Merve. 'What about some bulls-eye, then?'

'Coming!'

Gaunt as a pile of haunches and shinbones is Lemuel the Shop, official of the English Copper Works at twenty-two shillings a week, and only Company tokens taken, remember, if the customers are Company employees, and half a crown a week stopped for the rent. And here is my Mavis having her first, God help her, and the first is always a bit of a squeeze, they tell me. A son and heir for Lemuel Samuel, another hand behind the counter, preferably in the butchery department where I have filed off the numbers on the weights.

'What shall we call him, love?' asked Lemuel.

'I know what I'll call him,' replied Mavis groaning. 'You can have the next one. For the love of God, go and fetch Eunice Night-Time.'

'She sleeps in the day, my lovely,' said Lemuel. 'Besides,

seven and six she charged Mrs. Billa Jam Tart for an assisted delivery, and that was her ninth—fairly slipped out. But Mamie Goldie's been sent for, rest assured.' Patting her head as he proceeded into the shop.

' 'Morning, Mr. Samuel,' said Merve.

'Good morning, Mervyn Jam.'

'Ha'porth of bulls-eyes, please, Mr. Samuel.'

Bright-faced and quiffed is Merve, aged nine and well soaped behind the ears by Mamie, who practically kept him, although he was the boy next door, and she always hoses me down first thing in the morning, said Merve. Up on tip-toe now, he examined the scales, for Lemuel Samuel had a name for sleight of hand; a trick so astonishing that gum-drops had been known to vanish up his sleeve. With the flourish of a high priest Lemuel dropped in eight to a halfpenny and Merve subsided with a grin.

'Oh, God!' gasped Mavis from behind the curtains.

'Mrs. Samuel don't sound too good,' said Merve, peering.

'Suffering, as you can hear, my son,' said Lemuel. 'Got a slight touch of the colic.'

'Oh, ay?' said Merve, 'I thought she was nine months gone.'

'There are various interpretations of the state,' said Lemuel severely. 'And for boys of nine the colic will suffice. Incidentally, is it true that you were recently involved in a shooting incident, Mervyn Jam?'

'Ay, sir—got me breeches heated with buck-shot. Four in me left cheek, two in me right.'

'And how might that have happened, Mervyn Jam?'

'Poaching down at Rhigos with Willie Taibach, Mr. Samuel, but don't tell nobody.'

'And Mr. Waxey Evans the gentry cobbler the fortunate eye behind the gun?'

'Ay, ay. And fair peppered us, he did, the old basket. Willie got off but I got it proper. Haven't told anybody else, see, for Waxey still don't know it was us on them night-lines . . .' and Lemuel Samuel interjected:

'Then let the punishment fit the crime, Mervyn Jam,' and he lifted out two bulls-eyes and dropped them back into the jar, saying, 'Never let it be said that I would inform on a customer. Where, by the way, is Mamie Goldie?'

'Down Taibach market, Mr. Samuel,' said Merve, glum.

'Excellent, and when might she be back?'

'Not till tonight, Mr. Samuel.' He added: 'You want her for Mrs. Samuel, Mr. Samuel?'

'Certainly not. If I need medical attention I will send for the expert, Eunice Night-Time. Good day to you,' and he shut the door.

Mavis stiffened on the bed. 'Was that Mervyn Jam?'

'It was, my lovely—how did you know?'

'I dreamed it,' she gasped. 'Send him for Mamie, Lem—she's a midwife, too, and she only charges half a crown.'

'That is just what I've done, my precious—she'll be with you under the hour.'

'Oh, God—an hour!' whispered Mavis Samuel, and bit at her fingers.

In the sweating sighs and prayers of Mavis, beloved spouse, Lemuel Samuel of the company shop sat in a dream of sonship —one, two, three, four—five big lusty sons—two in the butchery, two in the groceries and one in the drapes—good old Mavis: in a dream of profit he sat amid red garters for girls, crêpe for funerals, lace for weddings; tiger-nuts and liquorice all-sorts, also Glyn Neath horse tonic, which was excellent for morning sickness, said Mrs. Billa Jam, the expert.

'Oh, God! Oh, God!' gasped Mavis, twisting on the bed.

'I tell you Mamie's coming, girl—I've sent the half a crown. Hush you, for heaven's sake—it's very bad for trade.'

Mavis Samuel died at half past ten that night.

'Poor wee soul, he was cut up dreadful,' said Billie Jam Tart.

The morning was all over bright and merry with June when Gideon took the road to the mountains.

'You comin' back for dinner, Gid?' Mamie screwed at her hands.

'Of course not, Mamie, I'm taking the road.' He did a strange thing: bending, he kissed her face and she raised her hand to it and stared as if he had struck her.

'When the leaves turn I'll be back,' he said, and she lowered her head.

'Goodbye, Gid. God guide your feet.'

She stood at the door watching him tapping with his stick up the Row towards the mountain, and Mrs. Billa Jam next door came out wiping her hands on her apron, and said: 'The fella wants his head hooking out—leaving your cooking.'

'And mind the new ditch up The Side, Gid!' called Mamie. She wept then.

'Doesn't know when he's doing well, that one,' said Billa.

'May the Rabbi bless and keep ye, Gid,' whispered Mamie in sobs, and Billa said:

'I always said he wasn't a full pound. Ach, it's a queer thing—a man like that shootin' off at this time o' the morning.'

'You get ye face behind that door before I stove it!' cried Mamie. 'And cease your lewd remarks about a decent working man!' She shouted into the sun. 'Mind ye feet in the drams, Gid. And if there's a sickness in you—send for Mamie!'

He waved his stick against the sunny sky, and took the middle of the Brombil dram-road for Constant, and the mountain was waiting for him, blowing live and free in the wind.

Mamie wept, and would not be comforted.

Little Randy and Blod Irish, the ones in love, were spragging the coal drams up the Constant Incline past the Balance Pond, with Randy stripped to the waist and belted and buckled up to show her his muscles, and find me the man who can stick ten rounds with me and he's yours, girl. Down with three drams of Brombil coal and up with five empties before dusk, then home to Mamie and her ox-tail stew.

'Oh, Mam—Blod's a fine one—she's all right, I tell ye!'

'She's bad through and through, and I won't abide her!' cried Mamie. 'This is a decent, God-fearing house, and ...'

'Decent?' cried Randy. 'Decent, ye call it, with you and Dai End-On ...'

'How dare you!'

'But Mam...'

'Don't you mam me, ye good for nothing ... accusing your own mother of shananikins—and with Dai End-On—what the devil d'ye take me for?'

'But I thought ... !'

'Well, stop thinking, for ye haven't the brain. Me and Dai End-On, indeed! Never heard the likes of it. The fella's a lodger like any other of 'em.'

'I'm sorry, Mam.'

'You'd better be, ye wee devil. And lay some odds on this— that Blod Irish is never stepping foot in this house, under-stand? One day you'll learn, me son, that ye can always stoop to pick up trash—and that's what Blod Irish is—rubbish!'

'But ... but won't you just talk to her—Mam, just once ...?'

'Don't tempt me,' cried Mamie. 'Talk to her—I'll brain her, for she's the sweepings of an Irish gutter. Here you are surrounded wi' decent Welsh women and ye have to pick ...!'

'All right, all right!'

'Oh, Randy, now ye pa's gone you're the only decent thing I've got!'

The empty dram inched up the incline for The Side, with Blod and Randy heaving like horses, their fine slim bodies tight to the load and their bare arms like rods as they braced to the sleepers.

'Och, ye Dai Dafto!' cried Blod, her black hair flying, 'ye'll do yeself an injury, man—give it to the mare!' Laughing was she, in gasps, her head back, eyes shut to the sun, her sack dress ragged about her breast.

'Then stand clear and watch this particular one!' Randy wiped his hair with his hand and the sweat flew in diamonds of light. 'Missus, you don't know nothin'! *Hei up!*' He heaved the dram upward with sheer strength, and the wheels grated on the gradient.

'Gi' it the horse, man—don't be daft!' She ran beside him with the excitement of a child, laughing at the sky, and her teeth were white against the red curves of her lips, and she was

33

beautiful in her rags, her voice tinkling out above the thunder of the drams. And she found a stick and danced around him, making mock swipes at his rear. 'Whooah, *whooah* there!'

'You watch it, woman—marry me and you're marryin' a stallion! For there's no two fellas in Taibach can move this dram up Constant!' and he heaved and gasped and the sweat sprayed from his face and shone on his muscles.

'Dear me,' said Mrs. Moocher, half-way out of her top window of Two Constant, 'don't it drop the tone of the neighbourhood.'

'Oh, I love you, Randy!' cried Blod, her face alight, and she flung her arms round his waist and kissed him.

'Reporting it, I am!' cried Mrs. Moocher, and she leaned over the sill with her hair in crackers. 'Worse than that Perky Polly over in Blaina, then some.' She shouted down at Randy, 'You hear that—reporting you—disporting yourselves in daylight!'

'But we were only kissing, missus,' cried Blod, laughing up.

'Ay, but one thing leads to another—got the morals of a hen-run, the pair of you!'

'What bush did they fish you out from under, then?' asked Randy, grinning up, smudged with coal.

'*Well!*'

'Ay, bloody *well*, woman—what you want of us, just misery? A blutty old hen you are, and no eggs for broody.'

'Randy, do not lower yourself,' said Blod, sad.

'Then tell us what you want from us,' shouted Randy, hands on hips. 'What d'you need of us, you blutty old cockerel?'

'Nothin''—just nothing!' Mrs. Moocher waved her chemise and lost the stitches. 'Just eatin', sleeping and work—that's all your kind are entitled to.'

'See, we got nothing but each other,' said Blod, face lowered.

'Aw, dunna cry, my little honey. You'm so pretty laughing.'

'She's an old bag,' said Blod.

'Ay, with no tops or bottoms,' said Randy, and he put his arm about her. 'You got everything and I've got everything—

34

we got you and me.'

'Even your mam do not count for me,' said Blod.

'She will one day, my lovely girl. One day she'll sit you on a knee—you hear that, little chicken?' he shouted up. 'Marrying we are, Blod Irish and me.'

'And not before time, strikes me,' cried Moocher.

It is night: the June moon is flashing, the mackerel gleaming silver in the surging harbour of the Old Bar: doves are whimpering in the woods of Dinas where the sulphur has not stained the trees.

'Oh, Randy!'

'Hush you now, my pretty little Welsh ...'

'Don't be daft, man—I'm bog-Irish ...'

The ghosts of the otters are calling from Avan; the rotting fish of Goytre stink on the blackened banks of the rains of Duffryn Mill.

'Oh, come on, ye darlin' thing!'

'Och, no, Randy me soul. What d'ye take me for?'

Humping and heaving is Randy and I should have known better getting mixed up with you.

'Och, me sweet lovin' boy, I'd die for ye, but would ye have me the way they make me in Taibach ... ?'

The moon was in her face, brightening the high cheeks, undertaking shadows deep around her mouth, and her lips were black in the strange light: the leaves rustled to her bare arms.

'Oh, Gawd,' whispered Randy.

A baby cried from Eight Miners' Row, Billa Jam's ninth, and Blod heard it and closed her eyes while about her sang the tainted wind of the works. And even while Randy kissed her again she heard the sobs of Mavis who died.

'You scared, then?'

'Ach, no! Didn't God make me for babies?' She shoved in disgust.

'I'll do right for ye, girl.'

She saw the pennied eyes of Jarrotty of the wake and heard the rumble of the drams coming down from Brombil. She heard the shriek of the Mayo women aboard the *King of Ire-*

35

land when the boiler burst on the no-return ticket from the Connemara famine; she begged again along the road from Fishguard and drank in the lanes the oatmeal broth from the cauldrons of the Quakers. Through a rift in his hair she saw the moon and she smelled again the tang of copper as she came over the mountain to Taibach.

'Ach, Blod, come alive!'

He drew away from her and thought she was sleeping. For a moment, indeed, he thought she was dead.

But she was thinking, in the clenched darkness of her eyes, of Mill Yard Row that ran along the English Copper Works where they took her in at half a crown a week, and of Mrs. Halloran, where she first lodged. Plump as a wheat-pigeon was Mrs. Halloran but demented with thoughts of rising prices, and as clean as a new pin, with her breast and stomach all in one, tied with a little white apron.

'You married, Mrs. Halloran?' she had asked.

'In the soul, girl, but not in the body, if you get me,' said Mrs. Halloran. 'Two and sixpence a week suit you, Blod Murphy?'

'Do fine, Mrs. Halloran.'

'Leaves ye sixpence a week for the essentials, ye see.'

'Thank you, Mrs. Halloran.'

'It's the economics, see, Blod Murphy,' said Mrs. Halloran. 'You can't have copper without talk of economics, and it's these economical things that keep prices up, according to Lemuel Samuel, the Shop.'

'You got a husband now, Mrs. Halloran?'

'Ay, but he's been on shift these past two years, so I dunna see hide nor hair of him.'

'A two-year shift, Mrs. Halloran?'

'Och, I've known longer. Do ye recall when Popo Hopkin collected it and the fiddler Gideon Davies was blinded?'

'Sure, I've only been in the place a fortnight, Mrs. Halloran.'

'Ay, yes—well, my man Mike caught it then, an' died.'

'Whee, I'm terrible sorry, Mrs. Halloran.'

'But it's all right, girl, it's all right now. The mould spat, ye see, and the shed caught fire. They got the fiddler and Popo Hopkin out, but all they got from my Mike was copper dust.'

'Copper dust, Mrs. Halloran?'

'Ay, no flesh nor bone—just copper dust.'

Blod's eyes were like saucers in that red mill light.

And now, through the patterned moonlight of the woods of Dinas, she saw the face of Randy above her: his eyes were filled with a glaze of copper and his head was bald where the fire had taken him, and she saw in his cheeks a calcined whiteness, and between his teeth where the lips had melted was a finger with a splintered bone.

'*Randy!*' She shrieked and fought to escape him, but he had arms that bulged with the heave of the drams, and he pinned her beneath him while she stared in horror.

'What ails ye, woman, what's wrong with ye? I'm only asking for the lovin' of ye, nobody's going to eat ye!'

'Didn't ... didn't they find Mr. Halloran, Mrs. Halloran?' asked Blod, dreaming.

'But I told ye, love,' and she patted and preened at her hair. 'They got him in copper dust. A pound and three-quarters— weighed him meself.' Mrs. Halloran sighed. 'Hope you'll be happy here with the two of us—got him in the tea-caddy, see—a real gentry tea-caddy—can't afford tea, of course.' She fetched it down. 'Like to have a look at him sitting on the shelf?'

'Oh, God,' whispered Blod.

'Aw, hell!' exclaimed Randy, sitting up and shouldering.

Blod clung to him, sobbing without sound, and she cried:

'Promise me, Randy, oh, promise me—never take a job in the casting-house!'

'Mark, Mary and Joseph!' said Randy. 'What the hell has the casting-house got to do with a time like this?'

She sobbed on, rocking herself. 'If ye love me, man, will ye promise?'

'Ay, promise I will, woman—to kill a pair o' quarts. I'm away down to the Somerset to lie me under a barrel for I'm wasting me entire future sittin' up by here.'

Ashes to ashes, dust to dust, said Mrs. Halloran—'you listening, Blod, my love? But he is luckier than most, being buried in the kitchen, so to speak, for the nights are cold up in the bone-yard. But don't get your tins mixed up, girl—that's all I ask. This is the tin for my man Mike, this is the one for salt. Don't clean your teeth with 'im like the last girl did.

Diminutive, a hair on the chin of the mountain, Gideon walked north.

The Irish immigrants were pouring in from Kenfig Sands: in their hundreds they came, the men scarecrowed with hunger, the tattered women with their skeleton babies lurching on their backs.

'Irish, Irish!' The cry of alarm rose above Taibach.

Since the little winter famines they had been coming, striking the Welsh coast in their rotting boats, begging their way, like Blod Murphy, to the new Welsh industries of iron and copper. What began as a trickle grew into a flood of humanity that choked the Welsh lanes: they filled the barns, stole from the orchards, rifled larders: they ate their way from barren Connemara, giving birth in the frozen fields, finding graves in wayside ditches. The churches and chapels were filled with keening women and rebellious men: these, the descendants of the heroic 1798 Rebellion, whose fathers had forged their pikes for a promised land, now deserted crucified Ireland for promises of food in a country of brothers, all Celts under the skin; for the Welsh, they were told, were only Irish who had never learned how to swim. They came in droves across the sands of Kenfig and Margam and the industrialists cornered them and signed them on at starvation wages in furnaces of Merthyr to Swansea, Aberdare to Blaenafon: they put their crosses on the books of the company shops for the horrors of truck: they housed themselves twelve to a room and five to a bed, naked at times, to make more room. And the iron and copper-masters packed them in like herrings in a barrel; the dram-road sub-contractors bedded them in culverts and water-pipes, and bricked up bridge-arches for rooms, with tin chimneys going up through the sleepers where the drams rumbled overhead.

'Irish! Irish!'

The cry flushed like a forest fire through Taibach Copper Town: doors came open on chains up Constant, windows were slammed down along The Side. Up the Conk the dram-road navvies like Belcher and Blackbird leaned on their shovels and stared down into the valley at the crawling black snake of immigrants from Kenfig Sands where the boats were unloading. Fights began in the streets, with bottles going up and heads going down and it was raining Irish confetti between Colliers' Row and Granny's Hole, and half of Cotton Row lost its glass according to Mamie Goldie.

All this Gideon heard in the wind driving up the mountain, and he smelled the familiar tang of clothes drenched with salt water and sea-sickness. The invading, tattered Irish—Mary's Children, as Taibach called them, had been coming in for as long as he could remember.

Behind him, not fifty paces distance, the thief Sun Heron walked, and her bare feet were noiseless on the mountain grass.

Gideon knew exactly where he was and the direction he was taking, for these were the tracks of his childhood. This took him up the dram-road and past the Balance Pond to The Conk, Pillows Mound and Brombil Pit. Remembering Mavis Samuel, he stopped, turning in the early sunlight to face down on Taibach, which he loved. Even death, in this particular town, had its humour, he reflected: only in beloved Taibach could Mamie Goldie's flowered hat be buried as a floral tribute. And he recalled with a sudden, impatient joy the colliers thronging down the narrow streets of Pyle, and the hostile crags of Kenfig Castle outlined against the stars.

Taking a deep breath he slowly turned to face the sun.

The red surge of light illuminated the blood of his eyelids and he saw crimson: a spectrum of diverting colours flashed and gleamed. Deliberately, he momentarily opened his eyes to the glare until the tears ran down his cheeks, but he was smiling. It was as if a light was beginning to grow within his head: gradually, he saw a great canopy of gold and misted images of racing blue and purple as the mountain grew into shape about him. Out of the astonishing brightness, fraught with pain, there slowly painted on the retinae of his eyes faint colours of green, and this was the heather. Then he stared down on Taibach, seeing a flowing maze of crammed houses: the crazy, winding streets fed slowly out before him with a new, conspicuous clarity, and he could have cried aloud with the joy that he could momentarily see. Then the vision faded: blackness fell with obliterating speed. Dropping to his knees, Gideon put his hands over his face and waited for the surging pain. Had he opened his eyes above the red coals of a forge and struck white-hot iron the sparks could have caused no less agony, and as he knelt enduring the penalty for momentary sight the tears welled through his fingers and ran in hot streams down his throat, but he endured this pain in silence. There grew within him then an almost ungovernable elation as he rose; he could have shouted aloud with joy. Not only had he seen the mountains this time, but the streets, too. For a long time he stood with closed eyes, allowing the wind to dry his face, then he put his fiddle under his arm and his bundle over his shoulder and took the track through Quarry Dip to Mynydd Margam, and the wind changed with his new direction. Instantly, he knew he was being followed.

If it was a man, he was particularly light upon his feet, Gideon reflected.

After walking for over an hour Gideon rested, assured that his follower had gone. He took a track on the northern slope of Mynydd Margam to a ruined barn and tapped with his white stick along its entrance. With the sun low overhead he sat in the shelter of a wall and ate some bread and cheese Mamie had given him, then made a swaying path down to a stream near a tumulus of trees.

Sitting with her back to a boulder not a hundred yards away Sun Heron put her elbows on her knees and her chin in her hands and watched Gideon take off his clothes. In the graceless poise of the slattern she sat while he waded into the stream, arms outstretched for balance. A fox watched him from a bush: Gideon sniffed the wind, nodding. When he came out of the water his hair was comically tufted, and Sun

Heron smiled, hugging herself; then managed to stop herself laughing aloud as he suddenly lay flat on the grass of the bank, rolling over and over as a dog dries itself. She had seen men naked before and the sight had induced in her disgust. Once she had seen fifty dram-road navvies disporting themselves on the banks of the Nedd, playing leap-frog like little boys, and their chunky antics had defiled the day. The body of this man was different: it possessed in its lithe strength an almost feminine beauty. She stiffened imperceptibly when Gideon began, slowly to walk towards her. Fear grew in her as he approached: it was as if, in his blindness, he was attached to her with an invisible string and was winding himself to her very feet. She did not know that the fox had left the bush; that Gideon could now smell her.

Standing before her, he said: 'I would not have done it to you,' and, turning, walked up the hill to the barn.

Because it was lonely sitting by herself in the sun, she got up and followed him.

When she reached the entrance to the barn Sun Heron waited, for Gideon was still dressing. Squatting in an ungainly posture she watched him collect sticks for a fire, and did not offer to help. There was a fascination in watching him do these things as accurately as a man with sight. His hands, she noticed, were long and slim, the fingers tapered, the nails cut square. Going deep within the barn he returned with an iron tripod and a boiling-can: this he suspended over the sticks, then brought out an earthenware jar and rose to fetch water.

'I'll get it, mister,' she said, and took it from his hand.

Breathless, she returned and knelt, facing him, offering the jar: he did not move, so she placed it against his knee. She did not offer to fill the boiling-can, and for this he was thankful. Filling it, he fumbled for matches, and struck one: the sticks flared into life.

'You got a good fire there, mister.'

'Why are you following me?' He spoke for the first time.

'For food.'

'And you think I will feed you again?'

41

'God help us, what's a bit o' bread?'

Sighing, he reached behind him and hooked in his bundle: the girl watched him unwrap it: a trickle of saliva ran from her mouth.

'Christ,' she said, 'cheese. You givin' me some?'

'I will give you what I can spare,' he said, 'then you must go.'

She wiped her mouth, watching as he broke the bread and cheese: he offered this and she snatched it from his hands across the fire.

'Oh, Christ,' she said, tearing it with her teeth.

'Please do not swear,' said Gideon.

'Who's swearin'?'

'You are.'

'I didn't!'

'You blasphemed; it is the same thing.'

She stopped chewing, staring at him. 'You a minister, or something?'

He said evenly: 'It is ridiculous to do it; it is nothing but a waste of breath.'

'Saints preserve us . . .' She swept back her hair.

'They might if you don't blaspheme.' He paused, listening to the simmering of the can. 'What is your name?'

'Sun.'

He peered at her, and she said, swallowing: 'Sun Heron.'

'Is that your real name?'

'No. Me ma called me Mari.' She put the rest of the bread into her mouth, chewing and gasping with hunger.

'How old are you?' asked Gideon.

'Eighteen.'

They sat silently, listening to the water.

Suddenly it boiled in noisy spurts and he took the can off the chain. The tea died in a sigh of agony.

'You never burn yourself?' she asked.

'Often.'

She spoke again but he did not reply because her presence was beginning to disturb him.

'You givin' me some tea?' she asked.

42

Gideon nodded.

'You got milk?'

'We will have it without milk.'

'I passed a cow down in the farm. Sure, if ye want some I'll milk the bugger.'

He sighed. 'There is only one mug—you drink first.' He swept the earth floor behind him, found his mug and filled it from the pot. Taking it, she sipped, blowing at the steam.

'You looked good with no clothes on.'

'I'm obliged,' said Gideon.

'But you anna the first man I seen without clothes on, though.'

'No doubt.' Rising, he went into the barn, and she called:

'I saw the navvies washing in the cut down Resolven way once, when I was twelve.'

He did not reply. There was a straw bed within the barn and Gideon knelt beside it, sweeping it rough with his arms. Tonight he would stay here, but first he must get rid of the girl: he was wondering how to do this when she said, coming to the doorway: 'An' I saw Dai Docker with his clothes off when I were five.'

'You started young.' His back was to her.

'You know Sker Rocks at low tide?'

He nodded, still on his knees: there was a stub of a candle somewhere; he was trying to find it.

'Dai Docker and his missus took me down the rocks after cockles, wi' a donkey ...' She sat at the doorway, cupping the mug against her and looked down the hill to the brook. 'The sweet virtue of the cocklin' was in them, an' they took me because I cried, I reckon. She was a fancy piece was Dai's gipsy missus, they said, but she worked good and carried me on her back in a shawl, like the Irish back home. You say ye know Sker?'

Gideon got to his feet; there was in her a new melody, and he was intrigued. She said: 'When the tide goes out at Sker on the flats there's white bones growin' out of the mud and antlers they grow on stags, all white and shinin' in the sun, like a burned-up forest. Folks say they come from when the world was ice, but Dai Docker said that were daft.' She suddenly laughed at the sky. 'His gipsy missus carried me while they cockled and cockled and the bloody donkey was fair up to his belly wi' the weight of them when Dai led him back to the shore. He took his clothes off to cockle deeper, I remember, and the gipsy missus said, "Have ye no thought for the wee one, ye dirty old thing?" and he said, "to hell wi' the wee one for there was nothin' in nakedness, and she'd best learn young, anyway ..." ' She looked into the barn. 'Are ye listenin'?'

'Yes.'

'Then the missus carried me in her arms and there was macassar oil on her hair, I remember, for it was shining bright black in the sun. Dai led the donkey an' the woman was chewin' tobacco and kept holding me off and spitting, an' the spit hung on the top of a bone, and the sun made it bright and beaded in the drips, like diamonds—you ever seen that?'

He was standing close to her now for her voice was quiet. 'So we went on, the three of us and the moke, wi' the gipsy chewin' and spitting and Dai in his birthdays up in front, an' I saw the muscles of his behind all bulging and shining wi' the sweat, an' mud was on him, but I never saw his front because his missus said it weren't decent for the child, an' put ye trews on before we get to the rocks, ye tuppenny thing. An' then she started swearin' and cursing to raise Satan, an' when the poor old moke got deeped in the mud she kept reaching out and thumping it wi' her fist. Can you see that?'

'Every bit of it,' answered Gideon.

'It were savage,' said Sun, and started to drink the tea.

A silence came: the wind whispered between them. Gideon said:

'When ... when did you come here?'

'Taibach? About three days ago.'

'With the other Irish?'

'Ay, out of Stallcourt Barn. You know Blod Irish, Randy's piece?'

'Yes.'

'I come over with her first, with me ma on the *King of Ireland*—that was a hundred years back, but we starved, so Ma

44

took me back for she couldn't get no work up in Merthyr and suckle me, too, for I was two and needed feeding. Blod Irish came back, too—we knew her back home in Wexford County. Then me ma died and Blod came again an' brought me wi' her—the fare was a penny on the *King of Ireland* for she had holes in her decks ye could put ye feet in. She pitched five overboard outside Carnsore, an' though it was summer we were freezing solid on the decks, and some people hugged round the boiler, an' the damn thing burst just off Fishguard and people were scalding an' some jumping off with their clothes alight an' screaming blue murder, an' ye've never heard such a commotion since they lowered the gang-plank on the Ark.'

'And then?' Gideon sat before her.

'Ach, the pair of us walked and ate on the Quakers—you ever seen Quakers?'

'Yes.'

'We come up The Top first, to Blaenafon, but they didn't need women, d'ye see? Then we tried for Merthyr and Aberdare on coal-cropping, but it was bad in the groin wi' me, said Blod, an' ye've got to consider the childer ... A fella gave us sixpence for nothing on Cardiff dock and took us on a coaster, for I think he fancied Blod. But he got nowhere wi' that one—ye realise her?'

'I do.'

'That Randy's lucky—she's firm on the point.'

'So I understand.'

'And last Monday we come in on Kenfig.'

Gideon said: 'There must be a mistake here. I know for certain that Blod Irish has been here a fortnight.'

'Is that so?'

'It is. You could never have come over with Blod Irish.'

She rose, giving him the mug. 'It's near enough,' she replied. 'It'd be a queer old world if ye got the truth all the time.'

'So you've been telling me lies?'

'*Arrah!* Not lies, they're only imaginings.' She got up, wandering about on tip-toe, smiling at the sky.

Gideon said: 'I happen to know that Blod Irish doesn't come from Wexford, anyway—she hails from Mayo.'

'Is that a fact?'

'It is. Now tell me when you first came to Wales.'

'Yesterday, with the Kenfig Irish.' She paused, staring down at him. 'But you're not the first fella I've seen wi' no clothes on—I swear it. As we came past Giant's Grave on the coaster I saw the navvies up the Nedd River . . .'

'And all that about Dai Docker and the cockle gipsy—that was all lies, too?'

'Ach, what's the odds? Sure to God, you've got to mix the gold wi' the dross, as me ma used to say, and ye must admit it made a wonderful story.'

'Good God,' said Gideon.

4

THAT afternoon Gideon rested, awaking at dusk free of pain in the barn straw. Astonishingly, in that sepulchral light he could see even better after the punishment of the sun glare: this was unusual, he considered. Previously, as if in revenge for momentary sight, his darkness lasted many days.

Lying motionless he listened to the rhythmic breathing of Sun Heron on the other side of the barn. He was surprised to find her sleeping.

Rising, Gideon went to the barn entrance and stared into the dusk. He saw, with a leaping excitement, the glare of the ironworks of Aberafon and Bryn flickering in his curtain of blindess, mere pin-points of red glow that brightened and died in faint rainbows of crimson and white.

Hearing him, the girl sat up. 'You there, Gid Davies?'

Gideon did not reply: already he was sick of her presence. She was a liar and he hated lies. The obscenities of the taverns touched him less than lies.

'That you, Gid?'

He wondered how she had discovered his name, and hated the familiarity. Scrambling out of the manger Sun joined him at the door.

'We going now, then?'

'I am going. You're staying here.'

'Here—alone?' Fear was in her voice.

'You are not coming with me,' he retorted. 'You will be quite safe here. In the morning you can go back to Taibach.'

'Why can't I come with you? God love us, I'm doin' no harm!'

'I am not your keeper and you are not following me around.'

'I'm only wanting for friends!'

Gideon said evenly, as to a child; 'Look ... it's all I can do to feed myself. I don't earn enough to feed you, too.'

'I anna going to eat much back in Taibach.'

'Yes you will. I can get you a job.'

'You'm a hard bugger,' she said.

'Hard? Ever since you came here you've been a pest to me. You thieve from my room—food at that. If Zimmerman had been there you'd have finished up in Swansea. I've fed you once today and you're getting no more. Now, out! It's the wrong way round—you ought to be keeping me.'

'You let me, Gid Davies, an' I'll do that,' she replied.

'*Out!*' he cried, and seized her arm but she twisted away into the barn, and he shouted: 'Come on, out of it. You're not even clean, woman, I can smell you from here!' He walked into the barn, hands outstretched, feeling for her, following the slurring of her feet on the earth.

'That's a cruel, damn wicked thing to say!'

'It's true. You're nothing but a thief and a slut ...'

Suddenly, to his astonishment, she ceased to evade him and began to cry.

'Oh, for God's sake, don't start that!'

She wept on, slipping down to her knees against the wall, rocking herself and beginning the Irish keening. Gideon turned away in disgust, mainly with himself.

'I anna a slut,' she said brokenly. 'Don't you ever call me that ag'in, Gid Davies—I anna a slut.'

'Are ye even Irish?' Turning, he yelled it at her.

'As the bogs, for I'm Connemara!'

'A couple of hours back you were County Wexford and you don't even talk like an Irish to me ... !'

'I see ye once an' I'm made for ye, Gideon Davies,' she said. 'I could have got food from the chapel, or even up Constant where the folks were out, for I tried the doors. But I got it from you because I've been wantin' ye—from the moment I saw ye down on the Bar three days back when I come in from Kenfig. And I followed ye every moment: I see you at the

48

Somerset an' I watched ye playing in the Jarrotty wake and come out wi' that fancy piece in the navvies' hut, for I looked through the window and a lad told me who you were.' Suddenly reaching up, she gripped his arms and drew him closer, whispering, 'I'll be no pest to you—I'm arming ye this once but never again, till ye bid it—if ye'll let me stay, for I'm empty without ye.'

Gideon turned away. She watched him as he knelt on his bed. Tying up his bundle he reached for his fiddle case and rose.

'Because of that fancy navvy, isn't it?' said Sun Heron.

'I am going now,' said Gideon. 'Stay here tonight. In the morning go back to Taibach. Go to Nine Miners' Row and ask for Mamie Goldie. Say I sent you, and she will take you in. Blod and Randy will get you a job on the drams, Mamie will give you a bed. Here, take this shilling.'

'Bloody keep it.'

As he went through the barn door into the dusk, Sun said; 'Jobina, eh? You ask my opinion and I'd say she's a tart.'

'How old did you say you were?' asked Gideon.

'Eighteen.'

He grinned despite his thoughts, rubbing his chin.

The moon was a glass marble when he reached Maesteg.

Light, smoke and hops struck him in the face as he opened the door of the Maesteg Old Swan Inn, and there exploded from momentary silence the roar of men and the shrieks of women.

'Love ye soul, Gid, come you in!'

They were the customers of the Jarrotty wake, from Taibach, and they thronged about him: there was Belcher, the hut foreman who stopped picking a fight with Curly Hayloft over Mercy Merriman: Skin-Crone, the cook was there with Tilly, and Big Bonce dragged Lady Godiva and Moll across by the hands. And they badgered and shouted about Gideon as he shouldered his way to the light, and the bar. He knew Dai Posh still kept the place because of the smell of his macassar oil: Sid Blump Boxer was there, too, for Gideon heard him

49

as he shadow-boxed and snorted in a corner: Shoni Melody, the hare-lip tenor he instantly indentified, and the presence of Jobina he sensed. She, from a chair in a corner, watched Gideon enter and straightened imperceptibly.

'And isn't it time you showed yourself, man?' cried Lady Godiva. She fluffed up, hands on hips, breasting through the men and her teeth shone white under the lantern. 'Where's Blackbird?'

'I'm here, me darlin' thing!' cried he.

'Tell him now, Blackie—weren't ye breezing it over Mynydd Margam and see him splicin' it with a wee Irish maid from Taibach?'

'As sure as Fate, I saw him,' Blackbird, chirping.

'You did not,' shouted Gideon. He elbowed his way to the counter, and Jobina sat unmoving, her fingers playing with the cross at her throat, her eyes glowing in her dark face.

'Is it a quart, Gid?' asked Dai Posh.

'Make it a pint.'

'Is it true, then?' asked Tilly, all five foot of her, fussing up on tip-toe. 'Come on now, fiddler, you can tell ye heart to Tilly!'

'Tell Tilly and ye tell the country,' said Skin-Crone. 'You keep your own counsel, Gid. What's ailing you, ye daft numbskull, bandying wi' toy women?'

The amber brew flooded over his mouth and he saw through drowning gold, and the room was submerged in hops and gurgles, cold to the throat after the dusty mountain. Gasping, he wiped his mouth with his hand.

'Is it right, Gid, boyo?'

'She was a child,' he replied.

'She dunna look much like a babe on the breast to me,' remarked Blackbird in his queer falsetto.

'Depends what you call a child,' said Jobina, but nobody heard.

They elbowed and pushed in the raucous vapouring of the near-drunk: they had come off at dusk and the shift was hard, with four-ton boulders levering out and stone sleepers going in, and the culverts were three feet diameter and the men were stained with sweat to their yorks, and the skirts of the navvy women painted yellow a foot up the hems with the bright clay of the vats. Soon the embankments would be sloped and the cuttings cleared and the mule-drams would take over for the end-on laying, with the long-handled barrow drams taking down, which was the way Jarrotty died, for they took six tons. The work was safe in the early stages, but it was hard. Spills and accidents would come later.

'But he always comes back home,' cried Big Bonce, swaying, 'for he's sweet on our wee Jobbie. Isn't it true he carries a reel o' cotton in his pocket and winds his way back to her skirt?'

'Not this time he didn't,' said Jobina, and sipped her small-beer.

'What's the odds, woman?' cried Moll. 'The man's here, isn't he?'

'Will you give us a tune, fiddler?'

'If you pay,' said Gideon.

'Have you eaten proper, Gid?' This from Dai Posh, flat-faced, smoothing his parting.

'I'm rumbling for pounce-thunder, but I'll last,' and Gideon opened his case on the bar: then he deliberately turned to face Jobina, lifted his pewter and drank steadily: smiling, he imagined the toss of her head and the pout of her lips in profile. Amid the bawling of the room he called:

'She was a child, girl; a child.'

'And how old is that?'

'Eighteen, so she said.' He smiled at his thoughts.

'Oh, ay? Blackie said he wouldn't trust her with his latest son, and he was two years old last Sunday.'

Shoni Melody, the hare-lip singer, took the middle of the room and the navvies backed away to give respect: he cupped his hand over his mouth to hide his deformity and made a sweet consoling sound, listening for the key.

Jobina said: 'You're nothing to me, fiddler—what makes you think it?'

'I just hoped you would be pleased I came to Maesteg.'

Shoni Melody began to sing, a beautiful counter-tenor, and

the tune was *David of the White Rock*: the navvies, though Irish, listened in a fumble of ale and tears. Jobina wandered over to Gideon, mug in hand.

'Where is she now, then?'

Gideon said: 'I sent her to Mamie Goldie...'

'Irish, is she?'

'You cannot trust anything she says.'

'Good for you, and I'll tell you something else. I'm Welsh, and have an eye for you. So if she crosses me with her fancy tarts I'll put one on her ear that'll land her back in County Cork.'

The hare-lip tenor sang on, even when the door went back on its hinges and the colliers of Morfa Pit flooded in, grimy with coal, and noisy with banter. And they thronged through the Irish navvies, pushing them aside and hammering the counter for quarts, with the dram-lads stumbling around their thighs begging for half-pints to settle the gob and Dai Posh going demented with the mugs: the home-brew flooded over the counter.

Jobina said to Gideon: 'Where you bound for now, then?'

'Merthyr.'

'You settling there, then?'

'It's a town of real people and the place is alive. It's the music I am after.'

'Music! In Merthyr?' she laughed.

'In the people,' said Gideon. 'You've never seen such people.'

'If you come at the right time you'll be following me around.'

'You bound there, too?'

'Within the month. Nipper Tandy's sub-contracting us on canal dredging—the Old Cyfarthfa. Anything's a change from the dram-roads—there's not much life under a two-ton boulder, but you can't drown properly in ten inches of water.'

'But it's hard,' said Gideon.

The noise of the room beat about them: Belcher was doing a clog-dance with Sid Blump and the Welsh colliers were clapping the time; a cock-fight was beginning in the sawdust, the birds being groomed, their feathers flashing, their spurs like jewels in the lamplight and the pitch-and-toss dram-lads leaped to the new excitement.

Gideon said: 'You wait for me in Merthyr, Welsh girl?'

Jobina's eyes lifted to his face. 'Once I might have done, but these days I'm not anybody's woman.'

'Nobody said you were.'

'Hey, Gid, gi' us a tune for the dancing!' cried Moll.

'You heave off,' said Jobina, pushing her away.

Gideon said: 'I didn't ask you to live with me, only wait for me.'

'*Aw*, fiddler, come on!' cried Tilly, dragging at him.

Gideon held Tilly's wrist: 'Merthyr, then—in the fall?'

Jobina got up, smiling over her shoulder. 'Autumn? Good God, man, the gang of us could be six foot down long before then.'

'Gid, Gid, *Gid*!' the Irish navvies began the chant, and he reached for his fiddle, calling to Jobina, 'But you'll be there?'

'Ay,' answered Jobina, 'more fool me, for I've been had before.'

Despite the feathering shriek of the birds, Shoni Melody was still singing, his lovely counter-tenor sweeping over the heads of the milling, roistering crowd: with averted face he sang, his hand shielding his strung mouth, that it might not sully the beauty of his throat. And Gideon took up the air, playing above him a descant carefully phrased; a silence fell over the room; even the cock-fight was stilled. Here the flushed faces of ale, bulbous and nosed: the gin-parlour faces of a dozen bawdy towns; humped and brutalised stood the navvies, the colliers Welsh dark with tattooed cheeks and head-bumps of coal: Moll stared with bright blue eyes from the obesity of her blowzy face: Skin-Crone of the dram-lined mouth, yawned; the prancing buccaneering Belcher leered: Dai Posh was stilled in a pout of soap and macassar, impatient of a clientele drinking music. And Jobina, her slanted eyes shining, watched Gideon. The lanterns flickered, the only movement: Shoni Melody sang on, his shoulder against a wall, his face cast down, and Gideon played, his dark hair

53

falling over his brow. Lady Godiva, one breast bare in her rags, wept soundlessly into Belcher's coat: Mercy Merriman was nibbling at cheese with the furtive appreciation of a mouse.

The duet stopped abruptly: all heads turned to the door, which went back on its hinges.

The girl Sun Heron was standing there: smoothing her red hair from her face she looked around the room.

It was astonishing, thought Gideon afterwards, that he instantly knew she was there, for neither smell nor sound assisted him: he saw her in his head, standing in brightness. Straight and white were her legs below the hem of her ragged dress and her feet were bare.

'Gid...' she said.

Gideon pushed through the men towards her. 'I sent you to Mamie Goldie. Why didn't you go?'

Sun Heron's eyes were on Jobina. 'Because no gunk of a man's tellin' me what to do.' She came down the step into the room, pushing people aside. Expectant, the men went back, giving her the floor.

'So you're the fancy piece he talks about,' she said to Jobina.

'Ay,' said Jobina, getting up. 'And you're a cuckoo in the nest, girl, and he's pledged. So out.'

'Jobina, for God's sake...!' whispered Gideon, and struggled through the men.

Sun Heron said, smiling, 'Make a ring, boys, she's the clout I'm after.'

'Now, now!' cried Dai Posh. 'No woman fights in here!'

'This won't be a fight, mister, this'll be a slaughter.'

The Welsh colliers backed away to the walls, their bass shouts and falsetto derision battering the room. The navvies, riding the navvy rule of best woman win, made a circle around the tap, while two stood guard by the door. The event was not unusual: the women of their compounds fought for their men with the same ferocity of the navvies for their women. Jobina, also, had fought before, when she was nineteen, before she

54

wore a cross, but this was an event with the Welsh: it was a trick she had learned from the dram-road Irish. Up in an Aberdare tunnel she had lived with a North Country ticket-navvy—a travelling newspaper from Wigan—and his wife came down on a coach and claimed him. Jobina had fought then for him, her first man: she had intended taking a stick to him afterwards because he had told her he was single, but she fought for him first in a spitting claw of a fight that ended rolling in the yellow mud of the tunnel in a tangle of hair and skirts, and the navvies pulling her off a wife in rags. But the man, whose name was Clarence, went back with his wife just the same, prodded on the end of a Wigan knobkerry all the way to the coach. Now Jobina rose from the table and finished her small-beer, tied back her hair and tightened the big cro-belt at her waist, her eyes glowing at the prospect of a fight, and amid Gideon's agonised protests as the men held him, Dai Posh shouted, up on the counter:

'For shame, Jobbie Morgan! And you taken the cloth! She's scarce out o' her napkins!'

'She will be when I've done with her,' said Jobina, and Gideon cried:

'Belcher, Blackbird, stop this! Bonce, Bonce ... !'

'Make a ring!'

'Fives on the Welsh—I take fives!'

'Two to one against the Irish!'

Gideon shouted, trying to shake off the men who held him: 'Godiva! Tilly, Moll—in the name of God!'

Jobina took off her little crucifix and dropped it on the table.

'Belcher!' Gideon ducked and fought with the colliers, but they held him, laughing at the ceiling.

'I would if I could, Gid,' shouted Belcher, 'for I'd die in respect of ye. But this is women—would ye have me hanging on hooks?'

'See to her, Jobbie, the wee slut,' whispered Skin-Crone, her skinny hands twisting, and Sun Heron smiled wide at this and whirled up her hair and tied it in a top-knot, then stepped aside with the grace of a dancer as Jobina rushed. Held off by

55

colliers, Jobina turned: Sun took a last pull at the knot and stooped, hands out, feet splayed. 'Right you,' she said.

'Jobina!' Gideon's voice rang through the silence of Sun's slithering feet as she circled.

'You go to hell,' whispered Jobina, and her heavy navvy boots clumped on the boards.

'Sun Heron! Sun Heron!' gasped Gideon.

'Ach, don't bother yourself, me sweet thing,' said Sun, and wiped her mouth with the back of her hand, and feinted, going left, then twisted to the right and Jobina reeled away before her astonishing speed as the girl stooped with sweeping hands and fastened on to her dress. The pull sent Jobina's head back, then her shoulders, and her nailed boots skidded in the sawdust, the men opening behind her with wild shouts. Jobina slipped to the floor and Sun Heron ran around her, spinning her with the pull; the skirt ripped below the cro-belt, splitting up to the waist. And the moment she was upright, arms waving for balance Sun came in again, her darting hands seeking another hold, but Jobina braced her body and clutched her, wheeling her around with her back to the counter. Trapped, Sun went limp, threw up her arms, slipped through the grip to her knees and clutched Jobina's legs and rose, taking her feet from under her. And as her adversary fell Sun danced across her, one hand reaching to snatch at her bodice: on this she flung her weight and the rough cloth tore a yard down to the cro-belt. Jobina shrieked, and hung on to the sagging bodice: Sun leaped clear, and the force of her spun the Welsh girl. Jobina got up. Her hair was already down. She backed away, holding the torn dress high against her throat. A man said softly:

'By hell, she's a quick 'un!'

'Do her, girl!'

'Into her, Jobbie! What are ye gapin' for?' Tilly's plea was shrill. But Jobina, her face white, stumbled backwards in the clogs that were hindering her and Sun Heron followed, smiling.

Gideon was standing in the arms of the men, head bowed, and there was in him a sickness.

'Twos on the youngster!' A navvy bawled it, his silver held high: Jobina retreated still, trying to gather up her tattered dress, and Sun followed her, her feet noiseless in the thumping of the clogs.

'I'll give threes!'

'Taken!'

'Watch it, Skewen, she anna done yet . . .'

Deliberately, Sun Heron turned her back: Jobina leaped at her in a shriek of anger, and her rush carried her over for the trip: she fell, sprawling, and in a moment the girl was astride her, her fingers clawing deep into her petticoat. Legs braced, she straightened, heaving in gasps; the red flannel held first, then ripped in zigzags from neck to cro-belt, and in the instant before Jobina turned on the floor, her assailant snatched at the seam below the belt and flung her body backwards in a drape of red cloth: Jobina shrieked at the speed of it, and Godiva cried:

'Watch it, Jobbie, the thing's undressing ye!'

Jobina turned on the floor, and prised off her boots. Disdainful of her approaching nakedness, she flung her hair over her bare shoulder and rose, gasping.

'Come on, then, ye navvy heathen,' said Sun Heron.

The men shouted, backing away as the fighters tore into each other with clawing hands: locked together at last, they fell, gasping, rolling, with Sun underneath. But as Jobina pounced for her face she twisted away with the litheness of a cat, coming back instantly for wild snatches at Jobina's clothes; then the backward lunges, and retreat. It was a pattern unfolding more surely every moment: outwitted, outspeeded by the amazing agility of the younger, Jobina floundered before one attack after another, forced in the last resort to protect herself from nakedness. All this Gideon saw in the terror of his mind: garnering the progress of the fight by the shouted obscenities of the men and the hysterical shrieking of the women: the scuffling bare feet of the fighters, their gasping breaths beat into and branded him, and he felt unclean. Again and again he heard the ripping of Jobina's clothes, and he screwed up his hands as she began to cry aloud in her

57

distress as Sun Heron, soundless, darted in and out with snatching fingers, never for once seeking combat with Jobina's outflung arms; never, like Jobina, seeking to scratch. But with each lithe attack by lunge, run or isolated snatch, she came away with a little more of her opponent's dangling rags.

'Let 'em drop, woman—who cares?' cried Lady Godiva. 'What ails ye, ye stupid Taff!'

The crowd was roaring now as Jobina's clothing ripped and tore, and Gideon, in sudden fury, beat about him with his fists and broke from the ring of colliers: some were struck but none struck back as he hit out wildly and gained the middle of the ring. Colliding with Jobina, he gripped and held her.

'Leave her!' he commanded.

But Sun Heron came sneaking past him for what was left of Jobina's petticoat as she slipped and fell. Gideon knelt, gathering her into his arms.

'What ails ye, man—leave them! It's woman-fighting—leave 'em or we haul ye off!' This from a big North Country man with a cropped head.

'Merriman, Moll, Tilly!' shouted Gideon, and rocked Jobina against him.

'We're here, ye honour!' shouted Godiva.

'Get a hold on the girl!'

'You touch me,' gasped Sun Heron, backing away from their hands, 'an' I'll not be responsible!'

'Would you tear her to pieces, then?' cried Gideon from the floor.

'Ay, in strips, if she comes between me and you.'

'You stupid bitch,' whispered Gideon. 'Get out. You mean nothing to me.'

'Do we up-end her, then, Gid—will ye make up your mind?' said Moll.

'Let her go,' he commanded. 'One of you give me a shawl,' and Tilly obeyed.

'If you put that round her,' said Sun behind him, 'it's about the only thing she'll be wearing...'

'I told you to get out!'

Money chinked about him: the colliers grumbled deep, like

bulls nosing an empty manger.

'Heaven above,' said Tilly, 'rather Jobbie than me—the thing anna human, is it, ducks?' and she lifted Sun Heron under the chin.

Sun said: 'I fought fair an' decent. I didn't use a nail on her, an' just look at me face . . .'

'She's scraped bad, Gid,' whispered Mercy Merriman.

'The kid's gone on ye, fiddler,' said a voice.

'Gawd,' said Godiva, 'our Jobbie's fainted . . .'

'She skinned a wench and found herself a lynx,' said Belcher.

Gideon rose with Jobina in his arms. 'Will somebody lead me to the kitchen?' He was worried; he could feel her heart thumping against his chest.

'In by here, fiddler,' said Dai Posh.

After they had gone Sun Heron tied back her hair and smoothed down her dress in a circle of the men, and none spoke but all watched her.

'You'd best go before Gid gets back, child,' said a woman.

She smiled at them, tightening the girdle around her waist, and a collier said lightly, 'No odds to her, *fach*—won't you stay awhile and drink with the Welsh? The night's young for a tot or two of gin, and . . .'

But Sun was at the door. 'And share the likes of you? Hell's alight, man, I'm choosey where I do me drinking.'

'Yet you fight for the likes of the fiddler—half a man.'

She opened the door and looked round the room. 'Ay, for there's not a fella in here comes up to his shoulder.'

The stars were bright over Mynydd Margam as Sun Heron went out into the night; the wind was chill for June, and she pulled the rag dress closer about her. 'Dear me,' she said at the moon, 'there's an ache deep in me for you, Gid Davies.'

Faintly, as she climbed the hill out of Maesteg she heard the full, sweet voice of Shoni Melody singing a tenor aria from *Judas Maccabaeus* and although she did not know it, she thought it was beautiful.

Kneeling by a brook she washed the blood from her face and dried herself with her hair. Later, on the bank of the Avan she

59

met a cow clear of the farm, and milked it, drinking from a cupped hand.

The young Welshman who had greeted Gideon in Taibach was sitting cross-legged on the bank, eating from his bundle. He gave her a happy grin in the light of the moon as Sun, suddenly aware of a presence, looked up.

'I'd try that myself if they milked home-brew,' he said. 'What's your name?'

Sun did not reply; she was tying back her hair.

The young man said: 'I'll walk you if you like, missus. You on the iron for Tredegar?'

'If I tell ye that you'll be as wise as me, boyo,' said Sun, and left him.

She struck east along the old pack-horse trails, making for a great redness in the sky that outshone all others, and beneath this redness was the town of Merthyr.

5

GIDEON walked slowly through Pontypridd, making his way to the market in sunshine so brilliant that he, too, could see it. For the last week he had been playing in the inns of Gower, Kenfig Hill and Cymmer, and the rising industrial towns and villages had greeted him with song. The Staffordshire specialists of Neath had welcomed him, dancing in the taverns to his fiddle in round North Country oaths. The Welsh colliers of Resolven had sung to the hymns of his youth—Robert Edwards' *Caersalem* ... Smart's *Bethany*, *Rhuddlan* and *Ar Hyd Y Nos* the Welsh traditional. Fresh in their grime along the River Afan they had sat at the benches with closed eyes and roared their harmonies at the tap-room ceilings. And Shoni Melody, who travelled with him as far as Tonna, sang with a shielded mouth. In Clydach, after he had sung *Bethlehem* the colliers went to his corner and drank from the mug from which he had drunk with his deformed lip, and passed it slowly round the company for each man there to sip, while Gideon stood, his head bowed. Here he had preached Reform and the aims of the young Union, and they had been avid pupils, cheering him, and distributing his political tracts. It was south of Clydach that he had played to the Spaniards; a rushing Tarantella in which the Italian labourers had joined with tambourines; one black-haired gipsy girl from Catania dancing in her red shawl and buckled shoes, acting the death-spider in the rhythm of her castanets, and Gideon had longed for sight as dancer after dancer succumbed to her bite. In the inns of the pack-horse trails he had fiddled out the tramping songs of the drovers, whom he hated: expressionless to their bawled obscenities, he had played, and strangely they paid best, though wanting nothing of his political speeches. But his pamphlets were being read; his placards crying for Parliamentary Reform were pinned up like a white snake over the mountains. He was coming into Pontypridd one sunny morning, wondering how Zimmerman was getting on in Merthyr, when he met Mrs. Duck Evans, once of Aberdare, with whom he had lodged.

'Good God! Gid Davies.'

He stood before her, beaming, his hat removed.

Mrs. Duck Evans was so named by her neighbours when her husband was arraigned at the Sessions for the theft of a duck. The punishment ranged from between two years hard labour in the House of Correction to seven years transportation to the Colonies: Mr. Evans got off with a flogging and eighteen months.

'*Diawch!*' she cried. 'You on the road again, Gid?'

'Ay, this past week or so.'

'Good pickings?'

He nodded. He imagined her correctly, thinner than when he lodged with her, but still fat and cherubic; her chattering greeting to everyone a part of the repayment for social misdeed, but he sensed that behind her cheerful ingratiation lay the crucified features of her soul. Her days were shot with disdain when she lived in Aberdare, her nights were haunted by fat ducks and thin ducks, ducks feathered and plucked, perching on the window-sill, easing their feet on her bed-rail; roosting on the brass knobs, hanging from the sampler, their red beaks and gory eyes floating in her nightmare of the public whipping and the shrieks of Mr. E., with a king duck sitting on the bench with a wig on its head, and the stolen duck a squawking first witness.

'Good weather we are having, isn't it, man?' She turned up her face to Gideon.

'It is a beautiful July, Mrs. Evans.'

She touched his hand in mute appeal as they stood there with the people pushing around them: bowed her head as Mrs. Windy Jones went past them with her nose up: next door but one in Aberdare until twelve months ago, and very good friends until ducks came into it.

'You see that, Gid?' said Mrs. Duck Evans. 'Won't speak, see ...'

'Are these people necessary to your happiness?'

The drovers came, beating the calves past them to the pens where the butchers were waiting with red hands and knives: the dust at their feet was beaded with saliva.

'How is he?' asked Gideon.

'As well as can be expected on bread and water, an' his poor back that cut with the whip.' Tears were in her throat.

'I know, I know.'

'Not ... not fair, I reckon. Never did anything like it before —eighteen months hard and a whipping in public. Just tempted, you see—saw the blutty thing and picked it up, and he's got a soul as white as a bedsheet—very gentle with me, you understand ... ?'

Gideon nodded.

'No lust nor sloth in him—sidesman at the Ebenezer. And there's a few buggers I know you'd 'ave to pull up a chimney for a clean.' She blew and wiped on a rag.

'Do not hang your life on a duck, Mrs. Evans. There are people in this country stealing souls.'

Distant fumes moved on the wind; Gideon felt physically sick; it reminded him of Taibach where there was no escape from the appalling garlic stink where the land had died under the tawny orange deposits that stained the roofs and laid waste the people who expired prematurely from chronic bronchial complaints, and a halfpenny a week was deducted from the 'long pay' towards defraying the cost of a white pine coffin made at the Company saw-mill.

'Ah, well,' said Mrs. Evans, 'I expect I've got to go. Me an' the kids are on our way to Merthyr—nobody knows us there, you see.'

Discovering her hand he pressed two shillings into it: the people jostled them in market chatter and smells of hot cloth.

'No, Gid, no ... !'

'Once you helped me—take it for the children.'

'Not badly off, you know.'

'You are now. Please ...'

She screwed the coins in her hand. 'God grant ye sight,' she said.

He bowed to her.

'You come across our girls in your travels, Gideon Davies?'

It was Mrs. Afron Hewers at the market vegetable stalls, wife to the limestone cutter. Gideon paused, smiling into the sun: he recognised them by smell. Gran Lloyd was there, too, in her carbolic; Mrs. Hewers was onions.

'Megsie Lloyd, and Anne Hewers?'

He always mixed up the latter with Annie Fewers of Taibach, recently married, thank God, said her da: the Hewers and Fewers, he reflected, had one thing in common—their daughters were wild. Gideon shook his head.

'Been out all night, see, Mr. Davies,' said Gran. 'God knows what will happen when my man comes home—granddaughters is very difficult, mind.'

'And my fella,' added Mrs. Hewers, gaunt and sallow and five feet ten. 'He raised lumps on my Annie last time it happened—drew blood: she got the buckle not the belt.'

'It is not what they take out that matters,' interjected Gran Lloyd. 'It's what they're inclined to bring home, see—that's the problem. My Megsie will 'ave to sort it out, though, and so will Annie. If they burn their backsides they'll 'ave to sit on the blisters.'

Gideon had always pitied Megsie and Annie; for years he had been coming to Pontypridd on the circuit, and watched them grow up. Now, about sixteen, they were the unhired mothers of their mothers' children, the nurse-maids, unloved, of a new generation of squallers, bawlers and sobbers. In the thunder of Ponty they changed, bottled and babied from dawn to dusk: neither could read nor write, both took in washing.

'Can't do more than bring them up decent, can you?' asked Gran Lloyd.

'Had better chances than we had, mind,' said Mrs. Hewers. 'Taking after her grancher on my husband's side, is Annie.

64

And the pair of them not too prominent in the head but very passionate, if ye get me—very, very passionate.' She tied a bundle of carrots and tossed them on the side.

Gideon smiled. Earlier, coming down from Hafod, he had heard Annie Hewers and Megsie Lloyd laughing gaily as they took the road to Merthyr.

'Oh, Gideon Davies, do not tell on us—promise ye will not tell!'

Mrs. Hewers said now, counting eggs, 'Don't forget, Gid Davies—don't forget, if ye see 'em . . . ?'

'Not on your life,' said Gideon.

On the corner of High near Pneumonia Alley a little dog accosted him, and he stooped, fondling it. Once he had possessed a dog and it had begun to serve him, but then it died, and he had sworn to himself never again to bring such a scourge to his affections.

'Away, now,' he said to this one, pushing it off: tapping with his stick he entered the sweet shop: the mongrel watched him, scratching in the sun.

'Good morning, Miss Thrush,' He removed his hat; the door-bell jangled behind him.

'Good morning, Mr. Davies,' said Miss Thrush, 'and a pleasant day it is for sure.'

Gideon had never been able to formulate a shape for Miss Thrush the Sweets, so named because she had a sister called Miss Thrush Hen who kept chickens six doors down.

'Last person in the world I expected to see,' said Miss Thrush.

'I am usually in this valley at this time of year,' replied Gideon.

She knew it, to the day: often, wandering in town she would casually enquire about him from the drovers, and marked his progress towards Pontypridd with the accuracy of a steersman plotting a course by the stars.

'What can I do for ye, then?' Her voice was broad North Country: she would scream, she thought, if this year of endless waiting for him ended in a request for laces.

Her hands, her arms ached for him.

'A pair of laces, if you please, Miss Thrush. Nowhere can I buy the laces I get in Pontypridd.'

Earlier she had seen him coming to the shop, and had rushed behind the trays of sweets to the cracked mirror of her parlour, and there smoothed away the lines under her eyes, patted her hair, tightened the white, lace-fringed bodice over her breasts and closed her eyes to the panic of his step, forgetting in her haste, that he could not see. Sometimes, when he played his fiddle in the Market Tavern she would walk up and down outside, listening in the dark despite her fear of men.

'Are you well, Miss Thrush?' He took the laces and paid the money, not noticing the trembling of her hand.

'As well as can be expected. One thing's sure—I've only myself to think about.'

Gideon smiled and she clutched at her hands. His teeth, she thought, were incredibly white, his face burned brown by the sun and wind. His eyes, too, were beautiful: no man, she reflected, had the right to be blind, yet so handsome. It induced in a woman an unbearable pity to add to the unbearable desire: once, in winter, he had called to buy and their hands had touched. He was shivering, and his fingers were blue with cold. Had he but asked he could have warmed them between her breasts.

'Somebody in here asking about you a few days back,' she said, eyes closed.

Gideon paused on the doorstep. 'Asking about me?'

'A navvy woman on her way to Merthyr.'

He nodded. 'That would be Jobina. Poor Jobina.'

'Didn't look poor to me—fancy boots and scarf—scarlet stockings: saw what she was the moment she came over the step. It's the same with 'em all, Mr. Davies—like that Annie Hewers and Megsie Lloyd—very hot below the waist, if you'll pardon it. Don't hold with it, cheapening yourself.'

'Thank you, Miss Thrush.' Gideon paused at the door.

'Men are all the same, too—never met one different—not one, you understand?'

'I understand.'

'Big, useless oafs, swillin' their stomachs with ale on pay nights, and fightin' like animals. Take decent women like they take their dinners—no respect for person or privilege, don't give a nod to the community.'

'Goodbye.' But he did not move, being captured by her vehemence.

'Wouldn't give 'em house room. If I was fool enough to treat one decent I'd do it and die of shame. Drink-sodden bunch of randies. I wouldn't raise a finger to point one the way.'

The bell clanged as Gideon opened the door wider.

'No, *wait*!'

He said at the street. 'Yes, Miss Thrush?'

She lowered her face. 'It ... it don't matter, Mr. Davies. Goodbye, Mr. Davies.'

'Goodbye.'

The slam of the door pole-axed her dreams for another twelve months. Miss Thrush made a mental note to order more leather laces and size nine boots. After a few moments she wiped her eyes on her apron. Going outside she watched him tapping along the railings, the little white dog trotting at his heels.

'Oh well,' she said aloud, 'time soon passes. Thank God he's got company.'

Doing it while she remembered it, she hurried inside to order the boots. The first thing she noticed on the drapery tray was a pair of scarlet stockings, and she picked them up.

Vaguely, she wondered as she stared through the window, if he was on his way to Merthyr ... ?

6

'It is my proud boast that no soul in need is turned from my door,' said Mrs. Nancy Thomas of the Somerset Arms Inn, Taibach.

'Then for the love of heaven, woman, have pity,' cried Mr. Waxey Evans, gentleman, of Rhigos Farm.

'Dear me, there is nothing so touching as threadbare good breeding. All right, fella, but when you going to pay?'

'I have a rich relation with ten thousand acres in Hereford; I know a London merchant who can stand bond!'

'I'd rather have the deeds of Rhigos, Mr. Evans.'

'But it has been in my family for three hundred years—what will Grandfather say?'

'What would Grandfather say about one thousand six hundred pints, eighteen cases of whisky, thirty-five bottles of rum and twenty-four cases of dandelion and burdock, Mr. Evans?'

'Madam, I beg you!'

'Assist him off the premises,' said Mrs. Nancy Thomas, and posted the deeds of Rhigos down the front of her.

'Gadarene swine!' yelled Waxey Evans. 'May you rot in the pit of hell, Mrs. Nancy Thomas. May you be pestered in the loins by your own iniquities and a scourge of scorpions plague your guts!'

'Dear me,' said Mrs. Thomas, 'Grandpa wouldn't like that. A bucket of pig-wash ought to shift him, boys.'

And Mr. Evans, late of Rhigos Farm, left, leaving behind him the heritage of Grandpa.

Miss Grieve, more than a bit above the neighbours, sat in

the empty window of Number One, Brick Row, and wrote in her diary:

'Lemuel Samuel failed in business; his dog ate the letters as fast as they arrived.'

'Mrs. Goldie's new hat was buried as a floral tribute last Wednesday.'

'That Polly Perks called Perky Polly is a very tarty piece.'

'Saw Aunty Sally Sara hiding behind the clothes-horse when the rent man came.'

'Joy sings within me at your touch, Ianto. By the strangest coincidence Mr. Waxey Evans, heir to the Herefordshire estate, is also moving to Merthyr ...'

Done up and polished in his best tunic and hunting trews, resplendent in brown leggings and chapel boots, Mr. Evans, his hair smarmed down with goose fat, waited outside Number One, Brick Row, Taibach, and every neighbour in the street was either hanging out her washing or sewing her nose to the glass.

''Morning, Mr. Evans!' cried Merve Jam, his face bright with sun.

Said Waxey: 'What the hell are you doing here?'

'Only helping Miss Grieve to pack, Mr. Evans. That right you sharing her trap to Merthyr, Mr. Evans?'

Waxey bowed low again, his cap sweeping the gutter as Miss Grieve appeared. Dressed in black was she; dark and lovely in expectancy of ten thousand acres in Herefordshire: stately as a maharanee to a funeral pyre she came.

'Dear me,' said Billa Jam, 'don't they look lovely together? One thing about the gentry, they always do things different, ye know.'

'Can't say I've noticed it, mind,' said Pru Knock Twice, fluffing up her hair. 'Give me a collier when it comes down to the essentials, dearie.'

Merve said, excitedly, 'Eh, Mamie Goldie was right, Mr. Evans. You and Miss Sarah Grieve seem very suited to each other, you don't mind my saying? You got a penny for me, Mr. Evans? For holding the 'orse's head, Mr. Evans?'

'But you had a penny for that, you darling child!' said Miss Grieve, and bent to kiss his grimy face. Her serene beauty, the very softness of her seemed to call him within her embrace. Miss Grieve's perfume swept his nostrils, and he would have gone to her then had he not remembered his mother, Billa Jam: to kiss another would seem like infidelity, but he closed his eyes and held his face, beaming with pleasure. Reaching out Miss Grieve caressed his hair, smiling beautifully.

'Get going, you little runt,' she said.

'Aw, Randy, for the love of God stay and tell her—don't write!' whispered Blod Irish.

'Are you light in your top?' asked Randy. 'If I stay to ask she'll fetter and bind me, and I'll not get away to Merthyr this side of ninety.'

'But it'll wound her sore, just going off and leaving a note.'

He sighed on the rack of decency. 'Ay, all right, then—but you keep out of it—you keep away or you'll get her jaw. Where will ye be?'

'A hundred yards up from the Somerset with me bundle.'

He smiled at her in the dusk. 'Ye love me, Blod?'

They fought in whispers of breath and kisses.

'Wait, then,' and he was gone.

Blod Irish looked up and down the dark streets: redness was flickering along the vents of the copper works.

Mr. Billy Jam turned the end of Miners' at that moment with his donkey and cart, and his voice was shrill:

'Old iron, cans and pegs, rags, bones, pots!'

The door came open in Number Eight and Mrs. Billa Jam came out, her head shawled black. 'That you, Billy Jam?'

'Ah, dear wife!' Stopping the donkey he bowed low to her.

'Gawd, are ye drunk already?' she peered at him in the flickering light of the copper vents.

'How dare you!' Outraged, he stared back at her, staggering.

'Oh, God in heaven,' cried Mrs. Billa Jam, bringing up her apron. 'Oh, God, what's to become of us? There's scarce a penny in the house an' you're swilling your belly with quarts.

And we got ten kids need feeding and on tick at the Shop!
Oh, God!'

The children came out then, wailing around Mrs. Jam and
tugging at her skirts; but she wept in dishevelled wetness, and
the night echoed her sobs in the garlic reek of the copper while
Mr. Billy Jam did an Irish reel in the road in a drunken,
staggering beat of hobnails.

Then Mike McTigue came out, one of their three Irish
lodgers, and he took Billa's hand.

'Don't cry, girl,' he said. 'Please don't cry ...'

Blod Irish watched.

Randy went into the kitchen of Nine Miners', sat down by
the glimmering lamp and licked the stub of a pencil: in a big
round hand, he wrote:

Dear Ma. Me and Blod Irish do love each other and we are
away off to Merthyr after the iron, for marrying decent. I'll
do good for you if ever you come. Love from Randy, and
Blod.

He looked around the faded walls, the earth floor: standing
in a corner was a crate piled with washing: on the table
Mamie's ironed sheets were piled high. A faint, savoury smell
touched his nostrils and he knelt, opening the oven. A bowl of
Irish stew was within, and he remembered then that he was
supposed to light the fire. This he did, kneeling and staring
into the flames, remembering the days of his childhood before
the obscenity of Dai End-On. He saw a clean man sitting at
the table, a man of few words and who carried a candle-tack
and a bottle of cold tea: in the dance of the flames Randy
saw the red glow of the fire on this man's back and Mamie
kneeling beside him, swabbing, swabbing, and he heard the
hiss of the hob and there were black hairs on the man's chest,
and his shoulders, streaked with coal and suds, were wide.
Snow lay thick on the sill and rimed the man's eye-lashes and
brows when he came off shift from the casting-house. Then
one day he did not come and Mamie cried. He had never since

71

seen anyone cry like Mamie, in a blueness of face, a slobbering grief. The man had been caught in the copper works rollers between the cog and the line, with only his foot sticking out. His boot, the only thing left, was still upstairs in Zimmerman's old room. Randy reflected: it had been lying there ever since he could remember. On a sudden impulse he rose from the fire and ran upstairs three at a time. Opening the wardrobe he took out the boot: downstairs now, he stuffed it into his bundle. Once more he looked around the kitchen, sniffed, and ran his fingers through his hair.

'Goodbye, Ma,' he said.

Blod was awaiting him up near the Somerset.

'You told her, boy?'

'Ay.'

'You explained as to how there was nothin' left to do?'

'Ay.'

She looked at him and he lowered his face before her. Blod said, 'Randy, you got ... you got to say goodbye to your ma!'

'How can I say goodbye to her if she anna there.'

'Hei now, me sweet boy, listen to me.' She clutched him against her. 'For me, Randy—for me, trace back ye steps, find her, and say goodbye to your ma. For me, will ye?' She stared into his pale face.

'Leave me alone, ye set bitch,' he said.

'Randy!'

He strode away and she hurried beside him, tearful, her hands beseeching along the road that led to Merthyr.

7

EAST of Tir-Phil the old Gitos Farm squatted black and shape-less in a covey clear of the drovers' track, its square thatch flashing at the moon. In a derelict coach by the barn Gideon rested, sinking back gratefully on to the ripped upholstery. Weariness began to sweep over him after the plundering heat of the day. Not even bothering to eat the last of his bread and cheese from the shoulder bundle, he lay staring through the window at the extraordinary brilliance of the night; in growing excitement he examined the phenomena that threatened to consume him; it was a realisation of increasing sight that for-bade movement. Not since the screams and dousing buckets of the copper works had he been able to see so well, and he allowed the full light of the moon to merge into shape and growing brilliance.

Drifting into the buoyant haze between nod and sleep Gideon listened to the songs of the farm; the bass grunting of the sow, the snorting of piglets. Cattle muttered; feathered images of moonlight barged each other on perches in cluck, clack and an easing of feet. From the open top window of the tumbling farmhouse came the snores of humans. These were the last sounds Gideon heard before the drovers came through.

They came from the mountain farms abounding between the little town of Cardiff and the thriving iron centre of Newport, from the packed cattle pens of Caerphilly, Pontypridd and Risca. Ten deep over the mountain road came the cattle, seek-ing the track of ancient Sarn Helen and the Midland towns. And they came in a whisper of sound that later grew in power, bringing Gideon upright in the coach, and longing for sight. Sun Heron, lying on her stomach in the cover of a nearby thicket, also watched. In the reviling shouts of the drovers the cattle ran; bucking, shouldering, leaping upon one another in a mêlée of flying bodies and dust. And their hooves beat a rhythmic thunder on the flinted road to an accompaniment of cracking whips and a shrieking of cow and heifer. Barging, leaning, horning, the mad pack came, and the night was filled with the agony of the passage: whips curled and flashed against the moon: men stood at out-stations with braced legs and cracked their flails in the faces of the beasts to maintain the herd; Welsh collies raced through the bordering heather, barking and snapping at their heels, others lay like quivering arrows in the grass, waiting for the command that would send them into battle. And the drovers, bow-legged and heavy with ale, bawled their obscenities and raucous oaths to keep the mob in being, fists thumping into the faces of oncoming heifers, boots swinging to maintain the line. Six hundred head of cattle were streaming over the breast of Old Pantlattyn, heading for the slaughterhouses of Hereford, Welshpool, Chester and Liverpool. And after the cattle came sheep and these numbered more than two thousand; a crawling, maggotty mass that blanketted the common. Fringed with racing dogs and shepherds, they followed the mad stampede of the cattle at a slower pace, thronging the pens of the wayside inns in a cacophony of bleating and baa-ing, and from their sweating bodies there rose a billow of heat and breath shot brown with dust. Carrying on their backs the wool for the factories of Cheshire, these were the packets of walking meat bound for the knives and killing-boards of the west. In the vanguard ran the fittest, in the middle the majority flock, and at the end of the heaving mass fell the footrot stragglers, the old ewes, the blind rams baa-ing pitifully in their limping, staggering pace, for to fall meant death: this they knew by instinct. And the killing shepherds walked in file behind them with blood-stained crooks and gullet knives, and behind them was a donkey-cart filled with carcasses for market sale or eating at the next inn down.

'Get up there!'

74

The night was filled with shrieks and the cracking of whips.
'Keep 'em going, Bounder! Keep at 'un, Nell. . . !'

'Hey-whey-*up*! Hey-whey-*up*!' The cattle stock-flails flourished against the stars and cracked down over the heaving backs. Dust billowed as a heifer went down, instantly trampled under the milling hooves.

'Get 'un on his cheeses, Towzer, me lad! On 'is tail, me lucky lad! Up, up. Where the blutty hell is you, Dai Downer? Ye get up front afore I shift ye! Up front, *up front*!'

Gideon heard the innocents crying under the thumps of men called human: this, the stinking refuse of the tramping trails— North Countrymen mostly, but their numbers swollen with brutal Welsh, the prize fighters and vagrants of the Welsh gutters, the sweepings of the dissolute inns; old soldiers from the French wars, still wearing the uniforms of their discharge; the tattered dregs of the ironworks, burned out in eyes and brains twenty years before their time. These were the drovers of industrial Wales; murderers who had escaped the rope, thieves who had swum from the transportation hulks—the *Leviathan* of Portsmouth, the convict ship which lost shackled prisoners by crew corruption; the *Captivity* lying at Devonport, whose captain sold felons at a guinea a time and took their wives to the brothels of the East.

'*Hey-whey-up!*' The stock-whips rose and cracked in shrieks. An old ewe fell; pause, kneel, slit her throat, and she is flung up in a blood-shower. The trampled heifer bellowed to the slash of the knife; two drovers on her threshing legs and stained in gory disembowelling. Of these, thought Gideon, a romance will be woven for new generations. Their songs will be told as the songs of the road, and the old drovers' tracks will snake into history, revered in lilt and doggerel. He bowed his head as the procession of torture passed him, making north. And behind it were trails of blood. Once, when he was young, he had seen the drovers pass, and wept. The bedlam grew fainter as the cortège took twin paths to lower ground; the night was murmuring in sadness to three thousand fainter throats; now all was silent save for the distant cracking of the whips. Then the handle of the coach door turned in a faint squeak that few but Gideon would have heard. The wind moved, bringing the stench of urine and the droppings of bowels turned to water: had he sight he would have seen the multitudinous tracks of saliva criss-crossed in silver on the moonlit road.

'You there, Gid?'

He stiffened imperceptibly, then sighed, running his fingers through his hair.

Sun Heron said: 'Are ye hogging both seats in there, or is one going free?'

He did not reply, so she entered, closing the door softly behind her. And sat on the seat opposite him with her hands between her knees, smiling into his face.

'How are ye?' she said.

Gideon was not surprised that she had come, he had been expecting her. Strangely, too, there was solace in her presence after the appalling cruelty of the droving.

'I waited for ye for a bit after doin' the navvy, but you didn't come,' she said.

The warmth of her crossed the coach and touched him; also, she smelled clean for once, and this pleased him. Anticipating his thought, she said: 'I was in the farm pond washing meself when the cattle come by: there's neither dirt nor scum on me, for I hooked a bit o' soap off a stall in Ponty and I washed meself twice since then—here, smell me hair ... I cut off a hank and sold it for a shillin'—in case you're short o' money.' She bent towards him. 'See, I'm all scented and washed—I'm as bright as a steel bodkin.'

Gideon did not reply, and she said: 'You shirty with me?'

'No.'

'The night's hot and I'd be weathering it outside, but I'm afrit of the Cefn boys.'

'There are no Cefn boys round here.'

'Ay, there is! I heard tell on the road that they got a church fella near Blackwood—and he pick-a-backed seven o' them till he fell, and they cut him cruel with the sticks, an' his legs black and blue, poor sod.'

76

'Blackwood is a long way south from here,' said Gideon.

'Ay? Well I'm frit o' them, for if they catch me I'm lucky if I'm pick-a-backing, for they do a terrible offence, dear me.'

Despite himself, he had to smile. She said: 'You let me stay by here?'

'If you please.'

Her voice lowered. 'Then I sit like travelling baggage? Or do I come over there beside you?'

Gideon moved over on the seat and they sat together, unspeaking.

There was growing in him a need of her; it was a new and startling emotion that dried his throat. The dog was panting under his hand and he could feel the beating of its heart.

Sun Heron said: 'You going to Merthyr, Gid?'

'Of course; you know that.'

'You doing your politics there, then, and handing out the pamphlets, and fiddling?'

'Ay.'

'What's the politics, Gid?'

'You wouldn't understand.'

'But I would!' She turned, speaking into his face. 'Ye treat me like a kid, but I'm not a kid—I'm turned eighteen and fending for myself. Didn't I act like a woman when I did that Jobina?'

'It's men's business, Sun.'

She interjected happily, 'You said me name! *Well!* I've been waitin' for that—just to hear ye say me name. Ach, come on, don't that stand next door to a kiss? Aw, kiss me, Gid Davies.'

In seconds it happened.

She was suddenly against him, her arms about him, and he heard the convulsive sobbing of her throat, and her strength beat about him in vigorous beauty. He held her, kissing her, but his need was spitted with bitterness, because he did not truly know her age. Pushing her away he got up and leaned, head bowed, on the door, his hands gripping the glass.

'Aw, be a sport, what ails ye, Gid?'

From the corner of the seat she examined him, her legs

crossed, trying not to giggle, while he stood in a brooding quiet, ashamed. Anger and need, tempestuous and rioting, were burning within him.

She said: 'Mind, it's a pretty shame after ye've done it, but the mood soon passes. Billy Ugmore had a word for it—like a rogue elephant was Billy, but he made a radiant woman out o' a girl just off me father's knee. Ach, come on, Gid Davies!'

'You are evil,' he said.

'An' that's for truth!' She threw back her head in elfin laughter. 'I'm upright and daisy, because I'm alive. But you're dead, fella! Sure to God, I thought if I smartened meself up you'd have an eye for me, for I've a sweet little leg on me and a yearning for wickedness. Can ye see out o' that window?'

Gideon raised his head and saw the light of the moon. She cried, gaily. 'Ye taking it all too fearsome, man, and it anna that important. And if it isn't now it'll be later, for ye need me deep in your breast. Look at me pretty legs—come on now— shall I give ye ease, for that's what you're wanting.'

'For God's sake leave me alone,' he said.

'I will not, for you're set on me. I'd be thick in the head if I didn't know that. The moon's got a hunter's polish on him, boy, and he's fair for kissing and loving...?'

He sighed, eyes closed, like a candle going out, for he was one with her in his mind but his body was standing by the window; the thought of her nearness rose hot within him, and he turned. Instantly he was in her arms, her kisses eager on his mouth. Mute and clasped within himself, he held her while her gay joy beat about him: he was experiencing a strange indifference that was making him selective and apart from the demand. Also, there was about her a sort of bastard rudeness that eased the wanting: rather more than love-making, hers was an assault on dignity: in the very gust of her breathing he saw a smile, and stood removed from the panic of her loving. Presently she went limp in his arms and began to cry, and the crying broke into a wild disorder of sobbing, and she sank back on to the seat and beat her fists upon it.

'For God's sake hush,' he said, 'you'll have the farmer out!'

'An' bloody good luck to him!'

'Be quiet, Sun!'

'I wanna!'

'*Whist!* Or I'll turn you out!'

'You try!'

He sat beside her, holding her hands. Dolefully she said: 'Billy Ugmore was a right good fella. More'n once he leathered me, but he never turned me down.'

'Nor have I,' said Gideon. 'Please do not cry.'

She said: 'You turned me down, you blutty turned me down, Gid Davies.' She raised a tearful face to his. 'An' I washed special for you.'

'Stop shouting! You're making too much noise!'

'I'll shout when I like!' Her voice rose in defiance. 'You'm a belt an' braces man, Gid Davies—you'm too careful.' She pulled her hair over her face and loosened her tears. 'Beyond my damned exertions, you are—you a preacher, or somethin'?'

He shook his head wearily: now that the wish had left him all he wanted was peace. She said, bitterly, 'Well, you dunna give much away, Gid Davies. I reckon they weren't all born in Jerusalem.'

'You are a child and I am trying to be a man,' he said softly.

'I'm eighteen—ain't that old enough?'

He turned away, and she said bitterly, 'I canna help meself with ye. A night out wi' some high-stepping girl would have cost ye a fortune, but it all comes free with me.'

'Perhaps that is the trouble.'

She sighed and put her hands over her face. 'Dear me,' she whispered, 'that were a close one: somebody's been gnawing at me with no teeth.'

'It will pass,' said Gideon, sitting down beside her.

As if to herself she said: 'You'm not like Billy Ugmore, though. A woman didn't ask twice off him, though he had no time for dark behaviour...' She stared at Gideon, her eyes moving over his face. 'An' he had no time for the preachers, neither. Pious brains they do have, said Billy, but no minds. You understand that?'

79

'I expect so.'

Warming to him she fluffed up and prided, hooking her arm through his and nudging on the seat. 'Ah, well,' she said brightly, 'got to make the best of it, like Billy Ugmore says . . .'

Gideon interjected: 'I am becoming a little tired of Billy Ugmore.'

She settled back. 'In time you'll come to it, Gid. Then shave off your eyebrows and I'll eat ye alive. Dear me, boiling oil's too good for me. A painful and troublesome day it's been, me lovely boy, so we'll say good night to it. But before we sleep— are ye sure you won't change your mind, now I'm all scented and clean?'

'I doubt it,' said Gideon.

'Dear me,' she said, hugging herself. 'Grow your hair, Samson, and we'll have the roof down on the pair of us. Good night to ye.'

Gideon stared sightlessly at her in the cold-breathing air, then lay down opposite her, and slept; to awake almost instantly, it seemed, to a garrulous argument of courting hedgehogs beneath the coach.

Then the scent of a wood fire struck his nostrils and he raised himself to the window; Sun joined him, staring out. At the foot of a tree not fifty yards away a fire was burning and beside it, stirring a cook-pot, was the young Welshman she had seen outside the Swan, Maesteg. He was on his way to Merthyr from Pyle, and the cottage *Penderyn* where he was born.

Now he began to whistle a quaint, happy tune.

'Who is it?' whispered Gideon.

'Ach—some gunk I passed on the way—like as not he's bound for Merthyr.' Cupping her hands to her mouth, she yelled, 'Will ye stop the birdies so decent people can get to sleep, ye noisy fella? D'you realise it's past midnight?'

Gideon hauled her back. 'Hush, you'll raise the farmer!'

The whistling ceased.

The moon was full on her face, and as she settled down again Gideon leaned closer to her, for the brightness had given her shape. Taking off his coat he put it over her, smiling.

'Good night to ye,' he said.

Annie Hewers and Megsie Lloyd, late of Pontypridd, arrived in Merthyr two days after Gideon had met them on the road; they came down through Georgetown in Sunday best and as large as life, and thank God we are finished with babies, bottle and bottoms, and is there work in the biggest town in Wales for two lusty girls?

Down Dynefor Street they came and along the canal, bonnet streamers blowing, and the brickfield women were chattering on the doorsteps and look what is coming down now, good God; the burned-out miners of an earlier generation of Crawshays stared through red-rimmed eyes and champed their toothless jaws on clays, remembering their lost youth and the legion of their lovers.

'Dear me,' whispered Megsie, gathering her shawl about her.

'Looks pretty savage, don't it?' said Annie, and on they went, bowing left and right to the grimy refuse of the Ynysfach ironworks that leaned on the corners of Bridgefield Terrace. On the cobbles outside the Miners' Arms the off-shift colliers of Lefal were sitting on their hunkers winking above their quarts, and Shan Shonko, the big-nosed puddler from Carmarthen was crossing her thick legs and waving a scarlet shawl and whooping like a Sioux Indian. Bedraggled, ragged children who had escaped the ravages of the early cholera in Georgetown and Williamstown, played aimlessly in the gutters amid the cracking of the mule-whips and clattering hooves. Shafting through the squalor rode the stately barges of the Glamorgan Canal loaded with the iron of Cyfarthfa, gliding for Newport and the ports of the world. And all around rose the cinder tips: the hot-drops of Ynys were glowing and filling the air with the acrid stink of sulphur: the straggling dramroads wound in and out of the alleys and working compounds like black vipers on the burned tumps.

'Where you bound for, girls?' This from an old crone; up to Megsie's shoulder was she, with a black shawl scragged round her head and her heavy-lidded eyes drooping in the folds of her broken face.

'Come for work,' said Annie.

81

'Have ye now, me little ones. And have ye an appointment with Crawshay, so to speak?'

'We just arrived,' said Megsie.

'Ay? And can I ask where from, me lovely?'

'Pontypridd.'

'Well, then, you can take ye pick. You can mine iron on the tumps out on Hirwaun Common or coal-crop on the Old Glamorgan levels—are ye scared of healthy work, ladies?'

'That is what we are here for,' said Annie.

'Then the world's wide open for ye in Merthyr, for it's a town of work, heaven and the devil. Is it quick money you're after?'

'Quicker than that, for we've got to eat.'

'Well now, that's unfortunate, for the belly's the enemy, ye understand? With a full belly ye can pick and choose, but with an empty one you've got to take what's going, you see. Do you fancy going underground in the Cyfarthfa pits, for the fellas are always after dram-fillers at six shillings a week.'

'She's weak in the chest,' said Annie.

'Then you go below and she crops on top—sure that's a fine arrangement.'

'We're not being parted,' said Annie.

'Would ye like to have a word to Aunty Popi Davey in the Lodgings?'

'Who's she?'

'She sees to all the new female labour coming in, me darlings. And she'll fix ye up decent, with a good shift and a bed for a penny in the shilling.'

'You work here, missus?' asked Megsie.

The sunlight shafted between them, a sword of fire blading through the smoke-pall of Ynysfach. The old woman said, 'Well, not nowadays, for I've given me best, ye see, now I'm nearly thirty. But I worked for the old beggar up in Cyfarthfa when I was seven—come over from Old Ireland on the ticket —and I filled the drams down the Lefal with me pa. When I was ten I was shovelling on the levels, and after I was fifteen Crawshay had me on the face, but the screws took me when I

82

was twenty, being wet working, ye understand.' She sighed and grinned and her yellow teeth rolled drunkenly in her mouth. 'Now I work for Aunty Popi Davey in the Lodgings—don't ask much now—just a bit o' bread and a do on the gin when things come delicate in the limbs, see, me lovelies?'

'Aunty Popi Davey?' asked Annie, looking about her. The flame-hot chimneys of Ynysfach she saw and heard beneath her feet the rumble of the shot-firing underground: she saw the pit-wheels revolving in the swirling smoke: women were quarrelling beyond the steps of the Miners' Arms, their voices shrill. At her side, beyond her as far as she could see the land was upturned, the fields laid waste in blackened upheaval as if by the cannon of an invading army: bright flashes lit the sky above Cyfarthfa Works where the molten iron was pouring from the cauldrons.

'You on, Megsie?'

'Ay.'

Annie shrugged. 'We got to do something.'

'That's it, girls. Come on, we're away to see Aunty Popi Davey. You stick to her and she'll fix you right,' said Old Wag.

Madoc Williams, top Cyfarthfa puddler, stood on the corner of Bridgefield; off shift, he watched Megsie and Annie go by. He saw Annie first because she was bigger, and smiled. Like a princess she went, with her black Abergavenny shawl akimbo over her arms and her bright hair falling over her shoulders; she had a neat swing on her hips, he thought, and her breasts were firm and high. Megsie he saw drooping in the delicate beauty of the consumptive adolescent, aged sixteen; her eyes, round and bright in the pallor of her cheeks, seemed to rove within his soul; once he knew a girl like this drooping one, and she had coughed out her lungs on a bed of rags in the Irish cellars up at Pontmorlais. Dobi, his ladler, had a sister like her well-set friend going with Old Wag up to the Aunty Popi Davey Lodgings, and she ended as one of Sgubor Fawr's molls on the Iron Bridge, touting the drunks coming off shift on pay nights, until they found her face down in the Taff one winter morning. Rumour said an agent had her first for a sovereign

and her father got a shilling a week rise on the limestone hauling, but he never had the proof of it.

Shrugging, he turned away, caught Shan Shonko's hands in
passing and wheeled her in a circle to the shrieks of the squatting colliers, then, pulling her drum-hat over her eyes, he went
within the Miners' and hammered the counter for a pint. He
was due to meet Bron Babbie, his wife, but he had forgotten
this.

Miss Thrush the Sweets, looking younger than her forty
years, cried to the waiting coach:

'I will not be a moment, Mrs. Taibach. Tell Mr. Note that I
am just coming.' Outside on the cobbles of High Street the
coach for Merthyr, with Mr. Bottom Note's harmonium strapped on the back, stamped and lurched with expectancy: Willie
Bach Genius, his violin case under his arm, cried nervously
around the door of the shop:

'Got to get going, see, Miss Thrush. Mr. Note's got a revolution coming off in Merthyr: he don't like being kept waiting.'

'The revolution will wait another five minutes, Willie Bach;
it will be that much more effective if Mr. Note keeps calm.'
Before the cracked mirror on the wall, the sole furnishing of an
otherwise empty shop, Miss Thrush patted her well-groomed
hair and smoothed her hands over her body: now turning in
profile to flicker a wink at the glass, while her sister, Miss
Agnes Thrush cried in wet misery:

'I don't know what's got into you, I just don't. If our ma
was alive it'd drive her lunatic, and me feyther must be sittin'
upright in his grave this moment. Woman, see sense—you
can't just sell up at forty and land yourself in Merthyr un-
escorted—you know what'll happen don't ye?'

'Stand aside, sister.' Miss Thrush took Willie's arm.
'Kindly escort me to the coach like a gentleman, Willie.'

This Willie did, and held the coach door wide for Miss
Thrush to ascend, while his mother, sitting beside a fuming
Mr. Note, nodded and beamed her approval.

'Good morning, Mrs. Taibach,' cried Miss Thrush. 'Good
morning, Mr. Note. Let us pray for a safe journey and thank

84

you for suggesting I should share the coach and the cost.'

And Miss Thrush, late of the The Sweets on High Street, steadied her broad-brimmed hat with one hand; with the other she drew high her voluminous black skirt, exposing to Willie's delighted gaze a long, shapely leg from bright buckled shoe to suspender as she stepped up. According to Willie later, even the horse looked round.

And in the doorway of the empty shop with its notice 'Sold' on the window, Miss Agnes Thrush clasped her kerchief to her throat in growing panic, and cried:

'Save us! She's got nought on! Why, ye scarlet huzzy, Milly Thrush. And to Merthyr, in scarlet stockings...!'

Percy Bottom Note, commanding a good view of the ascent, rose from his seat with a shivering smile and bowed low. 'Pray enter, good lady, pray enter...!' Vigorously he dusted the seat with a red handkerchief, crying, 'I must say, Miss Thrush, although I have seen you many times before, I never dreamed... pray, pray be seated.'

As Willie Bach Genius observed afterwards, a couple of inches of Milly Thrush thigh and they stop the revolution.

'Welcome, I'm sure,' said Mrs. Taibach, and hooked Willie beside her, abdicating his look of awe. 'You sit by here, and I'll know where you are.'

In this fashion, with Willie Taibach Genius staring at his idol in utter disbelief, they took the road to iron, and Merthyr.

8

WITH the listless demeanour of a woman lost, Jobina walked
down Plymouth Street past Maerdy Gardens where the big
oaks stood, fighting their everlasting battle against the encrust-
ing residue of coke, their boles gleaming with sparkle-mine
under the July moon. Outside Dark House she rested against
a wall and bathed her feet in a gutter with water piped from
the works into the nearby Taff. An urchin watched her from
the shadows, one of many who had followed her in from
Plymouth Works where the Nipper Tandy gang were building
a dram-road culvert. Belcher and Big Bonce were working
there, also Skin-Crone and Godiva, and Curly Hayloft who was
nursing his grief for Tilly, who was dead. Merthyr had not
been kind to the Nipper Tandy and the new Plymouth dram-
road. Working for the navvy contractor Peto the Baptist, whose
tentacles ranged from Darlington to Newport, they had con-
tracted for the culvert on piece-work; twelve hour shifts at two
pounds a foot, and hit the rock strata north of Mae Level on
the William Davies land, and this meant blasting. Belcher
went in with the drills and Big Bonce followed with powder,
and they charged the bore-holes in wet working up to their
arm-pits, said Lady Godiva.

'Where's me Tilly?' asked Curly Hayloft, and they said she
was on top.

'Has anybody seen me darling girl?' Curly asked again.
'Will you hold that match, Belch, until I discover me woman?'
but Belcher had lost an ear-drum on the Stockton barrow runs,
and his side to Curly was deaf.

'Away to go!' he cried, and fired the fuse. 'Take cover, me

lovelies, for it's two pounds a foot, and this should fix it!' and he scrambled behind a rock.

'In the name of God, where's Tilly?' shrieked Curly, and he stared down the hill while Tilly, whistling with her face up to the sun, went into the tunnel with the nose-bags.

'Tilly!' shrieked Moll. 'Tilly, Tilly!' screamed Godiva.

The tunnel barked fire like the muzzle of a gun: the morning sang with the whine of boulders: black smoke billowed and blinded the sun. They found Tilly in the mouth under a six-ton rock, and Curly went on all fours like a dog, burrowing in the drift, then lay beside her on the blood-stained ground and reached into a fissure and touched the tips of her fingers.

Tilly died in the tongue of Wigan, where she was born, and only Curly understood when she spoke from her tomb, though he was from the south.

'There's nought but you in a mile o' dinners,' she said. 'An' I threw the nose-bags clear as I come in, Curly. Are you with me, lad?'

'Ay, me sweet one.'

'Ye'll do well by me ma back home, Curly?'

'I will that,' he said. 'I'll skin me fingers for her, since she touched me with a good woman.'

'Eh, me chap, it's comin' awful dark,' she said, and died.

Now Jobina looked through the smoke at the moon, and the memory of Tilly was like cutting the stitches of a partly healed wound. It took Blackbird and Skin-Crone, Moll Maguire and Mercy Merriman to pull Curly off Belcher when he got him by the throat, and Jobina helped with a pick-handle.

'I'll give her one thing, she saved the dinners,' said Betsy Paul, collecting them up.

Now there was in Jobina an emptiness as she wandered, looking for Gideon, and as she went past the Angel into Court Street the children followed, though none saw them: these, the orphans of Cyfarthfa, Penydarren and Dowlais, lived in the disused workings of an earlier age. By theft they lived, for they lacked food. Denied poor relief or parish help, they had banded together for the common good, living like animals on the tumps by day, the ragged outcasts of an era of wealth and privilege: by night, in summer, they slept on the mountains. In winter, with the practised skill of trained soldiers, with lookouts in the vanguard and spies at the rear, they slept beside the coke ovens of Thompson, Ynysfach and Cyfarthfa until beaten out into the frost by the special constables. Within the shadow of the rope or cell, the transportation hulks or treadmill, they followed the easier prey like lame tigers: weakened by starvation, slowed by disease, they found strength in numbers. Aged from nine to sixteen, they roved in bands: twenty-four who lived in the old workings on the Meyrick and Davies land, were now following Jobina beyond the gates of the Unitarian where the Thompson agents were inside on their knees, and up the dram-road to Adulum Fields.

With her shoes in her hands Jobina wandered, wondering if Gideon would have come in on the Dowlais road: if he had, she reflected, he would likely be lodging in the Pontmorlais area, for he loved the Irish. So intent were her thoughts that she did not see the shadows moving about her, or hear the whisperings and the brushing of bare feet among the trees: for the Thompson works went into blast at ten o'clock and the world seemed to tremble, and a pillar of flame rose from the furnaces like a blow-torch fusing the stars. The red light played on the watching faces about her as she wandered, eyes half closed now to the sobbing of Curly. Then, realising that she was too far east, she stopped and rested. She was sitting there quietly in the shadows of the road when a hand brushed grass, a foot slithered on a stone behind her. The night was suddenly incredibly quiet: even the Cyfarthfa night-shift seemed to have died in sleep; the soil beneath her rumbled to the underground workings and the sprag of a dram five hundred feet below. A threat in moving hands and switching eyes grew from the darkness and the moon faded in a billow of smoke from Thompson. A finger of ice seemed to touch her brain, and Jobina slowly rose from the ditch, and turned, looking about her.

The ring of small faces were motionless above the grass of the berm.

Staring at them, she put her hands to her face and backed across the road, then turned and fled, weeping aloud as she went past the Independent and she heard them gasping in their swift pursuit. She shrieked as they came abreast of her on the edge of the new burial ground, the fleetest in the van: here Jobina stopped in prayers of incoherent terror as they closed the ring around her, and pulled her down.

'Ach, dear me,' said Blod. 'rest your wee self, Randy, me love, it's a tryin' time for the pair of us.'

Humping and heaving was Randy, with his fine body sweating in the straw of the barn and his eyes on sticks, and if there's one thing that drives a fella berserk it's a gorgeous filly like you diving around and never in one place long enough to pin ye.

'Listen, have you no pity? I could take me pick of the wenches from Merthyr to Aberafon, and here I am punching around in the dark and getting nowhere. Won't ye give a fella an outing?'

'I will not!' Upright and shocked was Blod, her head an inch from the barn roof, and he saw her eyes like diamonds in her face and the smudged shadows of her cheeks: golden as the straw was her hair tumbling in thick swathes over her shoulders and her skin was stained brown by the sun, her mouth shining with kisses: and he thought he had never seen so lovely a creature in a march from Merthyr to Penarth where the weekend coasters came in from France. Every Saturday night they came and anchored off the jetties in deep water, and the onion men from Breton would row ashore in their little sharp currachs with the Spanish immigrant women for the industries, and these they would land along the little stone quays, and he had never seen the likes of them either. For they were beauties from the eastern coast of Spain, many being of pure gipsy blood, the Gitano who fled inland from the persecutions of Gascony and Rousillon. They were hot women, this he knew, with siesta sun in their veins and their hair was black, their eyes slanted; their bodies were beautifully proportioned, and he saw them again in the sawdust of the Welsh inns, and heard the rattle of their castanets and the high shriek of their *tella tella hoi*! And he heard in the throat of Blod Irish the whispers of a girl called Marajeala, who said yes, yes, yes. She was sixteen, he remembered. Now he moved in the barn straw.

'No,' said Blod. 'No, no, *no*!'

'Aw, woman, gi' it a rest!' He sighed deep. 'Yes for a change, is it?'

'No,' said Blod Irish. 'If you want a girl for midnight sport you can seek her elsewhere. I'm standing before the priest or nothin'—didn't I tell you that before we left for Merthyr? When I'm wife to you and mither o' your children, could ye look me in the eye and call me decent if ye had me in barn straw?'

'Gawd help us,' said Randy, 'with speeches like that, and me setting fire to meself.'

'Aw, you poor little soul,' whispered Blod, 'tutty down here on me,' and she pulled his head down to her breast, but up went Randy like something scalded.

'Would you drive me deranged, girl? That's the last place in the world I can sleep.'

'What's the matter now, fella?'

'I'm off to the next door barn,' said Randy.

'Please yourself, I'm sure,' said Blod. '*Arrah!* If this is the start of it, what will be the end of it? The man's a heathen, a most temperamental creature.'

On her back, with her eyes closed at the roof, Blod listened to him going down the ladder; but he was back in seconds bending above her.

'No, no, no!' said Blod.

'Och, dry up, woman,' said he. 'Hush up, and listen.'

'God bless the Pope,' said Blod, peering down the road. 'Just look what's coming ... !'

Mamie Goldie and Billa Jam, Moke Donkey and the children were coming down Fishpond Street with the cart: Moke was walking behind with Merve and Saul pushing, the rest of the children were asleep on the cart with twin donkeys, and Mamie and Billa were harnessed in the shafts.

'Didn't I tell ye that moke was carrying for twins?' said Blod.

'Has the old girl been producing, then?'

'Like as not she's birthed on the road. There'll be hell to pay rent to when Mr. Jam finds that donkey kidnapped.'

Randy rubbed his face, saying, 'Will the damned woman never let me be? Will you tell me why I canna start a new life without her chasing me up with kids and donkeys?'

'It's a powerful love she bears you, Randy.'

'Och, go to sleep,' said he. 'I'm sick to death of females, anyway—the likes of you and mothers in particular.' He heaved over away from her and thumped the straw for a pillow. 'If I went down there what would it be? The same old tongue pie, the same old mythering, with you getting the sharp end of it as a good for nothing Irish quick-wit snatching at the first fine son that comes along—is that what you want?'

'You'll never change Mamie, that's for sure,' said Blod.

'Then why do you stand for her when she gives you nothing but jaw?'

'Because she's your ma, boy. And I've never yet come across an apology of a son who could bed himself down for the night while his mother does the work of a donkey—ach, you make me sick, Randy Goldie. Did you hear that—ye make me sick!'

Randy sat up and clutched himself; with flickering eyes, Blod watched.

'The big fat thing,' he said. 'She's not worth a second look. She's done nothing but moddle and coddle me, so I'm making the break. D'you hear me, Mamie Goldie? I'm done with ye— I've cut the strings for good.'

Blod waited, breath pent.

'Are you asleep, girl?' Randy leaned above her: through half-closed eyes Blod saw the sweat of his face, and breathed on with the rhythm of one asleep.

'Och, holy God,' whispered Randy, knuckling his mouth. 'Ma,' he said, and Blod watched him.

The hoof-beats of Moke began to fade.

'Ma,' he said again, 'eh dear . . . Ma!' and he leaped up and vaulted ten feet down to the floor of the barn: Blod rose in the straw watching him tearing through the moonlight up Fish-pond, and his voice came to her in flushes of the wind:

'Ma! Ma!'

Smiling, she looked at the stars.

Strident in her grief with Percy Bottom Note slipping away under her nose, Mrs. Taibach sat upright in the swaying coach and her soul snorted its fierce anger. In the vicious encounters of her mind, she clutched the libertine robes of Miss Thrush and tore them, shrieking, from her body, while Miss Thrush, done up in Sunday braveries, rocked on Mr. Note's shoulder like a captive butterfly: she swayed and bowed to the bucking coach and the drumming of hooves in a piratical dream. With the furnace glare flashing on her sleeping face and the stars of Dowlais Top spying in a rent of smoke, she nuzzled closer to Mr. Note in the comforting hollow between shoulder and starched collar. And she saw him not as one tattered in soul and frayed at sleeve but as a chevalier of high nobility.

'I'll blutty give it you,' whispered Mrs. Bach Taibach.

Mr. Note, Corresponding Member for the Merthyr Union Branch, nodded and dreamed in his plans for Miss Thrush the Sweets. Adrift from his ideals of property reform, the repeal of the Corn Laws and dissolution of the slave trade, he sat in a wicked, bare-legged crow of a dream. In a buccaneer pursuit of Milly Thrush, casting off a demand for higher wages, anti-shopocracy and pro-democracy, he exchanged the tub-thumped trumpetings of youth for a hunt along a palm-fringed beach while Miss Thrush, attired in red stockings, went in mecurial flight, arms up, her long hair flying. Removed from his castigation of the mine-owners, abandoning his resentment against Truck and the revenue of the Crown, the Poor Law coming, and parish relief, he cornered and caught her in a tangle of ribbons, bringing her down in shrieks of girlish laughter. And he heard Miss Thrush's cry as one of submission, a finale for the last chord of his new Gun Symphony, and he raised his fist high and brought it down, crying:

'*Diawch!*'

Miss Thrush awoke, gathering her things about her and eas-

92

ing her head off Mr. Note's collar with a smile of surprise at Mrs. Taibach and Willie, while Mr. Note blew his nose violently into a big red handkerchief.

'You 'aving nightmares, Mr. Note?' asked Willie, brightly.

Sonorously, Mr. Note replied: 'As a matter of fact I was conducting the last movement of my new Gun Symphony...' He twiddled his thumbs with delight.

'I'll give him Gun Symphony,' whispered Mrs. Bach Taibach.

The coach braked then, its locked wheels slithering along the rutted road opposite Adulum Fields: Willie peered out of the window. The gravestones of the new burial ground were standing white against the moon.

'We there, then?' asked Miss Thrush.

'We are not,' said Mr. Note, bass, and put his head out of the window. 'What ails us, coachman? What is wrong?'

The lights of Merthyr glowed in the valley; the furnaces of Cyfarthfa simmered on the night air. The coachman clambered down from his seat and came to the door.

'Been an accident, it appears,' said he.

'An accident!' Mrs. Taibach clutched at her throat.

'Kind of, beggin' your pardon, sir,' said the coachman to Mr. Note. 'Some poor vagrant found dead on the road. I suggest the ladies turn their fair 'eads as I take us past the gambo, for the sexton has got 'er.'

'Kindly proceed when convenient,' said Mr. Note.

As they lurched past the gambo Mrs. Taibach averted her head and pressed Willie's face into the folds of her coat: even Mr. Note lowered his eyes in respect. But Miss Thrush, impelled by some dreadful curiosity, looked out on to the road.

Jobina was lying on the gambo and her face was upturned in a drive of the moon.

The sexton wrung his hands and stared up at Miss Thrush, his great eyes brilliant in his cavernous face. 'Can't think how it happened; neither scratch nor bite on 'er, and beads and bodice intact, an' two shillings in money in her purse ... her heart must 'ave stopped, poor soul.'

'Oh, God,' said Miss Thrush, and bowed her head. For unmistakably, as she had suspected, projecting from beneath the tied-down skirt were the buckled boots of the navvy and the calves of two red stockings.

9

THE sun was nearly overhead when Gideon and Sun reached the outskirts of Pentre next day, and here rested in a ditch clear of the Merthyr road, and the mail coach for Cardiff passed them in a swaying gallop and horn-blast from a clowning postillion; the manes of the four big chestnuts were flying in the wind, their nostrils dilating red under the whip, their eyes wild.

Gideon eased himself up. 'Come on,' he commanded. 'I want to be in Merthyr before the sun goes down.'

'And me poor spags that blistered!' In the middle of the road she squatted, examining her feet. 'Man alive, you're as cussed as Moses with the tablets—we've got all day.'

Gideon did not reply but walked on, for there had come to him an unaccountable premonition of distaster; obedient to the warning, he strode on, while Sun followed, protesting. But now, the limp gone, she ran on tip-toe about him, crossing her feet in the manner of the Desmond gipsies and singing in a high soprano. Of a sudden, the mood of fear left him and he grinned and knelt, pulling out his fiddle, and played for her a merry Mayo reel.

'Are you dancing?' But he knew she was dancing, and played on, changing to a higher key and raising the tempo, and still she danced, madly pirouetting, and the dust rose to her feet. Then she stopped, and stared at the hedgerows. Gideon was still playing when the *Caro ar Cefn* appeared.

They rose slowly from behind the hedges: their game was at its height: six of them, and they approached slowly, their hands deep in their rags. Theirs was the sport of pick-a-back riding; and their prey was turned from human into a horse.

Gideon lowered the fiddle. 'What is it?'

'The *Caro ar Cefn*,' said Sun, clutching his arm.

The leader of the Riders smiled.

These were the hooligans of the Taibach industry, the re-fuse of the ironworks, pits and quarries who begged their way from one short-job to another, mixing humour and cruelty in their highway robbery; the pick-a-back riff-raff of the bawdy inns of Pyle and Kenfig Hill, who had drifted north when a victim died.

'How are you?' They ringed Gideon and Sun in the road. Dishevelled from rough sleeping and drink, they grinned, tossing a gin flask from hand to hand. The leader drank last, gasped, and wiped his mouth, saying, 'Dear me, we wink at the sky and the manna drops. A travelling fiddler and his prancer, is it? And pockets filled with gold?'

'You're a long way north, Rider,' said Gideon.

'You know us, and you blind?'

'I can smell you.' The dog began to whine at his feet and he stooped, picking it up. 'And what gold I have stays on me, but you're welcome to it if you can get it. Let us pass.'

'Have you right of way?' It was the age-old shout of the drovers, who fought for it for fun.

'The roads are metalled; the right is established,' said Gideon.

'If you shift us, blind man.' They ranged across it, barring the way.

Gideon said: 'I'll lay you this, Cefn Rider—you don't know who you're stopping. Stumble one of us and I'll come back with men who will tie you to trees and take blood from your backs.'

One shouted with laughter; the eyes of the leader danced in his face.

A dwarf of a man pushed to the front. 'Did you hear that, Iolo? The chap's going to cripple us!'

'The brutal fella!'

The Rider said: 'Well, there's nothing I like better than a bucking blind fiddler—down on your knees, boyo.'

'You are getting no lifts from me,' said Gideon.

'Then your missus might oblige?' They ringed about them, nearer. Another shouted: 'Ask natural and polite, Bando, and she might give you a lift of another kind.'

They laughed full-throated at this, stamping about. Gideon said, head averted, 'Run for it, run for it.'

'An' leave ye with these hooligans?' Sun shrieked at the men, 'Have ye no common decency—and him blind?'

Another cried. 'He's a fine set-up fella, missus. He don't need eyes to hand us poor weary travellers a ride!'

A big one, stark Irish, called: 'Is it too much to ask—a lift for a few of us—just a couple o' hundred yards?'

'Take his money but leave him in peace. Have ye no souls?' she yelled it into their faces as they advanced, drawing their short ash canes from their belts and swishing them in the air. Sun backed away, pulling Gideon after her.

'In the name of God, look, I'm begging ye! Leave him!'

'Ach, what's the odds? We're only after improving the manners of the community, don't ye see? If he takes the big ones and you picky-up the little ones we'll be half-way up the road to Merthyr without even swishing a cane—are ye on?' The Irishman was in the forefront now, the Welsh leader snatched at Sun's wrist, but she twisted free.

'God grant me sight,' said Gideon, and leaped, striking by sound. It was an astonishing blow and the Irishman took it square in the face, and sighed, slipping to the ground: with direction lost, Gideon flailed and swung, crouching and hooking vicious blows which the Riders avoided with laughing ease: Sun shrieked, fighting herself free of the leader in a tangle of hair and skirts.

'Ay, wang 'em Gid, the hairy bastards!'

'Get down the road, woman—run, run!' Gideon dived among them, caught one and clubbed him to his knees.

'Hey, Nevan, Will—give me a hand with this wild-cat!'

The men ran in a circle, taking Gideon from behind, tripping and bringing him down and they fought in grunts to secure him. He heard the cries of Sun Heron.

'Have ye got him?'

'Aye, an' settle his hash.' Face down, they held him.

'For pity's sake, Evan, can ye strike a cripple?'

'I can—look at me face!'

Gideon raised his head and his voice rang out from the struggles and oaths of the men above him: 'Sun Heron, run, *run*!'

The redness of the morning was fading in his eyes and there was a weariness in him; the blows and curses were dying in his ears. And he heard a scream, loud and clearly he heard it, then silence. They hauled him on to his feet, pinioned from behind. He said: 'In the name of Jesus, let the child go. I'll carry you, I'll give my money, but let her go.'

'Who's for harming her?' This from the Irishman, square and strong but still staggering from Gideon's blow. 'If ye'd come peaceful you'd not be on the end of a hammering now. Now settle yourself and enjoy the gallop. Are ye ready, for it's only a question of a morning trot, seeing you're delicate.'

Held by four of them, Gideon, inches the taller, raised his head. 'Sun Heron! Sun Heron!' he shouted. The woods echoed.

'Settle yourself, me son,' said the Irishman. 'She's in the very best of hands.'

'Just act easy with us, that's all we ask. Everybody's always after belting us, d'ye see, and us just polite travellers begging a lift on the way. Act civil, man, an' I'll speak for your wild-cat.'

'Down on your knees, fella.'

'Hold him steady, Daio!'

'Kneel, ye big mare—how can I mount ye standing—sure to God, the thing must be all o' fifteen hands!'

'Down, blind man, or it'll come worse for your filly!'

Gideon knelt in the road, eyes closed.

'Ah, that's better, eh, Will?'

'You on first, Bando boy, and give him one in the shanks if he don't behave.'

'Open your chops for the bridle, girl.'

They twisted a rope between Gideon's teeth: the man on his back now cried: 'Up, up! *Aw*, that's the daisy! Wheeah, there, she's a spirited mare. Are you steady, fella?'

On his feet now, with the man on his back, Gideon waited, holding the rider's legs.

'Right, away!'

They neighed at the sky, three of them dancing about in the manner of children playing at horses: the fourth man, on Gideon's back, lashed at his legs with the cane.

'Right, girl—gallop!'

With his head held back to the strain of the gag, Gideon broke into a swaying, staggering run with the Cefn Rider pick-a-back and the three pursuers thrashing at his calves, crying falsetto and urging him to greater speed. In this manner he went, brushing the hedgerows in his blindness while the rider heaved on the bridle yelling with joy. A boulder in his path and Gideon tripped, falling headlong, and the rider was on his back the moment he rose and the beating started again, but he did not feel the pain nor even the weight of the man upon him. There was growing in Gideon a fury that reached into the depth of his soul: it was all-consuming; a paroxysm of wrath that brought to him a new, vehement strength; crying aloud, he went headlong so that the rider fell: scrambling around, Gideon found him, caught his clothes and pulled him close, sought his throat and clutched; and to escape the blows of his tormentors he rolled over and over in the road, gasping with the effort to cut off his adversary's breath. In choking snarls and gasps they rolled to the verge and collapsed in waving legs into the roadside ditch. Gideon was underneath with the face of the choking man hard against his own, his whole being thrusting every moment of his strength into the cramping grip of his fingers. And although the fists of the other riders beat upon his head he still maintained the hold on the other's throat, pulling him higher as a shield, concentrating all his fading effort into the tips of his fingers: the body of the Cefn Rider began to stiffen and a trembling began, and Gideon heard the rumblings of his chest: his arms began to flail the air, impeding the efforts of the others who tried to haul him off. But even as they raised him out of the ditch so Gideon came too, stitched to his victim with a strength that made them one. Then he heard a shout, and thumping footsteps; cries of alarm began to beat about him and the blows of the Riders stopped; the man he held began faintly to gasp, weakly waving his arms as if in protest at the approach of death, and at that moment he was pulled from Gideon's grasp.

Sun came back to the edge of the road when the Cefn Riders left her, to face the new attack. With her hands pressed to her face she watched the young Welshman, recognising him instantly as the one who greeted her outside the Swan when she fought Jobina. With his bundle at his feet he was into the big Irishman first, fighting with the silent intent of the professional, and the man sagged before the sweeping hooks and swings, dropping to his knees as the Welshman left him, to bend and seize the bearded leader, pulled him over his shoulder; the man hit the road face down; and as two more Riders came storming in, the young man wheeled to face them; seeing Sun, he yelled, 'Don't stand there, woman, come on in!' He ducked a cane slash, took another on his shoulder and hooked a man solid, then backed away, tripped over the leader and fell headlong, but bringing down a third Rider as he went: they rolled, striking.

'*Arrah!* I'm comin', fella!' Sun shrieked, and stooped, picking up a stone. Gideon was on his feet now, seeking combat with sweeping hands, staring into the sun for sight. And through the vicious rays he saw the outline of fighting shapes and cried aloud, crouching towards them.

'That's the boy, Gid. Boot 'em, wang 'em, the big oafs!' and Sun stooped and cracked a Rider with a stone as he staggered up, and ran around the Welsh boy who had another on his back and stoned this one, too. Gideon had found the big Irishman now, a swaying shape against the sun, and struck, missed and struck again, and the man took it square, and dropped, motionless: one was running, another was trying to take the Welshman by the legs until Sun got him from behind; freed, the boy straightened the Welsh leader with a left as he rose and pulled down his hands. The punch that felled the man travelled but a few inches; his feet came off the road, his shoulders followed, he hit the berm of the road and lay still,

100

eyes closed. Now Gideon was swaying towards them, seeking a new target for his aimless swings and hooks, tripped over a Rider, and stumbled blindly.

'*Bayo!* Gid, it's over!' shrieked Sun, and dragged the Welsh boy out of Gideon's lunging path. 'That's done 'em! Three down and two runnin'! *Hei wei!* Slow up, fella!'

The Welshman was gasping, leaning on Sun, but he was grinning.

'Ay now,' he said, going double, 'that was a good one!' He licked his knuckles.

'Good? Bedamn, I've never had such a fight since Derry and Billy Ugmore! Are ye hurt, Gid?' She reached him, turning him to face her. 'Ach, the dirty gobs—you've an eye fillin' up, man—look what they've done to ye!'

'Are you all right?' gasped Gideon.

'Just about! The young chap here beat them to it. Och, it was a joy to see ye doin' 'em—where are you from?'

'Aberafon.' He stared about him. 'By God, these Riders are a long way north!'

Two of the men were getting up now, and she shrieked at them, 'Ye pesky snakes, have done wi' ye!' and she raised her stone, but Gideon caught her, dragging her back.

'Leave them, leave them!' he said. He turned to the Welshman. 'We can find no words to thank you.'

'It's little enough. I heard the shouting, but I'd seen the Riders earlier, and slowed me down. It was the woman I was worried for—where you bound?'

'Merthyr,' said Gideon. 'What's your name?'

'Dic Penderyn.'

The man on the bank stirred, groaning; the one by the ditch had gone.

'Dic Penderyn, eh?' Sun looked him over, smiling. 'Sure, there's the sound of a bird in that.'

The young man said: 'I saw you in Maesteg, and again at Gitos Farm. You travelling together?'

The dog was whining at Gideon's feet; stooping, he lifted it against him. 'I'm for Merthyr, but I don't know about you?' He looked at Sun. To his astonishment, and joy, he could see

101

her quite clearly.

'Ach, one place is as good as another.'

'One thing's sure,' said Gideon, 'with the Riders this far north it would be safer to travel together, do you mind?'

The Welshman was wondering about them; he had seen Gideon in Taibach; Sun he had first met in Maesteg; outside Tir-Phil he had seen them sharing the coach. The girl was ragged, and he judged her age at sixteen; the blind man was well dressed for a man on the road, and at least ten years older; also, he was educated, and the girl was not.

'Aw, ye poor thing, Gid—they've broken your fiddle!' Sun picked it up, cherishing it against her. 'Now, if there's money in that fella's pockets he's goin' to pay for it.' She turned. 'D'you realise the little one lifted your purse?'

'Both can be replaced,' said Gideon. 'Leave the man be— enough evil for one day, child.' He put out his hand to her.

'Can I take another wang at that fat Irishman 'afore I leave, then?'

'You can't—come on!' Gideon pushed her in front of him. 'Merthyr.'

'Ay,' said Penderyn, 'Merthyr.'

Gideon, Sun Heron and Dic Penderyn came through the cellars of Pontmorlais where the labouring Irish lived when the sun was going down. Earlier, they had come down the Penydarren dram-road past the works, and here the setting sun was dimmed by the incandescent flashes of iron. The labourers of the slopes and inclines were outlined against a sky of scarlet; the barrel-loaders tipping their limestone, coal and ore into the furnace maws, brought to pygmy size by the fire-shot smoke of the open hearths, and the ground shook to the shot-firing. Now, farther down the hill, they saw the twin glows of Cyfarthfa and Ynys Works, and heard the roar of ironmaking, the air buffeting their faces as if from the velocity of surface explosions.

'The old Cyfarthfa stink,' said Dic Penderyn.

Yellow smoke filled with sulphuretted gases was billowing upwards from the roasting mine; shafts of fire pinned the

102

dusking sky, and from the inferno of light and smoke there came the hiss and venting of pistons, the clanging of bells and the whine of the mills. Here, with an almost total disregard for the human condition, the violation called Merthyr sent its finished iron to the ports of the world, its economics tuned to rate and price. Men were mutilated here, eyes put out, children worked in the pits here or laboured in their hundreds on the Hirwaun open-mining in all weathers; women gave birth at the face, youth was old at ten, and the expectation of life was the age of twenty. Here was no sanitation, no water supply save from polluted wells; here the cottages—a legacy of Bacon the Pig, an earlier iron master—leaned in their ricketty confusion along tortuous courts and alleys; a criss-cross, crazy mass of leaning roofs and hovels which, at their worst, compared to the slums of India according to distinguished travellers. Down the hill the cobbles were piled high with garbage, the gutters crammed with rubbish, and excrement spilled searching fingers for the lower ground. And there rose a smell so offensive that Sun had to cover her mouth; Taibach was as nothing compared to this destitution. Here ill-clad children played and ragged people watched from doors; old men with the quaking pallor of the prematurely aged, followed them with hollowed eyes as they passed; beggars cried shrilly to them for alms; dogs and cats picked over rubbish with furtive apprehension.

'God alive, Gid,' said Sun, 'is this your beloved Merthyr?'

Yet, through the little cobbled streets that rose to higher ground she could see lines of washing out to dry despite the smoke, and from behind the neatly curtained windows of the tradesmen came the unmistakable gleam of brass and the flickering of homely fires.

'What address you going for, blind man?' asked Dic.

'Eighteen Cross, you know it?'

'We pass it on my way home.' Dic glanced from one to the other. 'Are you both bound there?'

'Not me,' said Sun, 'I'm on me own.'

'I will speak to Zimmerman,' said Gideon. 'He will know what to do.'

'Nobody's asking favours,' said she tartly. 'I told ye before

—I'll see to meself.'

'A bed for the night at least, woman; please do not be stupid.'

A gentry brougham passed them and drew up at the entrance of the Castle Inn as they turned into High Street.

Here the workers were flooding in from the open-cast mining of Hirwaun Common: men, women and children, Irish mostly—scrabbling on the heath for the furnace food of iron mine; and they were happy in their banter on a shilling a day, brown-faced and chattering, for it was summer. Later they would work with frozen bodies in the icy winds of Aberdare mountain, labouring under the sights of the little brass cannon of the Crawshay tower, in the name of benevolence.

Dic Penderyn said as they pushed through the crowd to Cross Street, 'If it's only a bed for the night you're after, I expect my mam could do it.'

'It's two beds, make no mistake on it,' said Sun.

They turned right past the Lamb public and Dic stopped at a door.

'This is Number Eighteen Cross Street, blind man.'

'We owe you hospitality—this is my friend's house, please come in.'

'You owe me nothing, man—I'd have done it for anyone.'

'You work here?' asked Gideon, knocking on the door.

'Ay, hauling, mainly—but the last month or so in the Ynys compound, under a rodder.' He smiled down at Sun. 'Is it work you're after?'

'That's the last thing she's after,' said Gideon.

Sun jerked her thumb. 'D'ye hear that? He's always slandering me. I'll be getting work when I'm good and ready, but I'm not going back to Taibach, for I'm sick to me stomach of the place. Can ye coin it here, man?'

'You can earn your keep—you can pick ore on Hirwaun, and that's all right now, in summer, for a shilling a day, but it's hard. Or you can stack under Liz Treharne down the Ynys Compound, and that's one-and-six a day, but it's murder.'

'You work there, you say?'

'Ay, ay.'

'And you live where?'

'Round the corner in Islyn Court with my mam and dad.'

Sun smiled at him. There was about him a native charm; he was not handsome as Gideon was handsome, and his strength was uncultured, as was his speech. But his youth called to her tempestuous nature, possessing as he did the same boisterous arrogance. With his hands deep in his pockets he flickered a wink at her as they waited for the answer to Gideon's knock, and she slid her eyes over him so that he grinned of a sudden.

Gideon, for his part, was astonished that the Bolton Authority Lodge should trust Zimmerman with anything, let alone the South Wales circuit. To site the Union branch here, in Cross Street, was typical of the man's inordinate lack of care; it was rather like booking a hotel room next to an iron master: even from here he could hear the high-pitched voices of the gentry arriving outside the Castle Inn. Then the door opened before him, and Zimmerman cried, reaching for Gideon's arm:

'Ah, my old friend, you are here—and in such charming company!'

'Don't overdo it,' murmured Gideon.

'You will come in?'

'The young man, too,' said Gideon.

'It is nearly a regiment.' Zimmerman opened the door wider, and they entered; immediately they were within he turned and locked it, saying, 'Good God, man, what the devil is happening? I thought we were acting alone?'

'We are. Both these young people are workers—they will know of our existence sooner or later.'

'The man I do not mind, but the woman . . .'

'Had my young friend not guided me I doubt I'd arrived at all.'

'Right,' said the Pole, turning to Sun. 'Now goodbye, young friend.'

'Oh, no, Zim—she stays.'

'But you, of all people!' Zimmerman smiled faintly. 'And you admonished me when I brought home women!'

'They were in my room,' said Gideon blandly, 'it's a rather

different matter. The child needs a bed—give me a guinea!'

'God alive, Davies—didn't you earn on the road?'

'We met the *Caro ar Cefn*—come, it's a long story—give me the sovereign.'

'Och, he can keep that,' exclaimed Sun, eyeing it.

'Take it,' said Gideon, 'and don't be a fool. Penderyn, did you say you had a bed?'

'With my mother, but I'll have to ask . . .'

'Good. You see the trouble of her staying here?'

'It's damned good, isn't it!' said Sun. 'I'm not five minutes in the place and you're dumping me.'

'It is safer you go, so please,' said Zimmerman. 'You cannot stay here. In Tredegar the man Donovan kept a woman for cooking and mending, and she talked. Women are all right for the table and the bed, but not for the politics.'

'The politics again, is it? I might have guessed,' said Sun. Gideon said: 'Paste on the door that this is the Branch Union and Merthyr itself will know—are you off your head, Zim?'

'She must go!'

A silence came between them. Deliberately, Dic Penderyn reached out and took the sovereign from Gideon's fingers and spun it up in Zimmerman's face, who snatched it.

'We don't charge for the beds in Islyn Court,' he said. 'Come on, girl, away out of it.'

Hand in hand they went down Cross and through the arch into *China*. Dim lights were burning in the cottage windows and there was a flicker of firelight and the gleam of bare shoulders, for the colliers had come off the day-shift from Winchfawr, Cwmglo and Penheol where out of seventy men employed half were on parish relief. The older miners were squatting on their hunkers and women talking on the door-steps, and look what Dic Penderyn is bringing home, good God, and it is funny where they collect them for she don't look like Merthyr pits to me. But some of the men got up as they approached and the women dropped curtseys.

' 'Evening, Dic, boy!'

'God help her,' said Bron Babbie, shifting her latest on to the other. 'She do not know what is coming to her, eh, Dico? Seen my Madoc, have you?'

'Outside the Wheatsheaf, but coming now just, I think.'

'Ach, a devil he is, but good otherwise, mind.'

'Good night, Bron!'

'Good night to you, boy, for you're going to need it. You wait till the minister catches you with that in your hand!'

Dic took a deep breath and opened the door of Islyn Court. His father was reading *The Cambrian*, off shift from Ynys; his mother turned at the hob.

'I've got a lodger, Mam.'

His mother's look of expectancy changed to fear. She said, 'But we haven't the room, lad...' She turned to her husband. 'Dada, we haven't the room, have we? I mean, when Gwen, Morgan and the children come...'

'Is it a female?'

'Ay, Dad, and Irish—her name's Sun Heron.'

'Time you was settled. Time you took to a girl and gave up the politics, me lad.' His father turned in his chair. 'Bring her in and let's have a look at her.' Removing his pipe he looked Sun up and down. 'With a wash she'd come prettier—Irish, ye say?'

'Welsh, and my name's Mari Beynon, though me mother called me Sun.'

'Ay, she's winsome, Welsh or Irish. Bring her in. You're not the first, young woman, and like as not you won't be the last...'

'But Dada, we haven't the room...' protested his wife.

'*Diawch*, it's only for the night, Mam,' said Dic.

'Settle him down, woman,' said Dic's father, 'and we'll get more babies and less politics: I'd pay a king's ransom to ye woman, if ye just settle him down.' Rising, he took Sun's arm and led her within.

10

Sɪᴅ Bʟᴜᴍᴘ, lately removed from the apartments of Dai Posh of the Old Swan, Maesteg, to follow the iron, was engaged in deep discussion with Jump-Jackson, the one-legged landlord of the Wellington.

'You see this thumb?' asked Sid Blump, holding it up.

'I do,' said the landlord.

'Give me a gallon of best home-brew and I'll chop it off.'

Sid Blump, glassy with hop contentment, fixed Jump Jackson with a stare, seeing through the lined, cavernous face of the landlord the white porcelain jars of his youth; the gilt-lettered *Rum*, the funereal black inscription *Port* and the dignified Roman imprint *Whisky*, and these called to him down the lost legions of the years when the bouts were easy, the purses good and gin was a penny a time. Beyond the banded stomachs of the forty-gallon casks stamped *Hopkins Ale, Tanyard*, he saw, too, the hate-lined faces of four hundred opponents imaged on the mirrors of his soul; a soul in black tights and hobnails, a cauliflowered deformity of head-bumps, a flattened nose, and the criss-cross cuts of its pounded youth. In a confusion of ale and pain Sid Blump, mountain-fighter, mouthed back the threat of Knocker Pyle of Ponty and Tancy Boy of Newport, the one who hit him when he was down.

'You all right, fighter?'

'You bugger off,' said Sid Blump.

In a ruptured, blood-streaked brain made egg-shaped by the head smashes of men five stones larger, he remembered the sweat and white bodies, the leaping ropes, the douse of the reviving buckets, and the baying crowds on the tumps. In his little gobbles of ears beaten out of his skull he heard again the mountain wind and the thump of hobnail boots on turf. In his mouth was the taste of blood.

Dic Penderyn came in. His dark eyes switched from Sid Blump to Jump Jackson, the landlord.

'Old fighter,' said Jump. 'Quart as usual?'

'Ay.' Dic put down a penny.

Bleary, his fat face puckered up, Sid Blump raised his thumb. 'You see this, boyo?'

Dic nodded.

'For a gallon of home-brew I'll chop it off.'

'You'll chop it off?'

'I'll chop it off and eat a basin. You know Bull Skewen?'

Dic shook his head.

'I beat him up on Llanthony mountain—hit hell out of him. You done any, son?'

The landlord said: 'Watch who you're talking to, fighter—he's done a lot.'

'Ach, hush!'

'Is that a fact?' asked Sid Blump with puckered joy.

'Just with my mates.'

'Well now!' Sid Blump regarded him with the warm eyes of friendship; Dic winked at him over his jug. The old fighter said: 'Then you must have heard of Bull Skewen.'

'I have not.'

'But everybody's heard of Bull Skewen—the heavyweight Welsh?'

'Not me.'

'Before his time, I expect,' said the landlord.

Furnace flashes were playing on the window, staining red on the sawdust of the bar. Three men entered and the smell of iron came in with their rags. Two were ballers from Cyfarthfa, the other a rodder of Ynysfach furnaces: the right side of his face was burned scarlet by the dandy-fires, a growth.

'Three up, Jumpo,' said one. ' 'Evening, Dic lad!'

' 'Evening,' said Sid Blump.

They nodded briefly. The old fighter waited while they lifted their pewters and drank.

'My old pals,' said Sid Blump. 'Another quart, landlord.'

One wiped the froth from his mouth. 'You heard he's dropping ironstone again, Dico?'

'By how much?'

'Two shillings a week.'

'There'll be bloody trouble.'

'There will be if I don't get another quart,' said Sid Blump.

'I told you before,' said the landlord, 'you can't drink on the slate.'

'Down in Taibach we drink on the gate.'

'The gate?' Dic's eyes were shining.

'Down in the Burgess—now, there's a pub—not like this one hop sawdust. Old Nana, she was, and worked it on pints.' He raised his voice and shouted Irish, ' "Me foine fellas, me hairy handsome men, ye can drink five bars for the rate o' one, but when Nana crosses 'em out, that's the diagonal, and then ye pays ..." Christ, she was a landlord!'

Jump Jackson said to the furnace men: 'And what are the Oddfellows doing about the cut, then?'

'The Oddfellows never saw me short of a pint,' said Sid Blump.

'You think they'll call us out?' asked the baller.

'Not me, man, my missus says we can't afford it—got one and tenpence in the caddy a week before pay.'

'None of us can afford it, but we come out just the same. You heard about John Hughes, Bethel Street?'

'What about him?'

'Got his furniture restrained.'

'He won't be the last.'

'And they took Wil Goff's bed from under him a week last Friday.'

'They didn't!'

'They bloody did.'

'You see this thumb?' asked Sid Blump.

'Court of Requests?'

'Coffin's Court—they just rolled up with a cart and donkey and a paper from the beadle, and took it—near drove his missus demented.'

'And that Crawshay's worth hundreds of thousands!'

'One day we'll have that blutty court down,' said the rodder with the burned face. 'My missus reckons it's a scandal.'

'It's a scandal that you put up with it,' said Dic, looking into his mug.

'What you say, boyo?'

'I said it's a scandal you put up with it. Union representatives have been down from London and gone back without a hearing...'

'God, listen to it! Pin up your napkin, son, and leave it to your elders. If we listened to you we'd finish up at Monmouth.'

'Better that than sitting here whining!' said Dic. 'Twice this week Mason's been speaking at the Miners' and six turned up to hear him. If ye want the Court of Requests down you'll do it by collective action and in public; if you want your furniture back you'll get nowhere sitting on your backsides whining in private.'

'Crawshay has outlawed the Union, lad. Talk sense.'

'He wasn't so keen on the Benefit, but he's got one. God Almighty, if you're going to ask Crawshay every time you move he'll have another quarter of a million and you'll not handle a loaf.'

'Words, words, and they get you nowhere,' said the rodder. 'My dinner's in the oven; I'm off,' but he did not go.

The door went back and the day-shift furnace men of Cyfarthfa crowded in, sullen with the twelve-hour shift, and their shirts were stained with sweat; some had their arms tied with grimy bandages from old burns, two had scalds on their faces from furnace blow-backs: these were Jump Jackson's best customers, drinking the half-strength Hopkins malt ale that replaced in their dried limbs the loss through sweat. They were rangey men, and gaunt, hostile in their silence.

'You're just in time,' said the landlord.

'For what?'

'To see the old fighter eat a basin and cut off his thumb.'

The men did not speak, reaching for their jugs: one said, 'Where's the catch, Boxer?'

111

'I want a gallon of Hopkins.'

'It's a price to pay for that bloody stuff—are ye sane?'

'Sane as a judge, look at his ears,' said the landlord.

Dic said: 'There's a meeting at the Bridge tonight—at ten—Mason, the Union man is speaking again. Are you coming?'

'Watch him,' said the landlord, 'he's touting round the publics, and it ain't healthy. Don't mix drinking with politics, I say.'

'But the lad's right,' said a refiner. 'We ought to support the Union.'

'He's an Englishman and I dunna trust the foreigners.'

'He's a Union man and the last hope you've got,' said Dic.

'What about me thumb, then?' asked Blump, holding it up.

'God help us, fighter, give it a rest.'

'Join the Union and you get thrown out of chapel now—you heard?' a man asked.

'The Reverend Morgan Howells?'

'Calvinistic Methodist, and he's not the only one.'

'There's a bloody loss—thrown out of chapel. I'd take it as a compliment.'

'Not me, not with my missus. Anything frightens me it's the Streams of Loveliness: put the fear of God in me, they do, and she's a life member. She reckons our minister's God.'

'Black magic, and the Church is against us, too, mind.'

'And the Chapels. And in their spare time the parsons go rook-shooting. God alive, what a country!'

'Not the Unitarians, though—be fair, they're behind us, and old Tom Cothi.'

'Talk about the blossoms of Gethsemane. *Women!* A lot of shrieking banshees, I call 'em. They're either wearing out their knees or bowing and scraping in High Street—I'm always telling mine—you take a furnace shift, girl—do you good; a sod, she is.' He spat in the sawdust. 'Airs and bloody graces...'

'Not mine,' said another. 'If Merthyr rises she'll be up front with pitchforks. Very benevolent.'

'You'm damned lucky, Daio.'

'Though she can be a hot one for the fellas, mind, when me back's turned.'

112

'That's all part of the benevolence.'

'Be human, Daio, she's half your age.'

'Ay, ay, but she's bound to draw the line, I say. She don't go up to Cyfarthfa just to clean her teeth.'

They pushed, they spluttered in their ale, and one cried: 'Is it just young Francis she's entertaining, *bach*?'

'Nineteen, is he? God knows what he'll be like when he's ninety!'

'Ach, live an' let live, Daio man—the stallions have to learn on someone to find out tricks for the gentry fillies!'

The baller with the burned face said: 'Oh, ay? Well, I've got three daughters, and if they try their tricks on them I'll be up to see their father—come fair, he don't hold with it—the old man plays it decent—he'd give him Francis.'

A rodder said: 'Ay, well don't count my girl in wi' Daio's skirt, for I got a good one. We got eleven lodgers in one room and six kids in the other, an' she gets sick in her stomach because she can't expose herself—there's always somebody lookin'. Night time I take her up the mountain, an' then she can't go. And it's the same up and down our Row, poor bitches. Unions, ye say? I'd give my arm for a four-inch drain pipe.'

'Ay, and I bet the agents don't walk a mile for a bucket o' water,' cried another. 'What you say, Dico—will ye Union grant us sanitary and clean drinking?'

Dic said earnestly: 'You'll get all these things once you've got a Lodge. Trouble's coming, and you'll have to get a Lodge to speak for you. And it's not only in Merthyr, mind. The foresters in the Dean are on a meal a day. Some of them haven't seen meat in years and the stuff's flying round them— gentry game; everything belongs to the squire. Tread on a partridge egg and you're booked for transportation. The country's mad. Every time the price of iron goes up people like Guest make a fortune in the Shops. They tell me he's looking for a country seat at half a million pounds—no bloody wonder.'

'And another half million for its art treasures while Dowlais children starve.'

'No truck in Merthyr, give Crawshay credit, remember.'

'Ay, no,' said a furnace man, 'but what about the reductions —you heard there's another one coming for ironstone?'

'Twenty per cent,' said Dic.

'Don't be blutty daft!' A man spat.

'I got it inside—it's true, and I'm telling you. This time next year he'll be dishing them four shillings in the pound.'

'When that happens I'm marching on Cyfarthfa Castle,' said a rollerman.

'By the time that happens it'll be too late,' said Dic. 'Look, can't ye see the sense of it ... ye *must* have a Union!'

'I'll do it now, if you like,' said Sid Blump.

'You're not making a mess in here,' replied the landlord. 'I'm a one-legged chap and I jump off Jackson's Bridge every Saturday night for a wager, but I don't hold with performances that mess up people's property. That's why I don't hold with politics and riots.'

'You'd riot with the rest of us if you worked for Crawshay, Jump.'

'Perhaps. Meanwhile I pour ale for brutal gunks like you. Now will somebody give me a hand to ease this silly old bastard out of here?' He gripped Sid Blump's collar, pulling him along the counter. The old boxer steadied, palmed his face and leaned over the counter, hitting short. The landlord sighed, and disappeared; there was no sound but his heavy breathing. Dic looked over the counter.

'Now you've done it, Boxer—that was the blutty landlord.'

'He's only got one leg, you know,' said the rodder, peering.

'He's got none now,' said the baller.

'All I wanted was to chop off me thumb,' protested Sid Blump.

The colliers were thronging down from Lucy Thomas and the Tasker which served the nine-foot seam, and from the Lefal the colliers came out riding on the drams, sitting in blackened, disconsolate groups on their way down the dram-road from Dynefor. The horses pulled with the lethargy of near exhaustion, mouths skimming the stone sleepers. Dic

114

vaulted on to the back of the last dram down.

'You there, Hopkin?' He peered through the grimy men.

'Right, you!'

'Down the Bridge tonight?'

'You'll get us all blutty hung, you will, Penderyn,' said a man.

'Brecon Barracks will be spinning special hemp to dangle you agitators, when the old man calls 'em out.'

Dic Penderyn said earnestly: 'Look, lads, Mason's speaking at Bridgefield tonight. The Bolton Authority Lodge is sending down a representative ...'

'That's taking a chance, isn't it? Supposing we're raided ...'

'If you want a Union you've got to take chances, and if you want basic wages—without cuts every time world rates go down—you've got to have a Union. There's a dozen branches up in the Midlands—why can't we have them in Wales?'

'Because we've got Guest, Sam Homfray and Crawshay.'

'Don't talk soft. There's worse than them in Lancashire.'

'Ay, ay? Well, count me out, I want no black-list. My brother's been on it these past two months and all he wanted was a Benefit.'

'If he'd got a Union he wouldn't need a Benefit, but it's the men we're after, not the blutty mice—who's on?'

An old miner said: 'Your trouble is that ye talk too much, Penderyn, and you go too fast. If you buttoned up a bit and made less damn noise you might get takers. If I'm going to swing I'll do it in me own time, not yours. Take my word on it, son—they'll 'ave you one day.'

Dic said: 'If we did everything in your time, Grancher, we'd never get a Union. You lot have sat on your backsides too long.'

'How much will it cost us?' asked another.

Dic groaned and ran his fingers through his hair. 'God alive!' he whispered. 'Listen, lad, we can start on a penny a week like we started the Benefit. Now come on, make up your minds. Who's with me? Who'll be there?'

'Not me, boyo,' said a smith, 'I'm staying in one piece.'

'And the devil take the hindmost?'

'Ay, if you like. I've got six kids and I'm on fifteen a week. My missus says I can't afford to be transported.'

The dram swayed on, passing the cottages down Dynefor: here the doors were open for the men coming off shift; shawled women were feeding their babies on the fronts, children playing hop-scotch on the line, jumping from sleeper to sleeper. In old wooden chairs sat the grandfathers of Georgetown, the torn and mufflered relics of the old pits and levels; the worked-out scrap of an earlier generation of Crawshays and Anthony Hill of Plymouth Works, of whom heat and cold had taken their toll. These were the withered sticks of humans parched by the fire-boxes of Cyfarthfa, Ynys and Hirwaun; the red-blinking near-blind who had stared too long at the open hearths. And they moved their dried joints to ease them as the younger men went by, waving heavy greeting; champing with naked mouths at a new generation employed by William the Second, for the earlier Crawshay was an absentee iron master in London. They, the ghosts of Canaid Dingle and a dozen other drifts, mines and pits that had emptied trouser-legs and sleeves, gossiped at night about the Great Wheel and output, firm in the pride that they had made good iron and dug good coal under a meteoric master of the mountains, a man they feared but of whom they boasted. These were the tradesmen who had built the Farewell Rock upon which the industrial greatness of Wales was to stand, and Merthyr, to them, was the finest town on earth.

'Count me in, Penderyn, for I've had a gut-full,' said a collier now. He was young and his face was gaunt. He added. 'I lost my grandpa down bloody Cwmglo last month, remember?'

'That bloody slaughterhouse, eh?' said Dic. 'One day she'll give us a thumping.'

'He's only another grancher,' said the man Hopkin, 'they don't come no different.'

'Maybe, but he was mine, an' he shouldn't have been there at all. I was working short 'cause me woman was ill. So he strikes a tinder for a candle-tack, the old way, God help him—in the Cwmglo and she's chock full of gas. The fire went

116

round the face an' it took him full. They said he was the only one in the stall, but he wasn't, for when I went down with a sack to fetch him back up I found three hands, an' Grandpa only had two, as I remember: the other was small, like a boy's, but none claimed it.'

'Weren't he on the books?'

'Ay, but alone. Yet he must have had a boy because he'd got two drams.'

'And never mentioned it?'

'Never a word, for he swore to me missus he was only filling one, poor old bugger. Took him up to Adulum a week last Monday.'

'God rest him.'

'And God rest bloody Merthyr,' said the man. 'What time you say that meeting was?'

'Sharp ten o'clock—the Iron Bridge Inn.'

'Count me there, boyo—me an' my son.'

'It stinks,' murmured Hopkin in a sudden silence of the dram.

'So does the whole bloody country,' said Dic, getting off the dram.

As he walked home he began to think about Sun Heron. He liked her red hair and the way she screwed up her eyes when she smiled.

Dic took another pint at the Horseshoes, then walked slowly along Bridgefield where Ynysfach ironworks was belching smoke and soot at the sun, and over the narrow road that led to *China*, the slum of Merthyr's slums. Below him the black Taff brooded and sulked in her dirt-swims and dead cats; old washings from the great engines of Cyfarthfa stained her banks where once the trout and grayling fought their way up to their spawning beds in the mountains. Now all was dead. Momentarily, Dic paused, staring down at the Crawshay sewer: then, raising his eyes, he saw great flushes of ragwort and a redness of poppies along the banks, fighting for life, and he likened the colour to a stain of blood. Turning away, he grinned, hands on his hips, for Shan Shonko and Old Wag, the bully women of

117

the prostitutes were squatting against the trestles, their clays cocked up in their shattered faces, and four molls from the Aunty Popi Davey lodgings were whistling up the colliers as they came in file off Ynys shift. Seeing Dic, they barred the way and he lowereed his head, frowning up, weaving and sparring with his fists, threatening them.

'*Arrah*, Molly, here comes a fine big handsome fella, be God.'

He smiled with slow grace, putting his arms across their shoulders as they walked beside him.

'Aw, Dic, lad, haven't ye a kiss for wee Maurie here? And her pining to death for ye!'

'And no pay-day since four weeks Friday? Am I made of money?'

'Ach, man, give us the womanly grace—you're fair loaded wi' it!' cried Shonko, clambering to her feet. 'Is it true he keeps it under his bed?'

'Aw, Dic, me lovely fella, come on!'

Molly Caulara cried in mock weeping: 'Is there no pity for you, and me and Kath by here just dying for a big healthy collier.'

'How's your ma?' asked Dic, grinning still.

'Och, you're wasting your time here, Molly, the fella's incapable, and I got the personal proof of it.'

Leaning over he made a backward swipe at her and she ducked, flouncing along behind them in a lifting of her skirts, laughing at the sun.

'Mind, girls, he'd collect a leathering if his Elizabeth Gwen found out.' She added: 'She's home, ye know—the minister's brought her to visit.'

'Easy on his sister!' cried Old Wag. 'Leave his sister be!'

He laughed, but he was angry, and he was glad that they were not Welsh, though there were Welsh girls in plenty in the Aunty Popi Davey lodgings. James Abbott, the High Street barber, came over the bridge then, face turned up amid the clamour of the women: with his top hat firmly on his head and his stock arching proudly, he evinced the air of a man who was not to be tampered with, and the girl Kath cried, sauntering along beside him:

'Sure to God, it's the hair-cut man. Is it true, fella, you've nothing to do wi' the females?'

'Not your sort,' said Abbott.

'Dear me, we're the same as all the others, man, if ye care to look close enough.'

'Oh, don't waste your time, Kath!' shouted Shan Shonko, as the girls barred Abbott's way, stepping left and right before him, and Old Wag cried to shrieks of laughter: 'Will you gi' us a hair-cut, fello, or treat us decent, like young Penderyn do?'

'Scum should mix with scum,' said Abbott, and pushed the women aside.

'You mind your tongue or Shoni Sgubor Fawr and Dai Cantw'r will 'ave you, mind!'

'Leave him, leave him, girls,' said Dic over his shoulder, and he marched along with his arm around Molly Caulara.

'Is it true you've brought a woman home, Dico?' she asked.

He shrugged. 'Ay, she's come in with a friend o' mine—the lodging's convenient.'

'She's right pretty, I hear say—five feet an' with bright red hair.'

'Can't say I've noticed—ach, you're a wench for other people's business, Molly Caulara!'

'Sure, your dear sister Gwen'll be making it hers, too, an' all.'

He was faintly annoyed that she should even mention his sister's name, for there was within him a deep and abiding love for Gwen, who, before her marriage to the Reverend Morgan Howells of Newport, had mothered and brought him up.

'What you thinking about, Dico?' asked Molly Caulara.

He knew these Popi Davey women as few men did, for he had been crossing the Iron Bridge since he was eleven. Indeed, he had learned of womanhood from Molly Caulara when he was sixteen. Now, six years later, there was growing in her face the sullying alleys of Merthyr, and he pitied her.

'You got a kiss for me, boy?'

'If it's for free,' he answered.

A faint hurt touched her face, but she smiled. 'It's always free to you.'

He winked. 'Me ma's expecting me and there's bacon for tea if they caught the pig. Can I trifle here with you when the fine minister from Newport's visiting with me sister?' He imitated her Irish accent.

'Ye don't like him, do you?'

'Ay, sure, but he worries me with his talk of hell.'

She cried: 'Ach, boyo, but it isn't every day o' the week that a *China* family have a minister the size o' that one come to visit. And he's a fine fella, say I, though he's off the Pope.' She crossed herself. Do you know what he says to me once? "Molly Caulara," he says, "ye ought to be ashamed of yourself. Did God give you that lovely bit o' workmanship to sell over the counter like ribs of beef?" "Ay, but it's all right for the likes of you, Minister," says I, "for yer world's fat and dandy." "Ay, ay," he says, "and so's yours, if ye let God come in with the sun. In any case, have you realised you're selling yourself short? If you bought a kerchief for a penny, would you sell it for a farthing?"'

Dic laughed. 'Did he say that?'

'He did indeed! "Molly Caulara," he said, "I can go down the Shambles and buy meself a five-pound loin for a penny a pound, an' that means I'm paying out fivepence ..." Then he stands back and weighs me up for size, so to speak, and says, "Molly Caulara, I reckon you weigh a hundred pounds or more. Even at a penny a pound you should be charging eight shillings minimum, do ye realise that?"'

'Eight shillings!' Dic gasped.

'Ay—eight shillings for me—anna I valuable? That's what the minister told me. "Molly, me girl," says he, "you're going over the blanket for less than the price of meat, do you realise that?" So I asked him should I put up me rates. Do you know what he comes back with?'

'I can guess.'

'Just this—he says to me, "There's a price on every tag, there's a rate for every piece of goods, and there's a rate for you. I'd weigh ye in rare jewels, pay a sovereign a strand for your hair and a king's ransom for your love. No gold can buy ye, Molly Caulara; you're priceless in the sight of God." '

A silence came. Dic said: 'The minister's right, Molly.'

'Like as not, does it make any difference? You started me, remember?' She drew herself up; there came a coldness; he dared not speak.

He walked away. Looking back once he saw her standing against the rail of the bridge, ignoring the commanding shouts of Old Wag and Shonko, for the Spanish tub-men were coming in from the Old Glamorgan since this was the night of the six weeks pay. Later there would be drinking and fighting in the taverns. Molly did not turn to the shouts of Old Wag and Shan Shonko, but stood there smoothing back her hair.

'Fool that I were, you had me free, Dic Penderyn, and I was worth eight shillings.'

The furnace smoke drifted between them.

Dic went through the arch and into *China*. The alleys were crowded with workers from Ynys and Cyfarthfa. Wizened faces too old to die stared down from cracked windows as he passed: half-starved children, the waste of iron, stared up from crowded doorsteps. A beggar jeered at him, waving his stumps, Dai No Arms who wouldn't go through the rollers. A Catholic priest, rotund and neat in his black cloth, was washing the face of a woman in labour, and he smiled as Dic went by. All around was the incredible stink that was a part of Merthyr's *China*, the mud of the road stained yellow. But the air became cleaner as he walked, and as he neared Jacksons Bridge a little wind blew from the iron master's park, bringing the tang of Hopkins Brewery: the British Tip reared up before him and at its burned base new harebell was growing in astonishing profusion amid the usual cat's-ears and dandelion. Bending, he picked a flower, looking about him at the squatting cottages, the sagging roofs, the confusion of slamming doors and shouting humans. The ground trembled about him and faintly he heard the drop-hammers of Cyfarthfa.

Bron Babbie Williams, aged twenty, was scrubbing her doorstep; three behind her and one at the breast, and she sat

121

on her haunches and spread her fingers on the thighs of her sack apron. 'Oi Oi!'

He pulled her hair as he passed.

'Meeting tonight, Dic?' She wiped the sweat from her face.

He nodded. 'Is Madoc coming?'

'That he is, or I will want to know. But he takes the politics gentle, like. A regular prophet of woe, he is these days. Nothin' like his da, see? Nor me, I'd have Cyfarthfa Castle down—give 'em damn stick, Dico. Wages, is it?'

'Unions mainly,' he replied.

'You got visitors, you know?' She winked. 'You also got a red-head.'

He grinned at her. The chemistry of youth moved between them. Suddenly Bron said: 'My Yorri's got a stye coming, you see it?' She reached behind her and brought up a child all feeder and bubbles. 'He do get 'em—one after the other.'

'You tried the wedding ring on it, Bron?'

She said: 'My little brother had a strawberry nose and my mam licked it every morning before eating, and it went away —it's the sleeping spit that does it, they say. You think it might work on this eye?'

'You could try it.'

'He won't go blind, or nothing?'

'Of course not, you're his mother.'

She put her finger to her cheek and looked at the sky. 'I never thought of that,' she said.

He saw in her face the early ravages of children, and Madoc, her puddler husband. Madoc Williams earned good wages up at Cyfarthfa, but she didn't know where he was from minute to minute. There was a claim made by the masters that good wages brought drinking and idleness, he reflected: often he wondered if there was something in this. It transgressed his every ideal but it was a startling revelation—when things got better the drinking got worse: Madoc was a stay-at-home man when Crawshay had a cut, and a high-stepper when the rates were returned.

Bron said: 'You try to get Madoc home reasonable tonight after the Lodge?'

'I'll watch him.'

'I got to handle him, see.'

He nodded.

'And Dic—any chance of laying me on at Ynys compound?'

'Working?' He frowned at her. 'What about the kids?'

'I could get 'em off on to Grancher—very good with 'em, he is.'

'Only rail-stacking, and you're not up to that.'

'Good God, fella, I'm as strong as a horse! Things are a bit delicate in the larder, ye understand . . . ?'

It was ridiculous: Madoc Williams was on top puddling rates; he would rarely bring home less than thirty-five shillings a week. Rocking the baby against her now Bron smiled up. 'Do me good, I reckon—nothing but kids, kids, kids round by here.'

'Come tomorrow—first shift, and I'll try. The stacking foreman's needing new horses—Liz Treharne of Pendydarren —you know her? She's lent by Homfray.'

Bron shook her head, and he added: 'She's a tough 'un, mind.'

'So am I,' said Bron. Unaccountably, he gave her the flower, crossed the alley, took a deep breath and went into the back of Islyn Court. His father and mother were there, so was the minister, but the only one he really saw was Gwen, his sister.

'Ay, ay.' He nodded, and went out the back to wash.

He had changed his shirt when he returned, for Gwen.

' 'Evening, Minister.'

Always there was the air of expectancy when Gwen and her husband called: it was as if at any moment the silence might break by everybody talking at once, yet it never did. His father, as usual, was sitting by the grate; his mother, plump and cherubic, toiled patiently at the hob, smiling to herself in peace.

'What time did you come, then?' Dic asked, sittting down at the table.

'After you left this morning,' said Gwen. Strain had banished the usual serenity of her eyes. 'You . . . you had a good day?'

He lifted his head from his plate, meeting the minister's stare.

Nothing had yet bridged the silent antagonism between them in the four years of Gwen's marriage. Although outspoken in the pulpit on the subject of Reform and fearless in his condemnation of the masters, Morgan Howells did nothing to hide his hatred of militancy and the coming Union in particular. Small of stature, possessing the pallor of a man constantly ill, his massive intellect seemed to fill the room. To Dic the ranting *hwyl* that held the congregation on the tips of his fingers was an art that could be done without in the face of the squalor that possessed the towns; and Morgan Howells' constant cry for peace was too high a price to pay in flesh and blood: and the fact that Dic never entered a chapel although he was Wesleyan, did nothing to strengthen the bond of relationship. Yet, astonishingly, Gwen, whom he loved, was happy with this man; they lived over a bakery in Newport Stow Hill; soon Morgan Howells would be full-time minister of the famous Hope Chapel. Two children had been born to them, but Dic rarely saw them.

'How's Ebenezer?' he asked, breaking bread: this was Gwen's son.

'Not too good.' She sat opposite him, and her eyes were smiling into his: there was about her a calm and distinctive beauty he had known in no other woman; and there existed between them a love that survived despite the complications of family and distance.

His father said, removing his clay: 'They got more discharges today, down Tasker—you heard?'

'Ay.'

'Bill Tender's off—you see him lately?'

Dic shook his head.

'Folks say he's gone over to Nantyglo for Crawshay Bailey, then he'll have to work.'

'And Hope?' Dic raised his face to Gwen, as if he had not heard.

Gwen's eyes danced. 'Oh, she's wonderful. If Ebbie had half her vitality he'd be up and about—we left him with Mrs.

Evan Jones, the Swansea girl.'

As he ate in the silence he wished desperately that Morgan Howells would go and leave Gwen at home—if only for the night; he never saw her these days and he wanted desperately to walk with her, to engage her in talk of the coming Union, the new clubs for sick benefit, the chances of getting a hospital. The clock was ticking away on the mantelpiece, the sun was setting in the window. He said, swallowing hard. 'Are ... are you all right, Morgan?'

'Perfectly.' The reply came instantly; the elfin face puckered up and the minister peered at Dic as if suddenly aware of his presence. Dic's mother clattered at the hob, his father cleared his throat noisily, rustling the newspaper, squinting over the top of his glasses.

Gwen said hurriedly: 'She's a nice girl, Dico! She's ... she's rough but she's nice.'

He beamed at her. 'Sun? Ay, I'd almost forgotten her—where is she?'

'Out scrubbing at Cross, but she's been down the compound,' replied his mother.

'For loading? She's too small for that!'

'She can load, lad,' said his father, 'she eats enough.'

'Got pretty hair,' said Gwen. 'You know, Morgan, she's the image of that Olwen Rees in Hope...' she nudged her husband, '...young Maldwyn's wife, remember?'

The minister said, lowering his cup, 'You're wasting your time, you know that, don't you?' His eyes were full on Dic's face. 'Never in this world will you get a Union ...'

Gwen said immediately, getting up, 'Ah well, Mam, I think we'd better be going...'

She kissed Dic in passing; he momentarily gripped her hand. She whispered into his face, 'Please, Dic, please...?'

He took a deep breath. 'Ay...' he said.

11

THE iron was coming out at Ynysfach.

In a scene of beauty the iron came out at dusk. The drams were coming in from Tramroadside with mine already roasted in the ovens of Cyfarthfa and limestone from Penymeol, and the loaders seized and turned them on the tops, filling the long-handled barrows at half a ton a time, and the hauliers took them: these, the giants of the furnace-filling, wheeled them up the barrow-roads above the Miners' Cottages, their sweating bodies, bare to the belt, made pygmy in the heat and flash of the furnace mouths: and tipped, one after the other, into the white-hot maws. In the shouted commands of tellers and overmen more came, and the furnaces belched and moaned, alternatively simmering in hiss and billowing smoke, now blazing red as the gases ignited, wallowing up at the clouds the incandescent lighting that was Ynysfach, competing with the giant Cyfarthfa, her sister iron for heat.

'Tap 'un! Tap 'un. Rodders out!'

'Hopkin, you there?'

'Comin', gaffer!'

'Rod 'un, and lively! You ready, Goff?'

And Wil Goff, whose furniture was in Coffin's Court, spat on his hands and took the bright rod and wiped sweat from his eyes. The furnace brewed then; Number One, they said it was, for they had coked her high and she was moaning and sighing like a cow in labour. And she flashed then, bright at the plug as Tom Llewellyn slid up and hit out the stone.

'Hold filling up top!'

'You up there, Hughes?'

'Ay, Over.'

'Right, you—stand clear. Rodders, rodders—take 'un!' The overman stood barrel-chested against the blackened hearths, fists on hips, his bull chest jutting and his eyes alive with the fire, and there was a taste of rust in him, which is the taste of iron, the first boiling of the ore. The furnaces were bubbling now, impatient for the sow and the nuzzling piglets waiting at her teats for their suckling of the molten iron. And behind Llewellyn worked the drams; the hauliers, the streaky Irish, grunting out their song as the drams moved up for the loading of the pig. Before them the white lanes of the sand-moulds, clear and cool, awaited the deluge of fire.

'Number Two up, Llewellyn?'

'Lazy by her looks, Over . . .'

'Give her door, Hopkin—air she wants—give it her . . .'

The firebox swung back: Number Two, feverish with her choked vents, bayed white fire at the dusk, and the men went back, hands to their eyes, but the foreman stood his ground, and the simmering grew to a hiss and the hissing into a wreath of smoke that rolled from under her belly instead of from her throat, then she boiled of a sudden and spurted flame, and the red cinders shot skyward. There came to the compound a merry song of the iron bubbling, spraying up a geyser of calcining whiteness and a billion sparks.

'She don't look good to me,' said Dic.

'Best blutty furnace this side of Tredegar, an' I calls them furnaces,' said the overman. He bellowed then with cupped hands. 'Right, rodders again—up, up. You ready, tappers?'

'Ay, ay!'

'Skip drams up—boys ready. Where the bloody 'ell's them boys?'

'Here, here, Over!'

'Right, plug her out—One first, Goff!'

'She looks dandy,' said Dic. He turned to Sun. 'You stand quiet, now, and watch the iron, and you don't see it like this in Taibach.'

As if a blanketing hand with spread fingers had descended on Ynys furnace compound, the activity ceased; drams rolled to a stop; gasping, sweating, the hauliers leaned their grimed faces on the iron rims; the cokers stopped, drooping on their shovels; the barrow-men, the scrapers, the mould-fillers, the women labourers of the coke and mine-breaking, all paused, lowering their hammers to watch the miracle of the liquid iron. And Sun Heron narrowed her eyes to the white flashing of the aenus when Wil Goff crouched with the fifteen-foot rod and hit out the plug, and Number One, as if anticipating her release from a bellyful of molten iron, belched within, instantly agitated by the blow. Slowly, reluctantly, the water-iron moved at the hole, the excrement of the mix, and pus gathered in huge globules, cauterised by the cold air. The overman took a ladle and, stooping, reached for the scum and seared it off. Behind it was the bright gleam of the grate, the incandescent mass of the iron. A bubbling began deep within.

'Touch her up, Penderyn!' and Dic moved up, eyes screwed to points against the astonishing glare, and rodded deep into the stomach of the furnace and his rod came out in glowing whiteness, the iron on fire.

'Watch your eyes. Back, back. Stand back, there!'

For the watching workers, who had seen it all a hundred times before, were pushing in a mass around the shimmering moulds. Sun Heron looked about her at the expectant faces. These, the ragged, sweating specialists were the brothers and sisters of bigger Cyfarthfa, and they sent their finished iron to the ports of the world: Irish, Welsh, North Country stackers and men of the Cornish tin, all were here, their lean faces backed by Italian and Spaniards of the Spanish Row over in Ynysgau. In their seared faces and blistered eyes she saw the tragedy of a generation, yet a task well done, for these were the best iron-makers of their time, and they knew it: this, and this alone, kept them to their task when lesser workmen would have foundered: hammered by fluctuations of wages, for the rates rose and fell according to the prices of world iron, they lived out their lives in the squalor of the drainless, waterless houses, the putrid springs: within the shadow of Crawshay's Castle, built for thirty thousand pounds at a time of high employment; denied by their masters the Union representation that would put a bargain on their labour, harassed by threats of discharge and action by the civil power, they laboured under a system of paternal dictatorship that bled them white and chained them to a dynasty of masters whose succession served only to increase their workers' anger, if not dilute their respect. Trouble was coming: even the stranger, Sun Heron, knew this. The banquets and shooting parties of the Crawshays, the elegant assemblies and brilliant wealth in the midst of the sewer-poverty of Pontmorlais and *China*, where the shift beds of the workers never grew cold, stained Merthyr beyond the confines of its boundaries: bringing, in later years, only the literary apologists to fawn on a management that combined greed and force to make a fortune of millions from the labour of men, women and children of a dozen different nationalities.

The iron was pouring from the bungs now in cadent whoops of rainbow gold and red in the dusking sky, now smouldering, now flashing again with seething brightness in a volcano of sparks and fire: down, down, filling the giant pig-mould to the brim as the tappers and rodders stirred, now reaching out fingers into the sand-moulds, each beaming in gaudy scintillation, each bed merging and blending with the mother sow into a giant, smoke-swept conflagration. And still the liquid iron descended, a writhing globule of light hissing at the plug. The furrow of the pigs was filled, the sand-moulds steamed with their first damp breath of night.

'Right, plug on. And Two!' The overman bellowed and his command split the gathering darkness as the fires died along the moulds. The fireboxes spurted reproach as the bungs were stopped; smoke rolled over the compound; one fine, purple flame enveloped the base of Number One and shot up into the darkness, lighting Ynysfach with a torch that faded and instantly died; the town was torn by dusk. Dic cleaned his firing-rods amid the bellowed commands of Liz Treharne, the six-foot woman overseer just come down from Penydarren: hands on hips she stood, a giant of strength, taller than a man with her hair plaited high and the women stackers scurried about her on the cinders, their half-naked bodies shining with sweat in the dying light of the moulds.

'Right, you Biddies, lever out, shake it, shake it!'

'They'm not cold, missus!'

'They're cold enough for shift—out wi' them!'

'You come and try, Liz—frying hot down 'ere.'

'Ach, ye tarts! Stand clear, and I'll take 'em!' And she gripped a lever and straddled a mould and levered low, her bare arms bulging muscle, and the dull hot pig-legs came up. 'Pincer 'em—come on, come on, we ain't got all night. Bess Jenks, Phyll Wright, Bron Williams—forward—pincer, pincer!'

' 'Tis a four-woman load, girl!'

'Three while I'm around—come on, shift it—lose Crawshay a penny an hour an' he'll bleed to death—move, *move*!'

Bron Babbie came up to Dic's shoulder. 'Christ,' she said, 'she's a tough 'un. Back to the kids with me if this is iron stacking.'

He grinned over his shoulder. 'Well, you asked for it.'

'Got womb trouble, an' it's wearying . . .'

'God alive!' He swung to her. 'What are you doin' here, then?'

'Och, it'll dry.'

'You got womb trouble you get back home to Madoc.'

'Perhaps I come too early after having Nick, me last.'

She leaned on him and he sensed her weakness, and saw in the faint glow of the moulds the worn lines of her face and the dull shifting of her eyes, and he shouted: 'Liz, girl, this one's out for a bit.'

The big overseer sauntered over to them. 'If she is she's out for good.'

'Ach, be reasonable, woman—her old man's a toss of mine, and she's sore in the middle with her last.'

'So am I, an' I had twins.' Over her shoulder she shouted: 'Joe Gab, leave that woman alone or I'll take the ladle to ye!' Turning to Dic and Bron, she said, 'Listen, this is consignment, an' if it isn't off tonight Crawshay'll have a heart attack. In this cinder you're either in or out—take pick.'

'*Jawch*, be human—she's only needing an hour.'

'You frig off,' said Bron, 'I can speak for myself.'

130

'Well, give her ten minutes.'

'Just a breather, Liz,' said Bron, leaning on the iron, 'for I need the loot.'

'And your fella puddling on the bouncer rate? God alive—if he was mine I'd have him under the handle and tie him to the bed-post—all right, then—I'll gi' you an hour.'

'Down by here,' said Dic, and patted the cinders. 'Make a hole for your hip and sleep it out.'

'And put your legs up,' said Liz Treharne, and Dic gave her a glance as he settled Bron down under the iron, weighing her in at something over fourteen stones: down at Jackson's on a Saturday night she fought like a man with her chest banded and sacked, and anything under six feet was frightened to death of her. Bull Skewen reckoned he had seen her stripped for the pump once, breaking the ice in winter, and he laid a bet that she had hair on her chest, though nobody got the proof of it, for since she courted Abod of Penydarren, the strongest navvy in the valley it would have been hard to find out, but either Abod loved her as wife or he was too frit to say, said Bull. A year after the altar, she had a child—a sickly four-pound girl who died a week after the birth: the labour of it nearly killed her, said Abod. Now the woman smiled, her teeth appearing white and strong in her smoke-grimed face, and her eyes were good.

'An hour, remember, then you're up and into it, or out.'

'You're a hard bugger, Liz,' said Dic.

The other women were still heaving on the levers along the moulds, others hauling up the drams for the loading on to the canal, and Dic shouted a rough but respectful banter at them, handing out slaps for haunches as he passed the gangs, laughing at their shrieked insults. In a drift of coke drams just come down from the main works he found Sun bucket-washing, flinging the water high and swilling it over her face and chest in clenched eyes and bubblings, with her long brown arms caressing the sky as he stalked up behind her: with his hands on her waist he steadied and held her, and over her wet shoulder kissed her face.

'You anna decent, you fella,' she said, not turning.

'You coming home with me, missus?'

'Are ye friendly?'

'Ay for sure—don't ye even care who's kissing you?'

'Not as long as it's a man. And he's a rare one for the liberties—and me hardly dressed—can I raise me bodice?'

'If ye ask proper off Dico Italian?'

'The new macaroni from Pescara, is it?'

He put his face in the wet hair about her neck. 'That's him, and he's a devil with the women. You love-spoon with me, Irish girl?'

'Enough of that, ye foreigner, I'm Welsh.'

'You don't sound Welsh to me.'

They stood together and he did not turn her in his arms or look upon her, and the night wind was cold on their bodies.

'You scarce know me, Penderyn,' said Sun, her voice low.

'Who cares? You have to take 'em as they come today, for there's not a lot of choice.'

'You ever had other women?'

'Ay.'

'Like that little Molly Caulara from the Aunty Popi Davey?'

'Ay.'

'But not now?'

'Not now—long before you come. A man gets hot about women and Unions, I reckon. Then along comes one who takes his eye and he doesn't lay a finger on her, not even when she stands like this, half naked.'

'Put your hands about me if you like, Dic Penderyn.' She raised her face.

'Ach, no, I'm saving it for Christmas.'

She said at the dusking sky, 'You treat me respectful, but you don't know nothing about me ...' Pulling up her ragged petticoat she turned in his arms and he saw her eyes large and beautiful in her blackened face. 'Since I known you there come a difference inside me, you understand?' She held herself. 'And perhaps there's a lot about this woman you ought to know before you treat me decent, like this, and not like that Molly Caulara, a woman of the pave ...'

132

He said, softly, 'I just aren't interested, girl.'

Sun saw him in the light of the moon; his face was smudged, too; on him a smell of sweat and the tobacco he chewed and spat at the furnace hauling to keep the wetness on his throat. When he smiled at her she saw his teeth appear like magic in the grime of his face and he bent to kiss her, but she put her fingers on his mouth and held him off an inch, and he heard a whisper he did not understand, until she said:

'*Arrah*, me sweet one, Dic Penderyn.'

'You love me, Sun?'

'Ah!'

Breathless they stood enwrapped, and the drams rang and bellowed obscenely about them; panting, he held her away. ' 'Tis daft, Sun! It's no more'n a fortnight, and the devils are after us . . .'

'The devil take them!'

'The big man's coming tonight for Gwen. He'll be asking us to table soon, for the Welsh are ones for rumours, and we're in the news.'

Said she: 'Are we beholden to the churches and chapels?'

'You are when you're living in our house, with Morgan Howells, the minister, arriving.'

'Am I? Think again, fella—I'd spit in his eye soon as look at him.'

He quietened her with a gesture, but she cried: 'I can tell by his mood that he doesn't approve of me, and your pa's half the same. Say nothing for your mother, and I only keep me a still tongue because of your Elizabeth Gwen.'

'Then keep it happy for her, Sun—keep it happy for Gwen.'

She went tall and frisky, bothering her shoulders and Dic lowered his hands.

'If the old fella thinks I'm a whore, why doesn't he say?'

'The minister doesn't think that, Sun.'

'He damned near said it night before last!'

'He said no such thing. He only said that the soul was famished without the food of God, and asked you to come to the Calvinistic with him and Gwen.'

'And me attached to the Pope?'

133

'Are you religious, then?'

'No, but the Pope will do to keep the other fellas off.'

'So you don't believe in God?'

'Not in Merthyr,' she replied, and hooked her arm about his waist; together they went over the Iron Bridge: Annie Hewers and Megsie Lloyd were talking to a group of puddlers; vaguely Dic wondered where he had seen them before.

'I tell you what,' cried Sun. 'Let's go into the town to see the illuminations, for the little minister will be hogging it back in the house—it'll give him a chance to get off.'

The stars were big over Dowlais Top for the smoke of the Ynys tapping had cleared; the ragged workers of the pits and drifts were thronging in down the dram-roads, shouting their banter at the coming night.

Dic said: 'Shall we take a spell up round Castle Street for a peep at the gentry and the letters coming in?'

'And the agents booking in Brecon Bank wi' the loot from Penydarren! Sure, I love seeing the silk and lace of 'em, and the spotted pudding dogs an' blackamoors!'

Laughing, they pushed through the crowds jamming the arch by the Lamb. The boozies were already at it in there, parting whiskers and tossing the pots: the big drays were stamping on the cobbles outside the post office on the corner of Cross and the agents heaving bags of Crawshay money into the bank. On the end of Thomas Street the moody relics of the old Welsh fraternity went with measured tread into the Wesleyan, mournful with their love, their brass-bound bibles under their arms.

' 'Evening, holy Father!' cried Sun, and a Catholic priest, buttoned and booted in black, bowed over his beads on his way to the keening Irish in the cellars of Pontmorlais. Unmindful of the tipsy long-shift workers spilling out of the Wheatsheaf and Star went the Quakers with their soup-carts, trundling for Bridge Street where two thirds of the workers were on parish relief, discharged because of a drop in world rates of iron. High-stepping were the pony-traps of the agents along Graham, Front Street and Thomas Street, and the elegant broughams of the incoming gentry grinding behind their frisky

134

greys past the doorstep chatter of the out-of-work Welsh and Irish: women, shawled and babied at the breast or in the stomach watched Dic and Sun go by with expressionless eyes; the men, standing aimlessly with the moody indifference of the long discharge watched also, following the paths of the stuffed over-rich with resignation.

'How long you been out?' asked Dic, reaching a group.

'Nigh two weeks.'

'Tasker?'

One said: 'No, Cwmglo—this fella's Tasker.'

'What's the rate there?'

'About half and half—six in ten on poor relief in Lefal.'

A woman said: 'It's a bloody scandal, mind—not a crust of bread in the house, and my three begging up by Canaid Brook.'

'Like as not we'll be took on Wednesday, according to the agent.'

'That damned Crawshay—they said that last Wednesday. It's a stink, man.'

'It's a stink and it must stop,' said another.

'You getting Benefit money?' asked Dic.

'Don't talk to me about Benefit!' An old man spat.

'A shilling a week is better 'n nothing.'

'A shilling a week! What the hell are we—blutty animals?'

'You take the Oddfellows' oath and you'll get benefit club money—free bread on the quiet and free burial, remember.'

'What about free living, then?'

'You'll get that when you get a Union,' said Dic, moving away.

'Ach, talk sense, man—would Crawshay stand for a Union?'

'He didn't stand for the Benefits, but he's got them,' said Dic, 'and he might act easier than most.'

Beggars were crying shrilly in the gutters up by Quarry, and the Tanyard specialists were sinking it in noisy banter along the rails: wizened girl-mothers were coming down from Cyfarthfa, the mine-breakers of the Yards, their kerchiefs tight round their starved faces: amazons from the stone-grading,

135

straight of carriage and comely, passed them with the treble shrieks of girls at play: emaciated children from Sulleri played *Devil at the Window*, darting between the moving drams along Tramroadside and *Touch me Last* down Iron Lane where the brass and china dogs of the well-paid puddlers gleamed in the lamplight.

'Good God,' exclaimed Sun, 'would you believe it?' For on the slopes of the Trevor tips six lay preachers declared their joy of belief to nobody in particular, giving it out from Genesis to Revelation, all bearded and smoking with the fire of hell's damnation. Fists clenched and shaking, the political tub-thumpers of a new awakening denounced clergy, masters and workers alike, surrounded by apathetic groups of ragged Irish labour. And up High and down Clive the workers of the six weeks' long-pay flooded into the shops where collared grocers of the new shopocracy were weighing and scaling, short-changing and overcharging, and Abbott the Barber was cut-throating the customers in a flapping of sheets and suds; next door but three Jones Draper was doing good business in Abergavenny waistcoats and new woollens from the Penyrheol factory, Chartist design; socks long and short, non-tickle vests for under stays, belly-binders for colic babies.

'Wait a bit while I get some macassar,' said Dic.

'I'll come, too,' said Sun, and followed him into the Abbott shop.

Swarthy and thick was James Abbott, the barber, and he turned idly from a shaving and get that bloody tart out of here, and quick.

'Who's he addressing?' asked Sun, peering.

The man put down his razor, and said softly, 'You've a mite of cheek, Penderyn, to bring the Old Wag molls into a decent establishment. Shift her.'

'Who are you talking about?' asked Dic, and Abbott pointed at Sun. 'That Molly Caulara, for I saw her frisky on the Taff bridge with you not a fortnight back; now move her before I get my boot.'

Dic ducked low, frowned up, hit short, and the barber took it full on the chin, going backwards over the chair and the

136

customer was upended in shrieks and suds with *The Cambrian* going up and the colliers roaring their excitement; but one, Shoni Crydd, the cobbler boxer, came from the back.

'Watch him!' shrieked Sun, and Dic turned, feinted as the man came lumbering in, hooked to the body and switched the same hand to the throat, and the man croaked with the pain of it, falling clumsily: one moment peace, next a palaver, with women collecting in the barber's entrance and shrieking, hat pins coming out and boots going in, and the colliers and miners sparring up, delighted. And in the middle of it Dic paused to swing a left at Shoni Crydd as he got up, and down he went again on top of Abbott in a tangle of legs, customers and sheets.

'Run for it!' cried Sun, dragging at him.

But they couldn't get out of the door for customers, and Abbott, big and powerful, rose, flinging people aside. Laughing, Dic squared to meet him, but Sun barged out backwards through the door, dragging him after her. Abbott reached them in the road and swung a left at Dic, who ducked, feinted, and hooked hard. The barber took it full and went over, boots waving. He said from the ground while the people ringed them:

'By God, Penderyn, one day I'll be up with thee!'

'Then you'll have to move faster than this, Abbott.'

Now the illumination crowds were flooding down from the Bush and the special constables were running in from Cross Keys. Sun cried, snatching Dic's hand, 'Come on, boyo—run for it!' Hand in hand they skidded past the Castle Inn and under the Arches into *China*. Gasping, she cried:

'Och, ye stuffed him! Jebers, did ye hit that fella!'

'Ay, well he had it coming to him.' Dic licked his knuckles.

'But he'll be up wi' you—you'll have to watch him—did ye hear what he said?'

David Rees, the puddler preacher, came up then, laughing, and said: 'The wee woman's right, Dico—you watch that Abbott, or sure as fate he'll take you to task.'

Dic straightened. 'He asked for it, Mr. Rees.'

The man nodded, walking away. 'He might have, but you watch him.'

'Who was the moll he took me for, anyway?' asked Sun after Rees had gone.

'A friend of mine.'

'That fresh Molly Caulara, would it be?'

'It is,' he said, breathless still, 'and she isn't a moll.'

'But she's one of the Aunty Popi Davey girls, isn't she?'

'She might be, but she still isn't a moll.' Angry, he glared at her.

Sun shrugged. 'Ay, well I suppose there's more'n one name for a kidney pudding. You realise, don't you, that the second fella you hit out was a special constable?'

He grinned. '*Diawl*, there's no law against hitting out special constables—it's a hobby round these parts.'

'And he'll make it a hobby to see to you proper one day—take my word on it.'

'Enough trouble for tonight, girl: we'll see to special constables tomorrow—home to Islyn now, eh?'

'Let's hope it's quieter up by there,' said Sun.

'One thing's for sure,' said Dic. 'Gwen's chap will be gone.'

'Best make sure,' said Sun. 'Shall we take another turn round town to cool him, for I couldn't stomach the man just now.'

Dic kissed her, and she did not expect it: what began as a caress of friendship ended with hard arms and quick breathing, till she pushed him away. 'You're not clinching Abbott the Barber,' said she. 'A walk in the night might cool you. Away!'

Outside the Aunty Popi Davey lodgings Miss Milly Thrush, the new shopkeeper, was serving black shag to Wil Thomas and chewings to Little Dusty Wilkins, who was four feet six, and hundreds of thousands to the pop-eyed urchins with tear-streaked faces from Pen Yard: just come in from Taibach was she, according to rumour, and paid twenty pounds goodwill to Mrs. Rees the Lollipop of Cross Keys, and God knows what is going on behind the scenes with that Mr. Note the musician hitting up Handel and Willie Taibach on the fiddle and his ma on the hob.

'Ounce of Tanyard Light, please,' said Dic, and Miss Thrush fluttered her eyes and Sun hooked him out saying she could swear she had seen her before but couldn't think where.

'Good evening, sir,' said Dic, and bowed, for old Iolo Morgan-Rees was labouring up Bridge Street on a child's arm, spectacles on the end of his nose, stopping betimes to gaze at the stars, as fragile as his poetry. Bull-chested and surly, Shoni Sgubor, the giant Emperor of *China* before Redman Coleman, was strutting up Thomas with his retinue of women and mountain fighters, breasting a path through the colliers coming in from Cyfarthfa, And, up in the castle of the Crawshays light blazed, fingering golden shafts on the lawns, and the giant chandeliers beamed on the rhododendron clusters purple and white, shimmering on the parkland lake where the great trout lazed under the mushrooming redness of the works, for the night shift had come on and the furnaces were roaring again and the sky above Merthyr was exploding anew in showering sparks. Organ-grinders were rasping out their garish music on Jackson's, monkeys climbed sticks and did acrobatics along the parapets; one-legged Jackson was gathering bets for his Saturday night jump off the bridge. And the whole Top from Aberdare to Blaenafon was coming alight as on a signal; the whole cacophony of life bursting in the narrow streets and alleys as Dic and Sun pushed through them hand in hand: this, the Saturday night illuminations and revelry of the biggest town in Wales, with the Jews and hucksters pouring in for the market, the tipsters and touters, the priests and prostitutes and pimps; and the salvationists bellowing the harmonies of their pamphlet hymns, The chapels were full for special services to keep the congregation out of the publics, blending their voices into Tans'ur's *Bangor* and Giardini's *Moscow* and vying with the bawdy choruses from the Patriot, Wheatsheaf, Dynefor and Crown where a dozen men, stripped to the belts, were fighting bare-fist along the pavement: there was cock-throwing going on at Glebeland and tip-tap betting and Bandy being played on the tumps: as they passed Biddle's foundry old Snelling was at it, adding to the commotion with shoeing and hammer-

139

ing, for the chaise was up from the Castle Inn and the gentry were abroad for fishing over at Langorse with the Crawshays.

'Good night, Mrs. Evans!' cried Dic.

'Good night, Dic Penderyn, how's your Gwen?'

'Dandy, she is, Mrs. Evans.'

Fat and merry was Mrs. Evans, wife of Evan Evans who hoped for a dowry of a cow and a half from Six Bells when he married, and received her and the offspring, and that is the equivalent, think yourself lucky, said her dada.

'Your Gwen very lucky, eh, married to the famous minister of Hope, Newport! Best preacher in the circuit, they do say.'

'Ay, ay.'

'But mind your step, Dic lad—strong against the Unions—cast you out as soon as look at you!'

On, on, with Sun dropping curtseys, and they went down to Cross Keys Gaol where Mr. Stinkin Shenkins, brother to the beadle, was wriggling in the stocks for inebriation and bad language to the clergy: piled high with garbage was he and singing at the sky in his blue ruin doldrums, and serve the old soak right, said Mr. Steffan Shenkins to Dic as they passed: what the devil is he up to, with me a deacon—brother to Barrabas, I am. And in the black hole they call a prison sits the bowed and broken form of Mr. Duck Evans, just released on family request from the Swansea House of Correction, and due out next Friday and Mrs. Duck Evans, on all fours, is whispering down the grating:

'Oh, my love, do not take it hard—it is only another few days!'

'Woman, in God's name,' said Dic, and lifted her up, but she fought clear and knelt again, whispering:

'Do not cry, Mr. E. Things are better now. I got the kids in an attic up in Pontmorlais—taking in washing with old Nanny Humphries, and I earn a shilling a day. And you are being discharged here, ye know—that's fine, see—nobody knows us here, and that gossipy Mrs. Windy Jones is still in Pontypridd. Oh, Mr. Evans, give me a glance . . . ?'

She raised her voice saying this because Mr. Shenkins was

singing, his drumstick arms akimbo, his cackle of a mouth vapouring neat gin, 'There was a little maid and she loved a little man, hooray, me love, Abendigo! And he was a little ram and she took herself to bed...'

'Look at me, my love ... Oh, Mr. Evans ...'

'... instead of gettin' wed, hooray, me love, Abendigo, an' she didn't give a damn ...' Mr. Stinkin Shenkins subsided in slurps and bubbles as Dic pushed fruit into his mouth, and knelt again to Mrs. Duck Evans.

'Home, missus,' he said. 'Home if you love him, eh?'

'Oh, God, I cannot bear it,' said Mrs. Evans, and wept.

Blind Dick and Hugh Pughe the harpist were playing and singing outside the Boot, and Shoni Melody, the hare-lip counter-tenor was there, too, and Sun saw him and leaped to him, seizing his arm. Smiling at the sky, with his face alight, Blind Dick sang with the gaiety of his soul, and the pure, feminine voice of Shoni swept above him in the descant, and Hugh Pughe's thick fingers, the nimblest in Wales, swept the strings and it was beautiful with the lovely strains of Edwards' *Caersalem* soaring up into the night, and the publics came open and the rowdies tumbled out, with the ragged children of the cottages squatting on the cinders and the colliers, rodders, ballers and puddlers standing with their women ten deep, letting the godliness of it enter them. Out with the pamphlets then, with urchins selling them at a penny a time, and they went like Welsh bakestones—Blind Dick's latest composition, and if ever we have a workhouse up in Glebeland I will sing God Save William the Fourth at the Abergavenny Eisteddfod and damn my soul to everlasting fire, and who is dining on silver plate with Crawshay now, not the Whigs, by God, but Lord Reform ...

'Home?' asked Dic.

Sun nodded and he took her hand and drew her through the gathering crowd of the Boot, and the words of Blind Dick's chorus grew in beauty and power, for the sopranos had come and the treble children had joined in with the pit tenors, and the great sound grew into a crescendo, sitting on contralto and bass, and they sang:

141

O, Thou Who rides a chariot of glory,
Bring us to peace in the valley of coal.
Light in the eyes of Thy broken people
A rebellious flame of a stubborn goal.
Cry out! Cry out, Thou great Jehovah! ...

The stars were at their brightest over Dowlais Top, said Dic, as they went up Bridge Street and through the arch into *China.*

12

Asa aged six and Adam aged two were playing on the
dram-road and running off on a last across as the drams
went by up to Cyfarthfa: up Dynefor came the drams that
day, but coming from Ynys and heaped high with the glowing furnace slag, with the old horse plodding along in front
with a wet sack over his rear to stop him blistering, and you
could fry an egg on the doorstep when they were emptying the
hearths, said Billa Jam, who was settled with Mamie in
Number Five, and it isn't good enough and what the hell do
they think they're up to? If I had my way I'd have Mrs.
Crawshay coming down here to dolly up the sheets—what
about my blutty washing, then—all smuts, just look at it:
agents' sheets, too, mind, and nobody washes whiter than
Mamie Goldie and me. Some got tapestries on 'em—you ever
seen lace on sheets? Spit on the iron, girl, send up the steam—
bedsheets for Ynys, tablecloths for Penydarren—scrub, scrub,
scrub—working our fingers to the bone: eleven kids now, just
produced my Joab, the latest—spit and image of Mr. Jam, too,
he is. Here, hand me that dolly, woman—slash 'em on the
stones. How you doing, Mamie?—can't see ye for steam. And
just when we got going that morning along come these blutty
drams, soot and all, smuts an' all—oh, hell, Randy—look at
my washing . . . Hey there, Merve—mind you don't fall in that
canal, and watch the kids on the drams—where's Asa?'

'Under my feet,' sang Mamie, scrubbing.

'Long as he anna under mine. You got Abiah, Randy?'

'Abiah's on the pot, Billa?'

'Like as not, then we know where he is?' She added: 'The

143

drams're coming.'

'Dear me,' said Mamie, 'I got the sheet from under the Reverend John D. Ellison, bet that anna seen much fun: got a face like a turnip that Reverend Ellison, but then, being Church of England. *Diawch*, look at the soots comin' in. Seen who, Billa?' She sang tunelessly at the cracked ceiling of Number Five as the drams thundered by, for they were rodding out Three at Ynys, and she was choked with slag—should have been done a month back, said Foreman. 'As long as I never dunna see my old man. You miss yours, Billa?'

'He was here a minute back,' said Randy.

'Who?' asked Blod, washing under the tap, and her long hair was stranding her face and shoulders.

'By God, you look lovely,' said Randy.

'Ay, as long as you got him, then,' said Billa, scrubbing.

'Got who?' asked Blod, pushing Randy off.

'My little Adam,' said Billa, humming.

'He isn't by here, mind,' said Blod.

'He was a minute back, girl.'

'Who?'

'Adam.'

Mamie sang, pegging things out. 'Is that little one out there with you, Billa? You seen Adam, Billa?'

'God no! I've been asking!'

'Watch him on the drams!' shrieked Mamie, and as she said it the sprags went down: the brakes went on and the wheels whistled; up went the horse on his shanks and the glowing slag spilled into the backs.

'Oh, Christ!' cried Randy, and Blod covered her face. 'Oh, Christ!'

Billa said, swaying against the door, 'Get him out, Randy, in the name of God, get him out . . .'

The spraggers came running into the heat, knocking up the links of the one at the back, and they pulled it clear with scorching hands while Randy heaved with Blod at the back, and they opened the line and found him: Adam, aged two, crying for Billa outside Number Ten with his legs side by side outside Number Nine. And Randy went full length between the rails and clutched his thighs, one in each hand.

They got a doctor from Cyfarthfa, for the Company surgeon of Ynys was out with the cholera up in Ponty with the Irish.

'There's a boy,' said Randy. 'There's me lovely little Adam.'

'I want my mam,' said Adam.

'Don't faint, Billa,' whispered Mamie, holding her. 'For God's sake don't faint, Billa.'

'What happened?' asked the surgeon, kneeling on the cinders.

'He was sitting on the rail,' said Randy.

'Where's his mother?'

'I'm his mother,' said Billa.

The surgeon was young; his handsome eyes flashed up. 'What the devil are you doing letting your children run wild?'

'He was here a second ago, sir,' said Mamie, screwing her apron.

'You damned Welsh! If you thought as much about your children as you do about your ale ... Can you hold him, lad?'

'Yes, sir,' said Randy.

'Then don't move him: I'll trim him where he lies.' He glanced at Billa's stomach. 'Are you in milk?'

'Yes, sir.'

'Then bare and feed him; he knows no pain yet. *Drammer!*'

A spragger came running with his whip.

'Drop that thing and collect those legs. I want everything cindered and washed down the moment I've finished. And you ... !'

'Yes, sir,' said Mamie.

'I want clean clothes, and water—but plenty of clean cloth —and clean, you understand?'

'She washes very white, sir,' said Blod, weeping.

So they stood in a circle, did the people of Ynys, and Billa Jam sat on the rail with Adam at her breast while the surgeon trimmed and tied him. And the bed-sheet that enwrapped them like a shroud had tassles on, belonging to the agent, stained red in widening blotches; and the one they tore into strips was the one belonging to the Reverend John Ellison.

145

'He was a good little fella,' said Billa afterwards, 'he never made a sound. I just breasted him and he suckled and fed.'

'I'm sorry,' said the young surgeon, touching her face. 'He lost too much; your baby is dead.'

'An' that's how it happened,' said Mamie later. 'Now she's got ten.'

'Never mind, Mam, you always got me,' said Merve, aged nine.

'*Uffern Dan!*' exclaimed Zeke Solomon, next door. 'Everything happens to Billa Jam Tart: she scrubbed the next two months to pay for those sheets.'

Randy and Blod got married that September, the dear little souls, said Mamie Goldie. 'I could look the whole world over and never find such a daughter-in-law—gained a dear relative, I have.'

'Something to approve of your daughter-in-law, mind,' observed Billa.

'Wouldn't have her a mite different, wouldn't hear a word against her,' said Mamie. 'The day I set eyes on that girl, I said, "Mamie Goldie, fancy is as fancy does, but this dear girl comes different." Virtue is its own reward, as I told Randy, and there's nothing like a mixing of the blood to put some froth into the new generation. Like the Good Book says, "Look not upon me, because I am black, because the sun hath looked upon me," and what's good enough for Solomon is good enough for us.'

'Dear me,' said Billa. 'One thing about you, girl, you never bloody vary.'

'Wouldn't put a foot in their way, wouldn't raise a finger to impede 'em, so to speak. Irish, of course, but a handsome one, is that—full in the breast and narrow in the haunch, and shouldn't be surprised if she didn't milk well, bless her, too. You there, Blod, my love?'

'Coming, Mamie!'

'There now, my little lovely! All ready for the Rabbi, are you?'

'All ready for the priest, Mamie.'

146

Even Billa Jam, who saw her through tears, said she was beautiful.

'Oh, well,' said Mamie, patting her, 'we can't have everything, can we? Even the gentiles are equal in the sight of the Lord. Virgins and virtue do collect the just reward, I say.' She peered at Blod Irish.

'Yes, Mamie,' said she, peering back. 'You can be sure o' that.'

'God bless ye for the pure upstanding creature that you are, then,' said Mamie. 'And thank God for the foresight that I chose you for me son.'

She wept then and Billa handed her a cloth.

And so, with the big spiders doing night-shifts along the hedges of Vaynor and the mist of the Beacons weaving its patterns over the Glebe, Randy Goldie, haulier of Ynys but late of Taibach, married Blodwen Irish late of Derry, and God grant them the same happy marriage as me, said Mamie, in tears.

'Salvation to you and may God forgive ye, Mamie,' said Billa, and she raised her lost Adam up against the stars, and kissed him. 'Good night, my precious,' she said.

The furnaces were weeping over Ynys that night, they said, in the sheet of the rain, and the hiss.

'You there, my beautiful?' whispered Randy in the dark.

'Unless someone's lifted me,' said Blod.

Outside in the rain the roofs of *China* shone wetness and the moon over Brecon dripped and waned; the dram-roads lay in viper snakes among the tumps and cinders of Cyfarthfa. A lone light shone in the window of the castle: a lone lamp burned in the curved flats of the Iron Bridge, and the Black Taff groaned in his basin of cholera, seeping for the lowlands and the cleansing sea of Cardiff.

'Where you got to, then?' asked Randy, keen.

'Over by here, man,' said Blod. 'All waiting and expectant.'

The furnaces were simmering in Ynys, the puddling pits steaming in Cyfarthfa: Gideon lay in his bed by the window up in Eighteen Cross Street, enwrapped in the bellowing

147

snores of Zimmerman, and he was thinking of Jobina. Day after day he had hunted for her, questioned the navvies, caught Belcher by the coat and shook him to rattle.

'No sign of her, man, and that's the truth—no hide nor hair of her since the day wee Tilly caught it—we reckoned she was upping out Merthyr lookin' for you.'

The rain was washing down the window of Five Ynys Row: the vagrants were huddled for shelter under the dram-arches, the destitute Irish sheltering from the rain beside the warm coke-ovens, the agents bedding the feather-down mattresses in a haze of sleep and accounts, the masters under the canopied velvets and curtained gilts. Miss Thrush lay dreaming in a sleep of fauns with Gideon beside her on a bed of gossamer, and his lips were soft on her face. Down below stairs Mrs. Taibach was driving them home, with Willie the other side of the bolster up among the trebles: bass and booming was Percy Bottom Note, peeping over the top of his dream like King David at Bathsheba, gathering up the brass for the last, strident fanfare that would tear down the walls of Jericho, trumpeting from sleep an amorous Miss Thrush.

'You are not yourself tonight, that's for sure,' said Blod.

'Oh, dear me,' said Randy.

'What's come over you, mon?'

'Don't ask me,' said Randy.

In the cellar under the Crown in High Street Annie Hewers awoke, lit her candle and got out of her side of the bed, and her eyes were like rubies in the wavering light, her bright hair was tousled, the plaits tied with red ribbon. For a moment only she sat there and listened to the hoarse breathing of Megsie in the bed beside her. Dim moonlight was filtering into the cellar from a pavement grating overhead as she tucked her nightgown around her thighs and stepped into a foot of water. Holding on to the brass balls of the bedstead, she waded slowly to the grating and looked up at the misted night; rain instantly spotted her face and she wiped it away with her hair. It was a sheeting downpour of a night, with the wind whistling down from the Beacons and whining like witches among the crippled chimneys of the moon.

'You all right, Megsie?'

Megsie Lloyd stirred in sleep, and opened her eyes at the ceiling.

'Ay, what's up?'

'We got water coming in.'

Megsie sat up. 'Where's it coming from, then—through the grating?'

'Up from the floor.'

'Can't be.'

'*Diawl!* It is—only spots coming down the grating. You all right?'

'I just said so,' said Megsie. She looked over the rail. '*Jawch!* It's worse than Noah's flood ...' She coughed holding her chest.

'You got any pain, then?' asked Annie.

'No.'

'You must have pain, you've been moaning and sobbing all night.'

'You're hearing things. What are we doing about this water?'

'Can't bale it. If it comes any higher we'll be floating. Look, it's up me shins. Bloody hell.'

'No good cursing it,' said Megsie. 'It's like Old Wag said—that's why the rent is a shilling a week. You seen it up by the Star?'

'Can be five foot up in the cellar there, they reckon. Must have washed Lady Hamilton out of bed—bet that cooled old Horatio. Comes out of the graveyard, they say, after washing up the corpses.'

'God, no!' whispered Megsie.

'Ay, it do—they got Knights of the Garter up there doing the breaststroke.'

There was a silence broken only by the howl of the wind, metallic plops and the hissing of water.

'It's only two inches under the mattress,' said Annie, looking under with the candle. 'What we want is a barge, not a blutty bed.'

149

'I saw Gid Davies yesterday,' said Megsie at nothing.

'Who?'

'Gideon Davies—you know, the Taibach fiddler.'

Annie sat on the bed beside her. 'What about him, then?'

'Seems he's staying in town. " 'Morning, Gid Davies," I said, but he didn't hear at first so I shouted again. "Well, me one-legged aunt," says he, "if it isn't Megsie Lloyd! How long you been in Merthyr, then?" So I told him. I left a few things out, of course—what the ear don't catch the heart don't grieve for—I reckon he forgot how he saw us on the road: one thing's sure, he never told my Gran.'

'Nor my mam—or me dad would have been up by 'ere with Bibles and belts. Could never understand my dad, see,' said Annie. 'Used to read me a chapter on the Provocation of David and then hit hell out of me—got all this religion in his knees, my da.'

'Expect he meant well,' remarked Megsie. She shivered and folded her hands over her knees. 'Eh, midear, sometimes I think o' the good times we had in Ponty.'

'Whee, it's shivering cold with this water,' said Annie. 'Back into bed with me, is it?'

'Ay,' said Megsie, 'and mind your head on the ceiling.'

The candle guttered: outside in the night the wind began to whimper like a sleepless child.

Megsie said softly: 'You awake, Annie?'

'I'm floating, woman. Look, we got our own lake. First thing tomorrow I'm up to Mrs. Crawshay to borrow her paddles.'

'You reckon we're doing it right, Annie?'

'Depends, don't it?'

'No, it don't depend,' said Megsie. 'I told Gid Davies we were coal-cropping. He asked me where, an' I said up at the levels serving Cyfarthfa Yard, but if he looks up there he'll not find neither of us.'

'That were daft,' said Annie. 'They've got no cropping girls up there.'

'Up till now I always kept decent ...'

'Mr. Duck Evans is coming out of Cross Keys Gaol tomorrow, they say.'

'My mam would turn in 'er grave...'

'It seems they shifted him up here from Swansea because Mrs. Evans moved up from Ponty, poor soul. Doing all right, too—taking in washing with old Nannie Humphreys, I heard.'

'Perhaps that's what we ought to do—take in washing.'

'Poor soul, he just sits and looks. Aunt Popi Davey says he's had the brains beat out of him—poor soul—all for a duck.'

'Oh, God, make me clean,' said Megsie.

'You all right, girl?' Annie peered at her, holding high the candle.

Her face was flushed with the fever, her eyes large and sparkling, and there was in her a strange, unhappy radiance that lacked a smile: her hair was black and smoothed either side of her cheeks, which were stretched tight over the high bones of her face: her lips were crimson, her throat smooth and white against the rag of her vest. Annie said, shaking her head:

'Dear me, you look gorgeous—like Aunty Popi Davey said —it would be a crying waste to the customers to see you coalcropping or pulling on the drams or filling at the face. No wonder they always ask for you, Megsie. You all right, kid?'

Megsie nodded, her eyes closed.

'Sleep now, is it?'

'Ay, sleep,' said Megsie.

'You got no chest pains, or nothing?'

'No.'

'Nor blood?'

'No blood now,' said Megsie. 'I never felt better—must be the rain.'

'That's the girl.' Annie huffed down under the blankets. 'It's another day tomorrow—call me if the corpses come in, throw out the lifebelts.'

'It's none too warm,' said Megsie.

'What will ye do when winter comes?' asked Annie, and turned, reaching out. 'Come down by here, kid, tutty up with aunty...'

The Reverend Morgan Howells, minister of the Calvinistic Methodist, lay flat on his back in his bed in Islyn Court, and breathed with the sonorous serenity of the godly just: in the brass gleam of the room, with his black trews over the bed rail and his frock coat over a chair, his boots under the bed, toe-caps kissing, and his knee-length socks airing in the the window, he lay in a black starch of a dream mainly concerned with redemption and obedience, solemnities and benedictions. Horizontal in the Big Seat he floated on a mattress of Bach oratorio amid a great surge of Welsh choirs, gathering about him all the princes of Israel and the priests and the Levites, Chronicles 1:23.

And from the mist of this glory, watched by the sampler *My God and King* above the bed, there rose in his vision a woman of beauty whose name was Elizabeth Gwen Penderyn; and bringing her refinement this woman came to him and knelt before him and when he raised her face, she said:

'I sat down under his shadow with great delight, and his fruit was sweet to my taste. I charge you, O ye daughters of Jerusalem, that ye stir not up, nor awake my love, till he pleases...'

'Oh, Christ, Mamie,' said Billa Jam as Randy picked her Adam up from between the rails outside Ynys Row, 'Oh, Christ, Mamie—look, he's got no legs...'

And the Reverend Morgan Howells, bass in sleep, lay on his back with his spade beard staining the sheet, and said at the ceiling: 'Come with me from Lebanon, my fair Elizabeth Gwendoline, my spouse: how fair is thy love; how much better is thy love than wine!'

'That Bron Babbie, the silly bitch,' said Liz Treharne, the Pendydarren stacker, 'that Mrs. Bronwen Williams—begging your pardon, Mr. Coroner—don't know a smelting compound from a nursery. As God's me judge, I warned her, sir. She was actually walking backwards in a furnace area, sir, with the iron being tapped, ye worship—ye understand, sir? Take my word for it—the moulds were being filled and the blutty fool starts walking about. I shouted to them all for standing still—it's the rules, ye see, sir—beg your pardon for the language, sir, but

152

they gets me hot, ye see. The rules stand firm an' clear—the agents has 'em pinned up in the compound—everybody but the tappers stand still when the furnaces are tapped, but not Bron Babbie, and she walked backwards over a ladle, and trips and falls—there was a pain in her stomach, ye see—had a hard time with her fourth, ye worship, and the milk fever was on her, too, poor sod, beg ye pardon: an' she falls and put out her hands and the sand-moulds take her just as the puddlers were creaming off the sludge. Well, ye can imagine, sir, can't you? This is molten iron, and, naturally, there's only one lot supposed to be stirring that with their fingers, and even they use ten-foot ladles. I remember much the same thing happened when I was stacking for old Homfray up in Penydarren, your honour. There was a woman called Morris—come down with her people from Cardie; she was a wanderer, too—never could keep still ...'

The coroner said: 'Please confine yourself to the facts of this case, Mrs. Treharne—the inquest on the woman Mrs. Bronwen Williams of Ynysgau.'

'Ay, well as I was saying, sir, she trips over the ladle and falls backwards over the sand-moulds just as the pig is filling and running into the moulds, and she sort of turns over in fallin' and lands in the moulds ...'

'The pig, the pig ...? Make yourself clear, woman.'

'The sow taking the trickle of the molten iron, your worship: when it fills up it overflows into the little pigs—it's the piglets milking on the sow, as we say in the trade ...'

'I understand; please continue.'

'Well, she puts her right arm in one mould and a hand in the other—Christ, you can imagine, can't you? I couldn't believe it when she got up. She got up and just stood there for a second with one arm burned off and the other arm on fire at the elbow, and her bodice going up in flames, and she were screaming. Oh, God, your worship, you should have heard that woman screaming ... she made more noise than a gentry hunt. Did our best, of course, that's natural ...'

'Death by misadventure,' said the coroner, and entered it accordingly.

The rain was lashing the roofs of Merthyr, filling the Irish cellars of Pontstorehouse where the Spaniards lived, running down the embattled windows of the castle where the Crawshays lived: little James Crawshay aged four, who died aged eight, was asleep in his lace cot, his breathing whispering down the ornate corridors where generations of Crawshays walked under the splendid chandeliers: Selina Williams, aged one, daughter of Bron Babbie Williams who lately died of fire, the silly bitch—Selina Williams fumbled for the breast of Bron on her bed of wood and rags and her bawling kept the colliers awake as far up as Iron Lane and the lodgers of the Popi Davey, and I wish they'd gag that bloody kid, said Percy Bottom Note, getting out of bed and going head first over Willie's violin and I'll brain that Willie first thing in the morning: bellowing kids and woofing dogs do send me demented.

'Ach, get back to sleep,' said Mrs. Taibach.

'*Heisht, heisht,* my little Selina,' whispered Mr. Madoc Williams, husband of Bron, and he held his baby against his empty breast.

'*Diawch!*' said Mr. Note, wandering the room. 'Hours and hours that blutty kid has been at it!'

'Dear me, dear me,' whispered Madoc Williams. 'As God's my judge, I will never touch another drop. Oh, my love, my poor little Bron...'

And Selina bawled on, fumbling at his chest.

'Hark at it—just hark at it!' cried Mr. Note.

Mrs. Taibach sat up. 'Soon you will have my Willie up, you old fool. Get back into bed—his opinion do count a lot for me, remember. Disgraceful, it is, absolutely disgraceful, heaven forgive me.'

'Thy lips drop as the honeycomb,' said the Reverend Morgan Howells in the bed in Islyn, and, although he did not know it, an old vagrant in rags was wandering along the swilling gutter of his dream, his shining puddle of a face rising above the floods of Shenir and Hermon of a modern world of crucifixions. Thunder bellowed and reverberated among the great Van Rocks and around the fortifications of Brechain where an ancient woman was slain, and her name was *Tydfil*, the daughter

154

of a Brecon King who once ruled Merthyr. And Merthyr, under a king of commerce, slept in filth and tears and silver plate and laughter; a new land of promise, a Canaan of gorging sewers and cholera, the tapestries of Hebron and the damask-robed priests of Zion: and down in Morlais and the cellars of Ynysgau the Irish huddled four to a bed on mattresses that never grew cold.

'What's wrong with you tonight, then?' asked Blod, sitting up in bed.

'*Diawl*,' exclaimed Randy, sitting up beside her.

She giggled then, did Blod, thumping the pillow.

'A fella can come too keen, mind,' said Randy, delicate.

'Whee jakes! I'd never have believed it. When I were single I was galloping for me life: now I'm signed for, sealed and ready to be delivered, nobody wants me.'

'Nothing to laugh about, mind,' said Randy, glum. 'It could happen to anyone.'

'*Jawch!*' said Blod, rubbing it in. 'Here is your flower of desire all ringed up and respectable, the bride of your heart, and the groom's gone cold. *Jawch!*'

'You'm a rotten dog, Blod,' said Randy.

And Blod put her face down into the pillow to stifle her laughter and clenched her hands and thumped and thumped, and presently she tossed over on her back and pealed her laughter at the ceiling, and every neighbour from there to Court Street sat up in bed and listened, and Mamie Goldie, knitting downstairs with Billa Jam, said:

'You know, Billa, for happy newlyweds that pair upstairs are acting queer. First nights is no laughing matter, as far as I remember.'

But Billa Jam did not reply for the ghost of Adam was in her arms.

'You reckon I've caught a chill or something?' asked Randy, vacant.

'Could be,' replied Blod, spluttering. 'I'll have ye examined first thing in the morning.' She kissed him then. 'Good night, lad, don't take it hard.'

'I anna myself, that's for sure,' said Randy, and Blod, in the

155

act of turning over, fell out of bed and landed with a thump.

'That sounds more healthy, mind,' said Mamie, pausing in her knitting.

The moon flooded the wall of Blod's bedroom then, and as she climbed back in beside Randy she saw his face: it was pale, and she no longer laughed. Also, there was in him a silence she had not heard before, and a look in his eyes of a man lost.

'You all right, boy?' she whispered.

'Ay,' said Randy.

He was looking into a corner where the shadows were dark, and he was not in the bed with Blod, his wife. Unaccountably, he was standing in the rolling house of the Taibach Copper Works, aged ten, just as they stopped the ten-ton rollers and got his father out.

'You can have this, son,' the smelting foreman said, and gave him the boot.

So now he was not within the warmth of Blod Irish but sitting on the rag-bolts of the casting-house in Taibach with the smashed boot in his hand; and in his nostrils was not the perfume of Blod's hair but the smell of torn leather, and under his hands was not the satin smoothness of her body but the rough of his father's boot.

His eyes were fixed to the shadows of the corner where it lay wrapped in brown paper, and he remembered the foreman's voice, the bloody sawdust and the dripping rollers.

'They'm mighty quiet again, mind,' said Mamie at her knitting.

'You go on with you, you old thing,' said Billa, mending.

Blod Irish held Randy in the bed and stared at him, and he drew away from her, for her arms, round and white, were like the arms of one they were cutting free, and her face was a mask of blood in his sight; her breast he saw riven with the bolts, and the hands she raised to him were smashed. And he screamed, shrinking away from her on the pillows.

'That anna normal, ye know,' said Mamie. 'Noises like that just anna normal for a first night,' and Billa lowered the mending in her lap, listening.

Later, the rain stopped and the moon came out and flooded Merthyr with light, and Blod held her husband, and he slept.

'*Heisht* you, me little boy,' she said.

And Mr. Madoc Williams, teetotaller, held his Selina, too, and she no longer cried for Bron Babbie, her mam. The town was quiet under the rain-washed stars; the Taff River lay silent, smiling at the moon.

'About time, too,' said Percy Bottom Note, getting back into bed.

13

THE mist was wreathing the Penderyn woods outside Merthyr and the trees clustered in green moss amid the refuse of their lonely autumns. Field bindweed was opening its cups to the sun as Dic and Sun went hand in hand, singing up the lane for Tafern Uchaf and the church. From here the valley of the Penderyn quarries that served the trade was white with mist, but a smoke cloud hung over distant Merthyr, and Aberdare was sending flame-shot cinders into a bright September sky.

'Did you know lots of chaps before me, then?'

'Nearly a few—about two thousand.'

'Serious, though.'

She said, stopping him: 'If you keep talking about it, mon, you'll barge into a tantrum.' Going on tip-toe, she kissed him and he tried to hold her but she slipped out of his arms and ran through the trees.

'I've got to know, Sun,' he said catching her.

'Right, you asked for it; sit down by there.'

They sat in the leaves and stared at each other over the yards between them.

'Can you hear me, Dic Penderyn?'

He grinned, folding his arms about his legs, resting his chin on his knees: full length lay Sun, and turned on her back, tracing the pattern of overhanging branches against a bright sky. He could not see her face, only the homespun dress stretched tightly over her shoulders, and her hair, which was spare and tufted, bright red against the green.

'You after tying me up, Penderyn?'

'You know it.'

'Then you best know I'm a bad beggar, if you're serious.' She heard him move in the leaves, and added; 'No, you stay there and hear me out. You chase me through these woods, that's one thing, Dic, but you talk of crippling me for life, that's another. You know Gid Davies well?'

'Only met him twice.'

'He knows you and me are sparkin'—and he never mentioned a fella called Billy Ugmore?'

'No, never.'

'Not once—you swear?'

'No, not once.'

'Ach,' said she, 'he's a right handy one is Gid. You reckon I'm pretty?'

'Prettiest I've seen in Merthyr.'

'That's outside. Inside I'm black as thunder. Give you three guesses what happened between me and Billy Ugmore.'

'Same as what happened between Molly Caulara and me, I expect,' he said. 'That makes us quits.'

'Oh, no it don't. Six weeks I was on the Derry roads with Billy, doing the tinkering cans; knocking on the doors by day wi' the pegs and poles, and four weeks of that I was his woman.'

She heard him move again, and called: 'No, don't come, Dic; you hear me out. When you buy a waistcoat at Merthyr market you're entitled to know what wool you're getting. There were a sailor from Bantry off the cutters, a fella from Dublin working the inns wi' a squeeze-box, and another called Windy—you ever heard a chap called Windy? And there was a wee oyster-catcher come in with the tide on Waterford Head—he were just sixteen, though I never knew his name.'

'You got around,' said Dic, his eyes low.

'But no, that were the trouble—they got round me, and there's a difference—you understand?'

'Not much.' He plucked a blade of grass and put it between his teeth.

'It's the difference between a woman and a man—but I

din't love none of 'em, except perhaps little Billy Ugmore—
you want to hear about him?'

'No.'

The wind whispered in the wood: a hare watched them
under trembling ears, its ball eyes glistening in the filtering
sun of the wood.

'You gone off me now, Dic?'

'What about Gid Davies, then?' he raised his face and she
swung over on her stomach, and called:

'Ay, what about him?'

'Did he ever have his way with you?'

She sat up, appalled. 'The devil wi' you! What the hell
d'you take me for? You sit there accusin' me of shananikins
with a man like Gid Davies? You'm got a nasty mind, Dic
Penderyn!'

'I'm sorry.'

'And ye should be, bedamn!' Her anger swept between
them. 'You sit there dancing me up on that blutty Molly Caulara from the Aunty Popi Davey, and then accuse me and Gid
Davies of a fine insinuation—you're not fit to clean the fella's
boots!'

'*Did* ye!' He leaned towards her, and her laughter pealed
about him as she rolled in the grass again and flung the leaves
high in a shower.

'*Arrah!* I did not, but it weren't for the want of trying. I'd
have managed it likely if I'd got him outside a quart or two o'
porter!'

'You're wicked to the devil, Sun Heron, and I'm finished
with you!'

'Och, don't be angry, Dico—if you ask daft questions you'll
collect hot answers.'

'Not true, then?'

'Of course not! Gid Davies is married to a Union—anyway,
why bother yourself? Isn't it more important to know who I've
loved than who I've mated?' She added, sitting up in the
leaves: 'And you're not exactly a monk yourself.'

'But you loved that Billy Ugmore, didn't you?'

'Ay, but only his tongue, for it were golden. But the difference between you and him is that I love all of you. You listening?'

He lit his pipe and the smoke drifted among the leaves and touched her nostrils.

'I'm listening,' said Dic.

'You play an Irish love game with me, Penderyn?'

He gave her a sigh of disapproval.

She knelt then, put her hands together as if in prayer and lowered her head in mock shyness, saying: 'If I swear to being true, will ye kneel a yard closer, Dic Penderyn?'

He pocketed the pipe, remembering the Irish game of the Merthyr streets: linking his fingers behind his back, he moved towards her on his knees, and she said:

'And if I wash me body white for you and put sugar on me lips, will you come a yard closer, Dic Penderyn?'

He obeyed, shuffling nearer. The hare watched, an ear cocked in the distant spinney: a badger grunted and shouldered from his earth, waddling in heavy swerves among the late butterwort of a thicket. Sun said:

'And not to smile to break the pledge: if I cook red beef without a burn, nor soup to scald—will ye come a bit closer, Dic Penderyn?'

The badger heard him move, and turned, listening.

'And take ye in my arms and never touch another, save me mother—will you come a foot closer, Dic Penderyn?' This he did, and put out his hands to her, and she reached also, but their fingers did not touch, so she said:

'Kiss me this once, and fill me with childer. Will you kiss this body, Dic Penderyn?'

Raising her head she opened her arms to him and he came to her and held her: the hare scampered in a rustling of dead leaves; the badger lumbered into his earth: a dog fox barked from the covies of the common and the sun burned down.

'For I love you better than a gipsy from Derry, Dic Penderyn.'

He held her: astonishingly, she had tears in her eyes when he kissed her.

'And no more Billy Ugmores?' he said.

'I swear it.' She kissed his face, his hair.

'No Bantry sailors, nor oyster-catchers on Waterford Head?'

'None no more, nor Molly Caularas, and you swear, too.'

'I'll do me best,' he said.

'Right for me. Will you be me chap, Dic?'

For answer he leaned her back in the leaves and the boles of the big trees shone green with sun and lichen, their roots garlanded with bittersweet, and in their nostrils was the wood scent of the hawkweed and rampion flowering yellow and blue, and the bees hummed about the wavering harebells in the wind. From the distant road to Brecon came the faint clanking of cavalry, and Sun felt him stiffen momentarily, eyes switching.

'Ach, to hell with them,' she said, 'this is ours.'

The Hirwaun Works were thumping and the earth-trembling entered them.

'I love you, Sun.'

There was no sound now but their breathing, and a rustling of leaves. There was no reward for custom: his strength astonished her and she twisted away her face, gasping.

'Will ye ease up—I'm only five foot.'

A man shouted with laughter from Tafern Uchaf: faintly clanged the gate of the church and the trees were suddenly alive with a chattering of birds above the vaulted graves.

'You realise you're lying on your skirt, woman?'

'I anna forgot.'

'But I love you. Who's to know?'

The hare raised steepled ears above the gorse, peering.

'I shall,' said Sun, and heaved him off. 'You promised me decent, an' you're not lining me up for a Molly Caulara.'

The metallic clash of hobnails savaged the road and the voices of men came on the still air; rising, Sun brushed herself down, saying, 'If you're half as hot as me you're melting, but I'm away for me night shift and it's time for your meeting.' She suddenly clung to him. 'There's an ache in me for you, Penderyn, and I felt the strength in you. But keep us clean, is it?'

162

He held her away, smiling. Pushing clear she ran to the edge of the clearing, then turned, waving. 'Give me love to Gid Davies.'

Picking up his hat Dic beat it against his thigh, smiling as he watched her running with her dress held up to her knees, swerving through the trees, ducking overhanging branches.

With his hat on the back of his head, his clay cocked up in his mouth, he took the track through the Penderyn woods to Tafern Uchaf.

Most of the Oddfellows Lodge were already seated in the Long Room above the bar when he arrived and he helped Wil Goff Half Pint, whose furniture was in Coffin's Court for debt: staggering under a tray of a dozen quarts was Wil, and them's thirsty sods they are upstairs, this is the third bloody time I've been down. The landlord winked at Dic as he took the tray and shouldered little Wil aside. With the tray poised he climbed the stairs to the Long Room and booted the door. A dozen faces swung down each side of the ceremonial table as he entered.

'Hoi hoi, Dico, me lovely!' cried a man: others bawled greeting, banging their mugs and he grinned wide as the bedlam beat about him and elbowed Wil Goff aside and set the tray on the table, crying, 'I took this off the five-foot boy on the stairs—ye'll be twisting off his rollickers with this bloody lot—who's for tan and who's on blue ruin?'

Gideon, the chairman, rose. 'Easy with the language, Dic.'

The greetings died to a whisper: Dic frowned at the woman at the end of the table. 'Och, no, Chairman—not bloody women!'

'Watch that tongue, Penderyn.' Zimmerman got up beside her, running his fingers awkwardly through his mop-gold hair: his large, bald eyes blinked with apprehension: the Long Room tinkled with silence and breathing. Dic eyed the girl: rarely had he seen a woman so beautiful. Her black dress trimmed with white lace enhanced the fine upward sweep of her bodice, but it was her eyes ... they held his with a piercing awareness, and her face in its sweep of dark, plaited hair was

163

pale and lifted with a hint of questioning and challenge. The big man the other side of Gideon raised his eyes at the ceiling, fearful of an onslaught.

'Ay, well sorry, missus,' said Dic. 'No women, see—this is a Lodge.'

'You keep order, Penderyn,' said Zimmerman softly, 'or you're out.'

'I'm out on the vote of members not by you, foreigner.' Picking up a pewter from the tray he went to the door. 'Speakers from Blaenafon, you said, Gid Davies—not the Streams of Loveliness—is she a member?'

'Of course not, but . . .'

'If she's not a member how the hell can she attend?'

Zimmerman shouted. 'She is here with Mr. Bennet by the special request of the Lancashire Association . . .'

'I don't care if she's here by the express wish of Mr. William bloody Crawshay—this is a Lodge meeting, not an annual outing, and we don't brook women.'

The shouting of the men died when the woman rose. She said softly: 'But you brook them hauling drams—you take them on the cropping and you sign them on the pig-stacking . . .' He drank deep at the door, watching her. She continued: 'You work them on the ore and hauling on the ladders; you pay them under the rate—and Christ knows yours is low enough—you put them on their knees with chains through their legs like bloody animals and you work them on a twelve-hour shift, then haul them off to the hob and the bed. By God, Penderyn—whatever they call you, you're a cheeky swine for voting them out of a second-rate Lodge.'

He held the pot against his chest, and grinned.

'She talks like a man, I give her that,' he said.

'You've had it easy,' said the man called Bennet, 'wait till she gets going.'

The men whispered laughter at this: Dic said:

'English, eh?'

'Ay, and I'll trip you up north to the mill-owners, son, then you can thank God you're Welsh.'

'I am Welsh,' said the woman, sitting down, 'though God

164

knows at times I doubt it and God knows at times I'm ashamed.' She looked around their staring faces. 'You've got ten thousand working out their guts for the greediest masters on The Top and you can't produce more than twenty for an Oddfellow Lodge—do you call this Benefit? Do you call this the Union?' She pointed at the window. 'Over there is Blaen-afon, which is my town—one of the smallest—she turns out a tenth of your iron but she's got ten times your soul.'

'Mind your words, woman,' said a man.

'Words are nothing, boyo—they spit on the air. Mind my words, indeed—who the hell are you talking to? Are we in this together for plain words and fair arguments? Or do we sit and wrangle among ourselves while the masters coin the profits—you, Penderyn . . .' and she pointed, 'will ye give me aloud the Four Points of the Charter—you're handy with your mouth—now we'll try your politics—come on—the Four Points.'

'Six,' said Zimmerman, softly, 'all unpublished.'

'*Four!* And Lovett's—the other two are coming.' She put her hands on her hips and stared at Dic.

'Leave it, Morfydd,' said the big man beside her.

She shouted: 'Can ye tell me one—just one, then? Any of ye here? By God, if Wales is dependent on the likes of you, then heaven help Cobbett and Fergus O'Connor. Is ale and Lodge rules the only thing you have to offer? And Thursday night at the Benefit at twopence a week for the amputated and nothing for the scalded? Is this what you want? You listen here, Penderyn—don't you speak of iron masters and me in the same breath or it'll be the worse for you, and don't you talk of voting me out for a woman until you've crawled coal under the Coity—I've got the nephew, remember—I get paid by Crawshay Bailey.'

Dic pulled up a chair and sat astride it. 'Count me in, then, but don't call it a Lodge.'

'That's the last thing I'd call it,' said the man called Bennet.

'And tell that witch to put a peg on her tongue for she don't know the length of it.' He gave her a happy grin and elbowed Wil Goff. 'Slip down to the bar and fetch her a gin.'

The girl said: 'I'll drink with you when you've got a

wheeled stretcher in Cyfarthfa and you know the difference between Reform and the Reformation.'

Gideon Davies rose. 'Lodge meeting cancelled—the ayes first, please.'

Dic drank steadily, watching the girl over the brim of his pewter. Someone counted the hands.

'Thirteen—majority. Lodge meeting cancelled—Mr. Secretary, kindly note that in the minutes: political meeting begins —Tafern Uchaf, September the first, 1830—does that suit you, Dic Penderyn?'

'It suits me,' said Zimmerman, heavily, 'and that's all that matters. Guest speaker is Mr. Richard Bennet of the Workingmen's Association. I introduce his friend, Mistress Mortymer, of the Blaenafon Benefit—your chairman is present, I believe —Mr. Idris Foreman: greetings to new members as follows: Mr. Lewis Lewis, known as Lewsyn *yr Heliwr* of Penderyn, Mr. R. Goldie and Mr. John Hughes of Forge Side . . .'

The names droned on: Randy lifted his face and watched Dic Penderyn and the new man Lewis Lewis; and Madoc Williams, his eyes still swollen with weeping for Bron Babbie, watched the woman, Morfydd Mortymer, and saw in her form the mist of another. Dick Llaw-Haearn of the Iron Hand was there from the shambles they called Silluri also Will Johns, who later ran, and condemned his friend . . . Abednego Jones, aged fourteen who said he was older, sat beside Mervyn Jam in a corner and watched with smouldering eyes. Hancock called Han, and Richards the draper and Parry of the Penydarren grocery and Owen Davis who went mad through riot and finished with the lunatics of Llandisilio: all were there, together with others who later said, in evidence, that they were not, and Rowland Thomas who was afterwards shot dead for picking up a soldier's hat—he was also present (the jury called it *Excusable Homicide*). Strangely, Mr. Thomas Rowland, meek as always, sat beside him: he who later went in chains for seven years forced labour in Botany Bay (which needed colonising) for stealing a sixpenny bonnet, while David Morgan, who was not present, went to prison for two years for the rape of a little girl. Both men, according to *The Cambrian*, as

166

feckless as ever, were tried by the same jury: the value of a bloodstained child being worth something less than sixpence.

'Gentlemen,' said Gideon, getting to his feet, 'we are living in a terrible period of Welsh history. In a century from now they will try to excuse our treatment by saying that those who terrorise us are children of their time. But the forces of justice are organising against this evil. It is on this subject that our colleagues will address you...' The room fell to silence. Gideon said: 'It is true that the world price of iron is dropping; it is also true that the masters of the ironworks are standing in the heaven of an economic piety: the translation of the term is simple; economic piety exists among men when they possess private and industrial assets of round about a quarter of a million pounds and make rather less than the normal standard of profit.' He smiled, his blind eyes, brilliant with an inner fire, moved over the room. 'Owing to the generosity of friends in high places I am able to give you examples of how the piety of our iron masters is expressed, and from this you will be able to deduce the degree of paternal benevolence which they claim they shower upon us—the workers, the object of their affections...'

The men laughed; the woman Mortymer bowed her head, and Dic watched her intently; it was as if she was undergoing a private crucifixion. Gideon said: 'My source of information says that in the year 1815—twelve months before the last big riots in Merthyr—William Crawshay the First held in the Cyfarthfa Works a capital investment of ninety-five thousand pounds; a year later—the actual year of the riots—this figure increased to a hundred thousand pounds—a sum also returned for 1817, which was a year *after* the riots.' He smiled. 'And so, if the bank espionage is correct, and I am assured that it is, it would appear that this paternal master lost nothing in profit at a time of his workers' distress. In fact, and I wish to stress this point, his son wrote to Josiah John Guest of Dowlais, who extracts fortunes from his workmen by illegal Truck ... his son wrote this letter on October 16th, 1816, in which he admits to the hunger which the workmen themselves claimed as their reason for the riot.' Gideon paused. 'At last, it appears, we have an admission of hunger from a dynasty of death that lives on the lie of paternal benevolence: if this is benevolence then let us have tyranny. But let this bit be read so that we fully recognise the forces of greed which encompass us ... can the Welsh speakers understand?'

'Ay, but take it slow,' mumbled Lewis Lewis, and Dic glanced at the man. Dark-haired and surly, he sat glowering in his corner, with one clenched hand pounding gently against the other. Gideon raised the letter, and Zimmerman read:

'The enemy is in too great a strength to oppose with any probability of success; have possessed themselves of all our works and wholly stopped them. They are yet exulting in their victory and are about to proceed to Pennydarren and Dowlais. My spies tell me that they threaten hard your Shop, for they are hungry...

Should anything more serious threaten you, I shall be glad to hear from you, as I would gladly do anything in my power to assist you, but the enemy have not yet evacuated their possessions here.'

Gideon said blandly, 'I ask you particularly to note the term "enemy". This is the manner in which our masters think of us; this is the paternal benevolence of the gaoler to the prisoner and the hangman to his victim. I ask this company to stand in memory of Aaron Williams who was hanged for his part in this riot, though he caused no injury to any person; also, to remember the earlier martyr, the collier Samuel Hill, hanged in the knowledge of Richard Crawshay, the church-goer, for leading riots against starvation sixteen years before.'

The men stood, removing their hats: the woman Mortymer did not rise, but sat with her face in her hands. When the company was seated again, Gideon said:

'And how stand we now? The economic piety continues, the paternal benevolence streams unabated from Cyfarthfa Castle; wages continue to slide to maintain profits, and hunger and degradation stalks the slums: the expectation of life is round about the age of twenty-two—half our children die before the age of five: include these murderous figures and the life expectation of the average worker is reduced further. The facts are indisputable; later, when the Medical Board publishes findings, the indictment of this barbarity will be there for future generations to read for themselves. Give me Crawshay Bailey, I say, if I have to have the Crawshays, for at least he is honest. He spreads no words of benevolence, he brooks no charity towards his Nantyglo slaves: instead, he builds embattlements to protect him from the people he employs—knowing them to be his enemies, and accepting them as such: he keeps his thugs he calls his Workmen's Volunteers in a barracks to defend him from the Scotch Cattle, who are the heroes of the coming Union. But the masters of Cyfarthfa and Nantyglo are one and the same: they have the bone and flesh of those of Penydarren and Dowlais, Tredegar and Pontypool; Hill of Plymouth and Uncle Willie Tait, Fothergill of Aberdare, God forgive him, and the rest of the miserable train, who, surely to God, will find no seat in heaven. *Listen!* You know the terms, you know the consequences—need they be repeated? From the grain riots of Beaufort to the stink we call the iron towns of today, it has been a story of privation, disease, degradation—and miserly wage rates, too, from these pirates of industry, and the reductions are increasing. We are prepared to assess the state of the trade, but not to bow to these decreases without good reason. And there is no good reason when minor Windsors like Cyfarthfa Castle can be built at a cost of thirty thousand and Hensol Castle bought on a whim!'

'By God, blind man,' shouted Lewis Lewis, 'one day they'll hang you!'

'You lead us, Gid Davies!' bawled another, 'and we'll follow!'

Gideon said quietly: 'There can be no leaders in this fight —the people themselves are the leaders. And if I hang—if any here hang—let our names be as unknown in a hundred years as Sam Hill's is today, for we are but the few who speak in the name of thousands. And when the history of our time is told, let the hero be the hungry man, and his mistress Merthyr Town: let it not raise the unimportant one or two, as most

169

stories do, but the whole condition of our society that longs for change—the idealist and the drunk, the atheist and ranter, the refiner and the humble digger—let no man stand an inch above another.' He straightened, smiling. 'Now back to the facts—give me the names of the distrained of Coffin's Court.'

Wil Goff got up, and read from a paper: Lewis Lewis, by 'ere . . .' He indicated the haulier beside him. 'One chest and a bed; two chairs and a framed picture, the kitchen table and pots and pans—value six pound ten. Robert Jones . . . lost his bed and mirror, his grancher's armchair and a clock—collected and auctioned by the beadle at the court and bought by the mother of David Williams, Front Street: taken in debt for groceries—three pound eleven and fourpence—is the fella here?'

'He is,' mumbled the man Jones, 'and he'll get back every stick, mind.'

Wil Goff read: 'Tom Rees and Mr. Vaughan—he caught a tartar—you here, Vaughan, lad.'

'Here!'

'A bed belonging to Vaughan's mother and a stool and two framed pictures—one of the *Ascent of Venus* and the other of the *Whipping in the Temple*, also a commode for a nursing mother, two breast phials and a cloak; the hat and stick of the man Rees's uncle, while visiting, and two china dogs: taken on the eighth of August in recovery of a five pound debt due to two shopkeepers and one saddler for stirrup leathers: auctioned by the beadle of the Court of Requests and bought by Mary Phillips.'

'Last week I met her in *China*,' said the man Rees. 'Me and Tom Vaughan met her and walked her side by side, and I asked her if she'd heard of the Court of Conscience: we'll have that Court down, mark me, and Mr. Coffin wi' it. My missus don't stop weeping for them two little dogs.'

'Left her by her grancher, see,' said the man Vaughan, his glasses on the end of his nose.

Richard Bennet said: 'What are you all talking about? What is this Court of Requests?'

'My God,' cried Dic instantly, 'and they send him into

170

Wales to instruct the Welsh—get back up north where you come from man!'

'Not so fast,' shouted the woman. 'He's arranged the return of debts and fought for parish relief from here to Glasgow, so a little less old tongue, unless you know the inside of a Lancashire prison, for he's just come out of one.'

Gideon rose and said: 'It is quite simple, Bennet. The Court of Requests, administered by a certain Mr. Coffin, of Merthyr, has the power under the local magistracy to seize workmen's furniture and effects and auction these articles to repay private debts—usually groceries—and ale: be fair, they are not without their faults.'

'My God,' said Bennet.

'In depressed times like this,' added Gideon, 'half the furniture of the town is changing hands every month, and you cannot get through the streets for the carts and gambos...'

'So what happens?'

'We sleep on the floor and eat off bloody boxes, man,' shouted Lewis, 'that's what happens. My missus got tired of sitting on the step in an empty house, so she ups and offs to her gran in Brecon wi' the children, while I sleep rough in Penderyn woods.'

There was a silence. The woman said, her fists on the table: 'So what are you going to do about it?'

'We're having it down, missus, that's what!'

'And Coffin with it!'

'An' hang that damn beadle from a rafter!'

The boy Abednego Jones said, though none heard him in the ensuing shouts: 'My mam got moved back to Carmarthen by the parish, and she's breaking stones in Llandovery to repay.'

'You seen the transportation lists?'

'Hey, Bennet—you follow the hunt?'

'My old woman lifted a door handle down Duke, and they got her in the Swansea Correction...'

'And I got a girl of ten—working at the face under Cyfarthfa—that's what, you cheeky buggers—what we going to do about it, then, ye brass fools...?'

'Order, order!' shouted Gideon, his hands raised high. 'Try

171

not to get excited.'

'Excited? You blind idiot! You give us lectures on the luck of the masters and that clown don't know the Court of Requests? You got an Englishman up there, an' you got a Pole—will ye tell me when the hell we're going to get some Welsh?'

'I told you before,' shouted the woman Mortymer, 'you've got one here. Will you tell me what use a meeting is if it can't be run with order? Don't you know what will happen if you lay a finger on that court, or Coffin?' Silenced by her shriek they subsided, grumbling deep, and nudging, and she looked them over in their sullen anger and rags. 'You move too soon, you crowd down here in Merthyr, and the gaffer will be delighted.' She shook her fist in their faces. 'You raise one finger in Merthyr town and he'll bring the Military in . . .'

'Let him, an' we'll bloody show them how!'

Dic watched the raving anger of the man Lewis Lewis.

'With the redcoats on a six-hour tap from Brecon barracks —talk sense, ye gunk!' cried the girl. 'What chance have ye got against the forces of the Crown? You're prepared to go to street barricades for a few loads of furniture?'

'I lost a kid last month, missus, so mind . . .'

'And I saw ten die up The Top last week, man, and not by cholera!' She rose. 'Do you think you and yours are the only ones starving? Fourteen years back Sarah Hopkins built a school in my town, and taught in it, and she and her old Sam the Welsh were the best masters of the day. But the kids still die in Blaenafon, like they die in Ponty and Tredegar and up in Nanty under Bailey, where I work the Coity. But you can't expect to move before your time, d'you hear me? I came here with Richard Bennet to talk of the new Union, but you're not ready in this town for a Union of workers: you're not even ready for a decent Benefit, for you are nothing like the standard we're running on the Eastern. Before you talk of action, before you shout for blood and burning this and hanging that, you've got to organise. Christ, I was up with the Dowlais puddlers the night 'afore last and I thought them bad enough. Don't you remember what happened to the Luddites? Or don't you even know who the Luddites are? What the hell

172

have you been doing these past fourteen years since they
hanged Aaron Williams? Can half of you even tell me who
Aaron Williams was? He raised a flag and ye dropped it in the
dust, like Samuel Hill before him, but you lot let it ride: you
let it ride because times were reasonable—they dropped pennies in the good times and you scrambled for the pickings:
now you howl on the doorstep when they distrain your goods,
you go to the beerhouse when they drop your wages, you moan
to your minister when they lengthen the shifts. And all in ten
minutes you're shouting for blood. What are you planning to
do—march on London?'

'It can be done,' said Zimmerman.

They heard Tom Rowlands breathing, but he was weak in
the chest.

Gideon said: 'Not now, Zim, in the name of God,' and
Randy Goldie shouted: 'You see this paper parcel? I got a
boot in this paper parcel—all they gave me was me father's
boot.'

'Shut your snivelling! What's the Pole saying?'

'Here, Wil—fetch another round to moisten things up—ay,
put it on the five-bar, the landlord's all right.'

'I asked you what the foreigner said,' shouted Lewis Lewis,
up on a chair, and Dic watched him, sipping from his mug;
and knew in this man an affinity he had known with no other,
like a forging together in a fire.

'My missus has gone, do you know that?' cried Madoc Williams. He wept aloud, the only drunkard not drinking, and
shivered his fist in the air. 'She were on iron stacking, and,
and ...' He covered his face.

'Hush, Madoc,' said Dic Penderyn, pulling him down, and
the commotion of the men thundered about them, some bawling for the Pole to speak, others demanding to throw him out
for a foreigner when the door came open and Sid Blump came
in, and Belcher, and Big Bonce with Lady Godiva on his arm,
also Peg-Moll and Crone and Curly Hayloft, balder still, his
face low and griving for Tilly. And the customers from the bar
downstairs came in with shouts and splashing mugs, raising a
song of Reform that hit the rafters, and the landlord cried,

173

banging on a gong:

'Gid Davies, Gid Davies!'

'Ay?'

'Boy just run in—says a redcoat troop are going past the Lamb—down on the Brecon road—you hear me?'

'I hear you,' shouted Gideon and brought down a clay flagon, banging it on the table for silence. The room swayed with faces; whispers died and there was a shifting of boots on the boards. Gideon said:

'My God, I weep for Merthyr. A vote of thanks, then, for the London speaker who never got a hearing. But he will be back, for unless you're senseless you'll have to raise a Union. If it's the last thing I do in this town, I'll raise a Union—we must have a negotiating body to meet the new Reform. Away now, and quietly. Keep clear of the Brecon road or they'll be among you with sabres.'

'When's the next Oddfellows, Gid?'

'I'll let you know.'

'How?'

'By word. What do you expect me to do—pin it on the works? Mistress Mortymer . . . are you there?'

'Yes, Mr. Davies.' And she took his arm.

Dic was still standing by the door, the mug dangling from his hand, watching her. He thought she was the most beautiful woman he had ever seen. Pausing before him she lifted her eyes to his face.

'Good for you, missus,' he said. Then Lewis Lewis pushed up, and the woman moved on with Gideon and Zimmerman. Lewis Lewis said:

'You come from round here?'

'No, from Pyle—parish of Aberafon.'

'Then why call you Penderyn—like these woods?'

'Because the cottage that raised me was called Penderyn.'

The man grunted: hair from his chest, Dic noticed, was sprouting out of his collar; his arms were thick to the broad shoulders, and he looked drunk with strength. 'What's your real name, then?'

'Dic Lewis.'

174

'Same name as me.'

'Ay,' said Dic, 'that's the trouble with the country—too many blutty Lewises.'

'You reckon you could take me, then? I saw you looking more'n twice.'

Dic grinned. 'No real reason, but I like your style.'

'You ever sink a loose quart come Saturdays?'

'Sunday, too, if I get the chance.'

'Wellington?'

'By Jackson's—Merthyr?'

'That's it—old Jumpo's place. It's poison, but it's cheap.'

'Some time, mate—we'll see how it goes,' said Dic.

'And you fancy a swing for the fun of it—say a guinea?'

'If I swing you for fancy, Lewis, you won't need a guinea.'

The man grinned wide, and made a fist of his hand and put it on Dic's chin. 'Saturday night, then—we'll give them Merthyr.'

When Dic got back to the tap Gideon Davies, Bennet and the Mortymer woman were going down the hill beyond Tafern Uchaf. It was a pity, he thought, for he would have liked to talk to Gideon Davies about Sun Heron; also, he would have liked to have been nearer the woman ... He remembered Sun then, and her smile; the way her red hair tufted up under his hands and the laughing freshness of her, all over fizzy like parsnip wine: and he remembered again the mature and dark beauty of the woman he had seen; the slow lift of her eyes at the end of the table. Undefinably he knew that his destiny was linked with hers; the thought was more a sensation, and eerie. Smiling, he said softly:

'Paid member of Parliament, Secret Vote ... No property qualifications ...' he paused, scratching his ear. She had been right, he thought; he couldn't even name four points of the new Charter everybody was talking about. Then he remembered Lewis Lewis and next Saturday night at the Wellington, and he wandered back into the Tafern tap-room and slapped down a penny.

'Quart of the best.'

He looked around the little room. A few aged men sat in

solitary dejection, staring into their mugs, and he knew them for the generation that had been hammered on the anvil of economic piety, burned out by one agent after another: personally, he blamed the agents more than the Crawshays—anyone, he reflected, could blame the masters for they were vulnerable: blame was a commodity one could slice up and apportion just where the mood took you, and Gideon Davies, in his opinion was as bad as any when it came to this. He drank the ale slowly, wondering about this, and grinned to himself. He didn't like the Crawshays better than anyone else in Merthyr, but it always amazed him that when the mob burned anybody in effigy, they always chose the masters; the real enemies, he thought, were much lower down the scale ... The landlord's voice shattered his inner silence:

'Thank God that lot's gone. Get me bloody hung, they will —but he's all right, mind, that Gid Davies.'

'Ay.' Dic drank again; amazingly, he could hear the sound of the woman's voice still.

'But fella! Did ye see that beauty he brought over from Blaenafon?'

'Ay,' Dic drank again: her eyes, he thought, were the most beautiful he had ever seen.

'Like polar bears, I say—ought to be chained up: enough to drive a lad demented, and I'm nigh sixty.'

'I'd rather be in her than in the Union.'

'What did you say—you want to join the Union?'

Dic put down his mug and went out into the sunlight.

With his hands deep in his trews and whistling to have his teeth out, he went down to the Lamb. There he drank steadily, staring into his mug. The memory of the Mortymer woman of Blaenafon had completely obliterated his thoughts of Sun...

14

GWEN, Dic's sister, gave Morgan Howells his third child when the leaves were falling on the old church up at Vaynor, and the country was russet and the trees of Penderyn woods were tracing the skies with tapestries of black. The cold hand of winter laid its spell on workers and masters alike, and there came to Merthyr and the trade a vice of stagnation. The bitter winds of depression howled down the ricketty streets; ice grew in the windows and shone on the boards, the skies darkened over the Beacons and the leaves gusted along the alleys of Graham and High. With the coming of the snow—five feet drifted up Chapel Street and choking the gutters of the Wesleyan—the Irish huddled in the cellars of Pontstorehouse and Sulleri and sought warmth in the blessing of their priests. The ice-breakers were heading the barges along the cut, which was frozen from the Old Cyfarthfa canal right down to Cardiff, the water was solid in the polluted wells. But the Quakers under Tregelles Price sent in their little donkey soup-carts and the gentry in their screened pews sent up prayers for the distressed poor. From Staffordshire to Newport, Swansea to Blaina the furnaces simmered and died, the weakest masters going first to the wall: the great iron stocks lay rusting along the docklands in hundreds of thousands of tons from Cardiff to Gower, the naked cranes and hoists raked the empty sky. But the Tommy shops, made illegal by the Act of 1820, were flourishing as the masters bolstered their fading profits by raising the prices of goods: the old truck shop of Guest of Dowlais which once tied his workers to him hand and foot, was reopened in the face of legal prosecution: all the workers had fought for—the removal of the hated Truck—was swept aside in the free-for-all that swept the valleys of Monmouthshire and Glamorgan. But the Crawshays, to their credit, followed the policy of the founder Richard, and no truck shops existed in Merthyr, though, for convenience (but not profit), they paid in their own printed money. And the shopkeepers, the great middle-class of the town, seized on this loophole for personal benefit: price rises began which decimated the pay packets of the Merthyr workers: a new tyranny arose; a shopocracy that enriched the few at the expense of the many. The paupers increased and thronged the roads from Merthyr, lined the frosted pavements from Cyfarthfa to Dowlais Top, or lay in destitution around the furnace area of Ynys and Penderyn. Hunger and cold walked the empty streets of Merthyr: no longer the children played hopscotch along Thomas and Duke, no longer the women chattered over the garden walls with their black Welsh shawls over their heads and shoulders. The old ironstone miners, the sallow colliers of an earlier generation, took to their beds for warmth, babies wailed from the tight-shut cottages. With the works of Cyfarthfa and Ynys running at a loss, the shivering sale-coal colliers stood in dejected groups on the pneumonia corners and beat themselves for warmth. The trade of iron, falling since the boom of 1825, slid down the graph to rock bottom. The publics were empty; even Jump Jackson was down to a barrel in the Wellington, it was said. But the chandeliers of Crawshay's castle still blazed over the eighteen acres of park land: still the parties gathered on the lawns, still the guests arrived. While over the wasted land the little black processions grew into a processional hymn of death, the carriages of the gentry and the new merchant princes clattered along the deserted streets of The Top towns on Sundays. And the older workers, who remembered the lavish and amorous escapades of George and Richard, the high flyer of a new era, watched with burning eyes this show of blatant wealth in the midst of their poverty.

Trouble was coming. It was whispered down the alleys, it moved in motions at the secret Lodge and Union meetings: many workers left the district, evicted for non-payment of

178

rent, more were tracked down and sentenced to the Usk tread-mill for leaving their place of employment: others went to the houses of correction for debt, other for theft; some to the scaffold or transportation, for robbery in the face of hunger. To support the losses of trade rates of wages were cut again; stoppages, as eight years before, were instantly punished; the employers withholding from the workmen all wages due previous to the stoppage on the grounds of illegal combinations. Ringleaders were summarily arrested, their families left to starve. Troops were at hand in Brecon Barracks to quell all disturbances. Starvation produces wonders, this was the Clydach cry. A few weeks on the black-list when none of the masters in the iron masters' union would employ them, and the most determined leaders of the new benefit clubs and embryo Unions were begging for five shillings of work to feed their pallid children. And in the midst of these tears the new middle-class shopkeepers flourished on The Top; in Merthyr a new Crawshay, Robert Thompson aged thirteen, drove with his father in the fly down the dingy streets; he who was later to lie in Vaynor churchyard with *God Forgive Me* on his grave.

Yet, despite these indignities, Merthyr retained her soul. Every Sunday, and for many of the weekdays, the churches and chapels were filled; and if the inns and taverns were filled, too, and the bawdy shouts of ale vied with songs of praise, this confict existed in a melting-pot of thirty thousand people, the biggest town in Wales: a town which possessed but the nucleus of an ancient community of peace and law. For Merthyr was then the crucible of half a dozen different nationalities, and more—Spanish, Italian and the coloured populations; Hebrew and Scandinavian, some French and Dutch; English from almost every county flooded in under the magic carpet of 'following the iron'. And the Irish never ceased to come, cramming into the cellars of Pontstorehouse and Sulleri, bringing their new religion and the conflicts of their beliefs.

Gigantic problems, social, religious and economic, beset the masters of iron, who were indicted for every injustice.

Dic and Sun Heron, whom some called Mari Beynon, were

179

married in the Wesleyan by the Reverend Edmund Evans on the last day of September, before the coming of the cold. They went to live in Seven Ynysfach next door but one to Mamie and Billa, once the cottage of Joe and Marion Morgan, evicted for a relapse in the rent. But it was more'n a relapse, said Billa, it were practically a death, for Joe's missus hit the rent collector with her grancher's Irish shillelagh.

'She never did!' said Sun, on the doorstep.

'She did,' said Billa, changing Asa, 'for I saw her. And his 'ead had a hole in it.'

'Ay, but that weren't done by Marion,' said Blod, hanging out.

'It were—I saw it.'

'You didn't,' said Mamie. 'That was done by the Spaniard in Number Ten—don't hold with Spaniards, mind,' she said to Sun. 'Paying the rent wi' a dog spike can be a very dangerous thing, but it's all you can expect of a foreigner. You Welsh?'

'Ay,' said Sun, 'and proud of it, missus.'

'You don't sound like one,' said Blod.

'Chiefly come from Ireland an' the bogs, but me da was as Welsh as a leek, and me real name's Mari.'

'Mari what?' asked Blod with pegs in her teeth.

'Mari Lewis, but I expect they'll call me Penderyn, like Dic.'

'The handsome fella with the big blue eyes?' asked Blod, coming alive.

'Ay, ay, though it's me that's saying it, girl.'

'Does he treat you good?' asked Mamie, ' 'Cause I saw him coming out o' the Miners' night before last and there weren't a leg under him.'

'Ach, he's fine and sweet, and he don't lay a hand on me—and he's on good money, despite the slump. You got fellas?'

'I have,' sang Blod. 'He's only little, see, but he's winsome, ain't he, Mamie ma?'

'You got husbands, Mrs. Goldie—you and Mrs. Jam?'

'One apiece—down in Taibach, but it ain't far enough away —we wish it were Japan, don't we, Billa?'

And Billa Jam looked beyond the dram-road and its rusted rails and wrung her hands with cold. 'I don't know. Sometimes I miss my little fat old chap . . .'

'Got to go,' said Sun, and she buttoned up her cloak and pulled tighter her shawl. 'Mustn't be late: got a good little job up in Cross, and it helps things out—scrubbing and cooking for Gideon Davies—you know him?'

'Know him, girl—he's me property,' said Mamie. 'He lodged with me down in Taibach, and if there was room in by here with Billa's tribe of Israel, I'd put him a bed down to-morrow.' She sighed deep, closing her eyes. 'Ah, a good, fine fella is my big Gid Davies.'

'Give him my love,' cried Billa, her arms full of washing.

'And mine!' sang Blod, fetching more out of the copper.

'Tell him we're all right,' called Mamie, and peered round the wall at Mrs. Zeke Solomon in Number Four. 'You want anything, Solomon?'

'No, Mrs. Goldie. Only passing the time of day, so to speak.'

'O, ay? Lend me your ear and I'll pin it to the door.' She sighed. 'Blutty shocking, it is—no privies and no privacy. You put your head back in there or I'll land ye one—rabbi or no rabbi.'

'No offence intended, Mrs. Goldie.'

'None taken,' said Mamie, 'now vanish.' She waved, then, her breath steaming in the early mist. 'Goodbye, Mrs. Penderyn—do us right by Gid Davies, mind.'

'There's one thing about it,' said Billa in passing, 'with those Crawshay drams gone cold at least you can pin out the washing.'

'The trouble is that the washing don't keep ten, do it?'

'Thank God I fed my Joab, and thank God my little Adam is in peace, I say,' said Billa, wringing out the mangle. 'Moke Donkey and her twins brought six-pounds-five, but that's nearly gone. Break my old man's heart, mind, when he finds out I sold Moke.'

'We'll manage,' said Mamie.

'We won't,' said Blod. 'Randy keeps us but the washing don't keep you lot and we're all in it together, so I'm going

181

down the pit.'

'In your condition? Don't be daft!' said Billa.

'Effie Brown the Lancashire went down yesterday, and she's five months gone.'

'The Union will be after you—no women down while the men are off, they say,' observed Mamie.

'The Union doesn't mind,' replied Blod. 'Randy's been a paid up member with Gid Davies ever since he started.'

'Thank God for the Union,' said Mamie. 'Soon we'll be eating coal.'

'One day for Randy and one for the baby,' said Blod. 'And there's no real sweat to the job—opening a few doors—I can get on wi' me knitting.'

'What a blutty state we're in,' said Mamie, and pushed in more sheets, crying, 'Will you keep off, Asa—you'll burn your backside backing on to that copper...'

Miss Grieve, sitting in the bay window of Ianto House, bulging with woollens, headscarfed and ear-muffed, with her Abergavenny blanket over her knees, wrote with a black, mittened hand in her diary:

'In the last two months I have seen the following in Merthyr: Mamie Goldie and Billa Jam Tart with her ten small boys—they have left that Dai End-On and Billy Jam; there is no love in the marriages of the working classes, as is widely known in gentry circles. Saw Mrs. Duck Evans go past today; her husband was convicted of the theft of a duck; she looked like a woman with something on her conscience. Yesterday, passing Number One, Ynys Row, I noticed an astonishing thing. Miss Blossom Thomas was sitting in the window nursing a baby, but when I looked closer, I saw that it was only a rag doll; which is very strange behaviour.

Last week I saw Lemuel Samuel begging in the gutter down Front Street and throwing stones at passing dogs: this is understandable, the way those things have treated him.'

Miss Grieve sighed deeply, and wrote in her book:

'Oh, Ianto Phillips, do you forgive me for my flight from the path of virtue? The shares in Fothergill's you left me have gone down twopence because of the avarice of the workers—recently they looted his company shop. Just heard that Willie Bach is going down the pit; he is a big boy for eleven, and the pit is the place for him. O, Ianto, do not think I have trespassed our love just because I am sleeping with Mr. Waxey Evans. Only the other night I sighed your name in a kiss, but he is not very sharp. This house, these possessions, the six thousand pounds you left me is insufficient for my station in life, and with ten thousand acres in Hereford it is safe to say he is a good proposition; Merthyr, you'd agree, is a soft-cornered old place to live—everybody with black faces, and choke and smoke are brothers; better to cry in health than sickness. Nothing is clean here; even the walls are stained with idleness where the colliers lounge. But the mansion in Hereford has red plush chairs in the parlour, says Waxey. Met that horrid little Mervyn Jam with Mrs. Goldie last Tuesday; his face, I would say, had a suspicion of acne. Did you like the winter flowers I scattered on your grave last Sunday? I feign death when Waxey Evans comes to me, though he is a morsel lower than himself day by day ... the physic is safe, if inclined to be slow in action... If fortune is kind to me, soon I will be in Hereford...'

Miss Grieve snapped the book shut as Waxey appeared in the parlour: top-hatted and frocked was he, brushed up against the pile and polished, with his corsets tight and a gold-knobbed cane in his hand, and half a pint of blue ruin inside him at ten o'clock in the morning.
'Are you there, my love?'
'Yes, here, my darling!' called Miss Grieve.
Entering the ornate room, he kissed her forehead. 'I am wondering ... would it be possible...? The prices are up in town, as you know—a few sovereigns these days does not go

very far.'

'Another twenty, shall we say?'

'Thirty would be handier, mind,' said Waxey. 'For all is signed and sealed, and in your name, is it not? Soon you will be in Hereford.'

Miss Grieve smiled. The coffin lid opened, and shut.

Sun said, 'Make in me a little one, a little Dic Penderyn. . .?'

The moon was putting his fist through the window, icicles were tinkling down the crooked streets of Sulleri where the miners coughed deep in their chests from the sale-coal pit: Mr. Madoc Williams, puddler bereaved, spouse to Mrs. Bronwren Williams, gathered his four in his arms in the brass-knobbed bed of Islyn and watched the stars fall out of the sky; and the children breathed softly against him, their cheeks lashed heavy in the pallor of sleep. Madoc opened wide his eyes and shouted at the ceiling:

'Bron! Bron!'

Sun said: 'Ach, boy, do not worry, we will be able to keep him. And I shall feed him at six and two and seven o'clock, and his name will be Richard Jay, which, like yours, has the flight of a bird: if it is a girl I will call her Joy, which is the name of your touch. Lie deep to me, my boy . . .'

'Oh, God,' said Dic.

In the hot-head, madcap essence of the dream; in all the lost visions of the loves that never happened, he drew deep to her in the bed, and there was in her a tumult he had never heard before; a beauty removed from the skittish laughter of the half-tart girls of his rollicking adolescence: no submission was this, for she claimed him in a fury of love, and in her was made a hand, an arm and ten fingers, and her body was smooth under his hands.

'Oh, God,' said Dic.

'Jesus, forgive me,' said Mr. Madoc Williams, bereaved.

'You all right, Dada?' asked Olwen, aged eight, sitting up in bed.

184

'Oh, Bron, my little Bron,' said Madoc.

'No good shouting for our mam, Dada,' said Meg, aged six, 'for our mam's dead.'

And Dic drew from his wife in Number Seven, Ynys, and saw in her dark face the face of Gwen, who mothered him: and the moon cocked an eye in the glazed ice of the window, smiling at her breasts so strangely like the breasts of Molly Caulara, but with no hay-seed upon them, for she was loved in a field: the mouth of Sun was then the mouth of Gwen, his sister, so he did not kiss it, but leaned his cheek against its wetness; then turned his face and kissed the lips of Molly, and these were the lips of Sun Heron: he smelled in her red hair the rust of the iron and the hands that smoothed his shoulders were calloused with the stacking.

'Do not leave me,' she said.

'What you up to, Dada?' asked Olwen Williams, aged eight, the daughter of Madoc.

Sun said: 'Do not go, Dic; please do not leave me.'

Outside in the street the night watchman was singing the hymn they had sung together in the Wesleyan on the day of their wedding, though the Reverend Morgan Howells did not come, nor Gwen, his sister... Dic had wept for this, but Sun did not know...

And there came to him then the face of the woman called Mortymer: even in the tumult of Sun's breath he heard this woman's voice, and her lips were full and red and her teeth shining and white; it was as if she lay in the bed beside them, so clearly did he see her, and she spoke to him, and he heard her say; 'Die hard, Dic Penderyn, die hard, Dic Penderyn.'

And Olwen Williams, aged eight, the eldest daughter of Mrs. Bron Babbie Williams who died by fire ... Olwen smoothed back her Welsh-dark hair in the bed of her father in Islyn Court, and put her arms around her possessions, which were a baby brother and twin sisters; and opened wide her eyes in terror.

185

'No, Dada,' she said, 'Oh, no...!' and opened her lips for the scream.

But Sun Heron, bride to Dic Penderyn of Number Seven, Ynys Row, smiled at the man possessing her and narrowed her eyes in love and reaching up, she drew him down into her soul and there ravished him, while in her he knew joy. And there was about this man a great host of men with coloured banners and pennants which were streams of fire. Presently he sighed and was as clay in the hands of the woman, and there came from her then a sound that others before her had made; the sound from a throat that was not her own, but one this man had fashioned beneath her breast.

A scream chilled the bed and they tensed, then listened to the watchman who was singing along the streets of Islyn Court; his voice was bass and pure in the icicled wind:

> *'Let not Thy worship blind us to the claims of love;*
> *but let Thy manna lead us to the feast above ...'*

Hearing this, Mr. Madoc Williams, husband of Babbie who died by fire, peered with shining eyes through the ice-glazed window of Islyn Court, and rubbed off the frost with a razored fist.

And the children behind him bled to death.

15

MAMIE GOLDIE said, 'I reckon God knew He couldn't be everywhere at once so that's why He dished up mothers.'

'And we fell for it,' said Billa Jam, taking a swipe at Abiah. 'Where you off to, Randy, son?'

'Got a meeting at the Lodge.'

'What about your dinner, then?'

'Give it to Blod, she's the one working.'

'But she's just polished one.'

'Then give her another. Feeling like a mule, she is.' He swaggered to the door, his trews tight over his slim buttocks, his waist no bigger than Molly Caulara's and there was tightness in him.

Mamie said: 'And I cooked it special—scrag end o' horse, but it's red meat, and good.' She looked at him with large, wet eyes. 'You'm a collier, Randy—you got to eat.'

'I'm half a blutty collier now I'm on Relief.'

Billa Jam came up then with Saul on her back and Caradoc under her arm and hooked in Asa with a foot, and she said, bothered: 'Don't reckon it's right having Lodge meetings on a Sunday—even Ynys only simmers. What you up to at these meetings—putting everything right?'

'Finding out where it's wrong.'

'Oho, hoity-toity, eh? Kiss them under the Coity, eh? You'm wasting your time at those Gid Davies meetings, Randy Goldie.'

He swaggered to the door and there was in him bitterness. 'Not now, Billa Jam, though I've wasted too much before.' He opened the door. ' 'Bye, Mam.'

'You kiss me, boy?'

The lines of obesity had thinned into drags and the flesh hung loose on her pin-bone cheeks. But she stood with her face up, waiting and he slowly came back and stood closer, then bent and kissed her.

'You'm a blutty good one,' he said.

'How about me?' asked Billa Jam, coming up, eyes shut, lips pursed. 'Got one for aunty?'

'You bugger off,' said Randy and slammed the door and went out into the weak, December sunshine.

They were still making iron at Ynys and Cyfarthfa, thanks to Crawshay, but the output was low.

'I'll bloody kill somebody if I get my hands on 'em,' said Randy as he went up Cross.

Tap tap on the door of Number Seven.

'Come in!' sang Sun.

Welsh cakes for my Dic, sizzle them on the stone, flap-jack, black-jack, brown on the bottoms and sugared on the tops and sweat 'em over the griddle: got a good fella to live with, neither lip nor fist from him, not like that swine Billy Ugmore: Gawd, I'd give him Billy Ugmore if I saw him now. Rainbow in his head, indeed? Can't think what got into me, ought to be ashamed of meself, should have had me head looked in: should have kept meself free for me big, strong Dic. She sang then, her voice like an angel: 'I got a big chap and his name is Dic, *Whee-hoi-hoi,* Abednigo! But it's a pity he drinks so much—got a gullet like a horse. Never mind, girl, can't have everything . . .'

Bang bang on the back.

'I said come in!' yelled Sun, wiping her hands on her apron.

Bang bang . . . and she swung the door wide to heat its hinges.

Dai End-On and Mr. Billy Jam of Taibach were standing on the step. Side by side were they, done up in Sunday best, hats on ears, alpaca suits, boots to shave in, starched collars under their whiskers, and smelling of peppermint, and never a quart had passed their lips.

' 'Morning, missus,' said Dai End-On, screwing at his fingers.

' 'Morning,' said Billy Jam, taking off his hat.

'Ay, and what can I do for ye?' asked Sun.

'Well,' said Dai, 'me and me friend—that is, Mr. Billy Jam by 'ere have been recommended to come to ye . . .'

'You've got the wrong house,' said Sun, 'you want the Popi Davey.'

'Actual,' said Dai, 'we called on Gid Davies, but he is out, so the big Pole Zimmerman sent us down to you.'

'Did he now, and what ails ye?'

'We want you to speak for us, missus,' said Billy Jam.

'To speak for you—who do you belong to, then?'

'Me lawful wife is next door but one,' said Dai, stuffy in the nose.

'And mine,' said Billy. 'Mrs. Billa Jam.'

Sun rubbed her chin, looking them over: repentant schoolboys, they lowered their eyes before her strict, unsavoury stare.

'I've heard of you two,' said she.

'Ay,' mumbled Dai End-On, broken.

Under the floor a mouse was in tears.

'And you, too,' said Sun.

Billy wiped his nose with the back of his hand. 'She left me months back, and she took me moke,' said he.

'Is it your moke you're after, then, or your missus?'

'Oh, ma'am!'

'And you're off the glass?'

'As God's me judge,' said Dai. 'Strike me dead, may I never move from here . . .'

'Not a drop, not a smell,' said Billy. 'I tell you this . . .'

'All right, all right. I'm daft, but I'll speak for ye. Wait by here.'

Taking off her apron Sun patted her hair, which was smooth to her head and bright red, tightened the scarf at her throat and went next door but one.

Returning in minutes she put her hands on her hips and breasted up to them, showing her teeth, her eyes bright with success.

189

'You're back,' she said, simply.

Incredulity struck Billy Jam. 'She's taking me back, woman?'

'I spoke well for ye, mind—I made a few promises—no ale from now on, no Lodge, no hammerings.'

'Ach, God bless ye soul,' said Dai, and kissed her hand. 'You're the loveliest sinner I've seen for a mile. An' Mamie, too?'

'And Mamie, too,' said Sun, 'you're in!'

Dai removed his hat in an act of reverence. 'Och, to hell, she's a wonderful woman. And she cooks the best blutty ox-tail that's gone past me lips this last five months.'

'Dear me,' said Billy, 'I'm all of a fumble. Are the kids there, too, girl?'

'All lined up and waiting,' said Sun, and tip-toed up to them. 'Smell your breath—ay, that's as sweet as honeysuckle.' She tightened Dai's muffler and smoothed Billy's hair, spitting on her fingers. 'All groomed up and dandy, there's a couple of handsome fellas. Next but one down then, and act respectful, tap on the door, lads, not too loud.'

'Eh, by Tanyard Light!' said Billy, 'you're a beautiful little lady,' and they marched out. And within ten seconds they were going down the dram-road with Mamie and Billa Jam Tart after them with the Irish confetti, and the kids hurling everything from cinders to fire-bricks. Quite fast went Dai End-On and Billy and they did not stop until the range lengthened, and there was a lump on Mr. Billy's head like a walnut, and sparking.

'Well, I never,' said he, rubbing. 'I never ever had that one before—that were the handle off the mangle.'

Mamie Goldie wiped her hands on her apron, disgusted. 'The pair of heathens! Of all the blutty cheek! What do they take us for—getting folks to speak for. 'em, indeed!' She yelled: 'Out, out, Dai End-On. You brute for treating a decent woman so! If my Randy were here he'd hand you an outing!' Turning, she stared at Billa Jam Tart. 'What's wrong wi' you, then?'

190

'You hit him,' said Billa, glum. 'You hit my Mr. Jam on his 'ead.'

'On his head? I'll blutty decapitate him. The sauce of it!'

Disconsolate, rubbing, Dai and Billy mooched off to the Wellington via the Popi Davey: with the children clustered about their skirts Mamie and Billa went back to Number Five and every neighbour in the Row was either hanging out washing or scrubbing the doorsteps. Even Old Papa Tomo Thomas came down to dig the garden and he'd been abed five years with rheumatics.

Mamie shouted for all to hear: 'Pesterin' virgin women, indeed—I'll take 'em to law, eh, Billa?'

But Billa Jam Tart did not reply.

Things were not tight with Dic and Sun. He was working full shifts up on Two Cyfarthfa, and though the rates had been dropped by some twenty per cent and the streets were crowded with people on parish relief, his wage was good—twenty-two shillings on a full shift, sixteen and fourpence on a thin one, and Sun thrived. Good hauliers, as usual, were at a premium, and he gradually furnished Number Seven, being careful at the auctions not to bid for sticks impounded by Coffin's Court from others less fortunate.

'But others are not so choosey, mind,' said Mrs. Taibach.

'I know, I know, ma'am,' replied Mrs. Duck Evans. 'They've taken everything of mine except the bed.'

'Ought to be hung,' said Mrs. Taibach. 'Enough to make a woman go into Purdah, it is.'

'Where's that, love?' asked Annie Hewers, passing.

'If you don't know girl, it do not matter,' said Mrs. Taibach, and shouted, 'Mr. Note, kindly raise off your backside and sweep out the back. Appalling, it is, these harmonious musicians laying about—and me working my fingers to the bone.'

'That's what my little Megsie says,' said Annie, vacant, and her face was thin and pale. 'It do not matter—nothing matters any more, says my Megsie.' She smiled at Molly Caulara coming up.

191

'A blutty scandal, it is,' said Molly Caulara 'The rates are down in every trade; most of the furniture is being bought by the upper class while the working class sits on the floor—cannibals, we are—living off each other. The shopkeepers are rising the prices—a penny on this, a halfpenny on that, and the Government don't care—I can't find a name for these blutty shopkeepers—they don't give a damn for their customers.'

'One day they will,' said Annie, quietly. 'One day we'll have those shops down, and their keepers.'

'Nothing like a good company shop, I always say,' said Mrs. Penderyn, Dic's man. 'It would cut their profits, mind, if Mr. Crawshay opened a Shop.'

'Don't talk daft, woman!' cried Mrs. Taibach. 'D'ye want the same as Guest hands them in Dowlais? Get in debt wi' him and he pulls the blankets off the bed, an' his prices are even higher than the private shops. We had a Shop in Taibach —everything from a pin to a coffin and prices up fifty per cent when copper went down. Give Crawshay credit for once—everybody singes the poor so-and-so.'

Annie Hewers said at the winter sky: 'It don't really matter, though. Could you spare a bit for my Megsie, Mrs. Taibach?'

'Spare ye? Woman, what do ye take me for? I'm down to my blutty uppers.'

'I got some,' said Mrs. Duck Evans. 'All the time I got a loaf you can have a bit for Megsie—poorly, is she?'

'Christ,' said Annie. 'She do nothing but cough.'

'And my fella does nothing but starve. Never very strong in the constitution, mind, and it's skinny on the parish. Ah well, things will get worse till they get better—look on the bright side. You hungry, Annie Hewers?'

'No.' She smiled, holding her stomach.

'You'd be best back home with your da in Pontypridd, mind. Got good times in Ponty, they do say—copper's staying up well, according.'

'Ain't going home,' said Annie. 'Me and Megsie ain't never going home to be leathered.'

'She's poorly, remember.'

192

'Ay, but she's all I've got—I ain't never going to see her leathered.'

'Come from the wilderness,' said Mrs. Duck Evans. 'Like I say to my old man—come out of the wilderness and smile like Jesus my Lord, and it will all come right—come home with me for the bread?' Looking at the sky, she said in silent prayer:

'Oh, God, Oh, God, help me to get out of Merthyr.'

Arm in arm, scragging their shawls round their faces, they went over Iron Bridge and down to the Dynefor Doss.

'Are you ready, then?' asked Gwen Morgan Howells, smiling on the doorstep of Number Seven, Ynys Row. And her eyes danced brightly under her blue poke-bonnet.

'You look beautiful this morning, Mrs. Gwen Morgan Howells,' said Sun, closing the door behind her. 'You don't mind my saying?' She clutched Dic's arm, on tip-toe to his face. 'You agree, Dic—don't your sister look beautiful?'

He winked.

'Marriage to the minister do suit her, eh?'

Gwen took Dic's other arm. 'He is a fine man and a splendid husband.'

'He might be, but he doesn't like the Unions,' said Dic.

'Aw, stop it, Dico!' cried Sun. Three abreast they walked down Castle on their way to the Methodist. 'You're coming, you said, so don't spoil it . . .'

'I'm only coming to please you.'

Gwen bowed to the doors of Ynys Row. 'Good morning, Mrs. Goldie, good morning, Mrs. Jam!'

' 'Mornin', missus!'

Blod came out with a pile of washing in her arms and stopped to curtsey to the minister's wife.

Dic said: 'One thing, you raise the tone of the place. I've never noticed that one curtsey to me. Poor old Blod. Four months away and she's still down Cwmglo. If she keeps her first she'll be lucky, with Randy out. Now you tell me, Gwen, why your old man stands against a Union.'

'Now, if you start that again, I anna coming,' said Sun,

angrily. 'We are going to the Methodist after a kind invitation from the minister, so be kind to your Gwen.'

'Just this once, boy—for me?' asked Gwen. 'And I know it would delight Morgan...'

They went together past the Castle Inn where the Gentry broughhams and flys were standing, the horses stamping impatiently. Alderman Thompson, owner of the Penydarren works, paused in the act of picking up a piece of coal, and raised his hat to Gwen; Hill, over from the Plymouth, bowed. Even old Sam Homfray smiled from his trap.

'God's teeth, we're going up in the world,' said Dic, bowing back.

'And none o' that, ye skillet!' whispered Sun.

'Anyway, I'm Wesleyan.' He elbowed Sun. 'And you belong to the Pope.'

'Methodist this time, just for me,' said Gwen.

A procession of worshippers was coming down the street in the Calvinistic Methodist: Gideon Davies was tapping with his stick along the railings of High, smiling into the January sunlight; behind him came Mrs. Bach Taibach holding Willie's hand, and for God's sake watch out, Mam, lest my mates do see me; and these were overtaken by Miss Milly Thrush who was pursuing Gideon. Nobody seemed to notice Lemuel Samuel in the gutter, nor the passing, inoffensive mongrel he assisted along with his boot.

'Mr. Davies ...!'

Gideon turned, instantly recognising Miss Thrush's voice.

'Why, good morning, Miss Thrush! Whatever are you doing in Merthyr?'

Unseen, Shoni Sgubor Fawr, pugilist, the Emperor of *China*, went by in rolling strength with his tenor friend Dai Cantw'r, and Dai was singing in a sad, minor key unsuited to the morning. Milly Thrush curtseyed, also unseen, and said: 'Got a shop on River Side, Mr. Davies—didn't you know? I've been expecting to see you...'

'And you sell the same things? Is it a good shop, Miss Thrush?'

194

'Ay, fair wonderful!' She warmed to him in the passing glances of her customers: women were eyeing him secretly from under bonnets: the dark eyes of a young gentry girl lifted and narrowed, and Miss Thrush was pleased; it came naturally to believe him her personal property. Swallowing down the heated bumping of her heart, she said: 'Ay, business is fine. I've ... I've sort of been expecting you. I sell sweets and drapery—really, I took over from the Lollipop Woman, but I've extended, if ye understand—men's wear, mainly underclothes, and razors, boots, laces...' Her voice faded, and she raised her face to his and closed her eyes, swallowing dry in the throat.

'But ... but where is the shop, Miss Thrush?'

'Outside the Popi Davey lodgings—River Side. I share the rooms above with Mrs. Taibach and her Willie ...'

'Are they in Merthyr, too?' He was astonished.

'Came in with me—and Mr. Note of Taibach—they say they have been looking for you, like me ...'

'I ... I spend a long time away, Miss Thrush.'

'So do they,' said she, instantly. 'Mr. Note and Mrs. Taibach and Willie spend a lot o' time away—mainly with relatives back down south...' she began to twist her gloved fingers. A passing child stopped to stare at her. Miss Thrush said: 'I ... I'm on my own a lot, so if ... if ... if you'd ever care to ...' She wilted, head bowed.

Reaching out he gripped her hand. 'Are you going to chapel, ma'am?'

Her face brightened. 'Ay, for the big Morgan Howells!'

'Calvinistic? So am I. The pavement is difficult, would you help me, please?' Staring momentarily, she peeled off a glove in a frenzy.

Her hand burned in his. The urchin child watched. Hand-in-hand they went down High. She began to tremble; the trembling began to control her and she fought it away; she wanted to cry with joy.

Mrs. Bach Taibach stopped on the other side of the road on her way with Willie to Ynysgau Chapel.

'Well, I'll be damned,' she whispered. 'An' holding his

195

hand, the sneaky little bitch!'

'Who's a sneaky little bitch, Mam?' asked Willie.

'Never you mind!' Turtling up and breasty was Mrs. Taibach.

'Here comes Mr. Note, Mam,' cried Willie.

Among the passing crowds on their way to a destitute God Mr. Percy Note drooped head and shoulders like a fractured oboe, following the lavender of Miss Milly Thrush like a hound follows aniseed, automatically nosing up the steps of the Methodist till jerked on the leash of Mrs. Taibach's command.

'Mr. Note!'

Collared, he retraced his steps amid the bellowing, harmonium strains of Wesley's *Heathland* and beg-pardoned his way across the street. 'Yes, my love.'

'Are you or are you not Wesleyan, man?'

'Yes, Mrs. Taibach.'

'Then what takes you into the Calvinistic?'

'Miss Thrush just gone in there, Mam,' piped Willie. 'Miss Thrush . . .'

'Anywhere you like, then,' said Mr. Note, broken. He had been racked on the ardour of the Taibach widowhood; his new Gun Symphony had died to a whisper in a savage boudoir that had put paid to an earlier spouse.

'Right, you,' said Mrs. Taibach, gripping her Willie, 'we will all go into Calvinistic.'

And as they climbed the steps Willie looked into the eyes of Mr. Note, and said: 'No more music lessons, Mr. Note?'

Percy Bottom Note shook his head.

Willie's eyes clouded. 'But what about the Revolution?'

'No,' said Mr. Note.

Willie clutched him, bouncing the latecomers entering in a hurry. 'But you must, Mr. Bottom Note. You promised, you promised. . . !'

'No, my son. No more revolutions.' He lowered his eyes from Willie's face.

'But property is theft—you said so, Mr. Note . . .' whispered Willie.

'Come on, *come on*,' said Mrs. Taibach.

'It is finished,' said Mr. Note, and turned away.

Blod went down Cwmglo Pit on the morning shift, though it was a Sunday, for you can't have everybody praying, said she, and Randy's got to eat.

' 'Morning, Goldie,' said the overman.

' 'Morning, sir,' said Blod, going down in the cage. 'You got a decent dram for me today?' The cage descended with a whine and crash.

'You're down here for the doors—Six Stall, anna ye?'

'Ay, but I could do with a dram, Mr. Overman. Me fella's still off, you see.'

'He told me no drams, mind—he told me you were on the doors.'

'An' me as strong as a dray, then some—come on, Overman!'

The overman rubbed his chin. 'You need the money—I'll see what I can do—meanwhile they're lining up on the vents, so move.' He pushed his way through the colliers coming out of the cage, and Blod followed with her bottle and candle-tack of clay, carried in the press of their half-naked bodies down the gallery: stripped to the waist went the colliers in a clanking of picks and shovels.

'Ay, ay, missus!' Big Ned Tranter, the collier from Wigan elbowed her in the crush, pushing a path for the young labour; Merve Jam, for one, walked with May Harries, aged six, who was on Two Vent Door, with her hair either side of her face in coal curls.

'You seen my doll?' asked May Harries.

'Ach, no,' replied Merve, pushing it away. 'Blutty rags and bones it is.'

'It is not!' cried May, indignant, and she folded her candle-tack under her arm and held her doll high among the barging shoulders of the colliers. 'Look now—she has real hair from my gran and leather boots, see?'

'So's me Aunt Fan,' said Merve, shoving on. 'Anyway, dolls are daft, and if Overman catches you nursing that on doors he'll tan your arse.'

'Ah, ay? He tans my arse and me dad'll see to him—you know my dad?'

'*Heisht*, you!' said Blod, 'bad language, May Harries...!'

'You'll hear worse in Eight-One,' said Ned Tranter. 'We got five-year-olds down there who can singe the beard off Satan.' He looked her over.

'More bugger you for hearing it,' said Blod. 'Don't hold with it—bad language from the childer—mine aren't coming down this Cwmglo—die first, says my Randy.'

'Is he still off?'

'Ay, a month,' said Blod, empty.

They tramped on down the gallery, spreading left and right to the stalls and headings, standing on the gob when the drams went past, some with ponies, some pulled by human horses, mares mostly; and they came from the lower roofs of the four-foot seams, stripped to the waist with their hair sealed on their sooted breasts and their teeth white in their coaled faces as they heaved to the loads, hobnails scraping. The little cage-army rolled on, the men ducking to the roof and the overmen were following, striking up at the plugs to bring down the falls for the clearing gangs coming up behind.

'You there, kids?' cried Ned Tranter, turning, and the ledge candles flickered on his strong, smudged face.

'Comin', sir,' said Merve, giving May another shove.

'You sod!' shouted May, kicking at him, and Merve swerved and her boot went high and he caught it, upending her, and the children danced about her in shrieks as she picked herself up out of the road dusting her doll and he made a noise as he went off and she cried after him in a voice of tears. 'You'm a bastard, Merve Jam, you'm a blutty bastard.'

'Now, now,' said Blod, kneeling. 'Now now, May Harries, do not mind him. And no more swearing or you will not go to heaven.' She kissed her.

'Nor me,' said Ned Tranter over his shoulder. 'Any time you like I got an empty dram for you, little Goldie, an' fill you up, remember.'

'And any time you like my Randy'll see to you,' said Blod. Standing in the road with the door children she watched him disappear with Merve into Stall Eight-One, and there was a fine swagger on him that made her grin, being a chap for the girls, she thought, but not this one: not ever this one, Ned Tranter me beauty, for I got Randy.

'What you looking at, Blod Irish?' asked another, Dafydd Jones, aged seven.

'Nothing,' said Blod, and smoothed back her hair. The wake-lights of the ledges brought her face to a fierce beauty, danc-ing red in her eyes as she looked after Tranter.

'Get on, get on!' shouted the plug-man jabbing at the roof behind them. 'You want this lot down on your nuts?'

Lifting her skirt Blod pulled out the waistband of her drawers and tucked it deep inside, for the three foot seam was coming up and the air was thicker, for Cwmglo drifted ten stalls from the cage. One by one the children headed off into the ventilating stalls, there to sit by the doors and await the drams coming through from the face.

'You there, Mrs. Goldie?' called a voice.

Blod turned at the entrance to her door. 'Ay, sir?'

The overman wandered up, ducking his head under the roof and the candle flame flung black shadows into his bearded face. 'Just remembered—Ned Tranter's got a free dram—are ye on?'

'Just one day?'

'Could be two weeks—his boy lost a finger.' He hesitated, then added: 'Tranter b'ant every woman's dram, but ye can't pick and choose.'

'You leave him to me, I'll handle Tranter.' She smiled at the overman, for she liked this man. He rarely beat the chil-dren for sleeping at the doors and he never took a woman underground, or none that she heard complaint from.

'Why are you on doors, then—a big strong cow like you?'

'Because me man says so.'

'And now you want drams, eh?'

'I told you—me chap's off and I need the money.'

'It's a long haul with Tranter—you carrying?'

'Ach, no, man—only since yesterday.' She pushed out her stomach and he grinned at her, saying:

199

'Report to Tranter, then. You can take his Number Two. If ye yell loud enough you've always got Merve Jam on One.'

'It'll be Tranter yelling, mind,' said Blod.

He winked at her. He thought she was beautiful standing there in the candlelight: he was forty-two and had buried a wife up in Derby a year back, and he wanted a woman for his children. 'I'll book you,' he said, 'Six a week out of Tranter's pay, remember—up to you, girl—stick out for six.'

'You watch me,' said Blod.

She went back up the drift of the gallery to Tranter and Merve Jam in Eight-One. Naked as badgers, the pair of them, with Tranter cutting and Merve filling and coal sweat was painting them up already. Tranter turned at the face and lowered his pick; the muscles of his fine body bulged as he straightened: Merve rested, leaning on the shovel.

'You got a dram, says Overman,' said Blod.

'Now I got a filly to pull it, eh?' said Tranter, and came from the face.

'If ye pay—six, it is.'

'Six shillings for a woman? What do ye take me for?' He turned to Merve. 'Is that full?'

'Ay.'

'Then away with ye!'

Merve hooked up to his towing-belt and leaned to the weight; the dram moved, biting at the grit on the rails; thundering softly, it went down the track to the stall vent-door where May Harries opened up, and through it to the gallery.

'You dram for me and you strip,' said Tranter.

'Six shillings,' said Blod, 'and no odds to that. But don't tell my chap for I'm supposed to be on doors.' She pulled the coarse dress over her head and stuffed her bodice into her belt. Tranter sat down on the gob, his eyes moving over her. Warm air fanned them as the door of Eight-One opened up.

'Shakes alive, girl, with a body like that you're wasted on doors.'

She pulled off the loose string and put it between her teeth, scragging back her hair, and this she tied tightly pulling hard at the knots while Tranter watched the candleflame touching her breasts with leaping shadows of redness.

'Six shillings a week, and you're entitled to the look,' said Blod. 'Where's me belt?' She walked past him, peering into the corners of the stall.

'I'll give ye eight with you thrown in,' said Tranter.

'That's a fine rate for a decent woman—two shilling.' She found the belt and tugged it around her waist, pulling for the hook.

'Will ye?'

'I will not, but you can always try,' said Blod. 'Hand me that shovel and I'll split your skull.'

'I can make it easy, mind—the long haul or the short one —you or Merve. They're not fussed on the turn-out up the line: just as you like.'

'What are ye after, man—a woman or a dram?' Blod faced him, her hands on her hips. She did not want trouble with Tranter. She was starting the way she intended to go on. Soon Merve would be back with the empty dram, for he was on the short haul. It usually happened like this with the new women; she had heard the others talking. It was happening all the time, and often she thought it was astonishing that it did not happen more—men and women working together in the hot confined spaces of the stalls. Once Tranter got used to her it would be all right, and she needed the money, she thought. Also, if it got too bad she could shout for the overman, and he would give him Ned bloody Tranter, for that was one thing this particular overman wouldn't stand for.

Tranter spat on the line and made a face at her. 'Right, you—the long haul and five shillings—take your pick.'

'It's cheap at the price,' said Blod, and spat on the line, too.

With Tranter cutting like a demon, Blod was filling Number Two as Merve came back with his empty dram.

'Right, woman—out of here,' shouted Tranter, gasping. Never had he cut a dram-full so quickly, and he held a grudging admiration for the woman who had filled for him.

'Shall I shackle you up, Mrs. Goldie?' cried Merve, running up. Blod smiled, for he had got trews on.

201

'I'm shackled,' said Blod. 'And don't tell Randy—I'm on doors, remember.'

'She's good,' shouted Tranter. 'Give her a start.' and Merve knelt behind the dram and levered it with a mandrel as Blod hooked up the towing-chain to her belt, and heaved. Kneeling now, with the chain between her legs, she grunted, and the dram moved up the incline, for here the stall drifted up an inch a yard.

'And again so!' yelled Tranter, and came off the gob and flung his weight against the dram stock. Straining, on all fours, Blod Irish hauled; slowly the coal-dram followed, its heap spilling off as it touched the roof.

'You filled her high, Mr. Tranter,' said Merve.

'Ay, lad—on this stall we thin 'em down, eh, Blod Goldie— left on the turn-out, remember—on the long haul!'

'Hallo, Mrs. Goldie,' said May Harries as she opened the ventilation door to let her through. 'I thought you was on doors, Mrs. Goldie?' She held her doll against the rock as the mare went by.

'So did I,' said Blod.

Wesley's *Heathland* beat out the Methodist, over the large and small, the well-dressed, the ragged the fed, hungry, hypo-critical and holy: up in the front row was Petheric, the Cornish agent, and what is that fella doing in Welsh Calvinistic, asked Sun: Miss Thrush, with the coarse hassock pricking through her red stockinged knees, knelt beside Gideon, and moved her lace-frilled wrist an inch for the touch of his home-spun sleeve. Mr. Duck Evans, reliving the lash of the house of correction, winced and shuddered while Mrs. Duck smoothed and consoled him. Sid Blump came in and sat beside Sun and she saw with horror that he only possessed thumbs. They flooded in from Black Pins and Dynefor, Aberdare Top and Hafod where the old Brychan died, he who was sired by An-lach the Irish king who brought Christianity to South Wales; they poured into the pews from Dyllas Colliery and the quar-ries of Pennant, the rock which built Cyfarthfa Ironworks, and from the towering carn of firestone which built the Castle.

They shouldered in from the squat slums of *China* and the ornate little houses of the agents, washed and polished, and they took their seats in the Big Calvinistic and sat with stony faces in the pews of varnished silence while the melody smothered them. And Morgan Howells sat in the Big Seat facing them; with six deacons either side; fearsome in black, he returned their stare.

Deacons who were drunkards, hucksters who were saints stood shoulder to shoulder and raised their faces to the timbers and there burst from them the hymn:

> *Worship, honour, glory, blessing,*
> *Lord, we offer to Thy Name;*
> *Young and old, their praise expressing,*
> *Join Thy goodness to proclaim!*

Colliers, iron-miners, hauliers and puddlers, and the men of a dozen trades in iron: Welsh, Irish and Spaniards from the tumbling cottages of Sulleri with their swarthy wives and dark-skinned children, all swelled their chests and roared their praises in a great harmony of soprano, contralto, soaring tenor and bass, with the children piping treble. And the shout of concord rose above the chapel, soaring above the narrow streets and into the grimy attics where the burned-out colliers of Lefal and Tasker lay; into the swimming cellars of the old, the refuse of the great town: Megsie Lloyd lying beneath the five-foot ceiling of the Crown as far down as Swan Street, she heard it, and shifted, fevered, in the bed. Many heard it who did not hear it, such as those of the Catholic faith. From every corner of the biggest town in Wales there arose the sounds of worship; from the pews of the Baptist up near Fishpond, Bethel Independent and Bethania up in Georgetown, Zoar and Ynysgau, the Adulum Independent and Zion and Ebenezer there came the shout of praise, a harmony that rose above the squalid slums, and dominant above it all was the great melody of Boyce, the beloved *Sharon* of Osler, a doxology coming from six hundred throats, and a thousand more in the cottages around, for family on family was singing:

As the saints in heaven adore Thee,
We would bow before Thy throne;
As Thine angels serve before Thee,
So on earth Thy will be done.

Blind Dick was singing, shaving blind in the window, Shoni Melody was singing the counter descant, flat on his back in his attic in the Star, bare toes wriggling at the end of the blanket: Mamie Goldie was singing, too, dollying the sheets of the Reverend Evan Evans, and mostly out of tune; the night-shift colliers coming from Pit Tasker and the old Abercanaid, the furnacemen around the glowing bases of Cyfarthfa and Ynys were singing amid the clanging of the ladles: bowed in black and fragile, old Iolo Morgan-Rees was praying on the cobbles of Bridge Street. In the Aunty Popi Davey lodgings Molly Caulara was telling her beads, and Old Wag, in her doorway facing the Castle Inn, was knitting to the beat of it, her coal-scarred face leering at the winter sun. Merthyr, for the crucifixion that was hers, was giving praise amid the cradle song that had given birth to Merthyr—the shrilling of whistles, the roaring songs of the drunks and wailing of the beggars, the thunder of the furnaces and the hissing of the molten iron. And Dic Penderyn, raising his face from the hymnal, saw that the eyes of the Reverend Morgan Howells were fixed upon him, and in them he saw the threat. Dic glanced at his sister beside him; she was singing with her face turned up, her eyes closed, oblivious to anything but the glory of her God: but Sun nudged his elbow.

'You see Morgan watching ye, Dic?'

He nodded, returning the minister's owl-like stare.

Kneel and pray, stand and sing, and up into the pulpit went the minister. Dust motes crowded in a sunbeam from a window: Morgan Howells cried:

'May the Lord hear this prayer: let mercy and truth not forsake thee; bind them about thy neck, my people, and write them upon the table of thy hearts, so listen, you.' Gripping the brass-bound book, he cried: 'Today there will be no sermon, for we have a business among the deacons, and the anger shall engulf you. On one matter only will I address you, and I pray to the One Who hearest all that my words shall not lie in the stony ground: "while men slept, his enemy came and sowed tares among the wheat, and went his way..." Matthew 13:25. And the tares have grown high and consumed the wheat ... you hear me?'

His voice rang out, battering off the faded walls, and he shouted, his fist high. 'Neither sermon nor an earthly directive shall you have, but the Word alone, and this shall suffice you; this shall command you before I speak in the name of the head deacon of the Calvanistic Methodist, which is the true faith, and I read from the book of God, Isaiah 59, also 56, so hear this,' and he read, with a fist high: ' "Behold, the Lord's hand is not shortened, that it cannot save; neither his ear heavy, that it cannot hear. But your iniquities have separated between you and your God, and your sins have hid his face from you, that he will not hear." ' His voice rose to a shout:

' "Yea, they are greedy dogs that can never have enough ... and they all look to their own way, every one for his gain from his quarter. Come ye, say they, I will fetch wine, and we will fill ourselves with strong drink; and tomorrow shall be as this day, and much more abundant!" ' He brought down his fist on the pulpit. 'This is the cry of the new Unionists, this is the dogma of the "never have enough". On all sides there is sprung up in the land the banners of the ungodly who oppose the will of those whom God has granted domination over us. Their baying is heard on every street corner, in every inn and tavern where the drink is strong, in every cottage that lacks a bible. From all corners come the lackeys of the new order who propose force; the effeminate ones like Twiss have come down from Ruabon to preach sedition in your hearts, and to these evil men you have turned your ears. Illegal benefit clubs are the springboards of these outlawed Unions, and to these new associations you are paying your pennies in the name of a promised freedom that is the freedom of the gaoler. Illegal oaths are being sworn against the majesty of the King, illegal plans are being made for the overthrow of the legal Government...! Now stand and confess—all Unionists here!'

Up in the gallery a woman was sobbing: Gwen wept, her face lowered from Dic's accusing stare. He said, pushing away Sun's restraining hand: 'You knew about this? You knew?'

'I did not know.'

'You fool,' whispered Sun. 'Of course she did not know! Leave her!'

Men were murmuring in growing anger, the deacons shifting uncomfortably in the Big Seat, children being hushed into silence by astonished mothers. And all heads swung as Gideon rose at the back: Miss Thrush raised a hand to her face. Bringing out his book of membership, the head deacon cried:

'So, we have the first to confess. Your name, please.'

'Gideon Davies.' Gideon felt his way along the row and reached the aisle.

The congregation turned in its seat, in disbelief. The head deacon cried:

'Your name is not familiar. Are you a member of this chapel, properly listed?'

'Head Deacon,' said Gideon, 'I am not a member.'

'Then why stand you?'

'In the name of God.'

The muted voices grew in sound.

'Silence!' Morgan Howells got to his feet. To Gideon he said: 'You affront the name of God, man? Stand to confess or stay silent. You defy the principles for which this house stands.'

'I stand in defiance of those who betray those principles,' answered Gideon. 'Was this house built to defend the rights of master, but not servant?'

'How dare you!'

'I dare because I protest in the name of dignity, Morgan Howells...!'

'You will take your place—you will sit, fellow!'

'I shall not sit until I have challenged this injustice, and nor is there any man in here who will remove me. You speak of the scriptures, you quote from the Book, Isaiah fifty-nine, but how do you stand if I quote you fifty-seven?'

206

Morgan Howells drew himself up in starched anger; the head deacon tugged at his sleeve but he shook the hand away: his face glowed and his eyes shone at the prospect of a fight; he shouted:

'So, we have at last exposed the godhead of the evil about us, eh? The nests are flushed, the serpents rise. How dare you defy me when you sustain greed, and I sustain love? When I stand in the light of God and you in the shadow of the devil? Eh? All right, all right, then let me meet you on this ground. "The righteous perisheth," says fifty-seven, but shall I quote you fifty-eight? Does not this define my duty? "Cry aloud, spare not: lift up thy voice like a trumpet, and show the people their transgressions..."'

Gideon, smiling, replied: 'Indeed, the works of God are marvellous, but nothing so wonderful as the interpretations of his self-appointed disciples. Is it not also your duty to cry aloud the transgressions of the masters of this town. The people fast, and you do not see; they are afflicted in their souls, and you take no knowledge.'

'I once met a drunkard who knew his bible,' said Morgan Howells, blandly.

'And I a minister of the Church who beat his wife.'

'If you speak slander, fellow, it is of your own Church clergy, I vow: I charge all present to take little heed of it, the criticisms have been ours since the Reformation.'

Even Gideon joined in the laughter. 'Indeed,' continued Howells, 'if you still have complaint on this particular ground I suggest you lay it before your Ecclesiastical Commissioners, since we Nonconformists stopped beating our wives about the time of the divorce.' Unsmiling, Howells plucked his fingers deep in his beard while the laughter and applause beat about him.

Gideon replied: 'Your denigration is correct. The church runs on a system of rank where the bishops plunder the parsons and the parsons plunder the people, with the assent of King and State.'

'Beware your tongue, blind man.'

'Let the sedition stand, if it be sedition, and not Truth.

Because of a system where God was a politician, I took off the cloth that once I wore and considered taking yours ...'

'I doubt we had a gown to fit you?'

'The heresy did not fit me, neither the hypocrisy, Minister, for I witnessed a casting-out. Not a hundred men of political reasons, but of a child who stood in labour—they watched her beaten through the chapel door with bibles and sticks, in defiance of John chapter eight ...'

'You contest our laws, yet you are not of us—be silent!'

'I contend that your interpretation of your laws are wrong! Pervert the laws of your God if you will, but leave us the laws of Man. Make nonsense of the thing you call religion but stand aside from the rules by which we live, or these pews will be empty.'

'I command you to leave this house!'

'It is not Nonconformity; it is witchcraft, it is mumbo-jumbo, man.'

And as the deacons leaped up and the tumult grew in the congregation, Gideon shouted: 'Stand, then—stand all who are members of the new Union! Stand, too, all members of the benefit clubs, the Oddfellows and Ivorites—stand, men, and be counted!'

'If they stand they will be cast out!' roared Howells, fist shaking.

'Better than to sit with a crooked conscience in this house of the masters, for it is no longer the house of God.' Gideon felt his way to the door. 'Stand, stand and leave this place!'

And they rose in the pews; first Dic Penderyn and Lewis Lewis, who was at the front, then Randy Goldie, Wil Goff and Joseph Harries, the father of May who worked the Cwmglo doors. Ned Tranter stood, and Sid Blump, though he did not know why he was standing. John Hughes stood, he who had fought at Waterloo and later died in agony before the muskets of the redcoats: the man Hopkin also rose, though his woman pulled at him, saying she would give him hell when she got him home, and the customers of Jump Jackson rose with him, led by the man with the burned face. Belcher and Curly Hayloft got up, though they were not Calvinists, for many had come that day in challenge to Morgan Howells, who was doing what had been done in a chapel at Tredegar. Tom Llewellyn, the respected Cyfarthfa puddler, took the aisle with Abod of Penydarren, who was a Baptist. Many stood who were not even Unionists, but who felt compelled by the courage of those who were: and they thronged the aisles amid shouts and accusations from the deacons while Morgan Howells stood white-faced, and trembling.

'Take their names! Take their names!' and the deacons put their arms across the door and listed every man who passed through. Some went with their wives, who also stood in protest: many, grey-faced and near to tears, left wives who were fuming in the pews, or silent—shamed in the eyes of God. In the street Dic said:

'She knew! Gwen knew! That was why she invited us!'

'Don't be a fool,' said Sun, 'she did not know.'

She took his arm. Empty, unspeaking, they went back home to Ynys.

16

It was the weekend Dusty Wilkins died of the fever and came to life again, which was right and proper, said Mamie, for we don't usually die of the cholera in January. Quiffed up and polished was Dusty, with the lads from the Cwmglo pit filing past his coffin sniffing and weeping, and up sat Dusty looking around him and what the hell is happening, and you couldn't see colliers for dust. Hopping off the trestles in the front room he went down Bridge Street as bare as an egg, nothing on him but the boiled shirt front flapping and shouting blue murder, and everybody thought him a clay-cold corpse. And they were fanning them and patting the backs of their hands all the way up Glebeland, for the chapels were turning out; Mrs. Stinkin Shenkins, hard at it in labour up by Fish-pond Number Three, saw him rise at speed past her window, and she had an assisted delivery, and Sid Blump, coming out of Miners' took a header into the canal.

Blod Irish, however, died in January, but that was because they didn't really know the date, said Billa.

'We was never sure, see?' explained Randy. 'My Blod was queer in that respect—could have been three months away, might have been six ...'

'A month or two don't make that much difference, son,' said Mamie.

'Don't you blame me,' cried the overman at the Head. 'D'you think I'd have had her tubbing the heavies if I'd known she was six months gone?'

'Yes,' said Billa.

'Don't talk daft!' Lancashire pits, this one, with a fist on

210

him for stunning mules, and Randy had him a minute after he came up with Blod following on the stretcher board: down he went with blood on his mouth and it took four colliers to heave Randy off.

'They'll blacklist you, mind,' said a collier, 'striking the overman.'

'Oh, Blod,' said Randy, 'oh, my poor little Blod . . .'

'What's happening here?' asked the agent, coming up in his trap, and they stood sullenly, the whole shift, staring down at the body of Randy's wife. Tethering the pony the agent stepped down on to the cinders.

'She birthed at the face,' said one.

'What was she on?'

'Dram-hauling.'

'How far was she gone?'

'Could have been six months,' said Mamie, sobbing, 'could have been four.'

The men moved their feet uncertainly as Randy rocked Blod in his arms and none moved to take her away from him.

'Six or four, make up your mind, woman,' said the agent.

'My Randy don't know.'

'We will have to know it for the inquest. Where was she?' Pert and quick, he turned to the overman.

'Heading Eight, stall one.'

'That were a long haul on a heavy,' said a collier.

'Nobody asked her to haul, remember—she signed herself on.'

'Her man was off, they needed the money, and she was feeding for two,' said Billa Jam with Amos in her arms.

'Randy wasn't eating proper, you see,' said Mamie.

A collier said at the winter sun, 'That Eight-One is nigh two hundred yards in, remember . . .'

'Who was she dramming for?'

'Ned Tranter by here.'

The agent turned. 'Did she complain?'

The collier Tranter said: 'Not a word, sir—she was as strong as a horse. My boy was hurt so she stood in for him.'

211

Randy was still rocking her, kissing her face; her skirts, from waist to hem, were sodden with blood.

'Where did you find her?' asked the agent, and out with a notebook, official.

'I didn't find her,' said Tranter. 'My Number Two dram was coming up empty, and young Merve Jam got blocked on the line.'

'Where is he?'

'Here, sir,' said Merve.

He was in tatters and smudged with coal, his face impish but streaked with tears.

'How long have you been down Cwmglo, boy?'

'Two months, sir.'

'And you were hauling a second dram for Mr. Tranter.'

'Ay, sir. My mam says . . .'

'And you had taken a dram down to the turn-out and were coming back with it?'

'Ay, sir.'

'And you found this woman's dram blocking the rails?'

'Her name is Mrs. Goldie,' said Mamie, raising her face.

'Where was the woman?'

'She was sitting on the rail, sir.'

'Did she speak?'

'Ay. She said to run down to the stall and fetch Mr. Tranter, sir. She said she had cut her leg, sir.'

'And you fetched Mr. Tranter?'

'Straight away, sir, but when we found her she was dead.'

'The child was half born,' said Billa Jam.

'Did you see to her?'

Mamie said, 'I went down. I saw to her.'

The agent was writing.

Mamie said: 'But she had bled to death before I got there.'

'The cause of death will be established by the surgeon in due course.' Pencil poised, he said: 'What was her name again?'

Randy laid Blod back on the cinders and climbed slowly to his feet. 'You bastard,' he said, 'you bloody bastard!'

'Now, now, stop that!'

Tranter was nearest and quick, despite his size, and he got Randy coming in, the other colliers tripped and held him, and in their grip he began to cry, which was best for him, thank God, said Mamie, and they took him into Number Five with the kids, not Number Seven with Dic Penderyn's missus, for she was in there knitting a bellyband for Blod's new baby, which is pretty daft, you stop to think of it, said Sun, since I should be knitting for myself.

'It's a queer old life, though,' said Dic later. 'Blod Goldie, aged seventeen, kicks the bucket and old Dusty Wilkins, nearly seventy, comes back to life.'

'It's the way it goes,' said Sun, and wondered if she ought to tell him about the baby. She decided against it.

'One thing, it has got a couple of Billa's kids into school,' said Dic.

Sun knitted on in the lamplight and the fire was dying in the grate.

'The agent came to see them—Randy was a Benefit member: they're putting up the twopence a week for Billa's Amos and Asa to start with Miss Williams the School next week,' added Dic, looking over *The Cambrian*.

'The Benefit's wasting its time,' said Sun.

Dic said: 'Will you tell me why we plot and plan for a Benefit if the folks won't take the benefits they're offered?'

'Food she wants, says Billa, not education.'

'If we get education we'll have the food, woman. Can't she see that?'

'Billa's only concerned with bellies. Besides, the fairies will have 'em.'

'The what?' he lowered the newspaper.

'When they go to school they have to write their names on paper, don't they?'

'Ay.'

'Right, then—Billa says it's dangerous, and I agree with her.'

'Dangerous?' He removed his pipe, staring.

'Just the same in Ireland, and I agree with her. Bad fairies

213

read those names on paper and God knows what might happen.'

'You don't believe that rubbish?' He was on his feet now.

'Rubbish or not, I've seen it happen. You remember that Bron Babbie who used to live near you in Chinatown? The whole family wiped out. They was as happy as little fleas till her Olwen started school—and Madoc paying, mind. A week after that kid wrote her name on school papers nothing went right.' She knitted on; in, over, through, off; one plain, one purl, her mouth pursed, as if she had said nothing. 'Them's sods, those fairies.'

'Good God,' said Dic, 'heaven forbid that we have any if ye think like that.'

Sun did not reply but smiled in her stomach: her skin these days, she had noticed, possessed a new sheen and beauty, though it could have been imaginaion. Hooking his coat over his shoulders he went to the door: the barges were sailing past the window and the heaped coal was rimed with frost; breath from the horses spurted like smoke in the still, winter air. Sun shivered and pulled her shawl closer about her.

'You off out again?'

'Got a meeting at the Wellington.'

'That Lewis Lewis fella again?'

'Now, don't start all that, for Christ's sake!'

'Ale and Lewis Lewis will lead you to the devil, Dic.'

'So we sit down here and whine!'

'We sit down by here and save what money we can till things get better. You can swill your belly and shout your politics all the time we got money in the house, but what will ye do if they lay you off?'

For answer he spun up a shilling and snatched it in the air. 'Now's the time for Benefits and politics, girl—I'm laid off.'

She saw the dim lights of the Iron Bridge as he opened the door, and got up, dropping the knitting. 'You ... you what?'

'Got laid off Number Two this morning.'

'But you said it was shift-break.'

'Ay. Now I'm saying I'm off. The hauls have stopped to Vaynor.'

Sun raised the tips of her fingers to her face. 'Oh, Jesus!'

'Same as Wil Goff and John Hughes, Luke Pearson, Tom Williams—and he's got six—the Jones brothers and Phelps—all out.'

'And all Union men.'

'It makes no odds.' He looked out on to the misted terrace. 'They say Crawshay's blowing out—if he blows out Ynys, too, everybody will be off, Union or not.'

'But you could get down Cwmglo?'

'Not till they get some safety regulations—not that slaughterhouse.'

'It was good enough for Blod.'

'That's why she's dead,' he said, and went out, slamming the door.

Sun sat down and started knitting again. She would go up and see Gid Davies, she thought: Gid would know what to do. There might be work down Cwmglo getting coal, of course, but she did not want Dic down Cwmglo where week after week the stretchers were coming up. She knitted violently, thinking that it was a scandal. The town was in rags in the depth of winter because of over stock-piling by the masters, yet coal was being called for from abroad and they couldn't see the value of it. Dic was right, she reflected: now was the time to turn to coal—Gid Davies was always shouting this at the meetings. The Cyfarthfa collieries mainly served the iron-works, and, since there was no big profit in them, the coal inspector would not spend money on them, and the safety regulations were almost criminal. Years later, in the first big Gethin explosion forty-nine men were to die and about a hundred and fifty were injured: later still, because ventilation was inadequate, there was a second explosion when thirty were killed and twenty injured. Cwmglo was a pig, Sun re-flected, because of the parsimonious policy; it was legs and arms off because they were skimping the pit funds: rising, she went to the mantle and opened the tea caddy. Carefully, she counted the money; it was two pounds fifteen and eightpence.

She was frightened. In town the day before, five were found dead of exposure and starvation, and they were always fishing out dead Irish from the cellars of *China* and Pontstorehouse. She wondered how the Crawshays could sleep in their beds, but there was one thing about this lot, she thought—they had made their own money. Not so Anthony Bacon of an earlier Merthyr: according to Gid Davies, Bacon had built Merthyr on money from the slave trade: places like Pontypool and Blaenafon, built by money of the big London merchants, had been built on blood: Tredegar and Risca, Aberman and even the great Dowlais whose gigantic slag mountain was reflecting on the kitchen window as she stood there—even Dowlais of the iron Guest was a monument to the vicious Bristol traders who had made their fortunes catching blacks in Africa and shipping them to the American plantations. This, she reflected vaguely, was what Gid Davies always called the 'purity of profit motive'—a motive based on greed. Standing there watching the barges go by in the frost Sun rubbed her face. It was words, words, words, talk, talk and more bloody talk. On one hand the workers were drinking themselves silly in the beer-houses: up the street the parsons and ministers were on their knees in the name of God, and up in Dowlais the masters were living like princes while the towns were full of vagrants and beggars: it didn't make sense to her. All she knew was that Blod Irish, Randy's girl, had miscarried while dram-hauling and that Dic had gone up to Jackson's Bridge for a meeting at the Wellington. Standing there at the window she held her stomach, wondering if she should try to get rid of it. Nobody knew, after all. If things got worse she wouldn't be able to feed it. Perhaps, she reflected, Madoc Williams had been right to kill his four, though it were a pity about that Olwen, for she was a beautiful little kid. They had sent him into the mad-house, she thought, yet perhaps he wasn't as mad as they made out... One thing she knew, they weren't getting her down Cwmglo: nor Dic—he wasn't going down Cwmglo Pit. She'd see this new one dead first.

A faint tap came on her door, and Sun turned.

Mamie appeared, her face pale, and she was shivering in her shawl.

'Come and see Randy,' she whispered. 'You got a minute, girl?'

'What's wrong?'

'Don't know. He just sits. Can't get him to talk . . .'

'Ay, wait a bit, then.'

Bending, she put some slack on the fire. Mamie said. 'You . . . you could always raise him a smile, Sun. He just stares. Mind, it'll be better when we can get our Blod up to Adulum. The house is at odds with her cold upstairs.'

Sun tightened her shawl around her face.

'Step easy on the ice, girl,' said Mamie. She caught Sun's arm and stared at her with red-rimmed eyes. 'Oh, God,' she said.

'Hush, Mamie.'

'Things would have been all right, see, if they hadn't loved for a baby.'

'Things will still be all right, you see.'

'Like you and your Dic. Got to be cool with a man at a time like this, Sun.'

'Ay.'

'You watch your fella, then.'

It had begun to snow again, painting up Sun's hair, and her eyes glowed at Mamie from the pale beauty of her face, reminding her of Blod when she was living down in Taibach with Mrs. Halloran. Mamie said:

'She was a good little piece, that Blod, ye know.'

'Yes, Mamie.'

'Billa was always on to me, but I loved her, ye know?'

'Of course.'

'I . . . I was a bit hard wi' her at first, but that's natural, like. After they was married I treated her like as a daughter, you remember?'

'Ay.'

Mamie gripped the door of the back, suddenly weeping.

'Don't take on so,' said Sun.

'I was a damn pig to her. One time I give her nothing but grunts.'

'All that's over, Mamie. Shall we go in now?'

Mamie raised her face. 'She would still be here now if it weren't for that baby. People like us can't afford babies at a time like this, ye know.'

'I'll remember,' said Sun.

They turned to footsteps. Lemuel Samuel, late of the Shop, Taibach, came from the darkness, and in his hand were some winter flowers.

' 'Evening, Mamie Goldie,' said he.

'Why, Lemuel Samuel!' Mamie peered into the rags.

'Just come to pay respects, Mrs. Goldie.' He gave her the periwinkles and snowdrops.

'But come in, man—you're perished, Mr. Samuel, come on in.'

'No thanks. Best to have his own people about him at a time like this; Randy, I mean.' His face was pinched and blue with cold.

'It was kind of you,' said Mamie, simply.

Lemuel sighed. 'Don't miss 'em till they go, do we?' He nodded at the flowers. 'I picked that lot up on the Beacons. Time was I could afford decent flowers—I started on my own, ye know?'

'Ay, we heard . . .'

'Bloody dog ate the letters—ate the orders as fast as they arrived. Very easy, it is, to fail in business. Did six months in Monmouth for debt—you hear that? I hate dogs now—blutty great woofin' things.'

'Ay.'

The wind of Ynys blustered between them, parting them; Mamie shivered.

'Best you go in, Mamie,' said Sun.

Lemuel said: 'I picked them special for Randy, them flowers. Give them to him from me and my Mavis. She died the same way. I was a sod to my Mavis, Mamie Goldie.'

They stared in the uncertainty of grief. He continued. 'All she wanted was an assisted delivery—cost half a crown,

218

but I wanted it free ... I wanted everything free, you see?'

There was sleet in the wind. Mamie put the flowers against her face, shivering more. Sun said quietly: 'Goodbye, Lemuel Samuel. Will you take sixpence from me?'

They stood listening to his footsteps echoing down Bridge-field.

17

'You there, Molly Caulara?'

Molly sat on the end of her bed in the Aunty Popi Davey and listened to the navvies and sale-coal colliers hitting it up in the Iron Bridge public just opposite, and the rumble of the carts on the cobbles outside. Earlier, walking the frosted streets she had eaten at the Quaker soup-urn down Bridge Street, and unless St. Peter's got a high hat on and dressed in Quaker black when I get to the golden gate that's one entrance they can keep, said she. Once, when young in County Mao, she had watched a child spit in the face of the Holy Virgin for a bowl of Protestant soup, and watched her father die in the corner of their cabin because he would not turn his coat, and saw her uncle eat because he did. But the Quaker of Bridge Street only smiled from the bearded gentleness of his face and the gaunt woman beside him filled the steaming bowl.

'Eat, child, eat.'

'You there, Molly Caulara?' called Shoni Crydd. 'I've got me sixpence, mind.'

'God bless you, woman,' she heard the Quaker say as she wandered away up the Taff to the Aunty Popi lodgings. And on the way she saw Dic Penderyn come out of Number Seven Ynysfach; face low in his collar, up to his elbows in his trews was Dic, and his brow like thunder. Vaguely, she had wondered how his life was going with that little Sun woman he had married; vaguely, too, she remembered a summer day and the laughing romp of the haystack up on the Brecon road.

' 'Evening, Dico.'

'Hello, Molly.' He made to move on, but she delayed him with a glance.

'How are ye doing?'

'Not so bad.' With a flourish he gave her one of his pamphlets.

'Are you still on heavy with the Benefits and the Unions?'

He raised his face to hers. 'Somebody has to be.' He waved a cynical hand. 'All this old lot's fit for is begging on their knees. You don't kneel and beg from masters like these, you up and take. The only language they understand is the wrong end of a gun.'

'They'll lead you to hell, you know.' She tightened the shawl about her face and he smiled at her pale beauty. She continued: 'People like that big Pole Zimmerman are chock full o' the gab, but you won't see them for dust when the Military come out. And they'll have you—pastin' up the *Twopenny Trash*.'

'It's the chance we take—look at the place. The town's in rags, half the folks here are starving. You heard about Blod Irish.'

'Ay.' She narrowed her eyes to the wind. 'It were a pity, that—a good little soul was that Blod Irish; how's her Randy doing?'

He wiped his mouth with the back of his hand. 'The man's demented; just sits and stares ...' He looked at the sky. 'God alive, what a country.'

'The country's all right, fella, it's the people.' She smiled, touching his arm, and the touch brought her to a sudden warmth. 'Some are lucky—you got a good filly, they tell me.'

He grinned wide. 'Ay, Sun's all right.'

'A jaunty piece, and pretty. But then, you could always pick 'em. Is she with childer?'

'God forbid,' he said.

'Keep her clear o' the childer, Dico—you'm a hot man, but keep her clear till the times get better:'

The wind whistled in from the Taff and the moon beamed over Sulleri where the criss-cross roofs slanted amid a crazy hotchpotch of gables and chimneys; the night bayed with cold, the frost flashed along the fozen road.

'Got to go,' said Dic.

'Ay. Take it slow, Dico—Merthyr's an expert in death.'

'Sufferin' saints,' he said, taking her off. 'You're a happy soul.'

'Just take it slow, especial with the politics. Things'll get better quick when spring comes in and the rate of iron rises . . .'

'God's blood, woman!' He turned, glaring at her. 'You're as bad as the rest of them, and I gave you credit for sense. When the rates of iron rise, is it? Are our bellies dependent on the rates of iron when Crawshay sits up there with gold in his bloody castle?'

'He's . . . he's got to keep going,' said Molly. 'You rook him now and he'll go bankrupt, and the town will starve. I'm telling ye, Dic . . .'

'Christ! When will you people learn?' He flung back to her. 'How the hell did he get the first half million—did he pick it off trees? No—he got it from us, his workers, and now we're wanting some of it back. All right, the world rates of iron are down, but that's not the workers' fault—can't you see that, woman? It's because Crawshay and Guest don't know their business—the fools overstocked. That's what Zimmerman says and he's right. And if they made their piles when times were good they should share it out now times are bad.' His voice rose. 'But mark me, things are changing, and you'll watch them jump. The Union is coming—Gideon says this, and he is right. This is only the beginning. All over the country the Lodges will rise, and branches form in every works. We are only hundreds now, but soon we'll be thousands, even millions —and we'll put a bargain on our labour that will make these buggers dance. The first thing we'll demand is increases . . .'

Molly laughed gaily. 'Increases, ye say? Don't be daft, fella!'

'Ay, increases, for we want a share of the profits—God alive, these masters make enough! Yes, it will come—perhaps not in our time, says Zimmerman—nor our children's, but it will come and swamp the country. By God, we'll wring the pockets of these employers! As Zimmerman says—we must cleanse it all, and start again . . .'

'You'm a hot bugger, mind, Dic Penderyn,' said Molly. 'Old Wag reckons she's got a witch fancy about you, so watch out—says you'll dance on a rope.'

'They'll have to move. . . . ! Got more suspicions than teeth, that one.'

They smiled at each other: there arose within her a small frenzy of love for him, and she fought it down.

'Good luck now,' she said, and walked away.

And she went back to her Popi Davey lodgings and sat on the bed.

'I've paid me shilling to Old Wag, and I've got your six-pence here, Molly Caulara,' said Shoni Crydd, and he closed and bolted the door.

Raked from the summer kisses of Dic Penderyn, she raised her head.

In the beery, blinkered gasps, the bed of rags, the yorked trews, buckled belt and riot baton of the gigantic Shoni Crydd, special constable, she saw on the stained ceiling a pattern of leaves in June sun: in the bearded scourge, the calloused hands, the floundering monstrosity of a thing called love, she remembered the laughter of that summer loving in a haystack up the Brecon road.

'Aw, to hell, girl, don't start that!' said Shoni Crydd. 'Now, what you crying for, Molly Caulara?'

They were collecting the rents outside the Aunty Popi Davey as well as inside, where Molly Caulara was paying hers. Mr. Steffan Shenkins, beadle in service to Mr. Coffin of the Court of Requests, was in attendance; it being necessary to remove the effects if the rents were not forthcoming, and a very dis-tressing business it can be, mind, turning out folks in the middle of February.

' 'Evening, Miss Thrush,' said Mr. Steffan Shenkins, deacon of the Big Ebenezer, and do not mix me up with that drunken coot of a brother of mine, Mr. Stinkin Shenkins, for we are as different as chalk to cheese.

'Good evening, Mr. Shenkins.' Amid her shelves of jars

223

stood she, shawled and mittened, and her cheeks were full and bitten red with frost. 'Four and sixpence, is it?'

'If you please, Miss Thrush, for the lower premises only.' Out with his little black book then, licking a stub of pencil. 'Are the other occupants available, Ma'am?'

'The other occupants are here,' announced Mrs. Bach Taibach, her arm around Willie. 'One and sixpence for the room above, Mr. Steffan Shenkins.'

'But there are two rooms above, Mrs. Taibach.'

'Only one occupied by me and my son,' replied she, and called up the stairs, 'Mr. Note, the rent man, if you please.'

'Oh, Mam!' whispered Willie.

Mr. Note shambled down the stairs and drooped before the beadle, his face low. With his rags hanging on his shanks and shoulders, he drooped.

'Music don't pay in Merthyr, do it?' said Mrs. Taibach, and Percy Bottom Note raised his head at this, saying:

'The people of Merthyr are very musical, Mr. Beadle.'

'But not prepared to pay for instruction, are they, Mr. Note?' said Mrs. Taibach.

'But you cannot buy music with money, Mr. Beadle,' and Mr. Note smiled.

'I will pay for the room,' said Miss Thrush, fishing in her purse.

Mr. Note straightened. 'Indeed you will not, Miss Thrush.' They stood together, silenced on the frosted boards.

'It seems we 'ave come to an impasse, so to speak,' and Mr. Steffan Shenkins awkwardly shifted his feet. 'Now, if you was Ebenezer . . .'

'I am of no religion, sir,' said Percy Bottom Note.

'Then . . . then are there any possessions? As you know, the court is most considerate . . . one and sixpence is not a large sum, and . . .'

'There are no possessions, Mr. Beadle.'

'Oh, but there is,' interjected Mrs. Bach Taibach. 'There's a silk-faced harmonium upstairs, made in Swansea in 1776.'

'Oh, Mam!' whispered Willie.

'It is not a possession, sir,' said Mr. Note, 'it is a harmonium.'

224

'Nevertheless of value, you agree?' said Mr. Steffan Shenkins warmly. 'I'm sure Mr. Coffin himself would treat it respectable. Indeed, I heard talk that the deacons up in Adulum are in need of a harmonium...'

'Please let me pay, Mr. Note,' said Milly Thrush.

'Then would you care to vacate...?' asked Mr. Shenkins.

'Yes, indeed, Mr. Beadle.'

At the door Percy Bottom Note bowed to Miss Thrush, saying: 'You have dignity and warmth, Miss Thrush, even in February.'

Hands deep in his pockets he mooched into the snowing street.

It was starlight on Dowlais Top.

Even the cats were in down the deserted streets of Aberpennar ... around the unborn town of Maerdy, later called Little Moscow, the snow was thinner, though the grass was shivering at being out all night: along the lonely, desecrated little valleys the warmest place was down the pit, and the *tylwyth teg* were skating on the ice of the Afan playing *Touch me Last*. Black and deserted were the streets of Taibach; the sheds and smelters of the English Copper Works were empty, the furnaces blown out down Mill Yard Row where Mrs. Halloran lives. Plump as a wheat-pigeon was Mrs. Halloran once, said Blod Irish who lodged there earlier, but now gone to a shadow because of the drop in prices. It is the economics that do beat us, mind, said Mrs. Halloran—when once you've got copper you're bound to 'ave the economics, like the agent said. But I'm quite happy, said Mrs. Halloran, for I've still got the rent. As I always say, love, you can empty the larder, they can cut off the coal, they can take the furniture, they can empty your stomach—nothing matters if you still have the roof. That Mamie Goldie—bless her, too, and I wonder how she's doing up in that Merthyr—she used to say the same: whatever they take, girl, your victuals or your virginity—ye got to keep the slates. It'll be a lot better, though, when we get the workhouse: that's what the agent says. You simply can't have copper without the economics.

'That you, Mr. Halloran?' she called.

With her back against the wall she sat; the moon over Dinas Woods shafted the empty room. Like a sack of coal propped up in a corner she sat, wife to Big Mike Halloran who once smelted for the English Copper in the Taibach casting-house : with her white hair down over her shoulders and a shilling held up between finger and thumb, she waited.

Footsteps echoed on the cobbles outside. She cried:

'That you, my lovely? Dinner's in the oven, Mike. Ach, wash yourself after, fella—you look weary to death.'

Never smelled of ale, mind—not like some I could mention —that Dai End-On, for instance, and that horrid Mr. Jam. Neither hops nor spirit passed his lips—don't hold with it, my Mike used to say. A good day's work for a fair day's pay, that's what he reckoned; big man, mind—topped six foot four : used to knit bed-socks special for him—they was always through the rails.

The door opened and the moon came in, bowing first.

'That you, Mike?'

'It is only me, Mrs. Halloran.'

'Why, it's Mr. Henry Chalk, the school-master! Come you in!'

'Rent collecting spare time, Mrs. Halloran. You got the rent?'

He stood as a blackboard blotting out the moon, his face chalk white, his mittened fingers making rabbits on the moon-lit wall, and he stooped over her, his easel legs astride her in the corner, his eyes flickering red in the etched shadows of his cheeks.

'Ay, I've got nothin' else,' said she, 'but I've got the rent—a shilling?'

'Are you all right, Mrs. Halloran?'

Bright and perky was her face. 'Right as rain, man—waiting for my Mike.'

Still at a stoop, Mr. Chalk wrote with a shivering hand :

'Mill Yard Row. Number Eleven. Mrs. M. Halloran. One shilling.'

And he took the shilling from her frozen fingers.

226

'I tell you she spoke, she spoke to me!' sobbed Mr. Chalk later.

'Don't be ridiculous,' said the coroner. 'According to medical evidence she'd been dead for a week.'

Mr. Steffan Shenkins knocked on the door of Number One, Ynys: it was opened by Miss Blossom Thomas, daughter to Papa Tomo Thomas who had been in bed over five years with the rheumatics, and I think it's a damned scandal, said Billa Jam; all over the country there's women like her taking care of the old 'uns when they should be sparking with the young 'uns, it's a waste of good human sport.

'She looks pretty fruitful to me,' observed Mamie.

'Courted and lost, so they say,' replied Billa, shaking out the smalls. 'Now all she's left with is Papa and rheumatics.'

'Good morning, Mr. Shenkins,' said Blossom Thomas, curtseying.

'Good morning, Miss Thomas; the rent, if you please?' He adjusted his spectacles and opened his book.

'I am sorry,' said Miss Thomas.

'So am I,' said Mr. Shenkins.

'D'ye want any help down there, woman?' shouted Mamie, her head out of the back of Number Five, and in crackers. 'Shall we pop up and see to him?'

'No, thank you,' said Miss Thomas, 'I can manage.'

'Who is it down there?' shouted Papa Tomo upstairs in bed.

'It's the Church of England parson,' called his daughter.

'Oh, ay? Well, tell him we're Baptist. And it's no good him patting the bloody dog for he only speaks Welsh.' He sang then, a bawdy sea-shanty of his youth, and the men of Ynysfach cocked their ears to listen. Mr. Steffan Shenkins said:

'It is now five weeks, Miss Thomas, and that is eight and ninepence. You have a framed picture of a deer pursued by hounds, I understand.'

'I have a water-colour of a mother feeding her baby,' said Miss Thomas.

'Ah, yes, I have mixed up the addresses: Miss Grieve, fortunately, will accept either. I will give it to the court collector, Miss Thomas—you will have a chance to redeem it if it is not auctioned by the end of the month.'

'As long as it pays the rent, Mr. Beadle.'

Mr. Shenkins ticked off her name in his book. 'Please fetch it. I will endeavour to persuade Miss Grieve to forfeit eight and ninepence, but she may prove unwilling, you understand?'

'I understand. Thank you, Mr. Shenkins. If I wrap it will you keep it private, Mr. Shenkins?'

'Of course.'

Strangely, he bowed to her before she closed the door.

'You can bugger off out of here for we've paid the rent,' said Mamie, as the gambo and rent cortège went by, and Billa Jam took the opportunity to empty her bucket of suds which sent the bubbles up the beadle's gaiters.

'Dear me,' said Mamie, her hand to her throat. 'Don't tell me they're in trouble in Number Seven...'

But on the door of Number Seven, Ynys, the beadle knocked.

Sun smoothed down her apron and patted her hair, which was now to her shoulders and tied with black ribbon. She opened the door.

'Mrs. Penderyn, I am sorry to have to inform you ...' began Mr. Steffan Shenkins.

'Yes, yes. But for God's sake take what you want before he gets back...'

'She's entitled to the bed and the table, remember,' said Mamie Goldie, leaning around the door.

After saying that she went back to Number Five, led Billa and the children after her and shut and bolted the door. And all down Ynysfach the people went inside and bolted the doors and drew the curtains while the Penderyn furniture was carried out to the Court of Requests, for debt.

One thing about the the folks of Merthyr, they can say goodbye to most things, but they are beggars for keeping their pride, said Mamie Goldie.

228

SPRING came in over the mountains bright and hot and the snows melted on the great Vans Rocks of the Beacons, and the land grew warm under a kinder sun. All over The Top from Abergavenny to Taibach the ice began to melt in rushing streams that began in trickles and grew into cascading torrents of ice-white water. In the glow of spring the land brightened, new tints grew on the trees of Cyfarthfa Park and the black, frozen streets of Merthyr were rutted with slush. As if at a signal of life reborn, the doors of the cottages opened, windows were flung wide to the warm air coming down the valley and a new chatter began: the whole kaleidoscope of sound and colour of the greatest iron town in the world burst anew over the streets in a rainbow of April showers and warmth. The streets were crammed with new immigrants, gay were the colours of the incoming broughams and traps of the gentry. As if at the end of a long hibernation sleep the aged workers of a lost generation tottered out on to the pavements; dutiful wives and daughters placed the kitchen chairs outside the fronts and backs for champing granchers and toothless grans: mufflered children danced the hopscotch down the chalked flags or trailed in viper snakes of lost hope to the penny a week private schools where they were not allowed to speak Welsh by order of England.

But a new hope and urgency was in the air: the whispers of Reform began in the tap-rooms and grew into a buffeting demand in every Lodge and benefit club. Political agitators were everywhere on The Top: tub-thumping in the Square off High, raising platforms outside Ynysgau and fists and banners down Graham and Duke. The Chartists met in the Three Horseshoes and discussed it; the new Unionists, meeting in defiance of the law, paraded their banners around the town led by fife and whistle bands and yelled aloud their songs of glory, Reform or Die with Lord Russell's Bill: the leaders of the new revolution ranted on the street corners their fierce denouncements of Church and State and the new ideology of pie in the sky. And the Church's leaders met the challenge head-on. Pulpit was thumped in verbal reprisals; with beard-trembling indignation the established servants of the Big Seats from the Welsh Wesleyan to Ebenezer opposed Reform in the name of God and the starving poor who would always be with them. This belief was confirmed by a new rush of famished immigrants from Ireland, wandering in from Bristol and the ports of Gower. Bare-footed and in rags, they ate their way like a locust swarm into the hills of Merthyr, went down on their knees in the mud of High Street and begged before the stalls where the groceries were spilling, till beaten away by the special constables. They offered their children for sale before the broughams of Penydarren and their daughters for prostitution before the Castle of Cyfarthfa, and the agents seized them. Turning away all but the fittest, they housed these in the cottages of the evicted Welsh and signed them on at cut rates. A rush of foreigners who were prepared to work for a jug of ale now swarmed into Merthyr and Dowlais and fought at the gates of the Alderman Thompson Works. And this was the new bargaining power of the capitalists who now joined in the shouts for Reform. For them it was a new banner to fly in the faces of the landed aristocracy; the great houses of Beaufort and Tredegar who had never accepted as equals these self-made princes of wealth. So the iron masters flouted their riches before this gentility; drove to church with coaches and fours and liveried postillions, gave banquets for the marriages of their sons and daughters and lavished dowries that vied with eastern potentates: blaming the old aristocratic influences and the heredity system for confining the rights of the working classes. And the new ferment of the working classes, the new demands for democratic ideals at a time of an eight hundred

230

million pound national debt, was projected by the industrialists as a direct result of a corrupt parliamentary system that threatened the sacred rights of capital and property. With a new slogan of Freedom, Justice and Equality the masters moved to the sides of their workers and thundered the cry for a Bill of Reform, blaming the new shopocracy and the old aristocracy for the plight of trade. And Crawshay, foremost in this fight for Reform, nominated a candidate to represent the people in the forthcoming May elections for Brecon. A new leader had appeared on the horizon of the workers' distress and they roamed the streets of Merthyr and Dowlais in torchlight processions, proclaiming that all who opposed Reform should be hanged on the gallows, stoning the houses of the Tories, burning in effigy prominent people who stood in opposition. Crawshay, the new hero of the oppressed, was eulogised and toasted in the name of Reform. His iron-stone miners cheered him in the streets.

He then cut their wages by twenty per cent.

Dic Penderyn came through the door of Number Seven, Ynysfach just as Shoni Crydd, the special constable attending the court beadle, was coming through it with two kitchen chairs, and Crydd went one way and the chairs another.

'What the hell is happening here?'

Sun said quietly: 'They have come for the second time.'

'I paid the rent!'

Mr. Steffan Shenkins said, consulting his book: 'You last paid it on the third of December; eighteen shillings is owing and the Court of Requests is confiscating your furniture both in this sum and a bill for twenty-two and fivepence claimed by Mr. Andrew Marsden, shopkeeper of Merthyr.'

'Oh, my God!'

'That's what I said,' remarked Sun, 'but you still went on swillin' ale with your fine new friend Johns up at the Lewis Lewis Benefit.'

'What are you taking?'

'Two chairs, the blankets received from Mr. Marsden, draper, the chest of drawers from the bedroom, the clock, and

231

the tub and dolly from the kitchen.'

'Take them and get out, it's cheap at the price.'

'And I am to inform you that the court will auction same articles in repayment of the debts unless redeemed within a fortnight from this date.'

'No chance of that,' said Sun, 'the way he's going you'll have the rest of it within the next fortnight.'

'You get inside, you noisy bitch.'

The beadle added: 'Further, Mr. Penderyn, if you lay hands on a constable of the law again, I will have you put in charge.'

'Don't worry,' said Shoni Crydd, brushing himself down. 'One day I will have him for it—me and Mr. Abbott, the barber—and personal.'

Sun slammed the door behind them; empty, they wandered about.

'Now perhaps you're satisfied,' she said, and went to the window. Distantly, she could see the court gambo lumbering over the bridge.

'I'm not breaking my heart over a few sticks of furniture, girl.'

She swung to him, furious. 'But I am! Will you tell me what else I've got? Night after night I'm sitting in here while you're up at the Oddfellows taking the oath—swilling your stomach with Jump beer and spouting your damned politics.' She held her stomach, staring up into his face. 'We've got a baby comin', or don't ye realise it? Nigh two months you've been off—the iron's still coming out—why aren't you working?'

'Because I'm laid off—you just said so!'

'Ay, and for why? Because of the politics. For all his shouting of reforming this and that, Crawshay don't stand for the tub-thumpers, and you know it!'

'Ach, don't talk stupid! Rowlands and Andrews were laid off, too, and they're both Tories—the politics are nothing to do with it.'

'Then are ye getting another job?' He turned away from her wrath but she gripped him and swung him to face her. 'God alive, time was I thought you'd make something of yourself—even Gid Davies said so. Now all you're fit for is kicking up the sawdust and laying on the cocks. From the moment you set eyes on that good-for-nothing Lewis Lewis you've been going to the devil, and me with you.'

'We've got to have the meetings. . . !'

'Ay, you've got to have the meetings, I grant ye that. But do you have to float 'em off on beer? Have ye any money, for instance, for there's not a bite of bread in the house.'

He laid three shillings on the table and she snatched it up.

'Benefit money?'

'It's as good as any other.'

'It won't be if the parish knows you're drawing it. Dic, Dic . . . !' She clung to him. 'Don't you realise the state we're in?'

'It will change soon,' he said. 'By God, it will change soon . . .'

'And who'll be doing that? You fellas are all the same. There's young Randy gone off and Mamie's half demented. Every man in Ynys is roaming the streets and shouting the politics, but where does it land us women? There's Mrs. Tranter with six kids to feed and her chap tub-thumping down Bridge and every agent in town booking down his name. Cwmglo and Tasker and Lcfal are on short time—at Tasker alone all but three colliers are on parish relief . . .'

'Aw, stick to your kitchen!' He pushed himself away. 'D'you think I don't know? According to Gid Davies and Zim, Crawshay's going to sack near ninety puddlers—that'll be the end of us—and there's good men getting out while the going's good . . .'

She shouted, following him round the room, 'And can you tell me why he's sacking the puddlers? Can the fella do anything right? Look, see sense—would Crawshay be laying off puddlers if he could afford to keep 'em. . . ?'

'He's laying them off because the trade is down!'

'Of course—can you blame him? Would he be cutting his own throat if there was profit in keeping them on? You say the fellas are going—of course—the tradesmen are getting out,

233

and Crawshay knows it. Would he be losing good puddlers to Beaufort and Tredegar...?'

'Oh, woman, shut it!'

'Ay, I will when I've had my say, for I'm not finished.' She pointed to the window. 'There's jobs going out there for hauliers and miners, and there's good men taking them. When anything goes wrong it's poor bloody Crawshay but it's never *you*—isn't it true that Fothergill's paying his colliers five shillings less than William Crawshay.'

'Ay, and we're seeing to that.' He roamed the room, thumping his fist into his hand.

'You're seeing to it, eh? That's a good one!' She laughed, her head back. 'And what will you do when you get there—blow him out? Where will that land the sale-coal people of Aberdare? All ye can think of is blowing people out and marching on this and that—you're not human, man—ye all belong to the jungle!'

'The jungle is the only thing they understand!'

'So you're fighting for it now?'

'Ay, if needs be.'

'Then God help ye all, for the Brecon garrison will cut you to pieces. In heaven's name!' She stared at him. 'Don't you realise that? Don't you understand that they'll bring in the Military? You've got that Tom Llewellyn dancing down the streets shouting about Reform, there's this Twiss fella you're always talking about twisting ye round his finger—but I've told you before—you'll not see the backside of one of them when the guns come out. Look—even Crawshay's backing you on the Bill of Reform—what else do you people want?'

'I've had enough of this, I'm getting out!'

She ran to the door and spread her arms across it. 'But you're not. You're not leaving here till you promise me you're done with that Benefit.' She thumped herself with her fist. 'I've a young 'un in here and I need food. I'm nigh seven months away and I'm having it decent, in by here, not out in the gutter on the parish.'

'We'll have changed things before you have that,' he said quietly.

His tone stilled her. Gasping, she faced him over the bare room. A man stumbled past the window, his hobnailed boots rattling on the cobbles but they did not hear him. A barge glided past with sale-coal for Abercynon, but they did not see it. Sun said, staring at him.

'You're fighting for it, then?'

'Ay, we're having the Request Court down for a start.'

'And then?' She clutched her shawl against her throat.

'Then a go for decent wages.'

'Is Gid Davies in this?'

'Gid Davies stands for a charter, and the Union . . .'

'Mr. Zimmerman?'

'Zimmerman stands for a fight, and he's right. Davies is wrong.'

She whispered, her face pale, 'So you're in with them, then. It's people like Zimmerman and Lewis Lewis and Cobbett's Trash from now, is it?'

He approached the door. 'It is the only way.'

'They'll cut you to pieces.'

'So be it. We're standing it no longer.'

She smiled. 'And this is what ye call Reform? You just go out and take.'

He said evenly: 'We've got London and Manchester people down with us now. We've got the backing of Morgan Williams and Zephaniah of Nantyglo: Cobbett pamphlets are coming in. Lord Russell's Reform Bill won't get through without a fight, and it will take somebody bigger than Crawshay who is only after the protection of property, he doesn't give a damn for the Reform. We beat the shopkeeper Stephens and Bruce the magistrate when they took Tom Llewellyn . . .'

'You call that justice? You broke the windows and threatened an innocent man—you were lucky to keep out of prison—that was the rule of a mob.'

'But we beat them; if the rule of the mob will change things, then it's that rule from now on, says Zimmerman.'

'God in heaven, ye must all be touched.' Raising a hand Sun wiped her sweating face. 'If ye go now, Dic, I won't be here when you come back.'

'I'm getting a shift-job with Lewis Lewis, hauling the timber over in Penderyn—Lewis knows people; he's well in with the Bodwigiad gentry, and he spoke for me.'

'If Lewis Lewis spoke for you I know you're bound for the devil.' The Great Hammer began to crash from Cyfarthfa.

He approached her and she drew herself up. Momentarily, he pitied her shapelessness, the black droop of her shawl, the way her dress lifted in the front, showing her legs. Yet, despite the pallor of her face there was in her eyes a brightness and beauty he had never seen before: vaguely, he wondered if she was about to cry, having lost most of the furniture now ... He remembered then that he had never seen her cry.

'Got to go, Sun,' he said.

She did not reply. A foot the shorter she just gripped her dress and stared up at him.

'But soon I'll be back, and bring you money for the ...' He touched her dress and she moved away, still staring.

'Not Lewis Lewis, Dic,' she said then. 'He'll bring ye to trouble. There's other jobs ye can get—even the parish, breaking on the road, but ... not Lewis Lewis.'

Bending, he kissed her face. 'Goodbye.'

When he had gone Sun leaned against the door and bowed her head.

And Mamie Goldie, standing by the window of Number Five watched him striding up the towpath towards Jackson's.

'And we think we've got trouble,' said Mamie. 'With Blod dead and gone and Randy God knows where ... bless my soul, here's Gid Davies coming ...'

'He'll collect an outing if he goes to Number Seven,' said Billa, stitching, 'for all he's the wonderful Gid Davies. Come away from that window, Mamie, it anna decent watching.'

'You reckon he's calling on Sun?'

'More'n likely.' Billa rose, drawing her away. 'Ye'll get a cold in your eye, woman—come away, now,' and she drew the curtains.

Tap tap on the door, and Mamie was up instantly, flinging the door open.

Gideon removed his hat.

'Number Five, is it? I am seeking Mamie Goldie.'

Mamie beamed. 'And you've found her, Gid, lad—come you in, and welcome.'

He sought her hand and the old warmth of friendship leaped between them.

'I've found Randy,' he said simply. 'I was up at Adulum with flowers for Jobina, and I found him with Blod, sitting by the grave.'

Mamie swallowed, her hand to her throat. Then she smiled.

'I'll come up and get him, Gid,' she said.

After Mamie had left for Zimmerman's up in Cross Street, Billa Jam said: 'Can you spare a moment for me, Mr. Davies?'

He nodded, smiling, and she fetched him a chair that faced the window where the light was on his face and she could see him properly.

'We're doing all right, Mamie and me,' said Billa.

'I'm glad.'

'We're ... we're doing fine, really—got plenty of washing despite the times—got plenty of kids about—you heard about my Adam, of course?'

'Yes, I am sorry.'

'And my two lads Merve and Saul, the twins—Saul's starting down Lefal day after tomorrow?'

'They are both a little young for the pit, Mrs. Jam. I was wondering...'

'My pa was down when he was six, and these are gone nine—they eat like mules and we need the money.'

'I see.' Gideon twisted his fingers in his lap. They blamed the masters for the early starts, but half the time it was the working classes. Education was the root of it all, of course. Education, he reflected, looking up at the light, was the only lever that could prise these people out of the vicious habits of years. Education ... If only Crawshay would open a school—a little one for a start—even a penny a week...

Billa said: 'You remember the three Irish lads who used to

237

lodge at my place in Taibach?'

'Mike, Tim and Joe? Of course.'

'Well, they're moving into Merthyr next week, and they need two extra drams. Good workers, mind, and fine lads, and they're lodging in by here with us. You remember Mike in particular?'

'The big handsome one, according to Mamie.' Gideon smiled reflectively.

'The one that is sweet on me,' said Billa.

'I ... I didn't know that, Mrs. Jam.' He raised his face.

'You do now.'

He was at a disadvantage, and knew it: women say much with their eyes.

She sighed and wandered the room. 'Don't know much about women, do ye?'

He sat and she walked about and he cursed his blindness. She said as from a distance. 'Disgusting, isn't it—me with ten kids.'

Searching for his pipe he filled and lit it, staring blindly through the smoke. 'You ... you want Mr. Jam back is that it?'

Her feet scurried over the floor and she was on her knees beside him. 'Oh God, Mr. Davies, oh God, I want my Mr. Jam...' She gripped his hands momentarily, then got up again, saying calmly, 'It ... it's for the kids mainly, ye see. Don't ... don't get me wrong, Mr. Davies, it ... it's nothing to do with ... with having a man around, if you get me. Just that it's bad for the kids having no pa, and ...'

'I seem to remember that he came once,' said Gideon.

She did not reply, and he added; 'They tell me he's off the bottle, too.'

'That right?'

'So they tell me. Even goes to chapel—Taibach, they say.'

'Good God, he's taken the oath.' She added: 'Will you ... will you mention it?'

'I'm due down there in a week—of course I'll mention it.'

'He can please himself, of course. I mean, I don't much care

238

if he comes or not—you realise that? It's just that...'

'I understand.'

'And don't mention it to Mamie, will ye, Gid Davies?'

Smiling, he lit the pipe again, shaking his head: a gang of colliers off shift from Cwmglo crowded past the window in good-natured banter and oaths.

'I've always kept myself to myself, ye see,' said Billa.

'That's how it should be.'

'That's what I mean. Thank you, Mr. Davies.' She opened the door. 'Goodbye, Mr. Davies.'

Despite the smoking furnaces of Ynys the spring air seemed suddenly sweet and clean.

When Gideon reached Zimmerman's house in Cross Street he saw Mamie Goldie standing outside, knowing her only by shape, for the sun was bright.

'Haven't you been in yet, then?' he asked.

'Ay, and just coming out, for he's sleeping. The big foreigner said not to wake him ... sleeping like a baby, he is.'

'He'll need good care when you get him back to Number Five, Mamie.'

She said, with a catch in her throat: 'Even while I were standing there he was calling for Blod ...'

'It will pass. He is young, and time heals ...'

'Gid ...' Mamie touched his hand. 'Do you ever get down Taibach these days?'

Gideon lit his pipe, trying not to smile. 'Not often.'

'Never get news of that good-for-nothing Dai of mine?'

'Sometimes I hear a mention.'

'Wouldn't ever have him back, mind—wouldn't give him house room. It's just that I'd like to know how he's getting on, ye see.' She caught his arm. 'Don't seem right to cast him off, as it were—especially if he happens to be in trouble.'

'Trouble?' He was not going to make it easy: according to Dai End-On even spare parts of the mangle had been thrown ... Mamie said then:

'Well, ye never know, ye see. Anything could happen—he

might even be dead.'

'If he is dead he is beyond assistance.'

Annie Hewers hurried past with averted eyes; people basketed and shoved on their way to the market; the hucksters were already quarrelling about the price of the stalls, the boozies searching out the taverns.

Gideon said: 'I'll do my best, Mamie, but I can't promise anything. But if I do bring Dai back I hope there won't be any violence.'

'Violence? Good God—what do ye take me for?'

'Well, last time Dai and Billy came...'

'Ay, I know. Well, I'll speak to Billa Jam—sometimes she's not herself, as ye know. She do tend to take the law into her own 'ands, so to speak, but I'll vouch for her.'

'That's generous of you, Mamie.'

'Granted. And I'd be inclined not to mention this ... this suggestion, if ye understand.'

The sun sworded down over Merthyr, lighting the faces of the cramming, chattering people; ragged urchins were looking for pockets in the crowds and diving under the bellies of the passing drays, for the ale was coming in from Hopkins' Brewery.

'I will be the soul of discretion,' said Gideon.

She peered up into his face. 'By the way—you heard about Sun and Dic?'

Gideon was instantly attentive, and Mamie continued: 'Got their furniture restrained again.'

'What!'

'Not an hour ago—Coffin's Court.'

'Did the beadle have a warrant for the distraint?'

'Search me,' said Mamie, 'ye know Steffan Shenkins—he just come up again and took.'

'But I didn't even know Dic Penderyn was off.'

'Ay—weeks—puddler's labourer down at Ynys, and hauling. Sun reckons it's because he's marching with them Lodges and things.'

Gideon was already moving away, and at that moment Zimmerman put his head out of Number Eighteen, and called:

'Ah, you have not gone, Mrs. Goldie. Come, your son is awake.'

Sun was standing at the door of her cottage when Gideon approached.

The old yearning for him moved in her again, blinding what should have been anger, and the child moved within her, too, as if stirred from sleep by the emotion.

'You come for me, Gid?'

'Sun!'

Reaching for his hand she drew him within the kitchen, and Mrs. Zeke Solomon in Number Four fell off the chair in the bedroom window and hit her head on the door and what the hell you doing standing on chairs at your age, anyway, said Zeke when he came back from the synagogue after instruction and observances.

'She's always standing on that chair,' said Billa. 'Next time I see her on it I am coming up there and blutty hit her off.'

'Better than the parish register, she is,' said Mamie. 'The very idea—counting up the groceries in the shopping baskets. You know she shaves, don't ye, Billa?' All down the Row the doors were coming open.

'She don't!'

'As sure as me eye—saw her lathering and shaving, didn't I?' she shouted up at the window.

'Oh, Mrs. Goldie ... please, Mrs. Goldie...' protested Mrs. Zeke Solomon.

'Right you, then down off that chair or it's going round the neighbourhood.'

'Who's in there now, then?' asked Billa, interested.

'The blind man—Mr. Gideon Davies, the blind man...' replied Mrs. Solomon.

'Not you—you hop off out of it,' said Billa and softly closed the door.

Gideon said, in Sun's kitchen, 'Mamie has just told me ... the Beadle has been here?'

241

'Why you worrying about me, then?' asked Sun.

'Because I feel responsible.'

'Don't you feel responsible for me, boyo, I can take care of myself.'

'Of course.'

The table was between them. Gideon said: 'May ... may I sit down.'

'Ay, on the floor—they've taken the chairs.'

'I am sorry, Sun.'

'You're sorry—that's a good one. What about me?' She patted her stomach. 'I've got this lot due soon and the fella who put it there is tipping his elbow and shouting about Reform.'

'It's the price we pay for freedom.' He remembered the colour of her hair.

'Freedom, eh? Och, you lot are nothing but hot air. My God, the women of this world would eat a fine stew if we depended on agitators. Before people like you and Twiss and Zimmerman got going my Dic was all right!' She walked about in pent anger. 'We were settling fine, with the baby coming, and all that—you can live in this town, ye know—Crawshay don't eat people alive, for all the slander ye give him!'

'But we need Reform, Sun—even the masters see that. We merely propose ...'

She swung to him. 'Ye propose? Ye propose damn all, ye only bloody talk. Were you at that Lodge meeting up at Tafern Uchaf, Penderyn, when he met Lewis Lewis, the haulier chap?'

'Yes.' Unaccountably, he remembered the road from Taibach, and her nearness.

'Well, it handed down from that night—he came home breathing fire and hops and Lewis Lewis on the brain: the agent heard of it and laid him off, and he hasn't been the same chap since. Oh, God!' She began to cry and he felt his way around the room and held her: the bulge of her carrying was against his loins and she shook with sobs and her tears were

242

wet on his hands.

'Come now, Sun, Sun!' Her nearness was bringing an emotion in him.

'Eh, I wish I was dead!'

'Don't say that.' His throat was dry and he clenched his hands.

'I wish I was back wi' Billy Ugmore!'

'And don't say that, either.'

She raised her face to his, thankful for his blindness. 'I do, I do. Ow ... I wish I was back with Billy Ugmore, for life were straight with him!'

'Hush, Sun, the neighbours will hear.' He held her and the child moved against him with a kick, as if in vehement protestation. She wept in tuneless sounds and wetness and there was no dignity in it; presently, she ceased.

'There now,' he said.

'There now me eye,' said she, wiping and sniffing. 'You'll go from here and start the same old thing again, and ye won't be happy till the blood is running in Merthyr, will ye?'

'We will not be happy until we get a Bill of Reform,' said Gideon. 'And this generation might have to suffer so the next ones live decently ...'

It angered her. 'Oh, ay? And it's the likes of us that have the furniture taken for debt, eh?' She clenched her fists before him. 'I told Dico and I'm telling you, Gid—you won't see your secret army for dust when the Military come out—they'll be away, away!'

Gideon said: 'You are wrong. In a fight they will discover their importance, and their courage. The Roman slaves were never numbered lest they discovered their strength and knew their power, and so it is with the workers of Merthyr and Dowlais.' He turned to her and she saw in his face a new light. 'Or are we all to wail, like you, over a few sticks of furniture. Is it the women who are going to hold us back in this town when women start rebellions?' She began to speak but he shouted her down. 'If the army of the government is attacked in these streets it will be for the first time in English history,

243

and the Welsh will show the way. Or are ye content to sit down under the injustices, snivelling to your neighbour while they grind you lower and lower? All right—your man drinks —but don't blame him, blame the masters who take his all and toss him a pittance.' He was walking about now, shouting as if addressing an assembly. 'Reform must come and men and women be prepared to die for it—for it is not only the iron towns we are concerned with, but the nation. Do you realise that in Oxfordshire the farm labourers are on one and two-pence a week? That in Lancashire the children are being kicked from sleep by the slubbers of the machines? And six-year-olds coming home with black eyes and broken noses; dying in their sleep? Being torn to pieces when they fall into the machines?' Finding the table he thumped it with his fist. 'D'you know, Mari Penderyn, how you stand in the fight? You carry a child in your belly—will you sit idly by in five years time and watch him go down Cwmglo Slaughterhouse on two shillings a week to give Dic another dram? God alive, woman —you're a mouse in a world of tigers, and that's how the churches, chapels and masters want you—a bloody mouse. But it's not for us, for things are going to change. And if we can't change them by my way—the recognition of the Union and lawful negotiation, then we'll do it Zimmerman's way, by blood.'

Sun said evenly: 'You will hang for it, ye know—they will find a scapegoat and hang him for it: in 1800, under Richard Crawshay they hanged Sam Hill; in 1816, under this Crawshay's father they hanged Aaron Williams for riot. And under this Crawshay they'll hang another, mark me . . .' She closed her eyes, gripping her hands.

Gideon said impatiently: 'They might hang a hundred of us, but what does it matter? Every year hundreds of us die in one way or another—pits and ironworks, child-fevers, the cholera. If a hundred of us were hanged for town drainage and another hundred for a piped water supply the price in death would be cheap, for the slums in this place are worse than the slums of Asia.' He levelled a finger in her direction. 'There's over thirty thousand people in this town and he hasn't provided a single school out of the profits; the accident rate is as bad as any town of The Top, and we don't enjoy even a hospital—there isn't even a stretcher at Ynys Works—did you know that? If Dic roasts his legs down there they'll cart him home on a board...'

Sun watched him: it was a new Gideon, one of violence, far removed from the gentle creature she had known. Feeling his way to the door, he opened it.

'By God, you've changed,' she said.

'And by God there's less in you than I thought. You're not worth a man like Dic Penderyn; you should have stuck to the likes of Billy Ugmore. Heavens above, woman—a few sticks of furniture...'

For a few moments Sun listened to him tapping his way down Ynys towards the canal bridge, then she ran across the room in sudden anger and slammed the door.

Later, when Billa Jam was putting her children to bed in Number Five, Mamie came up the stairs and there was peace in her face.

'Sun Penderyn's got her things back,' she said quietly. 'Gid must have bailed 'em out of the Court.'

'Ay, and you've got your Randy back. Can you tell me what this town would do without Gid Davies?' Billa smiled at the stars appearing over Merthyr.

'I don't know about that,' Mamie said.

Gideon walked slowly back to Cross. He was trying desperately to quell the emotion that threatened to consume him. It was astonishing, he thought, that on the journey from Taibach this girl had hardly impressed him, other than with an ability to lie. Slim and beautiful—in the coach at Gitos Farm on the night of the drovers—she had been in his arms and he had rejected her. Now another man's wife, shapeless with approaching childbirth, her womanhood called to him, and he hated his weakness. Reaching the door of Eighteen Cross he leaned momentarily on the railings, vainly trying to recapture the sounds of her, the smell of her hair; the memory of the time he saw her face after the onslaught of the Cefn Riders brought him to a trembling joy.

The door opened and Zimmerman appeared, concern on his broad face.

'Are you all right, Gideon?' he asked.

Gideon straightened. 'Of course, of course.'

19

ON Dowlais Top, violated by Sir John Guest who burned out the town, the wind wails among the slag-heaps like an old hag crying for her lost youth. But in summer the air is gentle in *The Fair Place*, which is the ancient name for Waun Hill, and here the parishes once met in the tap-rooms of the old Full Moon, which is as close to the stars as nearby Bedd y Gwyddel, the grave of the Irish Giant. Once the Ancient Britons lived here; near it the Prince of Brycheinog had his palace. Here, but later, walked Lady Charlotte Guest who translated the *Mabinogion*; she whose agent was the magnificent writer G. T. Clark ... Long, long before the creation of Penydarren, the cinder-pit the Homfrays and Thompsons jammed between Merthyr and Dowlais, there dwelt in these parts the gentle Tydfil who was slain on the spot where her church of glory now stands, once a celtic cross. This was the history, before the coming of the Magnificent Greed, that died under the bloodstained streets of Merthyr Parish: this was the Welsh culture that was sacrificed to hoard the millions of Hensol, Cyfarthfa and Caversham Park; that bought the art treasures of Canford Manor, the millionaire home of the Guests in England.

It was on the last day of May that the workers climbed the tracks and defiles from the crazy streets of Dowlais for the annual Waun Fair held up by the old Full Moon and Trecae Farm, and it is a wonder they had the strength, said Gideon, for even Crawshay said in *The Cambrian* that wages in Merthyr were low and that distress was prevalent among his workers.

'Think yourself lucky, girl,' said Dic, folding up the news-paper. 'Last week Jane Brace, aged twenty-seven, wife to Jem Brace of Epping, was sold in the market, pinioned and halt-ered, for the sum of two and sixpence by the Poor Law master, and he got sixpence interest.'

'Who bought her?' asked Sun, knitting. She closed her eyes to the pain of early labour.

'Doesn't say,' replied Dic, 'but no prosecution was offered by the Crown against her husband, Jem Brace, because it was discovered later that she was living in sin.'

Sun lowered the needles. 'Who with?'

'The fella who bought her,' said Dic, and got up, stretching and yawning.

'Poor little soul,' said Sun, at nothing.

'Ay—had she been a gentry bitch they would have been charged with slavery, rape and living on immoral earnings—but now you know your value—two and sixpence: you still tell me we don't need Reform?'

'I still say it'll lead ye to the devil. God, I'll make ye rub your heels together if I'm proved right—are ye off, then?'

'Ay.' He was standing by the door, grinning, and she thought that save for Gid Davies she had never seen a man as handsome.

'And you're taking Randy—keep him short o' trouble, now. Keep him away from Lewis and that new fella Will Johns.'

'I will, Sun.'

'He's ill, ye know—anything happens and Mamie'll never forgive you.'

Despite the obesity of her shape he thought she was beauti-ful; there was about her a new radiance now she had got her furniture back, and he was grateful to Gideon Davies. What with one thing and another he wondered how they had ever managed without Gideon Davies. As if reading him, Sun said:

'Have you heard that Dai End-On and Billy Jam are due back next door but one?' The child roamed within her and she gritted her teeth.

'No!'

'They're a pair of gorgeous old twisters—worse than your Union man from Bolton Lodge—when's he coming?'

'According to the Benefit, next October—staying at the Miners'. Talk is that he is meeting Crawshay for discussion.' He lit his pipe and blew out smoke in a cloud. 'Maybe if we get discussion we won't get riots—good fella that Bill Twiss, mind—got a good tongue.'

'Wouldn't trust him as far as I could heave him.'

'You're wrong, Sun—he's a good Union man.'

'So am I. He'll give ye Twiss by the time he's done with ye—you want to keep that bugger up in Bolton with the Authority Lodge.'

'Maybe so, maybe not—one thing's certain—all credit to Crawshay. Everybody's telling me he's set against a workers' Union, and here he is meeting a delegate.'

She said levelly, 'One day you people will realise that you can get a damned sight worse than the Crawshays though everybody's for skinning them. If you'd lived in Derry, like me, you'd have had the knackers off the Irish landlords.' Sweat suddenly beaded her forehead and she wiped it into her hair. She frowned up at him. 'Just you and Randy, is it ...?'

'Well, no,' Dic said uncertainly, 'we're supposed to be meeting Lewis Lewis at the Wellington.'

'More fool you ...' She thought: Please go, for God's sake go ...

'He got me a job hauling in Penderyn, didn't he?'

Sun nodded. 'All right, but keep Randy off the ale—and if you come back stinking of the stuff you won't hear the end of it.'

'*Whoopo!* Blutty hark at it! Goodbye, girl.' He opened the door.

'Aren't ye going to kiss me, then?'

He turned, grinning. 'And me smelling of ale?'

'Before you do,' she said, and put out her arms to him.

'My lovely,' he said.

'Oh, Dic!' she clung to him. The pain bloomed within her.

He whispered: 'When you're back to a reasonable shape, I

might even make love to ye.'

'That'll knock back your output.'

He looked at her as she smiled up from the chair. 'I'll pray you an easy time—but Mamie will be with you, won't she?'

'Good old Mamie...'

He kissed her again, and what began as a caress ended in heat and strength.

He winked at her as he went through the door, and she lay back in the chair with clenched eyes; never had she known such a pain. It had been on for the last five hours, now it was growing like an explosion within her, and she was glad Dic had gone. Getting out of the chair she went to the wall and knocked three times to Mrs. Solomon. Mamie Goldie came in moments.

'Are ye away, then?' she asked, her head around the door.

Sun stooped over the chair. 'God in heaven,' she said, 'what a pain!'

'Honeysuckle, you've only just started!' Mamie slapped her on the rump calling, 'Billa Jam, you there?'

'What you want?' the reply came faintly.

'Zeke called me—the Penderyn kid's away. Come on, come on...!'

'Can I help any?' asked Mrs. Zeke Solomon, peeping around the door.

'You've done your job—now get up on your stool again.' Mamie stood before Sun, hands on hips, grinning. 'I suppose you didn't happen to mention it to dear little Dico, did ye?'

'No point in spoiling his day,' said Sun.

'God help ye,' cried Billa, coming in with bowls and sheets. 'Eleven times I've been through this palaver, but Billy Jam is having the next one.'

'I told you to hop it!' cried Mamie, pushing Mrs. Solomon through the door. 'It's midwives we're after, not a blutty congregation.'

Just before midday a woman began to shriek in Ynys and the other women of the cottages, with their menfolk either charity-begging along the streets or attending the big meeting up on Waun Hill, paused to listen. The Spanish woman in

250

Number Ten, for instance, sat down in her kitchen and held her stomach, rocking to and fro. Miss Grieve, passing along Bridgefield Terrace in the pony and trap with Mr. Waxey Evans, heard it, too, and stiffened on the seat, her fingers clutched in her bombazine lap.

'You all right, my precious?' asked Waxey.

'Perfectly.'

Miss Blossom Thomas, daughter of Papa Thomas in Number One heard it as she was laying the table for dinner and gripped the cloth till the knuckles of her hands shone white, and when Sun cried again this woman raised her face, smiling, and said, 'Oh, it is wonderful, wonderful!'

'Can't ye stop that Penderyn wife braying?' shouted Papa Tomo Thomas. 'Worse than donkeys, some of the wives round by 'ere.'

'It is her first, it is her first,' said Blossom, with a light in her eyes.

'There there, me little love—give it hell for me,' said Billa, wiping the sweat from Sun's face.

Mrs. Duck Evans looking in the bins around Dynefor heard it, too. Lemuel Samuel standing in Bridge Street with coloured ribbons heard it also, and remembered Mavis who had died in shrieks that could have been bought for half a crown.

It is said that the new bride called Morvenna Doherty, married that very morning of Waun Fair heard it as well, for Sun is excellent in the vocals said Mamie, and right and proper too, for shouting do assist a birth: Ay, asserted Mrs. Zeke Solomon, these noisy labours may assist the brides, but it sets the fellas back on conjugal rights.

Bang bang on the back of Seven Ynysfach when all was silent.

'What you want, Zeke Solomon?' asked Mamie.

'Can I come in, Mrs. Goldie?' asked Zeke around the bedroom door.

'You're in,' said Billa, 'what can we do for ye?'

'You got that baby yet?' Her eyes were rimmed red in the plaster of her face.

Sun was lying on the bed as drained of blood as a corpse.

251

Billa, exhausted, was slumped in a chair surrounded by bowls and rags and buckets. Mamie, standing at the window, was letting down her hair.

'It's a boy,' said Billa, 'though God knows how. Jesus, I've never seen such a birth.'

'She's lucky to be alive,' said Mamie. 'Now goodbye, Zeke Solomon, we've had enough of ye.'

But Mrs. Zeke Solomon was scratching her ear. 'Queer, mind,' said she, 'how she kept on hollering for Gideon Davies. True, he's a friend of the family, but it's queer ...'

Mamie approached with business. 'You damned old faggot!' cried she. 'You ought to be ashamed o' yourself, making those insinuings—out, *out*!'

Very fast went Mrs. Zeke Solomon.

'The poor little soul,' said Mamie. The question was in her eyes.

'Don't you dare,' said Billa. 'Don't you dare, it ain't no business of ours, remember. She can shout for who she likes.'

Darkness fell on Waun Hill, and the workers gathered. With the fair over the crowd began to mass: they came from Dowlais, the puddlers and miners of Guest whose company truck shop was twenty per cent higher in prices at a time of depressed trade; they came from Merthyr under Crawshay, the iron-stone miners with their wages cut by forty per cent, the discharged puddlers; and they came from the shambles of Penydarren, the Alderman Thompson. But they did not only come from the three great works, but from Aberdare also, and Penderyn, Hirwaun and Abernant. In their thousands they came as if on a signal, arrowing in black snakes across the mountain tracks to the hill where their ancestors, the Iberian and Brythonic Welsh had met for centuries in debate. They came with black flags that signified their distress and white ones lettered with the words 'Reform in Parliament' and these petitioned their hope. And they gathered in a great mass with the falling of dusk, their numbers swelling as the torches sparked and waved, and there grew upon Waun Hill a glow of redness that was not the spilling of the hearths but the glowing fire of discontent that precedes rebellion. Agents were despatched at once by the masters to attend the meeting; spies for the Government finished their night meals and wandered carelessly from the surrounding inns and stared up at Waun Hill, and the hucksters ran. Gathering the spoils of the Fair Day, the smugglers of brandy and the poachers, the stall thieves, picaroons and pickpockets rove their paths through the oncoming workers and dived for the open plains. They blew out furnaces in Gelligaer to come, ragged and dishevelled; straight from pit and drift the labourers and technicians came in streams of ragged fire to the summit of Waun, their torches blazing; thronging into the stuffed tap-room of the old Full Moon, they hammered the teak for ale, or sat on the steps of the Waun Houses, spilling into the shippon of Trecae Farm. And the moon came out and blazed over the crooked streets of the iron towns far below them. John Petherick, the Cornish agent of Penydarren Works was there, Mr. Steffan Shenkins, the beadle of Coffin's Court was there, as was a young captain from Brecon Barracks, dressed as a collier, and these listened, and did not speak. A silence dropped like a curtain over the massed workers as Gideon climbed a rough platform on the highest point of Waun, and threw up his arms.

'Men of Glamorgan, workers of Monmouthshire, do you hear me?'

'Ay!' Oaths and shouts muttered into silence, and Gideon cried:

'We meet this day in the name of Reform, for it is only by Parliamentary Reform will we gain our just rights...'

Ragged shouts of applause and assent arose and the torches waved, and Gideon shouted in Welsh: 'The alternative is violence, and we do not seek violence, although our cause is just. It is a time of depressed trade and our wages are cut. But were our wages raised by Crawshay's forty per cent when times were good and he was selling at nigh six pounds a ton?'

The men roared encouragement, and he shouted: 'The anti-Truck Act of ten years back forbade the company shops, but Guest still keeps a Shop in Dowlais and charges twenty per cent over the odds for food. Did this employer cut his food

253

prices when the iron market was flourishing sixteen years back and a collier's wage was thirty-five shillings, compared with the twenty he gets now?'

The torches flared, and the men jostled for a better view of the speaker as Gideon raised his fist and yelled: 'They tell me Crawshay has eighty thousand tons of iron mine in stock-pile because of the state of the trade—are we to be penalised for bad management, for if this is management then give me anarchy! Must we live and die by the law of supply and demand? If the fortunes of the masters rise on the flourish, then they must expect to pay out in depression to the makers of their wealth, the people.' Gideon had got them going, and he knew it, stooping, his fist swinging within an inch of the nearest face. 'For the difference between masters and men is clear—depression of trade means for them smaller investment: for us it means food off the table and starvation for our families! How say you?'

They leaped to him. From the packed ranks came a great roar of agreement.

'Let him claim that he is stock-piling through generosity, to keep his men employed, and I will abandon the charge of bad management and substitute the claim that this is our entitlement, for if he stock-piled eight hundred thousand tons of iron he could still afford us decent wages and keep the bulk of the Cyfarthfa fortune intact! But more—he has begun to discharge us—were not eighty-four puddlers sent home six days back? Let the reduction of the wages of the iron-stone miners imposed but a week ago come out of the Stock Exchange investments which we have built. Let Cyfarthfa and Hirwaun be run at a loss, supported by the banking houses where these great fortunes lie, and which we have amassed for the Crawshays since the coming of the truly paternal Granfather Richard!'

They flung up their arms to this, stamping their feet on the mountain turf in a drumming like thunder, and Gideon cried: 'Churchman he might have been, ay, and autocratic—and he bowed his head when they hanged Sam Hill, God forgive him, but he was still one of us. And if he didn't open a school in the

254

place like Sara Hopkins did for Blaenafon, at least he gave us a Sunday one for the good of our souls and bought us corn when times were bad. But where is his absentee son this minute? Up in London—we never bloody see him. And all we get from the grandson in Cyfarthfa is "My Eye".'

They shouted with laughter at this, and Gideon cried: 'But "My Eye" doesn't quell us any more, because we are hungry— he admits we're distressed—read your *Cambrian*. But what does he do about it? He stands aside while the Court of Requests takes our furniture for debt. I advise you now—do not accept an abandoned stall except at an advanced rate—we'll teach him to drop wages. And go on parish relief if you can't get cheaper bread ...!'

'Talk sense!' shouted a miner. 'If we go on parish relief they'll send us back to our own parishes, and that will put us on the roads!'

'You've got to keep the roof!' bawled another.

'What happens come winter, me and six childer?'

Gideon yelled back: 'If you all apply for relief you'll break the shopkeepers by putting up the rates—can't ye see that? And if you squeeze their pockets they'll join you for Reform and not oppose you.'

'Don't shout at me about parish relief, man,' called a collier. 'I've had some, and the officers treated me and mine like dirt ... But Crawshay subscribes to support us—be fair!'

'Are ye with us or against us, blind man?'

'Are ye with this?' yelled Abednigo Jones, a fourteen-year-old five-footer as he climbed up behind Gideon with a flag bigger than himself. 'Can ye read, men, or shall I spell it out? Reform in Parliament, Reform in Parliament! And give three cheers for the House of Lords!'

Boos and groans accompanied this, and Zimmerman climbed up, too, and cried: 'Three cheers for the landed flunkies who sit in idleness in their palaces and watch your children starve—do you know the income of your Sailor King, or shall I tell you?'

'Send him back to Poland!' bawled a man.

'Or Moscow with the Tsar!'

255

'Give him a hearing!' shouted Lewis Lewis, scrambling up. 'For the people in his country are worse off than you!' Magnificent in brawny strength, his presence silenced them. 'Do you know the income of a belted earl, then? D'ye know the price of a bishop? For if you don't, then now's the chance to learn it, for some are getting more by larceny than Crawshay for making decent iron. Listen! The aristocracy of England derived their wealth from the spoils of the Reformation—and do ye know what the Reformation is, even? You don't, do you, because you're not educated. Do you realise that this man here has the facts and figures from the Black Book of Wade—have you heard of that, even—do you know any bloody thing? The salaries and incomes of the Dukes of Northumberland and Buccleugh and the Marquis of Stafford, Zim!'

'A million pounds a year,' said Zimmerman, and he straightened, pushing back his waving, bright hair. 'Foreigner, you call me? But I know more of your masters than you, you fools. In this year of 1831 there are three hundred members of the royal family—think what they cost you! You've got thirteen thousand nobility—though God only knows who made them noble, for they roister and fornicate away their lives—they cost you six million a year. Four hundred thousand gentry come next at fifty-two million, and up in Cardie the parish poor are getting three and sixpence a week for breaking on the roads.'

The crowd did not move; there was no sound save the hissing of the torches. Zimmerman's accent thickened, and he said: 'God alive, you're all half dead! Don't you care what is going on? Do you know that a lord receives the first hundred thousand of his income free of tax? That he pays no postage rate—nor do his recommended friends?' He drew himself up, dominant with his great size. 'If a peer obtains money by false pretences, can you imprison him? You cannot. Neither can you seize his estates for debt or render him bankrupt, for his property, like his person, is inviolate. But you can be sent to the hulks for a sixpenny fraud! He kills game at will, while you can be transported for treading on a partridge egg. You can be sentenced to the treadmill in the House of Correction for leaving your place of work without permission—the peer

256

can roam at will and never work at all, because you are keeping him. In the year ending last January there was a national revenue of fifty-five millions in tax—and nearly four fifths of this came from the industrial classes—*you*! Do you realise your importance, and power? Yet there is a nine hundred per cent tax on tobacco, but ale is cheaper for they want you drugged. Will you hear more, you stupid mules of Welsh, English and Irish, for if you want it I'll shout all night. Are bishops popular here? Are archbishops favoured by the mob? It would appear so, for you have two you do not need. In France they would receive a thousand pounds a year—in Britain you pay them twenty-seven thousand each. You have twenty-four bishops, you blind fools, who are worth six hundred a year each in Paris and over ten thousand pounds a year here. You have appointed twenty-eight deans, sixty archdeacons, three thousand aristocratic dignitaries of the Church and eight thousand incumbents—at a cost of ten millions. While a bishop I know is worth half a million and slept with Lady Hamilton, Nelson's favourite whore . . .'

Wild laughter broke out at this and Zimmerman raised his fist. 'You laugh, you stupid fools, when you should all be in tears: you drink when you should be sober, and you beg when you should demand! Aristocracy by acquirement is theft, and aristocracy by birth is feudal barbarism. You slave away your lives and beat the women who bore you in the temper of the rapacious thieves who rule you! "Receive the Holy Ghost," says the bishop, and then dresses up in riding habit, drinks a stirrup cup and leaps a five-barred gate. How can such a reveller claim the infallibility of the Holy Scriptures?' His voice rose to a cry. 'Listen! The times have passed when the lord is the despot of his domain—merchant prince or aristocrat—to tax, imprison, torture, rob, maltreat. Borough-English and Child-wit—Christ, but how can you know what these mean? —are monstrous usages of the past—the first night with the bride and a tax on women who gave birth without the squire's permission. Yet does not defilement exist in this town? Your furniture is distrained and you squat on your haunches and watch; in Poland, to which you would send me, that Court of Requests would not stand another twenty-four hours. You are to be soon driven to the polls to vote as you are instructed or go on the black list: you live in slums comparable with Asia, you have no hospitals or schools provided; the beauty of your women is being sullied by labour, the growth of your children stunted. The treatment of the parish poor by appointed officers in Merthyr parish is a public scandal and yet you tolerate it—you tolerate anything, because you are a broken people ...!'

'Mind that tongue, foreigner!' yelled a Welsh collier.

'And you your neck!' bawled Zimmerman, 'before I come down there and break it ...'

'You take us to violence and they'll bring the Military in, remember!'

'Then let them come, and use it to prove your manhood if not your nationality, for the Welsh, in my history, have never gone short on a fight. And do not talk to me of violence, my friend, for violence is the profession of good government. From the start of the slave trade until this day theirs has been the law of the whip and bludgeon—their revenge in Tudor times the bloodstained rack and in modern times the art of hanging, drawing and quartering—do you know they're bringing back the Anatomy Bill? Once more the turrets of London Bridge will be littered with the filth of decomposing limbs to satisfy a royal decree.'

'That is sedition,' said a man.

'And it is I who state it! You are the sheep-led tools who fly from the musket when you should be the liberators of a land born to be free! Lewis Lewis!'

'Ay, Zim.'

'Bring the calf.'

It began to rain then, breezing into the faces of the staring crowd; men previously aware, now seemingly hypnotised by Zimmerman's oratory. And the raindrops hissed on the flaring torches so that a drift of steam arose, rising from the white faces as if they were on fire. The mob jostled for better position as Zimmerman took in his hands a new-born calf and raised it high above his head, and he cried in the silence:

'See here this calf which will soon be sacrificed. And in its blood I will wash my hands; I tell you this, if we do not gain our ends by just means, then you will take to violence, and the white flag of Reform that flies here tonight we will stain red, as it was stained in the *Champ de Mars* massacre of forty years ago.'

All was silent then, save for the hissing of the rain and the faint bellowing, in its struggles, of the new-born calf.

And there came from the crowd then one called Tomos Glyn Cothi; bearded and grizzled with age was he and Lewis Lewis and Dic Penderyn helped him up on to the platform and he cried:

'Know me, you of the Welsh? Let us continue the talk in our tongue lest Cornish agents and London spies be among us. Have I not always charged you to fight against those who oppress us—in the name of God? Did I not sing you revolutionary songs from the bars of Carmarthen gaol? Now I say, take care!' He raised his skinny hands upwards and shouted above the growing clamour. 'Have I not, in company with Taliesin Williams preached the gospels of the great Orator Hunt, the advantages of Free Trade, and begged you to spread your activities among the populations of Lancashire, Yorkshire, Staffordshire and the labourers of the Forest of Dean? You who know me can vouch for my true radicalism. Was it not I who distributed to you the Welsh translations of Cobbett's *Twopenny Trash*? And pinned to your streets the placards of the Rotunda Radicals which denounce oppression and the misery of the poor? Men, it is such as I—so hear me—who, with the Unitarians of Heolgerrig and Georgetown, are the true spiritual advisers of the New Movements which hold the seeds of Moral Force Chartism, your only hope of freedom. You hear me?'

'They can hear you in bloody Swansea, man!' shouted one.

'Take him out of the pulpit, somebody!'

'Blutty past it, he is, and he will have us on our knees!'

The old minister shouted while they pulled at his clothes in laughter, 'You are the greatest force of men alive today, because you have a just cause. But is there Truck in Merthyr? There is not, for the master of that town is serving you in his way. Do not be swayed by any force of argument save the *facts*! In the name of God I beg you not to listen to men of violence, for they will use you to their ends and then depart, and your agony will be that of the Cross...'

The torches waved and sparkled and there rose about the old man a growing clamour, but this he pierced with his cry, 'I beg you—stay sober and *think*. Do not act while drunk with ale and power, for the iron masters are not your true enemies —the foreigner here is right!' He swung around, pointing into Zimmerman's face. 'Your enemies are not Guest and Crawshay—harsh these might be, think you, but these are your employers... and you do not do them justice!'

Bawls and jeers broke about him, but he shouted: 'This is a world slump in trade—would you break their banking houses? Do this, you fools, and you will starve! No, men—your enemies are the hereditary enemies; the pimps and ponces of the great estates and their hundred thousand wrangling lawyers. They patronise a Church Established, wage unnecessary wars, create employment for useless sons in the army and navy, conquer and retain useless colonies for the high office of half-wits in plumed hats, pay unmerited pensions to relatives in useless posts in the royal household, the Admiralty and the courts of law.' His voice rose to a shriek, and they were silenced by his vehemence. 'They live in a profusion of luxury— maintained by those who live in misery—but would you compare William Crawshay with the likes of these? Crawshay *works*! You hear me?—like you, he works. If you want blood then march on London in the bigger scheme, and tear these parasites from high office, but do not cut the tap-roots of your own employment...!' His last words faded into silence as men mounted the platform and pulled the old man down, but still he shouted and again they heard him. 'Moral justice will be served only by moral force. Does not your master support the Bill of Reform? Get your reform first, and afterwards bargain for better wages on the boards of a true democracy... If this fails, fight then—and fight like tigers!'

Strangely, hearing this voice coming from a mouth unseen, the men grew to quiet again, and Tomos Glyn Cothi sank down on the steps of the platform and wiped his bearded face with the back of his hand, and before him Dic Penderyn knelt in the crush of men.

'Are you all right, old man?'

'Ay.' The minister sighed and stared at the sky and there was in him a beauty, for his eyes were good despite the years.

'Shall I fetch ye a drink, Minister?'

Cothi smiled and put out his hand, touching Dic's face with the tips of his fingers.

'My God,' said Cothi, 'they are bound for the devil. But think of the challenge!' His fingers moved over Dic's features, resting on his lips. 'Just fancy being young at a time like this.'

And about them the mob was growing in anger; oaths and curses broke from the ranks of swaying men and Abednigo Jones, the boy, leaped on to the platform and raised his white flag which shouted for Reform, and he was joined by another lad, one named Willie Taibach who was shrieking at the sky, and together they chanted:

'Reform, Reform, Reform, Reform . . .!'

The word was taken up then, bellowed from thousands of throats and ceased only when Lewis Lewis yelled:

'Ay, Reform, Reform, but first the bloody furniture! Who's with me for Coffin's Court?'

'And burn it to the ground!'

'God help them,' said old Tomos Glyn Cothi.

Dic and Gideon helped the old man to his feet and there beat about them a great tumult, and from this disorder Tom Llewellyn, a Cyfarthfa miner, shouted:

'All who oppose Reform should be hanged on the gallows! And I will be the first man to do the hanging, free of expense, you hear me?'

'Ay ay!'

He scrambled on to the platform. 'Who's for a trip to Aberdare to wring the neck of Fothergill, the master? And loot his bloody truck shop—he who has publicly claimed that Crawshay is paying his men too much?'

They brandished their torches and mandrels, and flocked about him madly.

'By God, we'll hang him if he doesn't retract!' He quietened them with a yell of command, a natural leader risen from the ranks. 'Right you—a thousand men with me and we march on Aberdare—there the workers will join us. Lewis—where's Lewis Lewis?'

'By 'ere, Tom, lad!'

'Tomorrow lead the rest of them and burn Coffin's Court!'

They began to chant, swayed by his vehemence: 'Coffin's Court! Coffin's Court! Coffin's Court!'

And they streamed down the mountainside, with the Llewellyn contingent making west in a red stream for Aberdare. The night grew to quiet. At the platform Gideon pulled Zimmerman aside from a clutch of men.

'It went well,' said he, 'but it was not what I intended—neither is it what the London Association intended. Old Tomos Cothi is right, it is much too early—soon it will become uncontrollable.'

Zimmerman lit his pipe in his cupped hands. 'It is quite excellent.'

Gideon stared in his blindness. 'But they will riot—you have driven them into riot—don't you care what happens to these people?'

'Not particularly,' said Zimmerman.

20

'Coffin's Court! Coffin's Court!'

The chant thundered in the streets, and people came spilling out of their houses and throwing up the windows to the growing mob.

'What is happening, Blossom?' demanded Papa Tomo Thomas of One Ynys, and he sat up in bed. 'What the blutty hell is happening?'

'God save us!' cried she, tottering, 'it is a riot.'

'If it's a riot then I'm in it—what are they rioting for?'

'God knows!' cried Blossom, quivering. 'God knows!'

He eased himself out of bed. 'Fetch me the crutches, woman, and pull yourself together—heaven preserve me from the apron politicians.' He poked a stick through the window. 'Right you, lads, slow down, I'm coming!'

The sun bathed the June morning in precious smells of agents' simmering bacon. William Crawshay paused at his breakfast in Cyfarthfa Castle and turned his head, listening: Merve Jam opened great dark eyes at the stained ceiling in Number Five; the Spanish woman in the Row was already up, sharpening a knife on the copper. And down the alleys of Georgetown and Williamstown came the miners and colliers, the ladlers and puddlers and ballers, the washerwomen and coal-croppers.

They were spilling over the doorsteps down by St. Tydfil's, banging on pails up Duke and kicking tin cans down Graham, and the mob grew. Led by Lewis Lewis they came in a wave up Bridge Street and met the crowds from Jackson's and Quarry head on.

'What is that, Annie?' asked Megsie Lloyd in the bed in the cellar of the Crown, and Annie Hewers sat closer and wiped the blood from her mouth.

'It is nothing, it is nothing. You are dreaming, my lovely.'

Down Tramroadside came the rabble waving brooms and copper-sticks, and the Irish from Fishpond mostly had pokers, according to Sid Blump who went to earth in the graveyard, and Shan Shonko and Old Wag were going with their skirts up for speed down Swan Street followed by a crowd like the French Revolution.

'Coffin's Court! Coffin's Court!'

'Dear me, what is all the noise, Mrs. Taibach?' asked Miss Milly Thrush, coming up into the bedroom, and Mrs. Taibach opened bleary eyes, sat up and put on her wig, and her large breasts faltered under the low-necked night-dress till covered by six pounds of curls like black tallow.

'What's that you say?'

'The Devils of Gehenna are after us!' Miss Thrush gathered her petticoat against her throat as if somebody was down it. 'Listen!'

'Diawch!' ejaculated Mrs. Taibach. 'It's a riot,' and she waved out fat legs and went to the window, staring out at the Iron Bridge. *'Diawch!'*

For Mamie Goldie and Billa Jam were going over the Taff like runaway drams with Asa and Amos after them, Merve and Saul, Caleb and Caradoc, Abel and Aaron and Abiah carrying the chamber, and behind them came the Nipper Tandy gang off shift from the Tasker drainage—Belcher and Big Bonce, Skin-Crone and Godiva, top bare as usual, with Blackbird bringing up the rear and yelling for them to stop.

'Upon my soul!' ejaculated Mrs. Taibach. 'A riot it is— thank God the likes of us don't get mixed with the lower classes.'

'Willie isn't in, mind,' said Milly Thrush, and Mrs. Taibach swung to the bed.

'Uffern Dan!' She leaped as if lifted by a whip of scorpions, staring at the empty pillow.

'Heard him leave the house before light,' whispered Milly.

Mrs. Taibach sank on to the bed, fanning.

'Pray compose yourself, dear lady,' whispered Miss Thrush.

'I will, my girl, don't you worry! I'll have the skin from his backside if he's mixing with trash!' She sighed. 'Headstrong and wilful as a spring ram, he is!'

'Oh, dear. Perhaps I ought to go and see Gideon . . .'

'That anarchist? It's the likes of him and that Mr. Note that has got us into this revolutionary state.' She glared, baleful and Miss Thrush shrank. 'I'd gibbet the lot of them if I had my way—drawin' and quartering 'd be too good for 'em. Up the King and down with the labouring classes, I say.' She rocked herself in grief and blunt, surly anger and her great breasts swung to the blasts of a hunting horn coming out of the Popi Davey where Shoni Sgubor Fawr, the informer, was breezing into the sunlit morning with his fighters and molls. The streets were filling with the clamour of the mob, and Merthyr trembled to its thunder. But Blind Dick the singer and Hugh Pughe his friend, the harpist, were going with uplifted smiles for the Abergavenny Eisteddfod on their old pit pony, clip-clopping over Iron Bridge with the sun on their faces, oblivious to the commotion about them. Percy Bottom Note, sheltering in the coke ovens of Cyfarthfa bank, raised red-rimmed eyes to the sun and retreated back to warmth and the choking fumes: Lemuel Samuel beside him slept on under his counterpane of rags, but his fingers were moving in the hair of one called Mavis, who shared his dreams. Molly Caulara stood at the window of her Popi Davey lodgings and looked out on Bridge Street where the crowds were marching, and vainly she searched for Dic Penderyn. Vaguely, she wondered if he was at home with his wife, for whom her loins still ached, for it had been a bad labour—all the previous evening with the men up on Waun Hill she had listened to Sun crying. Now, faintly she heard the wail of a baby, and smiled. Above the snores of the man in the bed she heard this and smiled, wondering if it was Dic's. Now there came from the Taff a dull roar of the mob and she shivered in the early sunlight, drawing her shawl closer about her bare shoulders. Ned Tranter stirred in the bed and opened his eyes.

'What you doing, Caulara?'

'Just looking. There's a crowd down Bridge Street, and...'

'You come back in here.'

Dr. William Price was trotting down Pontmorlais in his goat cart, wearing the ceremonial dress of the Druidic Feast, the flowing white robes denoting purity of belief in the great Hu and the fox-skin on his head, tails flying, the elemental blessing of the earth: sunlight flashed on the bardic sword he held high, and Willie Taibach saw him coming while in the act of rifling potatoes from the shop of Evans Grocer and opened his shoulders and got the goat with a swede; his following salvo of potatoes missed the bard by inches. Very fast went the bardic cart round the corner of High Street, pelted by everything throwable since the start of Creation, for we have enough trouble with agents and politicians without having to put up with blutty druids at a time like this. All down Thomas Street and in Market Yard, the shopkeepers were battening down, but some got up too late. Andrew Marsden the draper lost three sets of silken drawers, and fifteen chemises were going like sails down to Gwern and Twynpin, and the conserves and loaves were rolling up Dynefor, while Abbott the barber was shaving and lathering free and Sid Blump lying back with his feet up smoking a cigar. Locked and barred were the doors of the taverns till confiscated by mob contingents in the name of the thirsty poor, and best home-brew was flowing down Plymouth Street in six inch waves, said Jump Jackson in tears. But there was little looting, said Mamie Goldie, only organised deductions, for we do not want the riot to get a bad name. But the Three Horseshoes lost two pins of burgundy and six flasks of gin, and it is a blutty scandal to say Papa Tomo has them under the bed, said Billa, for the old lad hasn't walked in years. The starving were flooding out of the culverts and cellars and the Irish marched down from Pontmorlais in a mob, forcing open the stalls and shops and handing out food, all very orderly, taking from the rich and giving to the poor, and Old Wag was seen going up Duke with two sides of mutton.

'Spots on your belly, my little lovely,' said Papa Tomo in Number One Ynys, and he tipped the bottle at the ceiling.

'Oh, Dada!' sobbed Blossom, in tears, clutching her rag doll.

Annie Hewers ran out of the cellar of the Crown, took two loaves that were lying in the gutter, and dashed back again to Megsie: Mrs. Duck Evans was seen with a new shirt for Mr. E., and down to thirteen collars he is, poor soul, said she; Mrs. Penderyn, the mother of Dic, took six pounds of potatoes off the stall of Mr. Onions in the market, and put down a penny as if it was gold. And Joseph Coffin cried from the window of his house: 'I will not rest until you are under lock and key!'

'Get your head in, you old bastard!' shouted Lewis. 'Dic, you there, mate?' And he led the rioters into the yard of Coffin's Court.

'Ay, man!'

'Run around the back and heave some cinders through the windows—they tell me there isn't a nail in the place, by God it should flare.'

Dic seized Randy's arm. 'Come on, man, come on!' and he towed him through the crowd down Tramroadside. Here he held out a handful of stones, but Randy only stared at them. Dic cried: 'Look, fella—are you in with us or not? Make up your mind ...!'

But Randy did not really see him. He was looking above Dic's head towards Adulum Fields and Blod. Dick shook him, shouting into his face, but Randy's expression did not change.

'Right, lad, sit by here,' said Dic, and took stones and pelted the court windows. Glass tinkled, bringing the mob in the front to momentary silence, then into renewed roaring as the shattering of glass rose to a crescendo in the hail of stones. Running round the front, Dic joined Lewis Lewis and a dozen others with a timber battering ram, charging the heavy doors of the court, staving in the panels first, then bringing up the bolts and hasps in splintering crashes; the doors went flat, and they were sprawling full length. Sticks and cudgels waved as a forest as the colliers streamed in, and the voice of Lewis rose above the shouts of triumph:

'The records first, lads—then the furniture. By God, we'll give him Coffin. In, *in*!' A giant in strength and purpose, he pulled them past him, yelling, 'Wil Goff, Wil Goff, are ye here?'

'Here, Lewis!' shouted Wil, jumping to heighten himself in the mob.

'Have you a list of the people's furniture distrained—the one you read at Tafern Uchaf?'

'I have, man!'

'Then hand back goods to every man who lost them!'

They were fighting to climb the narrow stairs to the loft and their furniture, they were overturning chairs and tables in the storerooms and dragging out beds. Tom Vaughan's *Ascent of Venus* was on its way up Court Street already and Merve Jam, escaped from Billa, was flying away under the *Whipping in the Temple*, and the Irish streaming out of the cellars of Pontmorlais came in especially for mattresses. Robert Jones's bed and kitchen table were carried out in whoops and his grancher's armchair was passed over the heads of the cheering men —special, this armchair, for the old man bought it in Canton when a seaman on the China Run.

'One chest of drawers, a bed, chairs and pictures!' shouted Lewis Lewis above the din. 'And I'm not leaving here till I get them—by God, I'm having the roof off this hell when I do.'

'You'll not find them here, man,' cried Wil Goff, reading from a ledger. 'Auctioned to Williams Grocer, it says . . .'

'I know, but have they been carted?' Lewis twisted in the roaring crowd.

'Collected by David Williams yesterday afternoon.'

Lewis fought a path into the yard. 'High Street, then—and collect it off David Williams—who's with me?'

'Lead the way!' A dozen gathered about him; another dozen ran through the yard for the house of Mary Phillips, for the two china dogs belonging to Bob Rees of Islyn. In all directions groups of men were running now, shouted on by Wil Goff who was calling out the names of people who had bought their furniture, and in the hubbub Tom Llewellyn arrived from Aberdare followed by his men, and he waved a paper high, shouting, 'Fothergill retracted, Fothergill signed a statement!' and his voice was drowned in thunderous applause.

Willie Taibach and Merve Jam were carrying out the records and documents and flinging them into the road. The flames leaped up, black smoke began to billow over Merthyr and pages of debts were blowing down the road to Maerdy Garden, pursued by pit-lads and torn to pieces. And at that moment Joseph Coffin put his head out of his window, shouting, 'All right, burn them, burn them! There's another set in here!'

'Is that a fact?' asked Tom Llewellyn, rubbing his chin.

'Well, I never!' said someone.

'Is he light in the head—telling us that?' asked Dick Llaw-Haearn. 'Did ye hear that, Row Thomas?' And Rowland Thomas, who later died, stooped and picked up a stone and Coffin's head disappeared and the window slammed down.

'After him,' said Abednigo, and he shouted for Willie Taibach. 'I say burn his lot, too.'

'One thing's sure,' said Dic, 'you'll always have debts while one set lasts!' and they ran. Led by Tom Llewellyn, they barged down the door, and as they came in the front, Coffin and his family went out of the back and up Court Street in their nightshirts. Storming into Coffin's house they flung out the copies of the debts and these they burned, too, piling out the furniture to add to the flames. And they swept up the stairs in hatred, stripping the paper off the walls, levering off the doors and breaking out the windows, then they set fire to the house. Many things happened which were not recorded, such as two stipendiary magistrates doing bottoms into the Taff and Shoni Crydd, James Abbott and two other special constables going up to Adulum Fields with a mob of Irish behind them; and Betsy Paul, Dick of the Iron Hand's mate, chased Mr. Steffan Shenkins up Bunker's Hill with a pair of scissors, threatening to bring him back two stones lighter, but this kind of behaviour do tend to drop the tone of the place, said Billa, mind, for a man's privates are entitled to respect, especially Mr. Steffan Shenkins'. The Riot Act was read outside the shop of Tom Lewis and the shopkeepers were cramming the entrance to the Talbot and Castle Inns, begging for military protection. The Nipper Tandy gang rigged themselves out in gentry finery, with Lady Godiva prancing back to the culverts in silk and peacock feathers, and Big Bonce and Belcher were done up to the nines in bombazine suits and grey tall hats, doffing them left and right to the neighbours hanging like beans on Iron Bridge. Carts and gambos were cramming the streets as impounded furniture was returned to its original owners. The sun blazed through the smoke of Coffin's house, drifting in a black pall over Merthyr.

Merve Jam, Billa's eldest, went up to the front door of Miss Sara Grieve and hit it with his boot to shift its hinges, and behind him came Abednigo Jones carrying his white flag of Reform and after that a crowd like the barricades of Paris. Nervously, Mr. Waxey Evans peered round the chain.

'Open up, Waxey,' demanded Merve. 'You remember me?'

'Unfortunately, my wife is indisposed...' said Waxey, white.

'No odds to that—do you remember me? I'm the fella you filled with buckshot...'

'It was a dreadful thing to do, mind,' said Abednigo.

'Absolutely blutty dreadful,' said Willie Taibach.

Waxey faltered, his hand to his heart, and Merve cried:

'Ianto House, eh? Doing pretty well marrying Sara Grieve, eh, Waxey? Has she got a picture of a mother and a baby?'

'Why, yes!' Perceptibly, Waxey brightened. 'The baby Jesus?'

'Bring it here,' said Willie Taibach, pushing to the front.

The picture changed hands with alacrity in glares and ingratiating smiles and Merve said: 'Next time you buy from Coffin's auction we'll have this place down, Waxey Evans—never mind blutty pictures—understand?'

'Yes, sir,' said Waxey.

After they had marched away Waxey lay against the door on trembling legs.

'Oh, my God,' he whispered.

From the hall he entered the drawing-room where candles were guttering on the drawn curtains, casting weird images on the coffin of polished oak wherein lay Miss Grieve with closed eyes in a perfumed intonation of death in red roses, and her will, recently read, lay on the table beside her.

'Oh, certainly,' whispered Waxey, 'I will have to get out of Merthyr.'

For, although the drains had been flushed out with caustic soda, the lotions and potions previously destroyed and a death certificate issued without thought of an inquest, it would be an act of God if one was convened by a People's Court, and the body examined for spirits of salts ...

Bending he kissed her face in all its marble rigidity.

'You shall have Ianto House and I the six thousand—draw it from Brecon Bank first thing in the morning; Australia, Africa—China, even—who knows? And you'll be in good company with Ianto up in Vaynor.'

Bowing, he shut the door.

A mouse watched him from a crack in the skirting as he went upstairs.

'*Caws gyda bara! Caws gyda bara!* Cheese with bread! *Caws gyda bara!*'

The cry for food thundered up from the milling crowds. The cobbles of Merthyr echoed to the boots of tramping men and women, and they went in a long procession around the town with their flags and banners; down High and up Bridge Street and along to the Castle Inn where the shopkeepers were sheltering; armed with picks, they went, with mandrels and rusted scythes, old flint-muskets pulled from the walls, old swords stolen from gentry museums: tramp, tramp, *tramp*.

'Cheese with bread! Cheese with bread!' They flocked down from Dowlais and Penydarren, they came running in from the nearby towns of Tredegar and Hirwaun, they marched in from Abercynon. And Sun Penderyn raised herself in the bed and covered the face of her suckling boy. The door slamed downstairs.

'That you, Dic?' But she knew it was not Dic.

Tap tap on the bedroom door, and she took a deep breath.

'Come in,' she said.

'It's only me,' said Gwen, Dic's sister.

'He isn't back yet,' said Sun.

'Morgan is downstairs, can I bring him up?'

'Do ye have to?'

'Please, Sun, listen to him—it's for Dic's sake. Has he been back?'

'Ay, once—just to see the baby. Now he's away again with the men.'

'Is he in his right senses?' asked Gwen, screwing at her hands.

Marriage to the fire and brimstone Morgan Howells, the big Newport Calvinistic, had done nothing to rob this woman of her beauty, thought Sun. She said, bitterly:

'Are any of them in their right senses? *Caws gyda bara*—one would think the whole place was starving—do you know that not a single man of those Lodge leaders is out of work? There's Lewis mining at Penydarren—eight shillin' a week, true, but at least he's working—Tom Llewellyn is still puddling for Crawshay on top rates ... *Duw Duw*, it makes me sick!'

'We've got to protect him, Sun,' said Gwen, sitting on the bed. 'Won't ye let Morgan come up?'

'Don't bother yourself, he's in.' Sun lowered her eyes from the man in the doorway, and buttoned her nightdress.

'Congratulations on the birth of your son, Mrs. Penderyn,' said Howells, simply.

'Thanks. When he's of age I'll bring him over to Hope for an official casting out. And ye can rave and rant against the Benefits and Unions, though we'll have a dozen of those before he's twenty-one.'

Morgan Howells said simply: 'It is happening as I prophesied, it is all coming to pass. Would ye have me serve a god of greed, as your man?' He drew himself up, as if containing with an effort the burning spirit within him. 'Ye realise he's in danger, don't you?'

'Don't tell me that, man—I've been living with it.'

'His companions will lead him to the fire.' The minister entered the bedroom. 'Were I not Gwen's husband I would now be in Newport caring for my people in Hope Chapel. You know sedition was talked on Waun Hill, at the meeting?'

Sun raised her shadowed eyes to him; she had been stitched by the works surgeon and the pain in her loins was a little fire that blazed with every breath. Gwen stiffened as the door slammed downstairs; heavy boots were coming up the stairs two at a time.

'Here he comes,' said Sun, 'you can explain it to him yourself.'

Dic ran into the room, and paused, eyeing Morgan Howells. 'What's going on?' he demanded.

'The big minister's just explaining about sedition.'

'The consequences of sedition, to be accurate,' said Howells.

'Dic, *please*,' whispered Gwen.

'Ay,' said Howells, 'you can rant your Union talk, you can spout your Benefit politics and threaten the masters of the town. But when you carry talk of Reform to the very gates of St. James's, the King is interested.'

'And about time, isn't it? God, we pay him enough.'

'Petherick's report is already on its way to London, did you know this?'

'Get out, the pair of you.'

Morgan Howells said: 'I beg you to listen, not for me, not even for your sister, but the sake of this woman and the son she has borne you. This riot, Penderyn, will not be contained within the boundaries of this town—it will spread its fingers to every corner of Wales. The Military have already been called out, do you know this? The Brecon Highlanders are on the march. A court has been rifled, its documents burned; the house of Coffin has been put to the torch, magistrates insulted and threatened. The houses of bailiffs have been ransacked, the possessions of decent people carted on exhibition through the town...'

'Decent people! Auction thieves, you mean!'

'I shall not bandy words on it, there is not time. Did not one of your own leaders on Waun Hill warn that Melbourne seeks the opportunity to strike at Unionism—where better than in Wales? The forces of law and order have been destroyed, greed and violence is on the streets. And, mark me, for this a

273

scapegoat will be found, and he will be a leader. I have a position of importance in the community of Newport...'

'And that's the bother of it, eh?' Dic shouted. 'You're here to keep the family respectable, man—you're not worried about the people in the street!'

'That isn't fair, Dic,' said Gwen, softly.

'I have a position of importance,' continued the minister, unperturbed, 'but I have no influence in this town, least of all in support of people who never see the inside of a chapel. If trouble comes, Penderyn, you face it alone.'

Faintly came the chanting of the mob as it marched up Bridge Street.

'Alone,' said Gwen, 'for Sun is coming back with us to Newport. Did you see Mr. Evans downstairs in the trap?'

Slowly, Dic turned and stared at Sun. 'You ... you're leaving?'

'What else do you expect me to do, man—sit here until the Military come for you?'

'It's the chance we take, all of us,' said he.

'Ay, for you, but not for me—I've the baby to think of. You're all mad, mad!'

'By Christ,' said Dic, going to the window, 'a man is best alone than mixing with friends and relations.' He swung round to her. 'Give us another couple of days and this thing will be over—it's only a wage increase we're after, ye know ... we're not killing anybody.'

'Crawshay will grant no wage increases under threat of force, he has already said so,' remarked Howells.

'Help me get me things, Gwen,' said Sun, pushing back the bedclothes.

They did not speak more for the mob had changed direction and was coming up to Georgetown: over the canal bridge it came in a waving of sticks and cudgels, led by Abednigo Jones with his white flag of Reform and Merve Jam blowing on a hunting horn; and they thronged along the towpath and Dynefor Street, making for the Cyfarthfa Works; under the windows of Ynys they went in yells and shouts, with Mamie and Billa in the van and the children dancing around them, and

274

Mrs. Zeke Solomon got off her chair and went under the bed, and they piled into the Three Horseshoes and hammered the counter for ale. In hundreds they came, like a black finger of rags, curving over the Iron Bridge by the Popi Davey and thrusting for Jackson's and Quarry on a visit to the castle where Crawshay was watching from his look-out turret. Dic turned from the window as the stragglers went past.

'What do ye want of me, Sun?'

'Just this, boy,' said Gwen. 'Go with Mr. Evans of Penrhiw; we brought him especially, for he knows Aberdare mountains like his hand—go with him to the mountain for the next three days, until the trouble's settled; his brother's deacon of Scion—remember? This makes it respectable, and it's Morgan's idea ...'

'If I had to choose between respectability and Lewis Lewis, I know who I'd choose.'

'That's not the choice,' said Sun, 'for I've had enough. It's between Lewis Lewis and us, and if you don't want us, we're off.'

Dic ran his fingers through his hair. He was thinking of Zimmerman and Twiss of the Authority Lodge; he remembered the words of Gideon, and the aged Tomos Glyn Cothi. Up at Waun that very moment there was a meeting of a council of war; that day Lewis Lewis had talked of fleshing swords to the hilt and ambushing the Brecon Highlanders, and he did not altogether trust Lewis Lewis: and Tom Llewellyn, the respected, had vanished.

'I've told ye before,' said Sun, shaking out her petticoats, 'and I tell ye again—you won't see 'em for dust when the bayonets come out.' She turned to the minister. 'Would you mind removing yourself while I get meself dressed, your worship?'

'Come, Morgan,' said Gwen, and took him to the door. The baby cried in gusty breath, fists waving.

Dic said: 'Sun, will you wait while I slip up to see Gid Davies?'

'Can't ye think for yourself, then?'

She thought he looked handsome standing there in his blue

275

coat and trews; it was a sort of ragged strength by which she would remember him.

'Will ye?'

Despite his strength there was in him a weakness, and she pitied him.

'Give ye ten minutes,' said Sun and began to comb her hair.

'And you'll stay if I go with this fella Evans?'

'I will.'

'For three days?'

'Four,' said Sun.

After Dic had gone Gwen came back. Sun lowered the comb. 'You've taken his soul, ye realise that? If he goes with Evans he'll never be able to look at his mates again.'

'But he'll be alive,' said Gwen.

Tap tap on the door of One Ynys, but Miss Blossom Thomas did not hear: sobbing in a disarray of straggling hair and wetness was she, and Papa Tomo well into his third flask of blue ruin and roaring his sea-shanties along the coast of Ushant full forty fathoms deep, and the language coming up was enough to take the varnish off the pews of the Ebenezer.

Tap tap on the back now; scurrying footsteps. Flogged by the cat of Papa's dissipation, keel-hauled and scuppered by tales of Annie Wong Lee of Hong Kong and an opium dream in Malaya, Miss Blossom Thomas peeped around the door of the back in distress, and every neighbour in the Row was either slamming the doors or pushing shut the windows as Papa's profanity blasted up the canal to Dynefor.

Then Blossom Thomas ceased to weep. Kneeling on the doorstep, smiling through her tears, she picked up her picture and rocked it against her; one of a woman tending a baby, and his name was Jesus.

21

On the common land of Hirwaun the farms and cottages were being turned into strong-points and the area into an armed camp. Gangs of men were coming in from Breconshire and Glamorgan, bringing with them weapons obtained from raided houses; Black flags were rising on high mounds and hills. Furnaces were blown out in Risca, coal shafts jammed and technicians forced away in Dowlais and Penydarren; the rebel army grew in numbers, the long black columns tramping over the mountains, an army of the respected furnace trades—the ballers and puddlers, shearers and blenders coming to join the colliers and miners of the pits, drifts and levels. They came marching to the beat of a drum or whistle, they came singly and in groups; armed with the trade tools, rusted swords and tappers, ancient pistols and fire-locks, they came from the Top Towns and advanced on Merthyr; they despatched outriders to distant places, they called on their Lodges and Benefits and scarecrow Unions scarcely born. And they gathered at a place north of Aberdare, following their instinct for the mass meeting, soon to be a part of their lives. They came from the darkness of a hidden people, into sunlight; an ancient race stepping over the shadowed threshold into a new and terrible awareness; they did not speak of this, they could not have explained it, but they knew that their history had begun. Flinging off the immaturity of centuries, they gathered, at dusk, on the lonely heath, and on a crag in that silent place a man was standing, and his name, for want of one that day, was John the Racer. In his hand was a knife and at his feet lay a calf tethered for sacrifice. About him were gathered men with great white flags, and one was Abednigo Jones, the boy: young men or boys mainly carried these flags, for another was Willie Taibach and yet another was Mervyn, the son of Billa.

'Bring the flags!'

The boys moved forward from the ranks of men, and these numbered thousands, and their breath was steaming in the stillness.

'Who with the basin?' cried the man, and a child moved forward with one in his hands.

'And one has the loaf of bread to be impaled?'

The wind whispered over the mountain and John the Racer cried, the knife held high, 'Let us announce this martial law! Let this flag fly in the name of the Welsh, as it flew for the French, our comrades in suffering under the 1791 massacre! Let this flag, when stained with blood, rise for the first time in Britain as a signal against authority!' and he knelt with the knife and severed the head of the calf, and the child with the basin caught its blood.

The men sighed as the basin was raised, and they heard him cry, 'Thus I wash my hands in the blood of this animal in token of the blood we will spill this day!' and this he did, raising high his stained hands. Next the flags he washed one by one, and on one standard he impaled the loaf now also red, and this banner he raised high as the moon broke over the hills.

'See this, then! The freedom flags that will strike off the shackles that bind us. Do you swear to follow them until the day is won, as did your comrades of the Bastille? For we have argued long enough, think you? Today, the talk is finished and we are in battle. *Bara neu waed!*'

'*Bara neu waed!*' the Welsh of ancestry echoed his cry.

'*Bara neu waed!*'

It thundered like a shock wave over Hirwaun, reverberating into silence.

'Bread or blood! Bread or blood!' The English among them repeated it.

Then all was still. Silently, as men with a purpose, they split into squads, and commands were whispered. Led by the boys with the blood-stained flags and the one with the impaled loaf in the van, they converged in ten thousand on to the town of Merthyr.

In St. James's the lamps were burning; with couriers from Wales galloping in every hour the King himself was engaged on this affair of State. In Brecon Barracks the 93rd Highlanders were drawing from the armoury their musket-shot and powder, for St. Tydfil herself was under siege. A ring of steel was closing around the hills, but Dai End-On and his mate got through. As Mamie said later, to do a thing like that you'd have to be as daft as Dai and Billy Jam.

'I'll not tell you again,' said Billa, covered in suds.

Here's the old tin bath slopping by the fire and Mam's got the lads into it, and where's the soap, Abiah, and who's got the towel? Auntie Mamie! Scrubbing like a washerwoman and looking twice as healthy, for these kids do give one a glow, mind, Billa was on her knees beside the bath, and will you stop arsing about, Caleb!

'Aw, Mam!'

'Get into that bath or I'll land you one,' said Mamie, handing over Aaron. '*Duw Duw*, woman—did ye have to have nine o' the fiends?'

Rub, rub, rub—got beautiful hair, mind, my Amos—anna you, Amos—got lovely 'air! and Billa upended him and kissed his bottom. 'Anna he got lovely hair, Mame?' Billa sighed. 'Just like his da, mind.'

'Mr. Jam hasn't got any hair!'

'He 'ad once,' said Billa. 'Don't you deny him, now—make two of your old soak any day, remember.' She sang then, her voice like an angel.

'Can I put me boat in, Ma?'

'You can't put your boat in—I want this over by curtains— don't ye know there's a riot on?' She belted Caradoc in passing. 'And stop playing wi' your pinkle. Got another one, Mamie?'

'Coming over!' Mamie stripped the trews off Abel and dropped him into the bath. Shrieks of joy and howls of soap in

279

the eyes, back-slaps and rubs, kisses, threats and cuddles; and Sun Penderyn, with Dic gone to Aberdare mountain, soothed her baby and smiled, listening, for everybody knew up Ynys Row when it was Billa Jam bath night.

'But I do miss my little Adam, though,' said Billa, and lowered her eyes, and instantly they were about her fighting for a place—in her hair, faces against her throat, down the front of her for warmth, and she knelt in wet limbs and kisses. The firelight was flickering on the cups and mugs; bacon was sizzling in the pan, best back straight out of Dai Rees's shop, and serve the beggar right, said Mamie, for he overcharges more than Guest of Dowlais. Borrowed ten pounds of cheese from the Grocery—saw it running down the hill—as God's me judge, Billa, I didn't loot it—it were blutty running, I tell ye.

'You'll get transportation for sure, you're caught—too light-fingered for my liking, you are. Did ye manage any eggs, Mame?'

'Poached half a dozen down the front o' me—nearly hatched out—come on, come on, lads, and not so much noise or you'll have the rebellion in.'

'Or the special constables,' said Billa, getting up. 'They can smell that bacon for miles, remember, and people our class don't eat bacon.'

Shirts on now, hair combed, ears examined and collars for ticks for there's funny people about these days, and up to the table they went, all nine of them, faces soaped and beaming.

'Good old Mame!' Out of the pan came the rashers, eggs for the oldest, dips for the youngest, and don't you bolt it now, Caleb.

'Ain't you having any, Mame?'

'Ach, leave it for the savages—you enjoying that, boys?'

Hoots and shouts and stop licking the jam-pot and look what Asa's doing under the table, Auntie Mamie!

Billa said, 'But I'm worried about my Merve.'

'Let him do the worrying—he's gone ten, ain't he? Probably with my Randy—look, forget 'em,' replied Mamie.

'He's in bad company with that Abednigo Jones. You think

I ought to go out looking?'

'You're staying here—it anna decent for virgin women on the Bridge. Coo—did Coffin's Court go up! Dear me, just listen to that old Papa Tomo—going up the yard-arm again—my heart bleeds for that poor little Blossom.'

'Somebody coming, Ma!' shouted Saul, his mouth full of bacon.

'And Dic gone up to Aberdare with the Seion deacon fella from Penrhiw, you heard?'

'Best place for him—I'll have to slip in to see Sun later.'

'People coming round the back, Mam!' shouted Caradoc.

'The Military!' cried Mamie, and peeped around the curtains. 'God save us,' said she, sinking down and patting.

'Who is it?'

'It's my Dai and Mr. Jam.'

'*Diwedd!*' exclaimed Billa, and whispered:

'You, Saul—pull yourself together. Round the back with you and ask them in the front. And do it polite, remember. Tell 'em we'll be down. The rest of you to bed.'

'Oh, Mam!' in chorus.

'Bed or I'll brain ye,' hissed Mamie.

Dai End-On and Mr. Jam sweating it out now, leaping to attention every time a board creaked.

'Treat 'em indifferent, remember,' said Mr. Jam. 'This is the time to keep your head.'

The door came open and Mamie and Billa were in.

Dressed like twins, with perfume behind the ears out of the herbalist in Cross Street; straw hats with wide brims tied under the chin with pink ribbons, black velvet bands around the throat and cameos of the Queen, black taffeta dresses caught at the waist and draped round the buttocks with pink cosey, corsetted at the waist and pushed up in the bust where white lace spread. They entered and sat delicately opposite Dai End-On and Jam.

'Well,' said Dai, 'I will go to my death.'

'You wanted to see us, we understand,' said Billa like ice.

'Well, ye see . . .'

'Well?'

'Gid, you see—that is, Gid Davies, sort of mentioned it last week down in Taibach, and we was thinking...' Mr. Jam faltered, his eyes on Billa. Lavender water swept the nostrils of Dai End-On and he sweated ominously.

'Up to you, of course,' announced Mamie, her nose up.

'Nobody asked you to come, you two—ye realise that, I suppose?'

'Ay, but, you see...'

'I mean to say, we're doing all right,' said Mamie. 'We managed fine these last months—even my Randy don't miss you...'

'I'm off the glass, though,' said Dai, snuffling.

The door moved in a creak, but nobody heard it, and the children peeped through the crack.

'I've done with the Oddfellows, too, see,' said Jam for no reason.

'Got a good rag and bone round now,' asserted Dai. 'Pulls the cart himself, too, having got no moke.' He looked at Billa. 'Very industrious. Somebody lifted his donkey, ye see.'

'Him, too,' said Jam. 'Doin' full shifts down Brombil back in Taibach. Doing good, ain't you, Dai boy?'

'Oh, well,' said Billa with business, 'we will have to think about it, won't we?'

'It's a big step, ye see,' added Mamie. 'When once ye make the break it's ... well, it's sort of tricky starting again, ain't it?' Snared by independence yet muted by habit, they stood, inarticulate, faltering in the gaze of the other until nothing was left to them but flight. Billa said, damp:

'Oh, well, I suppose you'd better be going, then,' and she saw a flash vision of Big Mike the Irish boy and his face was square and strong; years younger ... and the disgust swept her, but still her spirit yearned. Now she heard herself say: 'Ay, Mr. Jam, it was good of ye to call.'

'Goodbye, Missus,' said Mr. Jam, glum.

'Might see you again some time,' said Mamie.

'Ay,' said Dai.

Nothingness enveloped them, and Mr. Jam said, turning

away, 'Sorry about our lad, Billa—our wee Adam.'

'Oh, God!' shrieked Billa, and clung to him.

Mamie raised her eyes. Dai was standing with his arms open to her. The kids skidded round the door, in whoops.

The moon was sliding up the window of Number Five.

Before the moon was high the children of William Crawshay left Cyfarthfa Castle in the company of trusted servants, all disguised as beggars, and took to the hills. They took the mountain tracks, keeping clear of the roads where the men were marching, and by morning reached the town of Monmouth and the safety of the Beaufort Hotel.

Next morning Major Falls of the 93rd Highlanders marched in from Brecon Barracks at the head of his men, and they numbered but sixty-eight; later this rose to eight hundred. They were big men and their kilts and sporrans swung to the beat of their marching-drum; they came with muskets slung, looking neither right nor left at the tumult that lined the way, for cat-calls and jeers beat about them all down the Brecon Road. Here they were halted, joined by William Crawshay, Anthony Hill of the Plymouth Works and Bruce the magistrate carrying his Riot Act, and the workers pressed about them as they went down Tydfil Wells and into High Street. Behind them came an army of workers; those who had washed their hands in blood the previous night. Women were shrieking insults, children prancing along beside the soldiers.

'*Diawl!*' shrieked one, 'they've forgotten their trousers!'

'Ach, no—they've dropped them so they can walk the faster!' And this the Welsh believed because they had never seen Highlanders before. Some said they were Welsh struck dumb, and cried to them in the mother tongue; others called them foreigners. And from the crowds came the chant:

'Bread or blood! Reform in Parliament! Secret vote! No Court of Requests! Bread or blood! Reform in Parliament. Free Trade and cheese with bread!' Many carried weapons; hedge-stakes and shovels, mandrels and hammers. Abod of Penydarren, the giant husband of Liz Treharne who marched beside him, carried half a wheelbarrow. Lewis Lewis was there in the centre of the mob, and Gideon Davies was led by Merve Jam, his friend, who also carried a red banner. Abednigo Jones carried a flag, too, and on it was daubed 'Bread or blood'. Dic Llaw-Haearn also came, with Betsy Paul, his woman of the Nipper Tandy gang. Richard Evans the puddler of Hirwaun was there, too, but Tom Llewellyn, who defected, was not. Dai Hughes fought in Castle Square as well, with John Hughes who died of wounds, and with them were Tom Vaughan and Dan Thomas who were transported for life. John the Racer carried a red flag, and about him were his young sons, also David Richards, who got fourteen years. Among the thousands who pressed about the soldiers that day were some who should have stayed away. Many there were who should have come, but did not, such as William Twiss of the golden oratory and Zimmerman who, but a night before, had inflamed these men to violence, but was never seen again. Some there were, too, whose lives were being fulfilled that day—people like Randy Goldie and Mr. Waxey Evans, Mamie Goldie and Billa Jam, also Mr. Percy Note, all from Taibach, and Annie Hewers who came from Pontypridd.

But Dic Penderyn, who was put to death for being there, was up on Aberdare mountain, it was claimed, with the deacon of Seion as witness to this fact.

Reaching the Castle Inn, Crawshay, Hill and Bruce the magistrate, went within with Major Falls, and therein met Josiah John Guest, the master of Dowlais Works, among others. And the crowd bayed louder and pressed about the soldiers as they took refreshment handed out to them, and the baying grew into shouts of fierce anger as the Highlanders went into the Castle Inn by groups, and came out with bayonets fixed for action. Seeing this, Lewis Lewis climbed up on to the shoulders of his comrades, and shouted above the mob:

'See, we are threatened! We are come to discuss wages and Free Trade, and we are shown bared bayonets. Crawshay, Crawshay, Crawshay!' and the mob took up the name, and that of Guest, but neither of these men came out of the inn;

instead the high sheriff appeared, and, mounting a chair, he addressed the men in English, and read the Riot Act. Because many did not understand this, the magistrate Bruce read it again, in Welsh.

The mob was growing in numbers now, cramming like herrings in a barrel up and down High Street, down Post Office Lane, and over Glebeland behind the inn; they were rammed shoulder to shoulder on the waste land leading to the cindertip, they were forced by the weight of more coming in through the railings of Professional Terrace, and fainting women and children had to be passed over the crowd. And they pressed the Highlanders back to the wall of the inn so that it was impossible for them to use their arms: many joked with the soldiers, speaking to them in Welsh; but many, too, spoke in English, trying to suborn them; hearing this, Major Fall called from a window, ordering his men not to reply. It was half past ten in the morning when the Riot Act was read, and soon after this, the master Anthony Hill came out and stood on a chair, shouting:

'Now hear me out—hear me! You will get nowhere with your arms and threats—indeed, you may shout to bring down the town, but inside there we cannot hear a word. Will you appoint...'

His voice was drowned in fresh roars, but he cried, his hands held high, 'Will you appoint a deputation to lay before the masters your claim? How can we tell your requirements amid this disorder? Send within twelve of your leaders and we will talk with them man to man...'

Now fresh gangs of men were coming down Pontmorlais and over the cinder-tip from Jackson's, and those behind were forced forward so that those in front were jammed against the soldiers, and a voice cried then:

'Get between them and the wall of the inn, you fools—give way, give way—drive them free of the wall!'

Hearing this, the Highlanders outside the inn called to those at the windows above, in panic, and the windows were pulled open and muskets appeared. Gideon Davies, pushed to the entrance by willing hands, stood on the chair and shouted: 'I call twelve men who are of this town—David Hughes, Lewis Lewis and David Richards; Daniel Thomas and Thomas Vaughan, also Dai Solomon and Robert Jones—this is seven. These men come forward and join with five more waiting in the entrance. Declare the aims now, and clearly!'

'Make way for the deputation!' shouted Mr. Bruce, up on the chair, and the soldiers held him while the men pushed past him into the inn.

The shrieking of women was growing among the mob; many of these had come from the brick-fields and cropping on Lefal and Tasker pits, and some were ore-miners come from Abercanaid.

'Mind how you go now, love,' said Mrs. Duck Evans to Mr. E.

For it was a Friday and the day of the poor relief pay, and every week Mr. E. collected the five and eightpence from the office of the parish in Professional Terrace.

'There's rough old things happening in town, my lovely,' said Mrs. Duck Evans, and kissed him, 'so be careful.'

Mr. E. was shivering. Last night while the men were marching he had risen in the bed on the first floor of the Dynefor Doss and a duck had looked through the window. With a head as big as a coal bag, a beak like a shovel and lanterns for eyes, it had smiled as only ducks can smile and quacked to raise the graveyard, while Mr. E. gibbering, buried his face in the breast of his wife. Now, with morning, she went on tip-toe and kissed his gaunt face, saying:

'Now now, there's nothin' to be afraid of,' and she patted and smoothed him. 'Just tell the officer our circumstances haven't changed. You never know, he might shift us out of here after three months on the parish.' She beamed up into his face. 'You lean on me, my beautiful—everything will be all right.' Smiling, chattering, she hurried him through the door.

Deciding not to wake the children until she could buy some food, Mrs. Duck Evans, late of Taibach, went down on her knees by the bed and clasped her hands.

'O, merciful God,' she said. 'O, merciful God...'

286

Annie Hewers, late of Pontypridd, knelt by the bed in the cellar of the Crown and held the hand of Megsie, and smiled, and Megsie said, her voice bright with joy, 'But I'm better—I've never felt better, Annie...'

'Ay, ay...'

'Can I get up today, then?'

'We'll see,' replied Annie. 'Sleep now, is it?'

'Ay, sleep...'

'Mrs. Ned Tranter brought us a bit of butter and some milk, and I lifted some riot bread. We'll have a feast when you wake up...' Annie went to the grating, staring up at the boots of men pounding there, and their shouts enwrapped her in the soul of the mob. Vaguely, she began to wonder what she would do when Megsie died; go back to Ponty, more than likely. She would not have stayed as long as this had it not been for the neighbours. And God, what neighbours! Mrs. Ned Tranter, for instance—got a sod of an old man—nothing in skirts was safe with him. And old Shan Shonko—who would have thought she had a heart? And Gid Davies, of course. She wondered what she would have done without Gid Davies over this sickness. The cellar door rasped and Molly Caulara stood on the step.

'You all right, child?'

'Yes, Molly.'

'Your Megsie sleeping, is she?'

Annie smiled brilliantly. 'Don't know why, with all this noise.'

'And you're not frightened, or anything?'

'Not frightened at all, Molly. Not frightened of nothing no more.' Boots were stamping in metallic clashes on the grating.

Molly gestured at the bed. 'She looks better, but you know that, don't ye? They always look better...'

'Yes, yes, I know.' There was growing in Annie Hewers a fierce choking anger.

After Molly Caulara had gone she sat on the bed and looked at her shaking fingers.

The workers' deputation was coming out of the inn. Silence

curtained the mob; it began at the entrance where Gideon was standing and spread like a paralysis through the ranks of the men, extending up High and over Glebe until there was total silence, and in this silence Josiah John Guest, the Dowlais master, stood on the chair and cried:

'Now listen, and I will report the outcome of the discussion. Your deputation demanded, in your name, certain reforms which include reduction in the price of bread and all such basic items necessary to your daily lives ...'

'Ay, and about time, master! The price of bread is a bloody scandal!'

Mixed shouts followed this—cat-calls of derision and shouts of applause and Lewis Lewis, climbing a lamp-post, yelled: 'The price of everything is a bloody scandal! What are ye trying to do, Guest—starve us to death? What about your Shop? And where's Crawshay in this—doesn't he vote for Reform?'

Cheers and hurrahs now and the mob stamped its feet. Guest shouted:

'Your deputation has asked for higher wages, too, and I am to tell you this. If you disperse now we will give serious consideration to your complaints—have I not always done this ...?'

'Ay—with your prices up by twenty per cent!' yelled Philip Jones, the gambo man.

Guest spoke again, but his words were obliterated in a sudden rush for the entrance; the soldiers crossed their muskets; the inn door opened and shut, and within moments Guest appeared at an upstairs window, shouting:

'Now I am to warn you. You are rioting in the face of the King's law. The Riot Act has been read—disperse or take the consequences!'

A young man scrambled on to the back of a comrade and cried: 'If we disperse now you will give us nothing. For my part all I am asking for is a bit more bread ...'

There was a surge of anger about him, and he was pulled down into the crowd, and Abod, the giant of Penydarren, stiffened in the mob, yelling:

288

'Ay, well I want something more than bread! And so does my missus. We want cheese with it, and ale, and smokes—by Christ, you lot get enough. I want cheaper rent and no more bloody Courts of Requests, and we've waited too long already.'

A man yelled then: 'We want *everything*!'

The crowd bawled, and as the clamour mounted Crawshay came to the window and shouted: 'For my part I will not treat with anybody under threat of violence. Go home now. Send to me, within a fortnight, a deputation who can speak for you and I will give consideration to any injustices you think you may have ... But, by God, I will not treat with a rabble!'

Groans and moans burst from the men, and one shouted: 'Is this what ye call Reform?' The mob began to chant again:

'Bread or blood, bread or blood ...!'

And as Bruce the magistrate notified them that the hour of the Riot Act had expired, Lewis Lewis shouted from his position on the lamp-post:

'Now, ye see how much you'll get!' and he followed this in Welsh, 'We come here to get an increase in wages and all we get is soldiers set against us. We come here in the name of Reform and all they're prepared to give us is bullets. Now lads, if you're of the same mind as I am, let us begin by taking their arms ...!'

The sun was directly overhead, said Gideon later; the sun burned down, said Mamie, when she heard the firing.

'Come on, lads, into them!' yelled Lewis Lewis, and Gideon cried:

'No, in the name of God, wait, *wait*!'

The men rushed the Highlanders.

'Get behind them!'

'Trip the bastards!'

'Clear them from the wall!' and Lewis Lewis, in the van of the charge, shouted, 'On, on! Get them away from the wall!' And he leaped upon the nearest soldier and seized his musket as Major Falls ran out of the inn to take command, to fall almost immediately, being swung aside by Abod of Penydarren and clubbed down by another, some say Liz Treharne. Soldiers fell, sinking under the crashing mandrels as they

289

fought to use their arms. A worker shrieked and dropped, clutching at a bayonet which was sticking through his body. A boy fell, his head crushed by a musket-butt. Then a volley of stones smashed every window in the inn, and the crowd, forced on by unseen pressures, rammed the Highlanders against the entrance; the door flew open and the soldiers were carried within, sprawling. Women were screaming, men roaring encouragement to their comrades, a baby was crawling among the boots of the men. With a forest of stakes and mandrels heaving, the workers were fighting to get into the inn when a single shot spurted fire from an upper window.

Rumour had it in Tredegar at that time that William Crawshay fired the first shot of the massacre that followed, but none have proof of this. But now, with the order to fire shouted, volley after volley was poured into the massed people, and they slipped down where they stood, in screams. Gideon Davies fell early, being near the entrance, and a soldier clubbed him as he staggered blindly. Now ragged fusillades cracked out from the inn windows, and nearly all the soldiers in the forecourt were wounded and down. One, Private Donald Black, was seen by witnesses to be struggling with a worker; and in the mêlée of arms and legs, amid the swaying, cursing mass, a bayonet was seen to flourish; Private Black fell with the weapon in his thigh. According to the testimony of James Abbott the barber and Shoni Crydd the constable, the man who wounded him was Dic Penderyn...

Meanwhile, Mr. Waxey Evans, having had his trunks sent down to the Posting House, was ready to leave Merthyr. But, being in need of ready cash, he decided to call at the Brecon Bank in High Street opposite Professional Terrace and draw enough to tide him over the immediate future. So, with Sara Grieve safely interred with her Ianto up in Vaynor, Mr. Evans dusted the scurf off the shoulders of his morning coat, brushed up the pile of his grey hat, and with gold-knobbed cane, gloves and carnation made his way briskly down Bridge and up Thomas Street to Professional Square.

'This cheque, please,' said he at the bank counter.

The cashier was nervous, but not of Mr. Evans. With red-rimmed eyes twitching seriously, since he had been up all night in an attic down Post Office Lane, he peered at the door; here six special constables were standing with drawn batons.

'Anything the matter, man?' asked Waxey.

A volley of shots pierced the shrieks and screams. The cashier paid him in guineas, and these Waxey Evans stacked in little bags in his small travelling-case. The young man said: 'I can't think what's got into them. I really cannot think...'

Waxey was counting. He normally counted the money when drawing on the account, and it was necessary not to raise the smallest suspicion.

'My condolences on the loss of your wife, sir. It is tragic, absolutely tragic!' the clerk added. 'You will be back, of course? I mean... I trust this is but a temporary absence?'

Waxey Evans sniffed, snapped the travelling-case shut and departed, turning into Professional Square with his two hundred sovereigns just as Mr. Duck Evans was coming into High Street with his five and eightpence parish relief. And, as the mob came pell-mell down from the Castle, Corporal Joe McCann of the 93rd sighted down the barrel of his musket and pressed the trigger. He was aiming at the giant figure of Abod of Penydarren, but missed. The ball hit a lamp standard, ricochetted through a roof, cut through a king-post and whined down into the crowd, striking Waxey Evans an inch under the heart: dropping at the feet of Mr. Duck Evans, he died instantly. In the path of the retreating crowd he fell, and the workers leaped over him. When they had passed Mr. Duck Evans noticed the travelling-case; aimlessly, he picked it up, for the events had made but little impression. Vacantly, with the case held against him, he made his way down Thomas, over the Iron Bridge where Molly Caulara was waiting.

'Have you got the time?' asked Molly. 'Ye lovely handsome fella.'

'About midday,' replied Mr. Duck Evans, and raised his hat, and went up Dynefor to the Doss.

'What you got there, my lovely?' asked Mrs. Duck Evans, when he came in.

Giving her the five and eightpence, he wandered away.

'No, that I mean, my beautiful,' said she, and took the case.

Before the Castle Inn twenty-two people lay dead—men, women and children. Scores more were rolling and many were shrieking, and the cobbles were shining with blood. Sid Blump was lucky, for he died quickly. Pushing through the crowd he held a Highlander still with one hand and hit him flat with the other; an officer shot him personally; they were surprised to find that he possessed no fingers. Nearby died one, Mr. Note, who was once a revolutionary. But the spirit of war had surged in him again when he heard the firing, and he remembered in the lost ambitions the last movement of his Gun Symphony that had died in the arms of Mrs. Taibach. He came late to battle, for the mob was retreating even as he arrived with Lemuel Samuel, who fled. And hearing Willie Taibach shrieking in the folds of his blood-stained flag, he had stooped to succour him, and a soldier took him from the back. Percy Bottom Note died in Welsh, which was his father's tongue:

'*A gyrraf hefyd y prophwydi ac ysbryd aflendid o'r wlad!*' he said.

Amazingly, Curly Hayloft died in the arms of Tilly, who was dead. He had come into town to buy a physic for Mercy Merriman who had drunk Taff water, and had sheltered in the entrance of the King's Head hotel while the volleys of the Highlanders swept the blood-stained streets: then, in a lull of the firing he had run for it, and a musket-ball broke his spine. So he dragged himself along the cobbles of Professional Square like a wounded leveret while the insurgents leaped over him in flight, and here a woman was sheltering with a child. And this woman, who was an iron-stone miner of Hirwaun, gathered him against her, and her hands, which were calloused with labour, scoured his face: therefore, her touch, to him, was the touch of Tilly. She stared in wonder when he took her hand and pressed it against his lips.

Randy Goldie did not die, although he succeeded, with Lewis Lewis, in wresting away a musket from Private Alex

McGregor of Dundee. And with this musket, quite unnoticed, he wandered in a hail of fire, looking for Ned Tranter, who was in charge of Stall One, Heading Eight when Blod Irish died. Based largely on information given to him by Merve Jam, who spoke at the coroner's inquest, Randy's suspicions had flowered into fact. Ned Tranter, it seemed, was with a detachment of rioters sent by Lewis Lewis up to the Brecon Road to guard the northern approach of the town. In this direction Randy walked, climbing the cinder-tip behind *China*, and made his way up Quarry Street. Earlier, he had seen Dic Penderyn go into the Castle Inn as a member of the workers' delegation—or thought he had, and he had waited for Dic to come out, but he never did. Later still, just before the massacre, he was sure he had seen Dic standing by the tap-room wall at the side of the inn, but thought he must have been mistaken because when he reached this spot, Dic was not to be found. Now, with his stolen musket slung on his back and every Highlander in Merthyr beading him in the sights, Randy strolled across the line of fire that later shot down Mrs. Taibach, and the air was filled with the shrieking of the rico-chets, for Lewis Lewis and his men on the cinder-pit were now firing with glass marbles. With a bullet hole in his collar, two in his trews and one in his sleeve, Randy wandered aimlessly, thinking about Blod. In summer, he remembered, with flowers in her hair in Dinas Woods, Taibach, she was very pretty.

Gideon Davies was lying against the wall of Abbot the bar-ber's when Miss Thrush the Sweets found him, and he was not dead. Indeed, the blood of his wound was congealing and when she knelt beside him and gathered him into her arms he opened his eyes and smiled, knowing her, it seemed.

'Sun, Sun . . .' he said, and clung to her.

'Oh, God,' said Miss Thrush, 'whatever shall I do?' and she snatched at the legs of men running past her, and one paused, and knelt. A musket-ball struck the stonework of Abbott's shop above them and whined into space. The sight of the blood on Gideon's face held Miss Thrush with rooted force.

'Quick! Get him up!' cried Abednigo Jones.

Therefore, helping to lift Gideon, she did not notice Mrs.

Taibach walk past with Willie in her arms ... going round the corner of the Castle Inn oblivious to the shrieking wounded and the bawled warnings of men, and Willie's face was against hers and his bare arm hanging down her apron. She walked right through the volleys that shot down Rowland Thomas, he who had wandered into the High Street and picked up a soldier's hat. But the rioters were still firing from the cinder-tip behind the inn and she gasped to the smash of the ball and went to her knees, staring into Willie's face, until the next random volley laid her down with her arms about him. Jess Banks, who was English, died beside them, hand-in-hand with his wife, who was seventeen, and the neighbours took the baby, though it cried for two days. Mr. Stinkin Shenkins, the boozey brother of the beadle, he died also, in shrieks, beating his fists against the wall of the Baptist in Maerdy—the shot had taken him low. Shoni Melody, whose business was not riot, was humming a tenor solo from *The Messiah* in the attic of the Star when a ball took the window and struck him in the face, while poor Old Wag, who was knitting in a porch off Post Office Lane, died cleanly with the jersey in her lap, and she hadn't dropped a stitch, said Mamie. Some say Shan Shonko died also, but nobody got the proof of it, for she merely disappeared, while others said the Highlanders had eaten her. There were many who died that were not recorded, dragged into attics and cellars by terrified relatives; many of these died for want of medical attention, and were buried in secret graves. John Hughes, an old soldier who had fought at Waterloo, died in agony, for the ball took him in the back and came out of his navel, and he was concerned with the indignity, said the surgeon who signed his death certificate *Justifiable Homicide*. This verdict he also gave on the body of one, Annie Hewers, who died in tears, rushing on to the bayonets with her fists raised, crying the name of Megsie, her friend.

Some of the soldiers were wounded.

With Lewis Lewis and a small body of rioters firing on the Castle Inn from the cinder-tip behind *China*, the order was given to evacuate the defenders to Penydarren House, Forman's mansion built on the site of a Roman fortification. But the Military were converging on to Merthyr now, coming at the frantic commands of the magistrates' emissaries; the Glamorgan Militia came from Cardiff, the Llantrisant Cavalry galloped in and attacked the snipers on the cinder-pit, and were beaten off by salvos of glass marbles, for the rioters had run out of lead shot. The cavalry escorted the evacuating coaches of the iron masters up the hill to Penydarren.

And Merthyr, under the red flag, fell to the rioters.

22

'RIGHT, you, missus,' said Abednigo Jones, 'I got him by here, now it's up to you,' and he sprawled Gideon down over the bed in Miss Thrush's room, snatched the musket she had carried and ran downstairs and through the shop.

For many minutes Milly Thrush stood there with her hands to her face listening to the distant guns and Gideon's faint breathing. His head wound had begun to bleed again and was spreading on her pillow in a widening stain. She wanted to be sick. Once, when a child, she had cut her finger, and she was physically sick then; the sight of blood always did this to her. Now she swayed and held on to the bed-rail in a mist of horror, and Gideon groaned in his unconsciousness. Going to the window she looked through the Arches on to a deserted Bridge Street where smoke was drifting; nothing moved in Bridgefield. A sale-coal barge had stopped on the canal, lying askew from bank to bank, and the towing-horse was grazing peaceably nearby. To her right she saw smoke rising from the simmering furnaces of Ynys Works, but the dram-road was stilled, and the doors and windows up and down the Row were shut. It was as if the riot had taken Merthyr by the throat and choked it into death. Then a small figure carrying a red flag walked past Ynysgau Chapel, and Milly recognised it instantly as Merve, Billa Jam's boy; he walked in jerky sentences of pain, and the banner he carried high swayed and ripped in the wind of the Taff. In the middle of the Iron Bridge he fell, then rose, dragging the flag on the ground behind him. In this manner, falling and rising, he reached Ynys Row. The barge horse raised its head and watched him go to the house of Miss Blossom Thomas; there, beside the step he fell, and lay still.

Gideon groaned then, and turned on the bed, and Milly went to him, her hands screwing together, staring down. The wound in his head was bleeding profusely now. She began to bite at her fingers; sweat flooded to her face and she wiped it into her hair. Suddenly, she turned and ran downstairs, returning with a bowl of water and a cloth. With clenched teeth she sat beside him. The blood was on her fingers as she began to wipe it away. The coldness of the water stilled Gideon, and he sighed and did not groan again. Tearing up one of her petticoats, Milly put the soaked cloth over the wound and bound it tightly, flinging away the blood-soaked pillow. Then she heard footsteps on the road outside. Four special constables were marching towards the shop with drawn batons, and one she recognised as Shoni Crydd. Cleaning her hands of blood, she ran downstairs again and was behind the counter as the men entered.

'You been here all this morning, Miss Thrush?' asked Shoni Crydd.

'Ay, thank God.'

'You've had no trouble, then?'

'Only the firing, and the mob ...'

'You haven't seen a woman with a musket?'

She faltered, but he did not appear to notice. 'A ... a musket?'

'A woman carrying arms—she was seen on River Side, not more than half an hour back, with a wounded man.'

'God forbid they come in here,' said Milly.

'If they do, you yell, eh?' Crydd wiped his sweating face. 'The town's gone bloody mad. We got sixty specials and about that many Military—and they've gone up to Penydarren. You know Mrs. Taibach and her son are dead, I suppose?'

The shock she showed was real. As the men went through the door she leaned, bowed on the counter; faintly, from above stairs, she heard Gideon call, and she overturned a tin of paste brooches and began to snatch them up. A constable said from the door 'You see that woman with a gun, you call, remember.'

She nodded. 'Yes, of course.'

When they had gone she lifted her skirts and ran upstairs to Gideon and knelt with her hand over his mouth, listening to the retreating footsteps. Then, straightening him on the bed, she began to undress him, and this she did with the utmost care, so that he should not be exposed to her.

It took her an hour to get him under the blanket, but when this was achieved he slept almost immediately, breathing in the rhythm of one at peace.

From the floor beside the bed his little white dog stared up at her: bending, she fondled it, and it licked her hand as if in gratitude.

'You are not allowed in here,' she whispered, and picked it up.

As she went to the door Gideon spoke, and she turned.

'Sun... Sun Heron...' he said.

She straightened as one with dignity and gripped the door. 'I ... I am here,' she said.

That evening Randy Goldie climbed to the heights of Cefn, which overlooks the Brecon road. Here a body of rioters under the command of Abod of Penydarren had made their camp, awaiting the passage of an ammunition convoy coming from Brecon Barracks in support of the Highlanders. Of this body of insurgents, which numbered over a thousand, some four hundred were properly armed; the rest were mainly Irish, and these carried bludgeons. Road blocks had been set up across the road to Aberdare now, even mountain tracks were controlled by rebel snipers; nobody was allowed to leave Merthyr; farmers and their families trying to enter the town with goods were turned back. All this Randy saw, but did not find himself concerned. With the musket primed and the flint cocked he searched, in darkness now, for Ned Tranter. And, with returning sense, began to skirt the camp of the rebels up on Cefn Heights, shouting:

'A message for Ned Tranter of Dynefor! A message for Ned Tranter!'

And at ten o'clock, when the moon was high, Tranter heard this cry and came from a mass of men lying on their bellies on

298

Cefn Heights, and shouted.

'Ay, ay! Here's Ned Tranter!'

'The message this way,' shouted Randy, and retreated.

So it was that he came to a place of bushes which was away from the main body, and there he waited, shouting in the darkness: and Tranter came.

In the light of the moon Ned Tranter saw the face of Randy Goldie, and the musket in his hands, and Randy came to him close and touched him, then pulled him nearer, lowering the musket.

'You remember Blod Irish?' he asked.

And struck, and Tranter, who was big, went backwards, tripped and fell. Randy picked up the musket.

'This is from my girl,' he said, and fired.

When Abod, the Penydarren giant was called, he came with his wife, Liz Treharne, and they pushed through the ring of men where Randy was standing beside Tranter lying dead.

'What happened?' boomed Abod, and a collier replied:

'His name is Randy Goldie and he called from the dark for Tranter, and he went. And Goldie killed him.'

'She miscarried in Cwmglo,' said Liz softly. 'You know Tranter, he were a dog on the women.'

'Dear me,' said Abod, and rubbd his chin, and the moon shone down on the place of justice. Stooping he picked up the musket, cocked the pin and snapped it shut. ' 'Tis a light old trigger, mind. Some of these things do go off easy. Dear me, dear me . . .' he tossed the musket and Randy caught it. 'Now kill Highlanders—get back up there on the top of Cefn.'

At seven o'clock next morning Captain Moggridge of the Cardiff cavalry set out from Penydarren House to escort in the ammunition and baggage convoy coming from Brecon, and on their way through the town were fired on from many houses. And, after they had passed a narrow defile, the rioters came down from Cefn and blocked it with boulders, so that the cavalry and ammunition could not enter Merthyr by that route, but crossed the mountains from a village which was later drowned: this made the ammunition late for the defenders.

With the King both angered and dismayed, troops were now ordered into Merthyr from places as far away as Salisbury and Portsmouth, where the new steam-packet stood waiting to transport them, for it had been conveyed to the Government that the rebels of Merthyr intended to lead the rebels of England; that not only the Midland towns would rise to join the Welsh but London's east end, where the people were starving. Here, with parish relief down to a few shillings a head, the only Kingly assistance was a few tossed coppers to the Spitalfield poor: Reform would extend, said the Welsh, to the palace of St. James's, which was costing the country thousands a month.

At this the King was naturally concerned, and henceforth took more interest in the Merthyr correspondence from people like the Tory squires and the Marquis of Bute, much of which he personally annotated.

The iron masters besieged in Penydarren House were also concerned; for they learned that their ammunition convoy had been ambushed and the force under Captain Moggridge routed: that a hundred more cavalry sent in relief had been beaten off by musket-fire; that a troop of the West Glamorgan yeomanry under Major Penrice had been ambushed, disarmed and sent back to Swansea in disgrace.

What had begun as a riot was now a military operation.

Mrs. Duck Evans, late of Taibach, opened the travelling-case of Mr. Waxey Evans and counted on to the bed two hundred sovereigns. She had never imagined there to be so much money in Merthyr. And as she snapped the case shut and locked it, Mr. E. came into the room and looked out of the window.

'There is two hundred guineas in this travelling-case,' said she. 'Now tell me, Mr. E., where did you get it?'

'Ah,' said he.

'In the name of God, tell me, so I can give it back!'

'Ay,' said Mr. Duck.

'Where, then?' Shrieking this, she seized him and shook him, and he grinned amiably at this new game; from his throat came the sounds of the idiot; from his mouth the saliva ran in

300

streams while her vehemence and panic beat about him.

'You half-wit—*tell me*!' and she struck him in the face. Still he grinned, rocking to and fro on his heels, and she threw herself down on the bed, and wept, saying:

'Holy Father, have you no pity for me?'

After a few moments she raised herself, and said: 'You know what they'll do, don't you, Mr. Duck Evans—you a sidesman in the Ebenezer? Can you think what they'll do for two hundred guineas. They will cut off your hands, perhaps, and dip the stumps in tar, as they once did to the forgers. And they will blind you, and send you back to me.' Her voice rose to a scream, and the neighbours in the Doss raised their white faces, thinking he was beating her. 'Don't you understand— they'll flog you if you take their ducks, but they will kill you if you steal their money, you hear me? You can insult their women, you can shame their daughters, but you must not touch their money—can you imagine what they'll do to you for two hundred guineas? Oh, my love, tell me where you got it!'

'Ay, ay,' said Mr. Duck Evans, and beamed.

Later he left her and she went to the window of the Doss, looking down on to the deserted streets, seeing instantly a tiny figure crossing the Iron Bridge with a flag, and this was Merve, the son of Billa; and the figure fell and rose, and fell again; and rose once more, the flag held high, and disappeared into Ynys Row. And there came to Mrs. Duck Evans a new courage, and she lifted the travelling-case and held it against her. Her mind went back through the bludgeoning years, to the hungers and threats and evictions, the agonising births, the screams of the women trapped underground, and she was with them, aged six. She remembered the yellow pools of excrement outside the doors; the heat of furnace summers, the bitter winters of the rags, her washing burned to holes, her father coughing, the typhoid, the cholera, the rickets of her youth. And she remembered the time she starved a baby to the point of death, then placed a saucer of water near its mouth, and the lizards came tumbling over its lips. She knew again the bright explosions of her youth and the blood-stained stumps, and she saw, in a sudden beam of the afternoon sun the parkland of Cyfarthfa rolling in June green against a sky of strickening light. She put the case under her arm and said through the window at Merthyr:

'The way you've treated me it's cheap at a thousand times that much,' and she went downstairs to her sickly children, kissed Mr. E. on the cheek where she had struck him, and added:

'The parish 'ave paid a bit more this week. Come on, my lovelies, we're moving out of Merthyr.'

Later, she went to the door and looked at the sky, and said:
'I won't forget, and I'm very much obliged.'

In a tumult of exultation Lewis Lewis, commander of the rebel contingent which disarmed the Swansea cavalry, now led his forces south and east over the Taff River, and here, bristling with muskets and sabres captured from Major Penrice, joined forces with those of Abod who had ambushed the ammunition wagons on the Brecon road. And he addressed the massed thousands to repeated cheering.

'Now we are armed, who shall we fear?' He raised high his hands and leaped on to a crag. 'The soldiers are besieged in Penydarren, and they are few. It is we, the workers, who hold Merthyr for once, not this scum who call themselves masters!'

The rebels roared, stamping their feet; the afternoon was split by muskets fired into the air. Lewis Lewis continued: 'I say we mount an attack on Penydarren and flush them out...!'

'Unless they agree to our terms!' cried Abod.

'And the terms shall be restoration of wage rates at Cyfarthfa and Hirwaun, nothing less. Are ye with me?'

'Ay! Ay!'

It is said that they heard these roared replies as far east as Penydarren, and that one iron master collapsed with a paralytic stroke.

'And abolishment of the black list!'

'No victimisation!'

'Then let us treat with Crawshay, Lewis!' bawled Dai Solomon. 'Let Richard Evans, the puddler, speak for Hirwaun, and you for Cyfarthfa!'

'Wait you, Lewis!'

'Somebody is coming ...'

'A messenger—pull the bugger down!'

'Leave him!' commanded Abod, and shouldered out of the crowd, and men made way for him. And he stood in great size, hands on hips as the emissary from Penydarren, a young yeoman officer galloped up. He was small and fair, and the down of youth was on his face, yet he held himself well and was not afraid.

'I have a message for your leaders,' he said, and dismounted. 'I come from Penydarren. Mr. Guest and Mr. Crawshay, representing the masters, ask you to send a deputation to discuss terms of peace.'

Abod fumbled at this, but Lewis Lewis wandered up, his thumbs in his belt. 'How many more delegations, you think? Are we bloody children? You tell me how the last one fared.'

The young officer stood before him, unsmiling, and Abod said: 'He's a hearty wee cock. Shall we down his trews and check him for inches?'

But Lewis Lewis said: 'How many for this delegation? And what do we discuss?' The young officer said:

'I am only to inform you that you will be received, and treated with respect,' and he put his fists on his hips, like Abod, and looked him up and down.

'By God,' said Abod. 'He'd be rough to take, eh, son?' and he chucked the boy under the chin, and the young soldier said:

'It is not you I am worried about, Welshman, it's the other ten thousand.'

Men shouted with laughter at this, and gathered around him in cheers, and none laughed louder than Abod, who could have broken him with a hand. Lewis Lewis said then: 'Go back, sir. Tell the iron masters that this afternoon six men will come to parley at Penydarren. Touch a hair of their heads and we will tear the place to pieces. Now go.'

After the young officer had galloped away, Lewis Lewis, Abod and Richard Evans formed the insurgents into an order of battle, for the taking of Penydarren House, and there were eight battalions, each of one thousand men, and to them were appointed leaders; men like Thomas Vaughan and Daniel Thomas, John the Racer and David Hughes. And the great army formed up in the manner of soldiers. With Lewis Lewis at their head, led by the red flag in the hands of the boy Abednigo Jones, they marched down the Brecon road to the castle at Cyfarthfa; here they blew out the Crawshay Works, and sent their deputation on to Penydarren, while the rest waited, cleaning their bayonets and polishing their muskets, and many of them, especially the Irish of Pontmorlais, were drunk. Among them were women and children, some being the tattered orphans of the William Davies levels, who had caused the death of Jobina. Other small parties entered deeper into the town, especially to the north and west, and here requisitioned food, powder and shot from tradesmen; the powder chambers of the drifts and pits were also rifled for the muskets, and as far east as Dowlais twenty barrels were taken. Their look-outs, mounted on the horses of the West Glamorgan yeomanry, were galloping the hills from Trefil to Penderyn, north to Garn and south to Abercynon, and fire signals were smoking on the high ground. The encirclement of Merthyr was complete.

Miss Blossom Thomas laid down her doll and ran in a flurry of petticoats to Number Five Ynys Row and hammered the door: Mamie opened it.

'It is young Merve,' she began, white-faced. 'Oh, for God's sake, bring Billa!'

'Merve?' Mamie's expression did not change.

'In my house now, and wounded!'

Mamie shouted: 'Billa, Billa! It is Merve, it is Merve!'

'And near to death,' gasped Blossom. 'Oh, the blood, the blood!'

Billa and Mamie found him on the floor of Papa Tomo's kitchen, and he was lying like a compound accident, his bare arms outflung, and Billa went on her knees beside him, and, weeping without tears, ran her hands up his shirt and down his

304

trews, and the ball had struck him high, taking through the right shoulder in a downward path, and, spent, was lying in his chest. He was dying.

'Sorry, Mam,' he said.

'Quick, ring a surgeon!' cried Blossom, biting at her hands.

'Ay, but no,' said Billa, and she sat on the floor and took his head in her lap and there cooled his face with a rag and water Mamie brought. 'They are not putting him to the knife. I have seen the laudanum, and it does not work.'

'He will die?' whispered Blossom, kneeling.

'He is already dying,' said Mamie.

'Sorry, Mam,' said Merve.

'God,' said Mamie, 'This is no country for children and women,' and she walked Blossom's kitchen, empty. 'And not a word of my Randy...'

'There's me little boy,' said Billa, kissing him. 'There's me fine big Merve—fighting again, is it?'

'Sorry, Mam.'

And there came to Mrs. Billa Jam of Taibach a quiet that turned Mamie's face to her, and Blossom Thomas heard this, for it came after a small gasp from the child, and he shuddered once in Billa's arms, and died. And then she lowered her head and her hair, which was unpinned from a wash, swept over his face; she wept.

Then from the bedroom above came a roaring song, and the window went up and Papa Tomo Thomas hung out for all to see the red flag which Merve had brought, and he waved it at the deserted streets of Bridgefield, crying:

'Right you, come and get it and I'll blast ye into the sea! Roll me down to the Frenchies, me lads, and we'll show 'em what cannons are. Ahoy there, me hearties! By God, if I had decent legs I'd teach ye how to make rebellion! Shoni Crydd, Bill Tobbo and Mike O'Hara—ye call yourself special constables? Ay, well here's a flag of blood, and Papa Tomo is defending it—tell old Crawshay to come and get it!' and he tipped the flask of gin to his lips, belched and pardoned and waved his fist at a passing dog.

305

Mamie said: 'Blossom Thomas, if you don't get up there and stop that palaver I'll up and murder that old bastard.'

The riot was spreading. All that Saturday groups of men carrying flags and Cobbett's pamphlets journeyed over The Top to the towns of Ebbw Vale, Nantyglo and Tredegar, though Beaufort under the more benevolent duke was ignored, the workmen there being contented. To Blaenafon and Llanelli and Pontypool hundreds of Merthyr and Dowlais men and boys went next morning, seeking support of their demand for Reform. And the tradesmen of the Top Towns answered the call. They came in their hundreds, blowing out their furnaces and throwing down their tools: all that Sunday they travelled, carrying the banners of their secret lodges and infant unions, playing their bands of fifes and drums. And they arrowed like the fingers of a giant hand on to old Waun Hill, spilling down the narrow streets of Dowlais. These were not only the under-paid cutters, hauliers and colliers, but the men of the respected trades who, till now, had never caused disturbance. Their wives came too; armed with sacks to loot food from Guest and Fothergill's hated truck shops, they ran alongside the marching columns of men, adding their shrieks to the bawled threats; with their children on their backs they danced jigs over the mountain grass, tore shift bandages for wounds, spiking the heads of clubs and cutting food. Some there were in Monmouthshire who would not come, and many of these were visited by the dreaded Scotch Cattle, the enforcers of the new Union laws. Dressed in the skins of beasts, their leaders with cow horns strapped to their heads, these roamed the towns, dragging out men for beatings, burning the furniture of the black-legs. And so many travelled to Merthyr that night under threat of force, herded like cattle along tne tracks to Waun Hill by men with clubs and trailing ropes that prevented escape. In the morning, a Sunday, a great civilian army therefore converged on the Merthyr parish, and it numbered over ten thousand, according to the *Merlin*. With Merthyr and Dowlais already full of rioters, the deacons, shopkeepers and gentry went under their beds as the great rabble poured on to

306

Waun and raised its flags of Reform amid wild shouts. Ragged, hungry, unkempt from sleeping out, this new force was joined on the hill by that of Lewis Lewis and Abod of Penydarren, whose delegation to the iron masters had won victory: Crawshay had agreed to restore the wages lately reduced at Hirwaun and Cyfarthfa. And Lewis cried:

'Does not this only land us back where we started?'

'To hell with the wage restoration—we want an increase!'

'Ten per cent all round!'

They waved their arms, shrieking. 'Ten per cent! Ten per cent. What we want is Reform, not prattle! Reform, Reform, Reform!'

'Reform all round and wage increases, or we march on Penydarren House! By God, we'll teach them about old Forman's ready money!' And they prepared for the march. But already their ranks were splitting in dissent, and there came among them men who were not radicals, and these widened the split, dividing them, and one shouted, pulling down Lewis Lewis:

'And if they give you ten per cent after the restoration, what will ye ask for then, you fools? For you're already greedier than your masters! Listen—the Military are coming—we know this: not a few hundred, but thousands, perhaps, and they'll shoot you down like dogs. I say accept the terms, and thank your God, for they might not be offered tomorrow!'

Then this man, too, whose name is not known, was pulled down, yet his words were echoed and cheered by the ragged army on the right, while on the left came jeers and shrieks of derision, and Abod bawled, leaping up:

'And what of the blood they spilled by the Castle Inn? Do they die in vain? What of the children and women who have been murdered, shot down in cold blood? Is this what you sacrifice for wage restorations—your own flesh and blood? Rise here one man who has lost his own—here, Toby Garner, and let him be seen!' and he hauled up beside him a man wizened and small, and he was weeping. 'Does Toby Garner fight for restoration now, or does he cry for revenge for his wife and son?'

The man drooped before them, and they went quiet, remembering the Castle Inn and the bloodstained road, and Abod yelled: 'I say march on Penydarren and take the place by storm. Get signed documents for a ten per cent rise *after* restoration ...!'

'And when you've broken Crawshay's bank—what then, big man?'

Curses, cheers and jeers rose from the mob, which swayed, arms high. And for an hour they stood on Waun and quarrelled, and bitterness grew in the place of comradeship. Spies broke away and ran to inform the iron masters. And at ten o'clock that morning four hundred and fifty soldiers marched up Dowlais Hill with Guest at their head, to make the split wider.

It was on this morning that Gideon's fever subsided, but he was still delirious, and many times called Sun Heron's name. And, sitting there beside him, Miss Thrush knew that sight would have told that she was not beautiful, as Sun Heron was beautiful, she of the red-gold hair. With sight he would have known that her breast was too full, her hips too large; that her hands and feet were not dainty, as Sun Heron's, for it was by this name he continued to call her, not Sun Penderyn, another man's wife. In the onslaught of middle age Miss Thrush had wilted; obesity now was taking charge, and she would have recalled the defiling years only to be winsome, and gay, as the woman Gideon loved. Yet the passion in her grew for him even as she sat there, and his need called to her.

'Sun Heron ... Sun Heron ...'

And there came to Miss Thrush then an awareness of love, and a need that it be fulfilled; this awareness grew and brought to her throat a dryness, and a beating of her heart that no power of will could stifle. And as his hands roamed the blanket in search of Sun Heron, Miss Thrush began to tremble, and the trembling grew from her lips and consumed her.

'Sun ...'

Afterwards, she could die, she thought. After she had offered herself and known acceptance or rejection, she could leave him, and know herself to be defiled, as a stag defiles itself in its pit. Yet she would know the fulfilment of her love, this she reasoned, clutching at her hands. For a minute of her life she would be possessed, though in the name of another and in the bed of a loved one; and would give to this man the relief of love.

'Sun . . . Sun . . . !' It was as if his whole being was reaching out for her.

'Gid,' she said.

The sound of her silenced him and his eyes opened full on her face; she shrank away, exposed in the deceit. And then Gideon smiled and there came to his face a radiance she had never seen before; he raised himself in the bed and opened his arms to her. Kneeling, she touched his lips with the tips of her fingers, and the touch momentarily stilled him, as if he disbelieved. Then he grasped her hands and began to kiss them, calling her name, which was not her name but the one for whom his soul and body cried.

'Sun!'

He sought her; his hands moved up her arms and drew her down to him, and his lips swept her face and his fingers were in her hair; there was in him a passion of strength that brought her to momentary terror, for she had never been used before. And then fear left her in the knowledge that she would be his wife, and this brought her to a new, untainted joy. This joy was awakened by his kiss, and her mouth was one with his and there beat about them a great wind of oblivion as he drew her to the bed.

'Wait,' she said, in command, and he quietened at her bidding, as men do.

She did not speak more; indeed, she dared not speak again lest, through the mist of his sickness, he would have knowledge of her subterfuge, and cast her out. For her there was no taking, but giving; later, she thought as she undressed before his blindness, she would renew the laces in his boots, for they were worn, as she had expected. Laces, boots, razors, bodies—one was not more important than the other in the pursuit of his pleasure. And if she should die, broken by his strength—for he

309

was a big man—would not this be justice, because of her betrayal? she reasoned. Her dress ringed her feet, and then her petticoats; looking momentarily beautiful, Miss Thrush unpinned her long hair and waved it down to her waist, and this covered some of her approaching nakedness as she took off her bodice, and she saw, in revulsion, that there was little shape to her breasts, and she was thankful for his blindness, that she had so little to give. This confession of inadequacy chastened her, and she momentarily dropped before him in the window sunlight. But there was upon his face such an expectation of joy that she banished this; the knowledge of his need diluted in measure the sadness that her gift was small. Now she took his hands in hers and held them against her breast, and he closed his eyes and drew aside the blanket that she might enter into his warmth. And in the moment before his arms took her and his lips sought hers in gusty breath, she saw in a sky of astonishing blue the golden outline of the mountain flashing in the sun: the harvest of the world, she saw amid a growing, lovely music. She did not see the stunted trees and violated earth, but a bright river flowing down the sewer of the Taff. The wildness that consumed her then was the breaking out of her long captivity, the loneliness, longings, the fretful tears. He knew well of her, and she knew him as a man contained and strong in will, if unused to women. She worshipped him in whispers and caresses, and Gideon was good to her, because she did not defile them. And when the bright explosions of their union grew in the pace of love he cried aloud, yet did not call a name. Wondering at this cry, she held him, and he said:

'I love you. I love you.'

The words came as an echo in her soul, transcending in their simplicity any lovely sound she had ever heard. Nobody had said this to her before: not the man she remembered as her father: the child who had kissed her in a churchyard outside Wigan, nor the youth who had demanded her in rough-hewn strength, aged seventeen, in springtime on the banks of the Stour. They induced in her refinement amid the outrageous act committed against her; smothering with dignity the impropriety that she should be so invaded. Honour was laid in her husband and his kisses were sweet to her mouth. Vaguely, she wondered if she might bear his child, and in this new-found womanhood drew him down to her, telling in a gust of words that she needed him, too, in truth and love. Then no longer was she in the bed of a lover, but taken to a wild place which she had never known; a land of flowing forests laden with the tangled skeins of primitive flowers. And in this place the man's voice grew louder, louder; it was a command in which she died by conquest, in a strength greater than hers, and she knew that she was one with him, that the union was complete. She was astonished that it was so beautiful, so simple, and she could have cried aloud at this discovery, such was her peace, and joy. Presently Gideon sighed.

'Milly . . .' he said.

In a clubbed silence of disbelief, she held him, listening, but he did not speak again. Until now she had heard him calling for Sun Heron, so it must have been imagination, she thought; indeed, how could it be otherwise? How could this man have called her name when she was but the husk of the woman he was possessing?

Knowing this, she yet held him, cherishing his face with kisses.

23

Now for the first time the great forces joined; the insurgents came thronging down narrow Dowlais Hill, but they
were now without purpose. Having delayed the attack on
Penydarren House, divided over whether or not to accept
the wages restoration or persist for an increase and other
points of Reform, the rioters stumbled on with the most
militant in the van, and among these were Lewis Lewis and
Richard Evans; but other leaders such as Abod and Dai Solomon, Tom Vaughan and Dan Thomas advised for acceptance
of the masters' terms, and these, under their own banners,
followed at the rear. Thousands, too, their fire quenched by
the dissent, were drifting back to their homes—their great
numbers allowing them to defy the Scotch Cattle who guarded
the escape routes back to the towns of The Top. The story of
lack of union was being retold. The leaders were not the only
ones divided: collier was pitted against puddler in the grasp
of greed; baller opposed cutter and the behinders and picklers
of the Pontypool tinplate shrieked their arguments at the Vaynor hauliers, demanding respect for trade: Union branches
squabbled with the Benefit members, Oddfellows challenged
the Dowlais Building Society to see bloody sense. And the
clamour rose from them as they stumbled, hungry and dis-
organised, down the cobbles of Dowlais High; and they
marched in ragged contempt, distrustful of neighbour and
town, trade against trade, rate against rate. In this fashion,
with their red and black banners of Reform sagging on their
shoulders, they came to a place which was the narrowest on the
hill, and before them was a solid block of red and gold, and the

shine of bayonet steel. It was the 93rd Highlanders, their vicious enemies of the Castle massacre, and elements of the Militia. Some of these were lying side by side on the road; others were kneeling, a great body was standing; all had bayonets fixed, and their muskets pointed fifty deep. From the windows of the little terraced houses of the Irish projected muskets; around corners and from the grimy alleys the bayonets pointed, flashing in the morning sun. And before the soldiers their commanding officer stood motionless, his sword upraised, waiting to give the command to fire.

The van of the rioters stopped, flinging themselves back as those behind tried to force them on. Lewis Lewis spun to face them, crying:

'Ay, then what ails you? Rush them!'

The mob muttered and shoved; some lowered their faces: none moved forward and a man cried, dancing to the fore: 'Lewis is right—rush, rush! We are thousands, and they are under five hundred!'

'Are ye daft? D'ye want the same as ye got at the Castle?'

Another shouted: 'I say keep them here on guard while we get in the men from the Brecon and Swansea roads—we've got bloody thousands up there doing nothing!'

The soldiers did not move. The commanding officer was like a statue, the sword upraised, and in this presence of courage and training, the mob gibbered, its purpose waned. Still another—a man with one leg—came from the edge of the crowd on a crutch, and waved it, shouting:

'Are ye milk-sops or are ye Welsh? God alive, I come from the north—is this what ye call Glamorgan?'

'Talk sense, man!' bawled a woman. 'Half of your lot are running.'

'And what about the Merthyr workers, then? Where the hell they got to?' This from a Dowlais puddler under Guest, and he was eight pounds ten in debt to the Shop there, and on the black-list. 'Is this a Dowlais fight alone? I'm a Staffordshire man, and proud of it. One bang from a fowling-piece and you damned Welsh are off!'

'I say rush and to hell with what comes!' shouted Lewis Lewis.

They fumed, they pushed and muttered threats; they fretted, but they did not rush, and in seconds years were lost; Reform was lost; hopes, ambitions died. And they fell to silence, staring at the bayonets. From behind the soldiers came Josiah John Guest, and he cried, his arms high:

'See, you are betrayed! Most of you are from Dowlais and the towns of Blaenafon and Pontypool, Tredegar and Nantyglo under Crawshay Bailey. Is this a Top Town fight, then? Or is it your fight for the people of Cyfarthfa? For where are the comrades of Merthyr, for whom you have come to fight? Are they attacking Penydarren House? They are not! They have camped in thousands on the road to Brecon!'

'It is a lie!' shouted Lewis Lewis. 'Am I not here?'

'You might be,' said Guest drily, 'but what of the thousands? Are Dowlais men to die for Cyfarthfa?—if so, it is a strange form of riot. And I tell you this—I have come in your cause; for had I not done so these soldiers would have cut you to pieces. Earlier we told your deputation that Mr. Crawshay *might* grant a restoration of wages. Now you want even more, and he withdraws all his offers, for you do not adopt peaceful methods of negotiation. As for you Dowlais men—have I not always listened to your complaints?'

There was a roar of derision, about the last sound they made. Guest shouted: 'Bring all your complaints to me after a return to work, and I will listen again.'

'Ay,' said Lewis Lewis, 'I wonder where I have heard that before?' He swung to the mob. 'I say rush them! They can't kill all of us—rush them, and join the Merthyr men at Cyfarthfa!'

Guest said blandly: 'At Cyfarthfa, man? The last time I heard of them they were retreating along the Brecon Road.' They were not, but anything would do; it was stroke and counter-stroke. Now he turned to Colonel Morgan. 'Right, Commanding Officer, they have been warned, now you may fire when you care, even though they be my own men mostly,' and he stepped through the ranks of the soldiers and went into a house. The officer moved to the side of the road and pressed himself against the wall, the sword held higher. And the men stared into five hundred levelled muskets, then faced down, and broke.

It was Monday the sixth of June, the day of the Guest betrayal.

The soldiers did not move; the mob began to disperse into the hills, but many, braver than the most, crossed to the west and joined the insurgents on the roads to Brecon and Swansea, to help them keep control of the town, and here they underwent much drilling and parades, with a flying of banners, and two great black flags were seen flying on the turnpike road to the north. But, from his high turret in Cyfarthfa Castle, William Crawshay, the iron master, noticed a split in the ranks of even these rioters, for despite the crackle of their muskets and drilling, many were seen to be returning home, and there remained only the hard-core of armed insurgents. Some were seen throwing away their weapons or burying them. Soon, even the parades ceased; the banners were lowered, the red flags burned, the effigies destroyed. And Crawshay, to assist the return to peace, again abandoned the reduction in wages at Cyfarthfa and Hirwaun, or so it was reported: this he later, and publicly, revoked.

Sun Penderyn was sitting on the bed in Seven Ynys, looking out at the dram-road and deserted Bridge Street when Mamie came.

'How's Billa?' asked Sun.

'As well as can be expected, poor girl. God, she pinned her soul on that little Merve.'

'It will be better when old Dai and Mr. Jam come,' said Sun.

'And your Dic,' said Mamie. 'Did I tell ye my Randy's been seen?'

'No!'

Mamie beamed. 'Ay—seen up on Cefn night 'fore last—by old Nell Regan, the Dynefor Irish—ye remember Nell?'

Sun nodded. According to the reports coming in, anyone up

on Cefn above the Brecon Road was armed; one of these detachments of rioters had ambushed the 93rd, and the Highlanders were after every one of them: led by Captain Moggridge, the Swansea rebels were being brought home captive in batches: it was said that the new soldiers entering the town had immediately been sent to capture the outlying rebels, and Crawshay himself was preparing to assist in apprehending the ringleaders. Standing there at the window Sun began to wonder what had happened to Gideon. Zimmerman, they said, had fled before the first shot was fired, but it was inconceivable to her that Gideon would run, too: William Twiss, the Unionist she despised, had gone to Aberdare, boldly preaching the need of Unionism, she had heard. The puddler Tom Llewellyn, into whose hands most women would have delivered their lives, had been seen as far east as Pontypool. Turning away she thanked God that Dic was on Aberdare mountain.

'I am thankful to Morgan Howells, mind,' she said to Mamie, who was making the bed.

'Ay, ay, he do good intended,' gasped Mamie, bending. 'Be all right, won't it, when your Dico comes back with that Seion fella.'

Lifting the baby against her, Sun turned again to the window.

The men were crowding in now, made courageous by their very numbers. They thronged down Dynefor and Jackson's, through Dixon and into *China*. Sun saw Philip Lewis, the gambo man, come into Sixteen Ynys, his face blackened, as if he had just returned from a Tasker shift; a few days earlier he had clubbed down a Highlander with one fist and felled a second with a tapper: Blind Dick and Hugh Pughe trotted in on their pony, the harp over its rear—first prize for tenor and accompaniment at the Abergavenny Eisteddfod—and now they were looking for Shoni Melody... Among the men coming in from the Swansea road was Dai Solomon and Tom Vaughan, Dick Llaw-Haearn and Robert Jones, and these went quickly to their sobbing wives, already in earshot of the transportation hulks, yet unable to run because of children ... Molly Caulara was on the Iron Bridge again, chatting to the colliers who stayed at home, with the superficial gaiety of a woman lost: the radical Unitarians were flooding down the streets, fearlessly ranting the need of Reform in the face of defeat. Dragoons were galloping the lanes around Merthyr, bringing in the malefactors on their saddle cords, haltered like beasts. Militia squads were marching with the precision of conquerors, their blue and red uniforms a contrast to the ragged droop of the bearded conquered. The Castle and Talbot hotels were being prepared for the arrival of Mr. Evans Thomas of Sully, the chairman of the county quarter sessions; coaches and horses were being requisitioned to convey the accused to the county gaol at Cardiff. Men and women were being snatched from their houses as the pace of retribution grew. Shopkeepers thronged the streets with new-found courage, condemning and accusing, and whole families were examined for the presence of loot. Several of the murdered were claimed by mourning relatives from the coach house of the Castle Inn, and decently buried, but when the relatives returned from the funerals they were examined before the military court for participation in the rising. Therefore, many who died of wounds for want of medical attention were buried secretly, by night, in the open fields or cinder-tips of the works; therefore the total number killed by the soldiers that day has not been recorded. And the gambos and carts began again their endless journeyings, returning the furniture to their previous owners, though Miss Blossom Thomas never lost her picture. Clank clank up to the door of Number Five, Ynys, and Mamie Goldie opened it wide; the young lieutenant said, with soldiers at attention behind him:

'A man died who belonged to this house. I have orders to examine his mother for participation in the riot—Mrs. Jam, I am instructed . . .'

'Get out, you murdering swines,' said Mamie, 'the man was ten years old,' and she slammed the door in his face.

Strangely, although she did not see this, the young lieutenant bowed.

In her misery, when darkness fell, Merthyr tossed and turned: two inquests were held for scores of dead.

And Dic Penderyn did not come.

Instead, with darkness, Shoni Crydd came with three other special constables. The moon was shining over Merthyr when Sun opened the door. And they spoke no word, but pushed past her into the kitchen, and when she came, demanding, they slammed the door behind her.

'What the hell's the meanin' of this?' She gripped the petticoat against her throat.

'You'll soon know, Missus,' said Shoni Crydd.

The baby began to cry upstairs, but she did not hear it. And when Crydd eased his great bulk into a chair she stood above him, flushed with anger.

'He hasn't been near Merthyr, and you know it!' she breathed, bending to him. 'He's been up on Aberdare mountain, and you know that, too, don't you?'

'Ay, ay, woman,' said Shoni, and lit his pipe.

'Then what are ye doing here?'

Bill Tobbo and Boy O'Hara were Irish, and they leaned against the wall with easy confidence, coming to collect a Welsh; but Mog Morgan was Welsh from Swansea, and there was a sickness in him as he listened to the baby, and his bowels shrank in the knowledge of his perfidy.

Shoni Crydd said: 'There's evidence against him. Sworn statements have been taken from James Abbott, the barber, that your man was in the deputation...'

'A deputation—here, in town?'

'At the Castle Inn. Tom Darker confirms it, and he saw him again in the mob some five minutes later.'

'Tom Darker! D'you take the words of a paid Judas now, then?' A panic was growing within her. Soon Dic would come, and they would take him, these men would not be here unless they knew he was coming...

Crydd said: 'And the testimony of Jim Drew—this fella swears his life away, woman, an' he'll be hard put to deny it. For Drew says he was in the Castle deputation: that he saw him wrestling with the Highlanders, and stab a private soldier with a bayonet, and that's a hanging crime.'

'But how could he, fella, if he was up on Aberdare?' She gripped her hands and shouted into his face.

'Where your man says he was and where he got to are different things, Mrs. Penderyn. Shall I tell ye something else? I saw him, too.'

'You're a bloody liar, and Dic will prove it!'

'Me and the Private Black. God alive, woman—what else do you want—Guest, Crawshay and the whole army troop?'

She wandered about, holding herself, pausing before Mog Morgan, who turned away his eyes; the chair creaked under the bulk of Shoni Crydd; the two Irish Specials watched her with understanding smiles. To Morgan, Sun said: 'And you, did you see him, too, or didn't they pay you enough?'

'I'm only doing my job, woman.'

'And your job is a stink in the noses of decent Welsh!' She swung to Shoni Crydd. 'Have you sought out Lewis Lewis, for there's no damn mention o' him that I hear of?'

Crydd blew out smoke. 'They're fetchin' him. They're fetching them all, Mrs. Penderyn. And I call on you to tell your man to come quietly, or it'll be the worse for him.'

Sun sat slowly on to a chair, her eyes bright in her bloodless face. 'May God have mercy on ye soul, Shoni Crydd, and Abbot and Drew, and the man Tom Darker, for me chap was up on the mountain, and with a witness to prove it, and I tell you this. The truth will out and you'll be stained with it, you and yours down the generations, and you'll ne'er rub it out. How long are you staying?'

'Until your fella comes.' He grunted on his clay and cocked it up in his heavy face and folded his hands on his stomach.

'Then out and fetch another four,' said she, 'for if my Dic finds the likes of these in here, then God help you.'

Crydd did not reply; reaching out, he lowered the wick in the lamp and the room danced with shadows; upstairs the baby had ceased to cry.

'One shift out of you—one sound, and we floor you, woman —remember it,' said Boy O'Hara, the Irish, and Bill Tobbo, who hailed from County Clare, moved to the sound of running footsteps, and stood pressed behind the door.

The special constables ranged as far afield as Pembrokeshire and Carmarthenshire, pulling suspects from their beds and transporting them to Merthyr under escort: the hills from Waun to the Blorenge were combed for escapees; barns were pulled out and haystacks prodded, farmhouses were visited by night, and at ten o'clock David Hughes, Tom Vaughan and Dai Thomas were brought in roped—he who was known by the nick-name Dick Llaw-Haearn, and his woman, Betsy Paul, had to be beaten off by the constables. Then, before midnight came Tom Llewellyn of Cyfarthfa, and he was caught on the mountain of Caerphilly, trying to reach the sea, and the workers lined the roads and jeered when the Military brought him to the Castle Inn, in chains, because he had defected. Broad, handsome, bright in the eye, he came now with shuffling feet, his face low; and men shouted insults into his face, and women, who once adored him, spat on his clothes. Many there were who had not run away, but returned to their homes to await the knock; men like David Richards, whose wife was in labour even as the Specials came, and David Jones who was frightened of his mother, but no man alive: these were haltered by the neck, yet walked with dignity and smiles, despite the humiliation. Some were captured who are not recorded; broken men and boys, ragged and dishevelled, soaked with the dew of sleeping rough; thumped into wakefulness by the batons of the special constables, the ruffians of Merthyr, and many carried bruises, and blood was on their faces: some, too, were wounded, the injuries septic, and they stood in the Castle yard in aimless groups while the surgeons attended them. Joan Jenkins was brought in shackled to her husband and brother, and both these were men terrified while she walked cocky, spitting at the feet of the examining magistrate; these, with others, were taken for looting furniture, but claimed they were looting their own property, then, for it was furniture distrained by Coffin's Court, for debt. Margo Davies of Dynefor came weeping, with her hands over her face, unafraid of the possibility of transportation to the Colonies and the bloodstained sticks, but fearful of the anger of her outraged relatives. Twenty-six rioters were taken to Cardiff gaol by escorted coaches, rumbling out of Merthyr amid the cock-a-hoop Militia, the prancing yeomanry of boy-men on their big farm mares and horses: they went with manacled hands and feet, in the manner of felons, bowed on the juddering seats. Two there were, however, who were uncaptured just before this event, and both were to have their names written in the annals of their country's history; one was Lewis Lewis, and the other was Dic Penderyn.

When the mob broke on Dowlais Hill, Lewis Lewis ran to the village of Penderyn, the place from which Dic had taken his name to avoid confusion with other Lewises. It is said that his wife and family, with their furniture distrained, were living in Brecon; but he ran to Penderyn because it was his home, he was born there; also, at one time earlier he had been employed by Mr. Morgan of Bodwigiad, to whom it has been said that he was related, having been a huntsman on the estate. Indeed, many have claimed that Lewis Lewis was the illegitimate son of one of the local squires who abounded in those parts; some even said he was of noble birth, and that this is why he escaped the rope, but no proof exists of any of this. It has even been assumed that the English government mistook Lewis Lewis, aged thirty-eight, for the younger Richard Lewis called Dic Penderyn, since both men had connections with this village so named. One thing is sure; no man played a greater part in the riots of Merthyr, yet he did not die for this responsibility.

Hiding in the grounds of Bodwigiad, Lewis Lewis was taken on the road in Penderyn, for the special constables had a nose for cook-pots, and two named Eynon Beynon and John Selwyn lay in wait at a place of loneliness beyond small cottages; as he went past in the night mist these men took him from the hedge, and both were mountain fighters. One tripped him and as he sprawled the other held him, but he rose and flung them off; hands clenched, he awaited them, and they came with batons drawn.

'Come quiet, Lewis, or it'll come worse for you!'

And Lewis feinted and caught Beynon with a right to the head, ducked Selwyn's swinging baton and hooked him to the stomach, and as he fell Lewis dived for the open fields, but the man Selwyn, who had once fought with Abod of Penydarrén, went full length and caught his heels and pulled him down, and, holding him, awaited the truncheon of Beynon, who beat him. Yet the villagers of Penderyn slept on, for he made no sound, it was said. And they bound him on the road, being men of great strength, and took him to the Lamb Inn, and there detained him; and they sent a child to the Castle Inn to tell of the capture: William Crawshay, the iron master, hearing this, rode personally with Colonel Bush, the commander of the Pensioners, and Lieutenant Franklin with a large body of his yeomen cavalry, and took him from the Lamb Inn. With his hands tied behind him and a halter around his neck, Lewis Lewis came on foot into Merthyr with an escort of cavalry jogging about him and an iron master and a Colonel of the Pensioners leading the way in triumph.

In this manner Lewis Lewis came, and his was the dignity, said the people.

And on his way to the Castle Inn the prisoner passed within sight of Seven Ynys where Shoni Crydd and the other three Specials were lying in wait for his friend and namesake, Dic Penderyn.

Dic parted with his escort, the Seion deacon's son, at a place just south of Cefn Heights where the 93rd Highlanders' ammunition convoy had been ambushed; here, according to his family's belief he had been living in a cave, and did not return to Merthyr until they instructed. Mr. Evans returned to his home in Penrhiw and Dic walked in darkness across the tracks until he came to an inn, and there drank. Other inns presented themselves on the return to home, and at these he stopped and drank also; he was tipsy when he came past the simmering furnaces of Ynys and crossed the dram-road, unseen, and ran down to Number Seven Caradoc and Asa, two of Billa's boys were playing on the slag tumps as he came, and one of these he grasped and tossed high in a gale of laughter, and Shoni Crydd heard this laughter and rose from his chair in Sun's kitchen.

'Watch the woman,' he said, and Bill Tobbo gripped Sun

and twisted her against the wall and put his hand over her mouth. Boy O'Hara, the big Irish, got it first as Dic entered, because he was nearest. Gay with laughter, Dic burst through the door, his arms out for Sun, and he shouted, seeing O'Hara, ducked the baton and swung him hard to the jaw, and the Special slipped down the front of him with a sigh: three now, and Dic wheeled as Shoni Crydd came in, caught the baton and twisted it from his hand and pinned the big man against the wall as Crydd kicked and clubbed, but every blow took him clean, and blood was on Crydd's face as he got clear. Sun turned on Bill Tobbo who still had his hand over her face, and bit him, and when he yelled and got his fingers free she took her nails to him while Dic leaned over her shoulder and caught Tobbo square, and he fell.

'Run for it, Dic!'

'Not till I've done these bastards,' and he backed into Crydd who was rising and sent him floundering, then back-handed O'Hara as he was getting up. Sun was down as Mamie Goldie came through the door with a copper-stick; stooping, she dragged Sun to a corner, then belaboured Shoni Crydd with one hand while she threw the table cups at Mog Morgan, who was standing in a corner doing nothing while Tobbo and O'Hara were bellowing for help. With Crydd on his feet again, Dic attacked, hooking left and right to face and body with smashes to go through him, and the table went over in a crash of crocks, with Crydd between its legs and Billa, who had come through the back, hit Mog Morgan with a chair, and him still doing nothing but shielding himself. And, at that moment the three big Irish lodgers, Tim, Michael and Joe, who were due from Taibach to lodge, wandered along the Row looking for Billa and a bed, and heard the fighting, and a pot came through the back window to make sure of it, so they waded in, leaving their coats outside, which is right and proper, said Mamie after, for you can't let a good fight go by. This brought the neighbours, male mostly, and Mamie and Billa landed Shoni Crydd copper sticks for luck and pulled Sun outside while the men piled in, with more special constables running down from the Popi Davey. They've had some fights up and

323

down the Row, said Mr. Papa Tomo Thomas, waving his red flag, but nothing like the one they had in Seven Ynys when they tried to take Dic Penderyn, for most of the neighbours came out to assist the Specials along Bridgefield with rolling-pins and shillelaghs, and the Miners' Arms turned out, and the roughs came running in from Iron Bridge, and the worshippers got up off their knees in Ynysgau Chapel, for they were just giving thanks for the end of the riot. And then the Military came. The Military came with loaded muskets and bayonets fixed just as Shoni Crydd came out backwards with Mamie and Billa after him, and he tripped and fell at the feet of the sergeant.

'What's happening here?' the sergeant demanded.

Frozen, the Welsh stood, and Crydd said, from the ground: 'It's the man Lewis...' and he pointed at Dic who was standing in the doorway with his arms around his wife.

'How many more Lewises,' said the soldier. 'We've got one up at the Castle already.'

'Richard Lewis, this one,' said Crydd, getting up, and blood was on his mouth, 'but he goes by the name of Dic Penderyn.'

'And you are arresting him for riot? I've never seen the man before.' The sergeant was young, his accent broad North Country.

'For riot, on the testimony of James Abbot, Thomas Darker and James Drew.'

'This has not been notified, and he is not on the list,' replied the sergeant, consulting a paper.

'How could he be?' asked Sun. 'He was nowhere near the rioters, he was up on Aberdare mountain these past four days.'

'I saw him in the deputation,' said Crydd. 'James Abbott and I will bear witness—we saw him in the Castle Inn deputation. And William Williams, the tailor, saw him also. James Drew bears witness that he saw him stab your soldier.'

The sergeant's eyes immediately snapped up at this. 'Private Black of the 93rd?' He moved near to Dic and Sun. 'You stabbed one of ours, with a bayonet?'

'I was on Aberdare mountain...'

'Oh, God,' whispered Sun.

The young sergeant stepped aside and nodded peremptorily to his men. 'Take him,' he said.

The neighbours stood in silence. Only one voice was heard then—old Papa Tomo down in One Ynys, waving his flag and bawling; then another. Faintly, from the floor above, came the sound of the baby crying.

24

RANDY GOLDIE came back to Mamie two days after Dic was taken, and these two days after the ending of the riot he had spent up in Adulum Fields, with Blod. Mamie sank down on to a chair and Billa went out, taking the children, as he entered; he was soaked with dew and trembling with the sleeping out, despite it was June.

'Hallo, son,' said Mamie.

'Ay, ay,' he said, and he stood looking at her, not moving.

'Where you been till now, then?'

He shrugged. 'Up with Blod.'

'Anyone see you come in?'

He did not reply, but sat down and looked at his hands. 'You all right, then?' he asked eventually.

'Ay, fine. Old Dai and Billy Jam coming today, you know.' She warmed to him, trying to envelop him in her love, yet nervous to touch him lest the gossamer thread that bound them be broken by clumsiness. And as she moved uncertainly to get food for him, the door opened and Sun came in with her baby, Richard Jay. Her eyes switched from Mamie to Randy, and back.

'Randy's come home,' said Mamie simply.

'Ay, I see.' Sun kissed him in passing. 'You hungry, love?'

Randy nodded. The look in his eyes made her fight for normality.

'The kids will be glad you're back, boy.'

He nodded, his eyes distant, and said: 'I had Ned Tranter, mind—I saw to Ned Tranter.'

'Yes?' said Sun, and Mamie clutched herself at the fireplace.

'Oh, ay,' said Randy. 'I had him right enough—I shot him up on Cefn.'

'You ... you what?' whispered Mamie.

Sun reached out and gripped her arm, saying: 'You shot Ned Tranter because of Blod?'

'Ay, ay.'

There was no sound then but the ticking of the clock. Sun said: 'Have you told anybody else this?'

'Only the fellas—but Abod said it was all right, though. Dic said it didn't matter, neither—he said Tranter deserved it because of Blod.'

'Dic said that? When?'

'A couple o' nights back, up on Cefn. He'd come up from the Castle.'

Mamie was standing with her hands against her face; Sun said: 'You ... you saw Dic up at Cefn?'

'Oh, ay.' He grinned and wiped his mouth.

Sun said evenly: 'Randy, are ye sure it wasn't Lewis Lewis?'

His eyes were steady on hers. 'Lewis Lewis? Don't be daft—it were Dic, I tell ye. D'you think I don't know Dic from Lew Lewis?' Then he turned away and screwed his fist into his palm, saying, 'But I had that Tranter, mind—ay, girl, I had Tranter ...'

It was at this time that the iron master, Samuel Homfray, blamed William Crawshay of Cyfarthfa for being the cause of the riots; history relates this; the fact is recorded.

Gideon met Lemuel Samuel in High Street. And it was with a surge of joy that he recognised him from a distance of over twenty feet, for little identified Lemuel, in his rags, from the army of beggars in Merthyr at this time. Gideon was as a man revitalised with the return of his sight; as with the blows of the Cefn Riders a year ago, so the concussion caused by the musket butt had raised a curtain on his blindness, and he had never seen so well since the Taibach accident. Shadow and sun, however, alternatively fluctuated; the streets shimmered brightly, then died into blackness, but he saw Lemuel clearly.

' 'Morning, Gid Davies!' said Lemuel.

'Good morning, Mr. Samuel.'

'You heard about me, Gid Davies?' Lemuel beamed. 'Got a job in the Star slaughterhouse!' He seemed to have forgotten that Gideon should be blind, and he gabbled amid the press of the people going to market, 'Special on the calves, I am—I remember, I always used to say to my Mavie—get me around the meat an' I'm happy—there's money in meat, ye know. Just give me a good knife and a few fat pigs, and I'm fine.'

'Everyone to his own vocation,' said Gideon, and he saw Lemuel clearly for the first time; the creased folds of a gaunt face that had died, the pin-boned carcass, skewered and trussed on a skeleton draped with rags. The man moved furtively, nudging. 'You heard about that Dic Penderyn, of course—death by hanging?'

'I have,' said Gideon, head bowed.

'But Lewis Lewis got reprieved. Serve him right if he got it, too—don't hold with rioting and stabbing soldiers—only doing their duty.' Lemuel sniffed. 'But it was a pity about Mrs. Taibach and her Willie. Very fond of her, I was. And Percy Bottom Note—old enough to know better—I saw him, mind —you'd never believe it. He just walked on to the guns.'

'A man has his reasons,' said Gideon, blandly.

May Harries, the door-trapper, passed them, looking up at Gideon with large, serene eyes, and she returned his smile, her teeth missing in front: it was a red, gummy smile of milk and a freckled nose upturned, and he thought he had never seen anything more beautiful. Distantly, he heard Lemuel say: 'But Sun Penderyn's chap asked for it, though. I mean, you can't stab a King's soldier with his own bayonet and wound him sore, now can ye...?'

'Is there proof of this?'

'Oh, ay!'

'But how can you be sure?' asked Gideon. 'Do you believe all you are told?'

'Told me eye, Gid Davies. I saw him—I tell ye, I saw the lad at it!'

The street sounds died; for Gideon then sun began to fade, and the people pushed, chattering soundlessly like puppets. He said: 'But how could you have seen him stab the soldier—you weren't even here!'

'Oh, but I was, Gid Davies! I came with Mr. Note. We were sleeping near the beehives for warmth, and heard the firing.' He grinned delightedly. 'But Mr. Note, he stayed longer'n me, though!'

'You actually saw Dic Penderyn stab Private Black, the Highlander?'

'Ay, ay!'

Gideon swallowed down the sickness rising in his throat, and said: 'Are you ... are you quite sure it wasn't Lewis Lewis? No—don't reply at once, be careful. Have you ever seen Lewis Lewis, the haulier?'

'Ay. When Crawshay brought him back as a prisoner.'

'And that was the only time you saw him? Did you see him, for instance, during the rioting outside the Castle Inn?'

'Of course—when he was up on the lamp-post. And I saw Dic Penderyn go in with the deputation after you called for them ... I was at the back.'

'But did you see him come out?'

'Come out...?' Lemuel Samuel scratched his ear, frowning.

'Think, man—it is important. You saw Dic go in, you say. Did you see him come out with the rest of the deputation?'

'No, but Lewis Lewis wi' his hat off, cheering on the mob!'

'Did you? Private Black, who was stabbed, gave evidence that it was Dic out in front with his hat off cheering on the mob.'

'Well, well...' Lemuel Samuel was nonplussed, and Gideon said:

'There was ten thousand people in front of the Castle Inn, and you were at the back. Are you still certain that you saw Dic Penderyn struggling with the soldier, Private Black?'

'Oh, ay—I just said so.'

'What was he wearing?'

'Who?'

'Dic Penderyn—I asked you what he was wearing.'

'A grey smock and duck trews—saw him as clear as me eye. After he stabbed the soldier he fired at a window of the inn and ran off.'

'You are quite sure that the man who stabbed Black was wearing a smock and duck trews?'

'Ay!' Lemuel Samuel stared into Gideon's face.

'And you're prepared to swear this on oath to Mr. Tregelles Price.'

'Ay!' Lemuel grinned. 'I got the right fella, didn't I?'

'You did not. Dic Penderyn was wearing a blue coat and trousers that day, there is proof of this. You be careful, Lemuel Samuel—everybody is talking too much, everybody has seen too much. A man's life is at stake, and the only one who seems to realise it is Private Black, the soldier—even he can't identify the man who stabbed him. You watch that tongue, or somebody might try nipping off the end of it.'

'Dear me,' said Lemuel Samuel.

Merthyr seethed with bitterness and plans for revenge; the cause of Reform, which once unified master and servant, was now destroyed by the rising, said Colonel Brotherton, who gave the best official military account. 'It must be long before, if ever, this bad spirit is allayed,' he wrote; he who, but a few weeks later, met his death in the riots of Bristol.

In riot he was an expert.

The bailiffs came soon after Dic was arrested and evicted Sun and Richard Jay from Number Seven, Ynys, so she moved in with Mamie and Billa, though it's a bit inconvenient with Dai and Mr. Jam coming in, said Billa, to say nothing of Mike McTigue and Joe and Tim, his brothers.

'But Dai and Mr. Jam won't be here permanent for at least a fortnight,' said Mamie.

'I'll find somewhere else,' said Sun on the doorstep.

'You'll do no such thing,' replied Billa. 'Neighbours is neighbours, or so I've been told, and it anna a bad thing— we'll 'ave enough women in the place for a petticoat government. What you say, love?'

'Somebody's coming, Mam!' yelled Saul.

'Somebody's always coming to this house,' said Billa, and she took Sun's arms. 'You go inside, love, and make yourself at home.'

'Gid Davies been asking about you, you heard?' said Mamie.

'I haven't seen him,' replied Sun, and she smoothed her baby's face.

'Called twice, but you was out.'

Somebody took a fist to the door.

'That'll be Randy,' said Mamie, and opened it, and Dai End-On and Billy Jam were standing on the doorstep with beams.

'Good God, it never do rain but it pours,' said Mamie.

''Morning, missus!' said Dai.

'How are ye, Billa?' asked Mr. Jam. Solvent and sober were they, and returning to wives and lovers, eh; me darling, said Mr. Jam, and the two of them bowed with buttonhole posies on their chests big enough for a State funeral. Dai said: 'Come early, see—we know you'll be delighted.'

'It'll be a bit of a squeeze, if you get me,' said Mamie, shepherding them inside. 'We got Mrs. Penderyn staying a bit, see, so it's awkward on the beds, you understand?'

'Dear me,' said Dai, glum.

'I want to sleep with me da,' wailed Asa, jumping on tiptoe.

'The dear little soul,' said Mr. Jam, vicious.

'He's not the only one,' said Billa. 'You'll have Caradoc and Amos and Abiah too. I tell you, we just anna got the beds!'

'And the rest are in with me,' said Mamie.

'*Diawch*,' whispered Dai. 'I was hoping...' he faltered, looking.

Bang bang on the back.

'*Diwedd!*' said Mamie, 'I am in rags. Who's that now, then?'

Mike and Tim and Joe on the doorstep, handsome and dark in their Sunday best, and down they went in bows with bunches of Welsh poppies.

'What you lot want, then?' asked Billy Jam, weak.

'Come to lodge, Mr. Jam,' replied Mike, and he straightened his stock.

'Good morning, Mike,' said Billa, and there was a new beauty in her.

'Could ye come back a bit later, lads, while we try to sort something out?' asked Mamie. 'Things are sort of topsy-turvy . . .'

'I'll help you sort it, Mame,' said Mike, and came inside, but Dai End-On pushed him off.

'Away,' said Dai. 'We'll have lodgers when we grant ye, *away*!'

With clasped hands Billa roamed into the front room and stood before the window; she was shivering. Saul and Asa came in behind her, but she ushered them back into the kitchen. She was frightened, not of Mike the big Irishman, but of herself. And even as she stood there clasped within herself, he tapped the glass of the window. His hair was black and shining, she noticed; his teeth were white and even in his smile. She could hear Dai and Mr. Jam tramping down the dram-road, their hobnail boots chinking on the rails, and Mr. Jam was laughing. With trembling fingers she pushed up the window and Mike's hands closed on hers on the sill.

'What about me, then?' he asked. 'Oi Oi, missus, what about me?'

'Oh, God, Mike, leave me alone!'

'He's no good to ye, woman—you know he's no good to you!'

'Ach, please . . .'

'I love you—and I told you 'afore and I'm telling you now. I want ye, Billa.'

'And all me kids?'

'And all your kids. Look, I can have me pick o' the women

332

—I'm on good money and I'm as spright as a spring lamb. I'd work for ye, girl—I'd do late shift for you—say the word and I'll thump him out of it.'

People were passing down the cut; a barge went by and the bargees waved, but she did not raise her face, and Mike said: 'You make pretty men, and I want me own son—but it's got to be from you, Billa.' He emptied his hands at her. 'Now what have ye got in Billy Jam but a randy old drunk?'

At this she lifted her face and said to him: 'You get out of here, Mike McTigue. He's my fella and you've got no right to slander him! I think you're disgusting! Get out, you hear me?'

He straightened, and she held the sill lest she should fling herself against him, and said, with tears in her throat, 'There ought to be a law against it, pestering a decent woman!'

He looked at her. 'Didn't know ye felt like that ... Goodbye, Billa ...' He drifted away.

The door went back on its hinges then and three of the boys rushed in, seeking her in shouts, hauling at her arms. Amos, aged five, got a chair and stood on it and put his arms around her neck, kissing her with a wet mouth. Then Mamie came and stood with her hands on her hips, shouting:

'You know where that pair have gone, do you?—Jackson's —that means the Wellington, and they haven't even taken their boots off!'

Billa nodded. Mike, with his hands deep in his trews was going over the bridge.

'Goodbye, my darling,' she said.

It was a fortnight after Dic's trial.

Gideon said: 'Can you spare a minute, Sun?'

She was shopping in Georgetown with money Mamie had given her, and did not turn when she heard his voice, but stopped and leaned against the wall of the Horseshoes.

'Haven't ye caused us enough grief and bother?'

When she faced him she saw that his eyes held a new expression and colour, and she said, warmer, 'You can see, Gid?' and peered.

'More than a little.'

She smiled. 'Oh, I'm glad, I'm glad!'

'A soldier hit me with a musket butt,' he said simply. 'I have sight now, but it will fade—indeed, it's not so good as it was. How are you?'

Her face was pale, and she was thin. He was worried at her thinness.

'As good as can be expected.'

'And Richard Jay?'

She brightened into life and her eyes shone. 'Och, he's a wee fella! The spit and body of Dico, did ye know?'

'Yes, Mamie told me.'

'But ye never come to see him, Gid.'

He could not explain that he could never bring himself to do this. Not only did he feel responsible, in large measure, for her grief, and was ashamed; but this was Dic Penderyn's child, and the thought that another man had possessed her since the journey from Taibach induced in him an abhorrence. Standing there within reach of her was like reliving a dream: indeed, recently in a vivid dream he had possessed her, and her body had been sweet to his, so that desire and taste seemed to unify his need of her. Time was, he thought bitterly, he could have possessed her with a gesture: she had even offered herself, and he had rejected her. Now, standing before him in her soiled coat and the weariness of a heavy labour, he needed her infinitely more; the shadows were deep under her eyes, her hair was untidy, but he did not see these things; he knew only that he loved her, but she belonged to Dic Penderyn.

The smoke of Cyfarthfa moved between them. She said: 'Dear me, things do change, don't they? Not many of the old friends left save Mamie and Billa, and I don't give tuppence for Randy ...' She shifted the basket on her stomach. 'And it were a pity about old Waxey Evans—I mean, he was a wicked old soak, but he didn't deserve that.'

Gideon nodded. Sun continued, stepping off the rails: 'And Sara Grieve, the poor thing—that were quick, weren't it?'

'Yes.' By moving behind her he could get the scent of the wind; she never lost this strange and lovely smell, and he remembered that it came from her hair. Now he was thinking it strange that in his dream of her this same hair had been long and thick to his fingers, its perfume different. Such, he thought bitterly, was the sad incompetence of dreams; now he smiled, for he preferred her hair short and unkempt, like this.

'That right you are living with Miss Thrush of Taibach?'

'Not, it is not true. She ... she took me in after the riot, and I will never forget her kindness, but I'm back in Cross Street now.'

The furnaces of Cyfarthfa went into blast then, two great valedictory flames roaring into the sky and the old bell-clang of the naked iron beat down Dynefor and consumed them, forbidding speech. Gideon said, when the roar subsided: 'You remember when we came into Merthyr together, Sun?'

'After the Cefn Riders?' She rubbed her face, smiling. 'That were a hundred years back.'

'And now you're married to Dic Penderyn.'

'Ay.'

The silence came again and they lowered their faces and moved their feet. A new and stifling awkwardness was parting them.

Gideon said: 'You ... you've heard of Tregelles Price?'

'The Neath master?'

He nodded, looking at his watch. 'I was just coming down to Mamie's to see you. You've heard he is getting out a petition for Dic, I suppose—he and Taliesin Williams, the schoolmaster, are coming up to my place tonight. Mr. Price would like to meet you ...'

She looked at the sky. 'They are wasting their time.'

'Perhaps, but at least they can try. Listen, it is important that you know this. One petition is based on the fact that after the deputation in the Castle, Dic went out of the back door, not the front...'

Her eyes snapped up at this. 'Don't be ridiculous! He was nowhere near the Castle—you yourself advised him, with Morgan Howells, to go up the mountain with the deacon's son!'

Gideon said levelly: 'He was at the Castle right enough,

335

Sun—best you face this. He might have started on the mountain, but he didn't stay there long. Half a dozen people saw him in the deputation—Abbott, Williams, Darker...'

'That bunch of criminals!'

'Randy himself saw him outside the inn, as well as up on Cefn—remember?'

Recalling this, Sun stiffened, and Gideon added: 'Marsden the draper saw him in the passage. Nancy Evans, William Philip and Ben Davies all attest to seeing him standing by the tap-room before the fighting—even David Abraham, the Special, saw him there and cautioned him not to go into the fighting.'

'So he was not in the fighting ...?' She was suddenly, urgently aware.

Gideon replied: 'Half a dozen testify that he was not, but men like Abbott and the other Specials are swearing his life away. That is why we must have this final petition to send round Wales—we will get thousands of signatures...'

She interjected faintly, as if the knowledge of Abbott's testimony had tamed her, 'And I still say they're wasting their time. The King has been threatened, he will have to hang somebody...' She closed her eyes. 'Oh, what a fool he was to come down from Aberdare...'

'Did you ... did you know Tregelles Price has seen Dic, Sun?'

'Ay. It was more'n they'd do for me—they turned me away.'

He said softly: 'Don't lose hope, I beg you. Because he's sentenced to death it doesn't mean he'll die, you know. Lewis Lewis was reprieved, wasn't he?'

She raised her face, 'But there's a difference, isn't there! There's a difference now they've discovered he's of noble birth —the bastard son of this one or that one...'

'I beg you not to believe all the things you hear!'

Bitterly, she said: 'Morgan Howells came yesterday. The day before I was fancied up with the Church of England— these are the devils who are hanging him! Pray, pray, pray!' Her voice rose. 'While you're on your knees ye can't get the bloody size of 'em. My God, what a country!'

Gideon said: 'In this I agree—we are faced by a corrupt institution. The King himself has read most of the Merthyr correspondence—some of it he has personally annotated—the facts are clear, the perjury is proved, yet he will not even grant petitions for an interview...'

Sun said softly, her voice vibrant: 'Then the blood of my Dic be on his head.'

'Mr. Price is going to London to see Melbourne, the Secretary of State—don't lose hope, I beg you.'

'I have lost hope,' she said. 'I'll not come up to see Mr. Price, and tell him from me that he's wasting his time. They will have to hang someone.'

Strangely, as she walked away, he heard her gay laughter echoing through the woods of Tir-Phil. Gideon watched until she turned up Chapel Street for the shops in Iron Lane.

'That youngster Dic Penderyn's due for the long drop, then,' said Dai End-On, and he parted his whiskers in the Wellington up by Jackson's and poured in a quart without so much as a swallow.

'First quart to settle the dust,' said Billy Jam. 'Set 'em up again, Mr. Jackson.'

'You living here, you two?' asked Jump Jackson, pouring the ale.

'Just moved in,' answered Dai. 'That fella they're dropping used to live next door but one to us—in fact, his woman's living wi' us now.'

'She's a nice kid is that Sun Penderyn,' said the landlord.

'Mind, it's the least we can do,' said Mr. Jam, and lifted his quart. 'Down the hatch, Dai lad—here's to the next thousand —it's a good local this—very convenient, as the saying goes.'

'Then you'll be interested in what it says here,' said Jump Jackson, bringing out *The Cambrian*. 'But God, they're roasting old Crawshay,' and he squinted over the top of his glasses, and read:

'"In looking at this peaceable conclusion of an unusually dangerous and bloody transaction, we cannot avoid thinking that the patient and forgiving character of the workmen stands painfully contrasted with the despotic and avaricious conduct of the master . . ." '

The landlord folded the newspaper and put it under the counter. 'And that's an extract from the London *Observer*, remember—enough to give the poor old lad a heart attack—I bet his dad won't like it; meself, I don't think it's fair.'

'Drink up, me old darlin',' said Dai End-On. 'We might as well go home the first night wet—I intend to start the way I'm goin' on.'

'I'm with ye in that, me old soak,' replied Mr. Jam, and Jump Jackson said, reflectively:

'But 'tis a bit hard, nevertheless. The lad used to come in here, ye know. He were a bit heavy on the ale, and sharp with his hands on a drunk, as the saying goes, but I'd lay me life on one thing—he'd not take a weapon to a man—there was no need, see—his fists were good enough. Did ye hear what Mr. Sockett said for the defence?'

'Ay—another quart o' that excellent brew, if you please,' said Dai.

' . . . He said it was a cryin' shame to hold the trial in English. Dic Penderyn was Welsh—he'd not know if he was pleading innocent or guilty.'

'Nor me,' said Dai, pushing up his mug.

Jump Jackson continued: 'And Mr. Sockett weren't in full possession of the evidence, mind—and they'll never publish the trial, of course. John Guest of Dowlais don't think Dic did it, and Mr. Dillwyn, the foreman o' the Grand Jury 'as written to Tregelles Price to say he's changed his mind about the verdict of Guilty—think o' that, lads—he's changed his mind!— what the blutty hell's happening, I say? You know what I think?'

'I think it's a beautiful brew,' said Dai, gasping and wiping his whiskers.

'I reckon that Lewis Lewis did it—that's what I think,' said Jump Jackson. 'You know what Squire Morgan of Bodwigiad

338

called him—a devoted victim!'

'That's what they'll call you if I don't get this quart,' said Billy, pushing up his pot. Taking it, the landlord filled it, adding:

'A devoted victim, eh? Ye don't get squires talking like that unless they've had a finger in the pie, so to speak, if ye get me. I reckon Lew Lewis rose off a silk-lined bed.'

'Now you're talking,' said Billy Jam, 'a silk-lined bed—that's what I'm off to—comin', me love, Mrs. Billa Jam Tart!'

The landlord said: 'Don't ye care about a fella dying, then?'

'Ye've got us in tears,' said Dai End-On.

'God help your women, that's all I say.'

'Ay, ay,' said Billy, and lifted his pot. 'Bottoms up, me lovely.'

25

CARDIFF was like a town of the dead when they hanged
Dic Penderyn. Most of the shops were closed on the previous
day, curtains were drawn over the windows of cottages, doors
were locked and barred. Nothing moved on the deserted
streets; the scaffold awaited, its rope dangling.

But at first light a man on horseback galloped in from
Worcester, and this was the hangman—a novice who had been
found at the last minute since no professional hangman could
be induced to undertake the task. And soon after this a great
crowd of people began to move like a black finger in procession: first from the valley of the Taff these people came;
many from Merthyr and Aberdare; later, in smaller groups
came more, dressed in mourning black, and they made no
sound, these people, who had come to watch Dic Penderyn
die; this, the first Welsh martyr of the working class. Many
were Catholic Irish, and these told their beads in whispered
incantations; others were English, the Staffordshire specialists; most were Welsh, coming with measured tread, with their
brass-bound bibles under their arms, and they went with their
faces upturned to the dawn, as if to an early chapel. Sun and
Billa walked at the head of the Taff Vale procession, and they
were dressed in funeral black, for to attend the hanging of a
relative was the custom, to send the last goodbye. Mamie,
whose feet were bad, did not come, so she stayed at home with
Richard Jay, Dic's baby son: Randy did not come, because,
although he had been told, he did not know of this event; and
he rose early and went up to Adulum to visit Blod. Gideon
walked with Miss Thrush, that she could guide him were his

sight again to fail; Dai and Billy Jam did not come since they were drinking in the Wellington. Tim and Joe McTigue, the Irish lodgers of Taibach did not come, but Mike, the eldest, did, in order to be close to Billa at this time. Molly Caulara came, and walked at the back, alone, since she was of the Popi Davey, and people wondered why she wept, since Sun Penderyn was not weeping. Gwen, Dic's sister, did not come because she was confined by illness, nor did his father and mother, because they could not bear it. But the Reverend Morgan Howells had come the previous night, and now with others, was in the condemned cell with Dic, and here he prayed. Miss Blossom Thomas walked in the Vale procession, because old Papa Tomo demanded this, as he would have done from a son; and she walked with her hands screwing in fear, and men had to support her. Abednigo Jones was there, also, hands in his belt, and let's get this lot over and quick. Dr. William Price of Pontypridd came, perhaps in the hope of a body for cremation, for this he later invented. Many were there from the benefit clubs of the Top Towns, and the new leaders of the underground Unions, for whom, in part, Dic was dying. It is said that some travelled from London, and a few from the Bolton Authority Lodge. One whose name was Morfydd Mortymer came with Richard Bennet, and they journeyed over the mountains from Nantyglo, where they lodged. Many early Chartists came, the men of vision who later fought for the Six Points of Decency; John Frost, later the mayor of Newport, was surely present, as would be Zephaniah Williams, and perhaps even Jones the Watchmaker, but history has no proof of this. Many came who did not know who was to be hanged, until they asked; a few arrived to tell of the spectacle; to see a man die was what they sought. And they massed in a black mantle around the scaffold, these people, numbering over five hundred.

And of them only one was staring at the platform lest she missed the first glimpse of Dic Penderyn when he came, and this was Sun.

All over Wales people were praying; the chapels and

churches had been filled since dawn; and not only did the Welsh attend the early services, but the Irish, and these were keening in the packed terraces of the Top Towns from Swansea to Blaenafon. Of all nationalities and denominations, the people did not go on shift; but flooded into the pews of Calfaria and Ebenezer, Zion and Salem and a score of others; they packed themselves ten deep standing in the Roman Catholics and the Chapels of Ease: they stood in massed funeral black in the fields and knelt in the roads, furnace areas, smelting sheds and compounds; they stopped the barges on the Old Glamorgan canal and knelt in the fields as the time of death approached; they spragged their drams and tethered the mules and horses and knelt on the line, and many wept, it was said—some not for Dic Penderyn, aged twenty-three who lived in Merthyr, but the things he stood for, and a nation wept because he was Welsh. Wandering preachers, black-clad and trembling with indignation, declaimed the outrage from lonely crags to the empty places, demanding from their God an explanation of the injustice of the King and Melbourne. In the pits and drifts, the levels of coal and the limestone caves the colliers and miners gathered by candlelight, and knelt. On the Iron Bridge in Merthyr Blind Dick and Hugh Pughe sang eulogies of the man from Aberafon who was about to die; in the penny-a-week schools the children listened in pent silence, wondering why.

And so did Dic Penderyn.

In the cell in Cardiff Gaol he was sitting at a table, and about him were four men, and they were dressed in black; Joseph Tregelles Price, the saintly iron master of Neath, the Reverend Edmund Evans of the Merthyr Wesleyan, the Reverend Morgan Howells, Dic's brother-in-law, and the prison chaplain.

'Is it raining?' Dic looked at the high, peep-window.

'Since an hour, perhaps,' said Morgan Howells.

'The crowd down St. Mary's will get wet.'

Distantly thunder boomed and reverberated over The Top, echoing in dull claps and whispering into silence.

'Is the crowd large?'

'Many have come,' said Morgan Howells.

Rising, Dic put his hands in his pockets and stared up at the little square window, and said: 'My God, this is hard measure, but the cause was just. You think there is a chance of a reprieve now, Morgan?'

'There is no sign of it. Melbourne has already delayed it a week. I entreat you to make your peace with your God.'

'*Diwedd!* You don't change much! At the moment I am more concerned with my body than my soul. Is it for the surgeons?'

Edmund Evans said: 'Many care little what happens to the carcass after the soul has fled.'

'I care a great deal.'

'Then write what you will,' said Tregelles Price, 'and I will see that it is carried into effect,' and with this he took his leave; the cell door clanged open and shut, and Dic sat at the table and wrote to Gwen:

'Yr wyf yn deisyf arnat i ddyfod yn ddiatreg i nôl fy nghorff, oherwydd nid oes dim tebygolrwydd am ddim arall yn bresennol. Dos at Philip Lewis a gwna iddo ef ddyfod a chertyn i lawr heno, a chymaint o ddynion a allo, mewn rhyw wedd, i ddyfod gydag ef. Yr wyf yn credu fod yr Arglwydd wedi maddau i fi fy amrywiol bechodau a'm troseddiadau, ond am yr wyf yn cael nghyhuddo nid yr wyf yn euog ac am hynny gennyf achos i fod yn ddiolchgar.'

which, being translated, means:

'I entreat you to come without fail to fetch my body, as there is no likelihood of anything else at present. Go to Philip Lewis and get him to come down somehow tonight with a cart and as many men as he can. I believe the Lord has forgiven me my sins and transgressions, and as for the charge now made against me, I am not guilty, and for that I have reason to be thankful.'

343

This letter he gave to Morgan Howells, and the prison chaplain Jones and the Reverend Edmund Evans read it also, and Dic said:

'Now examine me for the good of my soul, as you put it, and I will tell you the truth of it yet again.'

Edmund Evans of the Wesleyan spoke first, saying: 'Do you continue to deny that you stabbed Private Black with a bayonet?'

'I do. At the time he was wounded I was not in front of the Castle Inn.'

'Yet,' said Chaplain Jones, 'you do not deny that you were one of the deputation of leaders who entered by the front door to meet the iron masters?'

'I do not deny it—I state it. This is in the Petition. I was with Lewis Lewis when the deputation was called for. I entered the inn by the front door and left it by the back entrance—there are witnesses to this.'

'Name them.'

'As I said at the trial—after the meeting I left with Will Johns. Mr. Marsden, the draper, saw us going through the back door; I nodded to him, and he acknowledged me.'

'Mr. Marsden has already testified to this. And then?'

'Then I intended to keep my promise to my wife, and return to Aberdare mountain. But I stood for a while by the tap-wall of the inn, on the Glebe side. There I saw Nancy Evans, who is with child, and her son, Evan Evans . . .'

'Who else?' interjected Morgan Howells.

'David Abraham, the special constable, spoke to me while I was there.'

'What did he say?'

'He warned me not to come round to the front of the inn since trouble was starting—did he bear witness to this?'

'He did. Anything more?'

'Ay. Ben Davies, the navigator, stood with me, and we talked—how many more witnesses do you want?'

'Kindly proceed,' said the chaplain, and Dic said, his voice low:

'I keep on telling this! When the firing started Ben Davies, the Evans boy and I ran down to Iron Bridge. As he went, Philip the Puddler of Two Furnace, shouted to us—he spoke in Welsh at the trial—I heard him swear to this...'

Morgan Howells said bitterly: 'Everybody in Christendom has sworn for you, but the evidence is not heeded. Only the evidence of the liars Abbott, Drew and Darker, appears to have weight ...'

'That is not fair,' said Chaplain Jones, sharply.

'But it is a fact!' Howells turned away. 'God knows we've had our differences, but I am disgusted at the handling of this boy's trial.'

The Reverend Edmund Evans said: 'Anger and bitterness will not help us. Only facts can help us now.' To Dic, he said: 'You speak of this man Will Johns. If he accompanied you through the back entrance he is a key witness. Why has he vanished, if he is your friend?'

'He is a drinking friend,' interjected Morgan Howells, 'there is a difference.' He swung to Dic, his voice raised. 'Had you kept your word to me you would have no need of such people now. I sent you with the son of the deacon... !'

Dic cried: 'What the hell do ye expect of me? You threatened to take away my wife and son. I am an enroller for a Union Lodge. How could I have faced the men again if I had not joined the deputation?' He added, bitterly: 'Best you three face the truth of it. I am a Union man; this is why I am going to die.'

There was a silence. Distantly from the town came the tolling of a bell; then the chaplain said: 'One question more, and we will leave you with your God. If, as you say, you were not at the front of the inn during the fighting, how is it that Private Black—though not identifying you as the man that stabbed him—said he saw you with your hat off and cheering on the mob?'

Dic shrugged. 'I cannot speak for Private Black. Perhaps he mistook me for Lewis Lewis; perhaps he is saying what he has been told to say; I do not know. But find Will Johns of Ynys compound, and he will save me. Even the deacon's son will swear that I left him for but a short time on two occasions—

once when we got news of the deputation, once later, when I went to Cefn Heights and met the son of my neighbour, Mrs. Goldie.'

'Why did you not mention such other meetings at the trial?'

'Because nobody asked me. Was Cefn Coed mentioned? The trial was in English, and the gabble so fast that much I did not understand.'

At this, Morgan Howells turned away. 'Oh, God,' he said.

'Ay, ay, well, thank Him, at least, that they will let me die in Welsh, even if it is for another.'

'Lewis Lewis, the huntsman of Bodwigiad?'

He did not reply.

The chaplain said: 'Let this be known officially to you, so that you may prepare your soul to meet your God, and know that there is no hope of release. The petition of eleven thousand signatures has been rejected: the Quaker master, Tregelles Price, has himself visited Lord Melbourne, the Home Secretary, and later took fresh evidence to London, when he saw Lord Brougham, the Lord Chancellor. The reprieve was rejected then, there is no chance of it arriving at this late hour. Do you still persist in your innocence?'

'I am innocent of the crime for which I am going to be hanged.'

And Morgan Howells said then: 'Let the record stand, that you take it to your grave. Joseph Tregelles Price, when rejected by Lord Melbourne, said these words: "I felt that this young man's blood was on my own head if I did not strive for him in every way. Now I put that burden from my conscience on to yours." '

The chaplain remarked, turning away: 'We are concerned with this man's soul, not the iniquity of the Whigs; let us stay with the subject,' and Howells replied:

'This man is my relative, and he has a right to know: let him know also that I petitioned the King, and that he would not receive me: the Whigs are not alone in sharing the guilt of blood.'

The Reverend Edmund Evans said then: 'I ask you to

swear before God, then, that you did not stab the soldier Private Black, and to state before Him, Whom you are soon to meet, that you are going to hang unjustly.'

Dic said: 'I did not stab the soldier. And I will continue to swear to this with my dying breath.'

Morgan Howells turned away at this and covered his face with his hands, saying:

'I cannot bear this. They are going to kill an innocent man.'

When the hangman came in and pinioned his arms behind him, Dic said:

'The hangmen are younger than I expected. Where do you come from?'

The man tied the knots, saying: 'I come from Bristol, but all last night I travelled from London, and arrived here at three o'clock this morning.'

'It were a pity you did not arrive later, I think.'

Later it was known that the authorities had scoured the neighbouring counties for a hangman without success, and that the professionals in London would not undertake the task. This hangman was a novice, and had undertaken this hanging because of his poverty.

Dic said, before they opened the cell door that led to the gallows:

'Morgan, I do not want to die.'

'We all have to die,' replied Morgan Howells. 'Do you but precede us by a year or two.' In Welsh he said this, which was their mother tongue.

At the door Dic paused, and said: 'You will care for my baby son, and my wife, to whom I have not been good, because of the drinking?'

'She sends to you her love,' said Morgan Howells. 'If this is the punishment for drinking then many stand condemned. Your sister Gwen says that she will be united with you, both now and in death. Your mother and father are in prayer for you; Wales itself is in prayer for you.'

And Dic Penderyn said again: 'My God, for all, and for

me, this is a bloody hard measure. Thank God I have had the Sacrament.' With this he turned to Morgan Howells, who had been joined by the sheriff and said: 'I am going out to suffer unjustly. God, Who knows all things, knows it is so.'

With this he walked to the scaffold. The Reverend Edmund Evans walked one side of him, the sheriff walked on the other; behind came Mr. Woods, the prison governor and he was with Morgan Howells; after them came the hangman and a gaoler. Nor did he lose his composure as he mounted the steps to the platform, but looked around the crowd as if seeking friends, while the hangman tied his ankles. It is said, also, that the rain increased and that thunder began to roll in from the sea; many of the people knelt, and bowed their heads. Perhaps he was looking for Sun, perhaps for his sister Gwen, but these he did not see, nor even the face of Molly Caulara, who knelt and prayed alone on the distant street. But, near the scarlet uniforms of the Red-coats on guard against disturbances he saw one face upturned, and it was that of Mistress Morfydd Mortymer, the young agitator of Blaenafon whom he had insulted in the Long Room above the bar of Tavern Uchaf, at the meeting of the Oddfellows Lodge. And he remembered her face with its glowing, dark eyes, and the way she held herself. Suddenly, she clenched her hand and swept back her hair, and as the hangman placed the noose about him, she cried, her voice shrill:

'Die hard, Dic Penderyn. You are dying for Wales. Die hard, Dic Penderyn!'

Legend would have us believe that lightning split the sky and that thunder roared as Dic Penderyn died; it is known only that it was raining, and that, in the moment before the trap was pulled, he cried with his face to the sky:

'*O Arglwydd, dyma gamwedd! O Arglwydd, dyma gamwedd!*'

Which, being translated, means:

'O Lord, what an inquity! O Lord, what an iniquity!'

And the thunder rolled over the town and the people bowed their heads, for they were afraid.

26

LEWIS LEWIS was heard by a gaoler to be crying in his cell when Dic Penderyn was hanged, and this man went to him, and Lewis said:

'Dic is innocent. I know him not to have been there. I was by the soldier. If I had been sharing the same fate I would have disclosed it on the scaffold.'

The statement has been recorded for history.

Also recorded for history is the letter William Crawshay, the Cyfarthfa iron master, wrote to his father a week later.

'As Bell and the children and Eliza were going to church on Sunday week a bitch of a woman called out from a party of folks who were standing on the path, "There go the devils..." '

Hatred for the iron masters seethed, not only in Merthyr, but the Top Towns. And Colonel Brotherton's prediction of a rift between master and worker that might never be bridged was coming to truth. But William Crawshay was not responsible for the hanging of Dic Penderyn, let history record this, too; for he, like others, had accepted the testimony of Shoni Crydd and Abbot the barber, whom the people of Merthyr ran out of the town.

Crawshay wrote:

'My conduct at all times to my men has been guided by the liberal and humane feeling ... I have ever been the last to reduce and the first to advance the rates of wages...'

This was true, but it would appear that he could afford it. For, at the wedding of his son a few years later a series of celebration functions took place for hundreds of guests at the Castle Inn, the scene of the rising; the King's Head and the Bush Hotel. And a great wagon shed in Cyfarthfa works was converted into a ballroom of magnificent splendour; draped with shrubs and greenery especially imported, decorated with squares and pennants, it was lighted by huge gas chandeliers and a polished wooden floor was laid for dancing. A banquet in this great hall attended by the ladies of Merthyr provided boars' heads and massive joints of beef, and waiters by the score in evening dress drew wine from casks for the entertainment of the guests. At a later festivity at the Bush Hotel for gentlemen the tables were set for three hundred; the menu began with turtle, soups, turbot, rounds, rumps, ham, tongue, venison haunches and fowl; it was followed by pheasants, woodcocks, partridge and leverets, and the meal, as reported in the *Cardiff and Merthyr Guardian*, was ended with pineapples, grapes, almonds and raisins washed down with port, sherry, claret and champagne.

Three years later, in the summer of 1849, over fifteen hundred men, women and children died in the parish of Merthyr for want of a decent water supply that would have cost the price of these dinners; the details of the cholera being given in the Report of the Local Board of Health under Dr. William Kay, which was read in Merthyr in 1854.

Let posterity judge, said Gideon, and if it be claimed by posterity that such masters were creatures of their time, then let me name others who were also children of their day— Robert Owen, Wilberforce, Lord Shaftesbury, and the iron master of Neath which is close to Merthyr—Joseph Tregelles Price.

Ay, said Gideon, let posterity judge, but let it also be fair; this was a fight for Reform, not against masters.

William Crawshay the Second was not responsible for the death of Dic Penderyn—even if he never raised a finger to oppose it: and no one man was responsible for the Merthyr Riots.

Now they took the body of Dic Penderyn back to Aberafon, the parish of his birth, and a great procession of mourning people followed the gambo that carried it through the lanes from Cardiff. Among those who pushed the cart of Philip Lewis, the gambo-man, was Mercy Merriman and Lady Godiva, top covered: those who later carried his coffin were Belcher, Big Bonce and Blackbird, the navvies; also Gideon. And the mourners, who numbered hundreds at Ely grew to thousands within reach of Pyle. Here crowds came to meet it, jamming the roads and flooding over the fields, even coming from the little whitewashed cottage called *Penderyn*, from which he had taken his name. With the Reverend Morgan Howells at the head of the cortège, it called at many churches and chapels on the way, seeking a Christian burial, but none, it is said, would take him in. But the vicar of St. Mary's Church, though Protestant, declared he would receive the body and lay it in consecrated ground, though he was forbidden by the authorities to hold his service within the church, since this, they claimed, was the body of a criminal. So Morgan Howells stood on the churchyard wall and raised his long, thin hands, and cried:

'See here an injustice, see here the coffin of an innocent man! Let it be known, and recorded, that the blood of Dic Penderyn lies on the hands of the Government and the King himself: and if this be sedition, then let this be recorded also, for I have a stake in this affair, I have a knowledge of the outrage... !'

Sun raised her face at this, and Howells cried: 'I have a knowledge of it because he was my relative. It was I who sent him away from Merthyr lest, because of his radical views and tub-thumping, he be branded as a scapegoat before a crime was laid. I have a stake in this affair because I am a Christian, and as a Christian I shall not stand silently while hostages are found and publicly put to death as an example to malefactors. For I tell you this—the malefactors are not here today—let agents present listen and report these words, and I trust they give offence ... the malefactors are those who sit on thrones, the lords and peers who govern, the Church dignitaries who

351

stand aside from responsibility—and to whom the life of a working man is of less value than a partridge egg, when an example is to be made of one to impress the mass. Did not the beloved Tregelles Price have two petitions rejected by the King even in the face of fresh evidence that proved the perjury of James Abbott and Drew? This man Abbott, in particular, has sworn away his life—did he not threaten to be even with him? I ask the people of Merthyr parish to remember this iniquitous man. In the face of this I myself travelled to London and the King refused me an audience! Let it be known that the death of this man is an offence, not only against the laws of the country, but against God...'

Sun moved, pushing her way through the crowd, and the people parted, and Billa did not follow her. And it happened that she came to the place on the edge of the crowd where Gideon was standing with Milly Thrush, and she raised her eyes to his face.

'Gid...' she said.

Seeing this, Miss Thrush moved away to a quiet place and stood, hands clasped. And Mike McTigue, seeing Billa Jam standing alone, came nearer to her, reaching for her hand. They stood together, listening to the oratory of Morgan Howells. Gideon and Sun also stood together in the drifting rain, and there was no sound but the wind, and the preacher's voice.

And Sun Penderyn saw again in her mind the young strength of the man she loved, and whom she had owned, but whose heart she had never possessed in full measure. She heard again the sounds of his laughter and remembered him in the compound of Liz Treharne, and his arms about her wet body:

'You coming home with me, missus?'

Now Sun smiled. The heat of the furnaces, she remembered, was warm on her arms and shoulders, and his chin was rough against her face.

'Don't ye even care who's kissing you?'

The rain was dripping off the brims of the black hats about her, and she smelled the people in soaked clothes; and she heard again from the bed of Seven Ynys the voice of the night

352

watchman singing bass on the night that Madoc and his four children died.

'Make in me a little one ... a little Dic Penderyn?'

And she closed her eyes and bowed her head.

Molly Caulara, who was standing on the road away from eyes lest she be discovered, did not see this, but came nearer to the gambo and reached out and touched it. She remembered a sunlit field that was a part of her youth and saw the face of Dic Penderyn bending above her and hayseed was in his hair and his teeth were white in the moment before he kissed her: she was sixteen, she recalled; there for the boys to learn on, but he had treated her with respect and dignity. Morgan Howells was still ranting at the sky, his face upturned in the fervour of his emotion; the rain was on her face as she touched the gambo again, for she could not get close enough to touch his coffin.

Miss Milly Thrush, amazingly, was thinking about Percy Bottom Note and Willie Taibach, and she did not see Gideon gripping Sun Penderyn's hands amid the intonations of the St. Mary's vicar. Vaguely, she was wondering what she would do about the harmonium she had saved from the beadle of Coffin's Court, for there wasn't really room for it in the bedroom—especially if Gideon Davies came back with her to the shop ... after all, she reasoned, there was nothing to keep him in Eighteen Cross now that fanatic Zimmerman had gone, and it did seem a waste of rent keeping two establishments. True, he was comforting Sun Penderyn now, but that was right and proper—they were old friends, after all. Not that there had really been anything between them in the past, she thought: how could there have been? Gideon was a man of honour, and Sun was married to Dic Penderyn. And in a fantasy of her own breeding Miss Thrush remembered, too, the sister in Pontypridd and the little shop there; the size nine boots, the laces he called for once a year, which was a lifetime away, now that he belonged to her. After all, she reflected, there was that navvy girl Jobina, or whatever he called her—there was no reason to think he had been anything to her, either. Only to

353

her, Milly Thrush, had he come for love; she straightened
amid the crowd, smiling joyously at the recollection, and
people standing nearby saw this smile, and were perplexed. It
was the fulfilment of all she wished for; for ever safe in his love
she could face the world; it was a banishment of loneliness
now that she was one with him. She would become his eyes,
and in his need of her his love would grow, and there would
flower from their union a greater, fuller life. Now he was coming through the crowd, seeking her; he called her name, and
seeing her bright expectancy and upraised hand, people
guided him. Now Gideon stood before her, his hand outstretched to her.

'Goodbye, Miss Thrush.'

Momentarily, she stared up in astonishment at him, then
bowed her head.

Gideon said: 'Or would you care to come back with us in
the first trap?'

'No thanks,' said she, recovering herself, 'I can manage,
thanks.'

'But you must ride home—please, it was so kind of you to
bring me.'

Her eyes were filling with tears now, but she smiled, saying,
'No thanks, Gid Davies—I'd ... I'd rather be alone, thanks.
Always been used to seeing to meself, ye see ...'

'As you please.' Gideon bowed to her. 'Goodbye.'

The rain struck her face as she watched him go back into
the crowd, and then she heard his dog whining at her feet.
Bending, she lifted it against her, pressing its wetness against
her cheek, and it was shivering.

'Goodbye,' she said.

She made a mental note to order more size nines and
laces ...

'Billa!'

On the very edge of the departing crowd Billa stopped and
gripped her hands. Mike McTigue touched her arm, saying
over her shoulder:

'Don't go off like that, girl.'

354

'I got to, Mike—ye know I've got to.'

'Not before you hear what I've got to say.'

'Oh, God,' said Billa. 'Won't ye leave me alone? Look, the trap's arrivin'—you know I've got to go with Morgan Howells and the rest of 'em, and . . .'

'You are going with me,' said Mike.

'Are ye mad, fella!' She swung to him. His face was smooth and unlined; his strength seemed to reach out and grip her, forbidding movement; she thought it was disgraceful that she should even be looking at him like this; she was at least ten years older . . . and a horde of kids . . .

'He's a drunk, Billa—you've took him back, but he's at it again up in the Wellington. God alive, girl—will ye never learn?'

'What do ye want of me?' She touched his face. 'In the name of heaven, what do you see in me? I've got nothing to offer you—can't ye see I'm done for?' Desperately, she pushed her wet hair from her face. 'I've had me time, can't you see that? Do you want a rag of a woman when you can take your pick o' the fillies?'

'I love you,' he said, and took her to the lych-gate, ignoring the staring people.

Billa said: 'God help us.'

The rain was sheeting down as they got to the trap. Morgan Howells had already climbed into it, and Mike confronted him. 'Mrs. Jam won't be coming back in this one, Minister,' he said. 'I'll get another from Aber.'

The minister's eyes switched over them both. 'It . . . it has been a tragic business. Are you all right, Mrs. Jam?'

'Ay, sir.'

She was soaked with rain and shivering; her clothes were clinging to her wet body, her hair was down now, stranding her dress. Mike took off his coat and put it around her.

Morgan Howells said: 'I am glad, Mrs. Jam . . .'

Mike led her away, and she turned her wet face to his. 'But me kids . . . me kids!'

'The kids, too—come on, my lovely.'

'You ready, Sun?' asked Gideon.

She nodded. Most of the people had gone now; the Church was deserted save for two labouring figures.

'The minister is waiting,' said Gideon. 'Come.'

'Ay.'

The sky was threatening with thunder clouds. Lacking a brilliant light Gideon could not see her face; only the outline of the bonnet, he saw, and the deep shadows of her eyes; he thought she looked even smaller than usual standing there before him. Suddenly, she said:

'Empty ... empty I am, without my boy ...'

He left her then and went to the grave and placed upon its mound a piece of paper under a stone, and Belcher and Blackbird, who were the diggers stood back, and were careful of it. Returning to her, Gideon said:

'But you have his son. You will always have Richard Jay ... Come. Morgan Howells is waiting.'

Molly Caulara was standing at the lych-gate and she put out her hand to Sun as she passed.

'God be with ye, Mrs. Penderyn.'

They looked at each other.

'Goodbye, now,' said Molly Caulara. She stood watching the trap disappearing along the road to Neath. Behind it, in great blades of gold and crimson, Swansea was making iron; the very ground beneath her feet was trembling to the shot-firing. After the two labourers had gone she went to the spoiled earth and there knelt, picking up the paper Gideon had left, and on it she read:

Ye see me only in my chains, ye see me only in my grave. But behind each forehead, in each heart, is not my place prepared for me? Am I not mankind's ardent breath that endless thirsts for liberty? So, I will rise again, before the people stride. Deliverer, judge, I wait to take the streets: upon your heads, upon your necks, upon your crowns I'll stamp. For this is history's iron law; conceit it is not, threats are none. The day grows hot, how cool your shade, O, willow leaves of Babylon ...

Rising, Molly Caulara looked at the sky, for the rain had stopped and from a break in the clouds a golden light began to shine. Then Morriston began to pour from the bungs, and the molten iron flashed its incandescent whiteness on the lowering clouds; Llanelli, too, was stirring in bonds of fire: beneath her feet the ground began to tremble violently to the underground shot-firers of Aberafon; above her the sky was glowing in rainbow colours as the cauldrons were stirred. And, as the clamour of the iron-making grew about her, she remembered Dic's words:

'All over the country the Lodges will rise ... we are only hundreds now, but soon we'll be thousands, even millions ...!'

Hearing his voice as an echo, Molly Caulara stood amid the growing thunder of the Aberafon hammers, seeing in the eye of her mind an army of men sweeping across the fields towards the towns of industry, their fists clenched: and from them came a great shout. The sky became brighter, brighter in her imagination, before shattering into nothingness and brilliant light. She heard Dic say:

'And this is only the beginning. As Zimmerman said, we must cleanse it all and start all over again ...'

Sweat was on Molly's face. Above Aberdare a great, valedictory flame was standing, shafting the Top Towns as with a beacon of hope for the future, and this sight raked her from her dream. Shivering, she replaced the piece of paper on the grave, and smiled.

''Bye, Dico,' she said, and took the road that led to a distant glow, and beneath this glow was the town of Merthyr.

THE CONFESSION

In 1874, forty-three years after Dic Penderyn was hanged at Cardiff on the order of the Home Secretary, the Reverend Evan Evans of Nantyglo was travelling in the United States. He was called to the death-bed of Ieuan Parker, a Welshman of Cwmavon, then living in Pennsylvania. This man confessed to the crime for which Dic Penderyn had been executed.

Historical sources: *The Insurrection at Merthyr Tydfil in 1831* by Professor Gwyn A. Williams, M.A., Ph.D., F.R. Hist.S. (Note: Professor Williams, perhaps the ablest authority, does not state the name of the Welshman who confessed but establishes the confession); *Dic Penderyn* by Islwyn ap Nicholas; *Dic Penderyn and the Merthyr Rising of 1831* by Harri Webb, who states Ieuan Parker's confession: 'It was I who wounded the soldier that Dic Penderyn was hanged for. I got away to America as soon as I could afterwards, but I could never escape from the memory of it. When you go back to Wales tell everybody that Dic Penderyn was innocent.' *The Merthyr Riots of 1831* (The Welsh Historical Review, Vol. 3, Dec. 1966, No. 2) by D. J. V. Jones. This historian states: 'As an explanation of his [Dic Penderyn's] death, it may be that the Government, which was shocked by the seriousness of the Merthyr riots, decided to make an example of this unwilling martyr.' (Neither the Marquis of Bute nor Mr. Justice Bosanquet, who sentenced him, seems to have expected him to be hanged—Home Office Papers 52/16: letter from the Marquis of Bute, 16th July 1831.)

An extract from *The New Newgate Calendar*, the Folio

Society, with an introduction by Lord Justice Birkett—*Riots at Merthyr Tydfil*: 'The soldier could not identify the prisoner [Dic Penderyn] as the party who had used the bayonet... The prisoner persisted in denying his guilt, and declared that he would do so with his dying breath... On the night before the execution, the unhappy convict was urged to make a confession of his guilt, but he positively denied... He continued firm in this declaration up to the time of his death...' The article concludes with the statement that Lewis Lewis confirmed this assertion, stating that he could have given satisfactory evidence of Dic Penderyn having been altogether absent from the affray.

NEW EVIDENCE CONCERNING THE EXECUTION OF RICHARD LEWIS (DIC PENDERYN)

INFORMATION about Richard Lewis (Dic Penderyn) has been obscured by the mists of time, largely because certain documents such as his trial record, the Tregelles Price petition and letters from the sentencing judge Bosanquet to Lord Melbourne (the then Home Secretary) have been lost to posterity until today. And, as is usual in cases where the historical facts are thin, what was not known about Penderyn's life has been invented by a succession of early historians. The name of Dic Penderyn has been enhanced by national pride and the man himself built up into a hero almost pantomimic in quality. Yet, as one eminent historian has remarked, it is astonishing how popular legend has in this case followed a pattern of sober truth.

Now, however, the curtain has been largely pulled aside by nothing less than a stroke of luck. After two years of research and another year of writing this novel, I received in December 1970 from the Departmental Record Officer of the Home Office a letter which informed me that '... the additional information given in your letter of the 23rd November has led us to the discovery of some papers about Richard Lewis ...

It was the sort of find a writer dreams about. Within a day or two I was at the Record Office examining Bundle Zp 37 of HO 17/128 Part 2, which contained the *Sentence passed upon*

Lewis Lewis and Richard Lewis, a *Transcript of the Evidence for the Prosecution*, *six* letters from the sentencing judge to Melbourne (hitherto it was believed that three were written, none of which survived), *two* petitions in respect of Dic Penderyn and *one* in respect of Lewis Lewis (hitherto it was believed that but one was presented), *one* Petition in respect of Penderyn in the form of a letter from his prison chaplain and surgeon, *two* letters from Tregelles Price to government officials; other miscellaneous documents.

Until this discovery most historians believed Dic Penderyn had taken no active part in the Rising; that, because he had brawled with James Abbott, he had gone into hiding during the riot and had been picked off the street and hanged by Lord Melbourne as an example to the militants and Unionists in Wales. Nothing in the new evidence argues this fact—indeed, his murder is further emphasised. But what is now discovered is that he was not innocuous, as has been claimed by historians. Richard Lewis, alias Dic Penderyn, was not only a workers' leader but one important enough to enter the Castle Inn on the day of the Merthyr Rising and negotiate on behalf of the working force of thousands with men of the calibre of Guest and Crawshay: before the inn that day was massed some ten thousand men, yet he was one of a deputation of twelve. He might not have been a trade union official in the mould of William Twiss of the Bolton Authority, nor a Zephaniah Williams who was being groomed to lead the later Chartists, but he was doubtless a young man of political importance and steeped in the fight for Reform. Indeed, the family from which he sprang must have been head and shoulders above their contemporaries—it is doubtful if the great Welsh preacher Morgan Howells would have tolerated an unintelligent woman for a wife, the elder sister who so influenced Dic's life.

Melbourne, at this time, was thirsting for action against the embryonic unions, as Cole and the Webbs relate—even Peel, at the end of his tenancy, was trying to ferment Union reaction in the North which would sanction the use of government forces to destroy them. The Merthyr riots quite obviously were

362

not government sponsored, but they provided the opportunity for the strength of action Melbourne sought. Dic Penderyn is now seen to deserve the laurels imposed on him by our ancestors' word of mouth; he died, and lives, in the sanctity of sacrifice—the first accepted martyr of the Welsh working class.

TRANSCRIPT OF THE EVIDENCE FOR THE PROSECUTION

(Taken by William Meyrick Esq., lawyer for the Prosecution; July 14th 1831).

James Abbott

'I am a hair-dresser at Merthyr Tydfil—I was sworn in a special constable 3rd March—I saw a crowd first from half-past five to six o'clock in the morning—they were then in the market-place ... by Mr. Jenkins, the druggist ... at first three or four hundred—increased much by ten o'clock—some thousands at the Castle Inn... I saw Lewis Lewis after the men went into the house, the Castle Inn ... I saw some of them return ... I saw Lewis Lewis hanging on to the lamp iron ... he was speaking in Welsh ... addressing the mob—I observed a rush from the mob upon the soldiers—the soldiers were beaten very much—many of the soldiers came in disarmed to the passage of the Inn... I was stationed in the passage of the Inn... *I saw a soldier coming up the steps—saw him struggle with two or three others to keep his musket—which he lost. Richard Lewis was one—and others of the mob. The soldier that had lost his musket was making his way into the Inn, and as he was on the top step or thereabouts Richard Lewis charged him with a bayonet and made an incision in the thick part of the thigh, somewhere above the knee considerably—* The bayonet was fixed on the gun. I took the soldier by the arm directly and led him to the brewhouse—I know the soldier —Donald Black—he is here—I left him in the care of a person dressing him, I saw a large hole bleeding like a pig—I have not the slightest doubt of the person I saw.'

Under cross-examination, Abbot said:

'The ironmasters desired the mob to pick out twelve to fourteen—I heard Mr. Crawshay speaking—ten or twelve persons
were to be sent in as a deputation to the ironmasters—I can't
say what happened ... Mr. Guest said he would speak to them
—treat with them ... the mob was perfectly quiet up to this
time—I did not see the ten or twelve go in, but saw them come
out again ... when they came out they seemed very dissatisfied ... I suppose some 8,000 to 10,000 workmen were collected—there were at that time soldiers in the Castle (Inn)—
they had arms ... there were soldiers outside the Castle (Inn)
... the mob seemed dissatisfied ... Lewis Lewis stood up and
attempted to speak after the deputies came out—the first time
I saw him was after the deputies came out ... he was higher
than the generality of the mob ... a man said ... he stated in
the presence of 10,000—he spoke as loud as he was able—I
did not hear any threat, he did it respectfully, he said they
wanted bread and cheese, that there were many families that
had not sufficient ... I did not hear Mr. Guest promise them
bread and cheese for their families—the soldiers were one
deep, the workmen were close to the soldiers ... I did not see
the soldiers do anything till the mob came upon them. They
tried to take care of their arms. The soldiers got mixed with
the mob ... the bayonets were upright ... some of the workmen seized hold of the muskets—the firing did not take place
immediately from the windows. Some person fired ... I saw
several (workmen) wounded before the firing took place ...
When the firing took place the consequences were very fatal—
none of the soldiers had been attacked—that I know ... when
they saw their comrades struggling below they fired from
above—there were Magistrates with them—Mr. Bruce was
downstairs in the passage at the time of the rush, and Mr. Hill
at the door. He was not off the first step. Before the wound
was given to Donald Black I had not noticed him at all. I saw
a flag in the crowd ... I saw three muskets in possession of
some of the mob ...'

William Williams

'On Thursday 3rd June I was a special constable—I was stationed with the other special constables, and Mr. Bruce and Mr. Hill in the passage—I saw a mob in front—I saw Lewis Lewis holding the iron of a lamp post raised above the rest of the mob—I heard him address the mob in Welsh "Boys, let me say a word—these are come against us—if every one of you is of the same mind as me we *shall force their arms away from them*, I shall make to so begin"—The other words I did not comprehend—then he got down—there was a rush upon the soldiers by the mob—I saw their bludgeons go up and the people rushed forwards—some of them were holloaing out for bread—"Squeeze closer, on, on"—I was behind some gentleman I assisted the gentleman to take the man in. A man was taken from the crowd that had one of the soldier's fire-arms ...'

Under cross-examination, Williams said:

'...When I heard the words "Squeeze on" there was a great crush in the crowd. I did not get out of the passage into the street. There is a flight of steps from the passage into the street—the foot pavement is beyond that. My duty and occupation prevented me from observing accurately where the soldiers were standing and what they were doing. What further explanation Lewis Lewis may have given I do not know.'

Under re-examination, Williams said:

'A rush took place in about half a minute after I heard the last words. The people at the front had bludgeons up in their arms.'

William Rowland

'I am a constable was on duty at the Castle ... I heard the High Sheriff read a paper. The gentlemen afterwards addressed the mob and requested them to disperse—I heard persons go into the Castle (Inn)—part of the mob and came out again ... I heard several expressions used by the mob—one in particular said "That the soldiers who were come there were no more than a gooseberry in the hands of the mob". This was said opposite to the Castle door loud enough to be heard at a distance—one "that they were determined to be revenged on the constables" and "Particularly would play the devil with the constables" or words to that effect. I saw a flag right opposite the Castle door—they had a great number of very large clubs, and some with small pit wood which they use in the levels ... I saw both prisoners there, I saw Lewis Lewis supporting himself on the lamp iron ... I could have wished to see more men—I thought myself in danger ... There had been a meeting before—a Reform meeting—I saw people passing through Merthyr with a flag on the 30th May ... I did not hear all Lewis Lewis said. He might have qualified ... They attempted to take me into the mob. They were very riotous. They desired to send ten or fourteen men in. The proposal came from the gentlemen. I let them into the room. I was sometimes looking one way and sometimes another—They said there was nothing settled. Everyone wanted to know the result of what the gentlemen had said—They could not be closer ...'

Thomas Darker
'I am a special constable. I was in the passage—I was there when the deputation came out—the mob appeared to be very riotous—armed with large sticks—some as thick as my arm. Nothing particular about them. A great deal of Welsh was spoken that I did not understand—*I saw Richard Lewis first in the passage coming out with the deputation. The first time I saw him after he came out was about five to ten minutes—I saw him in the front of the Castle* (Inn) *with his hat off he waved his hat and shouted*—I saw a flag—I had seen a Reform procession before—they had a flag then.'

Under cross-examination, Darker said:

'*Richard Lewis was standing by the door with his hat up*— What had been said from the window of the Castle (Inn) just before he *waved his hat* I did not hear.'

366

James Drew
'Special constable—I was at the Inn on 3rd June—I saw both prisoners—*I saw Richard Lewis wrestling with a soldier and one or two more—he pushed the bayonet at his thigh.*'

Under cross-examination, Drew said:

'It was but one struggle—more muskets than one were laid hold of nearly at the same time.'

John Bruce Esq. Magistrate of Glamorganshire
'I act for Merthyr—I remember the soldiers coming ... I sent for them in consequence of what had happened the night before ... So great a mob Mr. Hill (ironmaster) and I were unable to go the direct road to meet them ... we met them at Pandy ... came down to Merthyr with them to the Castle Inn ... a very large mob before us and following us—made use of many threats as to the paucity of their numbers (the soldiers) —exhorting each other to overpower them ... part of the soldiers went into the house ... the rest stood in the street. I placed the constables in the passage ... I stood at the door except when called in to consult with anyone in the Inn ... if the Commanding Officer had understood Welsh no musket would have been seized ... Expressions were used, urging one another to "Squeeze close, press upon them, keep between them and the wall ... don't let them have the wall..." The mob was armed with bludgeons—they had a sort of red flag ... I did not notice either of the prisoners ... proclamation of the Riot Act (was) read in a loud voice ... I explained the nature of it in Welsh and English ... they seemed to treat it with perfect indifference ... I saw the general scuffle and turmoil ... I saw the wounded soldier brought in bleeding— Major Falls was brought in with his head bleeding...'

Donald Black, Lance-Corporal in the 93rd Regiment (Previously a Private).
'I was one of the detachment that marched from Brecon to Merthyr on 3rd June ... I went inside (the Inn) and then turned out again ... the mob made a rush on us and I was

wounded—They tried to take my arms from me ... my musket was seized, it was wrested from me. I was wounded in the right hip—I don't know the man that wounded me—*I saw both the prisoners in the crowd*—I did not see them laying hands on anyone—I saw one of the crowd try to break our rank and get in our rear—Captain Sparks came out and turned him back, and Lewis Lewis said he would not do that to him. *Only saw Richard Lewis taking off his hat and cheering but not laying his hands on anyone in the crowd*... Great confusion among the men when the rush was made on us—it was *before the rush was made that I saw Richard Lewis*. After the rush was made there was so much confusion I could not identify any man—I was so much confused, I do not know who wrested the gun from me—I had a bayonet wound which bled very much—I was taken back into the brew-house—I have seen the man who took me into the brew-house (James Abbott). Saw him at Merthyr, and here...'

Under cross-examination, Lance-Corporal Black said:

'... I was on the pavement ... we had fixed bayonets ... Some person endeavoured to get into the rear, Captain Sparks laid hold of him—Lewis Lewis did not seem to like seeing one of the workmen to be laid hold of by a soldier. I believe it was in English that Lewis Lewis said "You would not do so to me." ... I did not like Lewis Lewis stand at the rear—we were trying all we could in our power to keep persons from the wall—It was impossible. I do not understand Welsh.'

Under re-examination, Lance-Corporal Black said:

'I was stationed by the door—the crowd was immediately in front—my object was to keep as near the wall as possible—Our guns were not charged.'

DEFENCE

RICHARD LEWIS said on Friday morning this riot began to get up.
LEWIS LEWIS said nothing.

The Jury found RICHARD LEWIS guilty. LEWIS
LEWIS not guilty.
The jury said they thought LEWIS LEWIS guilty of
encouraging the mob to *disarm* the soldiers.

DEFENCE

Author's note

I consider it technically correct here to point out that in the
Second Petition for Richard Lewis (Dic Penderyn)—which follows hereunder—the man William Jones (who heard James
Abbott's evidence read back to him) stated this witness's con-
tradiction of the evidence he had originally given. Abbot
originally stated that he was 'on the steps of the Inn'. He
altered this to 'in the passage of the Inn'. The reader's attention
is drawn to the evidence of Lance-Corporal Black who stated
he was *on the pavement* in front of the Inn, which was on a
lower level than the passage. Clearly, Abbott would have had
to be positioned on the steps to witness the actual wounding.
Joseph Tregelles Price, the Neath Quaker ironmaster, makes
much of this point in the Petition.

THE FIRST PETITION

To: *William the Fourth*   From Joseph T. Price
       King of Great Britain.
                    CASE OF RICHARD LEWIS—Condemned
                    at the Cardiff Assize July 9 1831
                    to suffer the penalty of Death.
Charged upon the oath of James Abbott of Merthyr Tydfil and
others with having (at the Parish of Merthyr Tydfil) with
divers others unknown riotously assembled and with having
feloniously attacked and wounded Donald Black of the 93rd
Regiment with a bayonet whilst the said Donald Black was on
duty.
   Donald Black, it is on evidence, was stabbed in the *Front*
Street, opposite the Door, the *front* door—that he was stabbed
by Richard Lewis—and therefore Richard Lewis was con-

victed—no evidence appears to have been given of a contrary kind.

Richard Lewis declares his innocence of this charge, in the full prospect of death—he declares that he freely and fully forgives his accusers from the bottom of his heart, and trusts solely in the mercy of God for pardon for all his sins and in this state of mind states that when he went out of the Castle Inn *as one of the Deputation who waited on their Masters*—he went out at the back door and another man named Johns went out with him—that he did not afterwards go round to the Front door, that he stopped for 15 or 20 minutes on that side of the Castle Inn—that on hearing the first gun-shot he ran off down a street (which is called Glebeland) through an archway over the Iron Bridge towards Kirkhouses' [the agent for W. Crawshay over the miners and colliers]—that Nancy Evans, wife of Evan Evans of Merthyr, saw him standing *there* by the side of the Castle Inn all the time after he came out through the back door, and saw him run away. That Elizabeth Lewis also saw him run away, and many others. On being asked if he had ever had any quarrel or scuffle with Abbott, the principal witness, he said that on the evening of the illuminations on occasion of the Reform question coming out, he had a scuffle in Merthyr Street—that Abbott was there and took part in it—that Abbott at that time said he would be up with him the first chance he had—that Will John David was with him that night and can tell how it was that night.

This simple declaration made to the writer induced him to proceed to Merthyr to ask the parties named questions upon the facts. These, in company with John Thomas, a Constable, without telling the parties what declaration Richard Lewis made to him, he first had the following replies from:

Nancy Evans, wife of Evan Evans.

She was standing with Richard Lewis by the Tap Room window of the Castle Inn for about twenty minutes before the first gun-shot went off (the Tap Room window is on the side of the Castle Inn, not the front) that Richard Lewis was not in the Front Street at the time of the firing (or for twenty minutes before). She saw him run away at the first shot and her

370

boy, Evan Evans, who confirmed it, was along with him—the boy says that Richard Lewis ran faster than him and ran before him through the Arches.

Elizabeth Lewis says she stood opposite the Tap Room window—saw Richard Lewis standing by the Tap Room window a quarter of an hour before the firing commenced, and when the firing commenced he ran away.

William Philip, puddler, works at Cyfarthfa—saw Richard Lewis run off as hard as he could at the same time with him on the first shot going off down the Glebeland to the Arch by the Iron Bridge.

Benjamin Davies, navigator, works at Penydarren—knows Richard Lewis very well—saw him standing by the wall (the Glebeland side of the Castle Inn) about a quarter of an hour before the firing commenced—he heard the firing and then they both ran through the Archway towards the Iron Bridge, and that he (Benjamin Davies) stood, and Richard Lewis went on—had nothing in his hand at the time—he was with him a quarter of an hour till they both ran together towards the Iron Bridge—that Richard Lewis had a *blue* jacket and trousers and waistcoat on at the time. Several others were ready to offer their testimony, but the writer considered it [unnecessary?] to take same; on the point he sought for Johns who is said by Richard Lewis to have gone out with him from the meeting in the Castle Inn of the Deputation and the Masters, but Johns could not be found—he is said to have gone off.

David Abraham, a special constable, was standing near Abbott at the time of the riot, and that though he knew Richard Lewis he did not see him in front of the Castle—he had seen him by the side of the house and cautioned him against going forward, and believes he was not forward in front—in that part of the crowd.

Thomas Cottrell, waiter at the Castle Inn, was looking out of the same (an upper window) saw the soldier who was stabbed in the thigh—saw the act of stabbing—that the man who stabbed the soldier was clothed in a coat of a sort of *drab* colour, *he is quite sure it was not a black or a blue colour*—and that if Richard Lewis had on a blue coloured coat or jacket it

371

could not have been he that stabbed the soldier.

Ann Morgan lives opposite the Castle Inn—saw the soldier of the 93rd who was stabbed in the thigh by a bayonet—*saw the act*. She knows Richard Lewis very well, that it was another man who stabbed him, not Richard Lewis—the man who stabbed him had on a *drab* coloured frock coat and duck trousers, and afterwards he broke a window with the gun and then went up the front street running as fast as he could, and the gun in his hand—she cried murder when she saw the man stabbed—she knows it was the same soldier that Richard Lewis is accused of stabbing.

Richard Lewis was wholly unknown to me till I saw him on the 24th Inst. in Cardiff gaol. I left my home near Neath Abbey that morning on purpose to see the condemned prisoners, Richard Lewis and Lewis Lewis—having heard his narrative I thought it right to ascertain whether it was susceptible on confirmation or not. I found it fully and correctly confirmed as the foregoing statements. I therefore yielded belief to them and determined in consequence to proceed to London to present the case to the proper authority. And now make my appeal to those authorities for the extension of mercy to Richard Lewis.

To William the Fourth
    King of Great Britain.

Joseph T. Price.
Watchets' Hotel. Piccadilly.
27th July 1831

Author's note.
This is the first mention of a quarrel between Richard Lewis (Dic Penderyn) and James Abbott, the principal witness. As a result of this Petition the then Lord Chancellor, Lord Brougham, wrote to Mr. Justice Bosanquet, the sentencing judge, expressing '... a serious doubt whether the credibility of Abbott, a principal witness, was not affected by the fact, if true, of his having entertained personal animosity against the Prisoner ...' Lord Brougham added: '... I deem it right to

transmit to you the statement of facts before mentioned and request you to take into your consideration and inform me whether you see any ground for altering your opinion as to the guilt of the Prisoner . . .'

In order to allow the judge to reconsider his verdict in the case, the Lord Chancellor then granted a stay of execution for a fortnight.

Mr. Justice Bosanquet took no positive action—in a letter dated August 1st to Lord Melbourne he dismisses the possibility of animosity on the part of Abbott, and dilutes the prisoner's allegation of a scuffle between himself and Abbott on the grounds that he was *asked* by Mr. Price if there had been one. Here is the judge's letter to Lord Melbourne:

Cardigan.
August 1 1831

My Lord,

I have the honour to send to your Lordship a report of the evidence given in the case of Richard Lewis at Cardiff and also to return Mr. Price's representation—your Lordship will observe that the assertion now made by the Prisoner that he was not in front of the Castle Inn after the Deputation went out, is inconsistent not only with the evidence of James Abbott, but also with that of the two special constables on duty—Thomas Darker and James Drew as well as of Donald Black the wounded soldier. It is very singular that the defence now made for the Prisoner should not have been suggested at the trial in any way, though the Prisoner was very ably defended, and I believe that on referring to the Petitions presented to your Lordship by and on behalf of the Prisoners Richard Lewis and Lewis Lewis, and which were shown to me before they were sent to London, you will not find the ground now taken relied upon.

It is also remarkable that the imputation now made upon the credit of James Abbott on account of a previous scuffle with the Prisoner and words of which were not referred (?) to in the cross examination of that witness, which was long and minute, and should now be remembered by the Prisoner 'on being *asked* by Mr. Price whether he had ever had any quarrel or scuffle with Abbott'. It is very probable that the Prisoner may have been at the back or side of the Castle (Inn) a quarter of an hour or twenty minutes before the firing, and have run away, as many others did, immediately after the firing, and that a person in a coat of drab colour may have been seen from an *upper* window of the Castle Inn stabbing a soldier in the thigh without suffering any part of the evidence for the prosecution to be untrue. I have the honour to be, my Lord,

Your Lordship's faithful and obedient Servant,
J. B. Bosanquet.

The statement of Benjamin Davies as given by J. T. Price is apparently inconsistent with the evidence of the prosecution as given by four of the witnesses.

Author's note
Mr. Justice Bosanquet wrote, in all, six letters to Lord Melbourne in respect of the case—hitherto it was thought that three were written, and that none survived. From this correspondence emerges Bosanquet's apparent determination that Dic Penderyn should die, and much of Melbourne's implacability is thus now explained. Only in his last but one letter—that of August 6th—a week before the execution—does a little of the judge's confidence begin to fail him under the weight of new evidence brought by J. Tregelles Price, and he states:

'... under the circumstances it may be a matter of your Lordship's consideration whether it is advisable that the sentence of death should be carried into execution, there being reason to think that the justice of it will be considered doubtful...'

The unhappy Bosanquet, hoist by his own insistence in rejecting all but Abbott's evidence, wrote:

'... one individual may satisfy the exigency of further justice.'

And, then, finally, in his last letter (August 6th) to the Home Secretary, he said:

'...If upon further consideration your Lordship should be induced to recommend a commutation of the sentence of Death...'

But Melbourne was already convinced that somebody should die, and it was too late.

However, out of this correspondence arises a strange occurrence that probably will never be adequately explained, and Bosanquet refers to it in the last letter. It appears that one, Henry Morgan, took personally to Melbourne a declaration of guilt on the part of the two prisoners—a document which was apparently presented to them for signature, and which was purported to have emanated from them. Certainly this 'confession' made an adverse impression at the Home Office, as Mr. Price was quick to point out in one of two letters to Lord James Stewart, an official there. The existence of this document angered the people of Merthyr, and the two prisoners, and, as a result of this, Mr. Price immediately forwarded to Melbourne, via Lord James Stewart, the following refutation of the confession presented by officials of Cardiff Prison:

Cardiff.
August 1st 1831

We hereby humbly certify that we have respectively attended Richard Lewis now under sentence of death in the Gaol of this place since his conviction, and that he has uniformly and solemnly denied any participation in or knowledge of the act of wounding, or endeavouring to wound the Soldier, for which offence he, the said Richard Lewis, is condemned to die.

(Signed Daniel Jones (Chaplain to the Gaol)
William Jones (Baptist Minister)
Lewis Powell (Independent Minister)

375

Joseph Tregelles Price, now in desperation, made a final attempt to secure the reprieve of Dic Penderyn (Lewis Lewis was reprieved by Melbourne on 3rd August) by sending his Second Petition, which, it is understood, was accompanied by over 11,000 signatures, mainly from the town of Merthyr. It is significant that he did not this time address it to the King.

THE SECOND PETITION

Petition—Glamorgan Assizes

In the case of Richard Lewis, the Prisoner respited until the 13th Inst—I stated before that he admitted that he was engaged in a scuffle in Merthyr Street on the night of the illuminations; that James Abbott, the principal witness took part in that scuffle and that Abbott then declared that he would be up with him the first chance he had, and that Will John David could tell how it was on that occasion.

I have seen this person twice—he states 'that he was present when Abbott the Barber and Dic Lewis quarrelled the night of the illuminations, and heard Abbott then declare "Come thee I will be up with thee again the first opportunity I can get" or words to that effect. 'That he saw him strike Richard Lewis in the street—that he has known Abbott about three quarters of a year.' Will John David mentioned another person who was present—this person was called Edward Mathews, a Pudler, he says he was in Merthyr the night of the illuminations—saw Richard Lewis and others in the street near the Bush Inn—saw Abbott strike Richard Lewis. David Rees also saw this, he is a miner, and he also preaches among the Baptists; he declares that he saw Richard Lewis and Abbott scuffling together—he thinks it was a little past ten o'clock at night—he heard Abbott in parting declare to Richard Lewis that the first opportunity that he should have *he would be up with him.*

I saw Abbott myself and mentioned these statements to him —he declares on the contrary that he did not know Richard Lewis previous to the time he saw him at the Riot by the

Castle Inn—that he never had a quarrel with him on any occasion—produced William Henry James, Adam Newell and George Williams, all of Merthyr, who admitted that they were present at the row in Merthyr on the night of the illuminations when Richard Lewis received blows, and returned them, but that neither of them saw James Abbott there. Adam Newell admitted that he might have been in the street yet not be seen by him.

Richard Lewis stated to me that a man named Johns went out with him through the back door of the Castle Inn after the interview with their Masters—this Johns could not be found. Marsden a respectable linen draper of Merthyr, says that he was in the Castle Inn at that time and *saw Richard Lewis* go out through *the back door*.

Rice, the wife of James Rice lives opposite the Castle Inn, in front of it, was looking out of their house at the time of the fight—*saw Richard Lewis* in the street *dressed in a blue jacket and trousers—before he went in as one of the Deputation—did not see him after.*

Thomas Burnell, a tallow chandler, was in the Castle Inn at the time of the riot—saw the Highlanders engage with the workmen in front of the doors, saw no such person dressed as Richard Lewis was that day stab any soldier—but saw some person in a flannel smock strike one of the soldiers with a bayonet, but from the confusion that occurred he could not take upon himself to swear to him—does not know Richard Lewis.

Henry Jones, a Gentleman residing in Merthyr—was in the Castle Inn at the time of the riot—saw the commencement of the attack and observed Lewis Lewis advance towards the soldiers—saw several others join him, but from the instant the confusion that prevailed was so great that he could not identify any—he did not see anyone clad in blue jacket and trousers as Richard Lewis is described to have been, and he considered it was extremely difficult to distinguish individuals from the confusion which existed—he described it as comparable to the rush and tumult of the waves of the sea.

Thomas James, a miner, works at Penydarren with William

Lewis, Master Miner—was outside the Castle Inn at the time of the riot—saw a man dressed in a *smock frock and trousers* by the front door stab a soldier in the thigh with a bayonet, and then he went off up to the front street.

There were one or two men killed at the time so dressed—killed a few yards from the spot, several persons declared to me they had seen such persons dead or dying. And it does seem probable that under the eyes and fire of the soldiers in the upper windows and below—any man stabbing a soldier would be picked out *as an object for them to shoot and be shot.*

William Jones, fitter of Cyfarthfa Works, was present in W. Meyrick's office on the Thursday before the last quarter sessions. [W. Meyrick was solicitor for the prosecution against the rioters.] James Abbott was there—he heard the evidence read over which he was then considered to have given—and which he would be expected to give in court. It stated that he [Abbott] was on the steps of the front door of the Castle Inn when Donald Black was stabbed; this statement, Abbott then declared to one of Meyrick's clerks named Davis, was *incorrect—that he was in the passage of the Inn at the time*, and William Jones says that he considers that if he was in the passage of the Inn (thronged as it was by soldiers in the front) it would be impossible for him to see so as to distinguish a person stabbing a soldier on the outside of the house at that time.

William Edwards, Master Collier and Miner or undertaker of Job Work in those departments at Penydarren Ironworks, states that he was in the Castle Inn at the time of the Merthyr riots—that he was standing near James Drew who gave evidence in the case of Richard Lewis—that they were within the passage several yards from the front door, that the passage was crowded with soldiers so that it was impossible for *him* and he is *sure* it was also impossible for Drew who was further *in* than he was, to see, outside the door, *who*, in particular, inflicted any wound on any soldier—and he declares that he, Drew the Barber, remained with him from the *commencement* of the scuffle, before the firing of the guns—until several hours *after* the same was over, with the exception of about an hour or

378

rather less—and which absence was stated by him to be for the purpose of assuring his wife of his safety; and he, (William Edwards) further states that Drew did not go from him *until a quarter of an hour or twenty minutes after the firing was over.*

William Edwards further says that as he spent several hours with James Drew that day in a neighbouring public house, it appears to him not a little extraordinary that Drew should not have mentioned to him his having seen Richard Lewis stab the soldier if it was a fact that he did see it, but he declares that Drew did not tell him.

On reviewing the several features of this case, considering that Donald Black could not recognise the man who stabbed him, that though he says he saw Richard Lewis he does not say he saw him *at the time* of the fight—that Richard Lewis passed in from the front as one of the deputation and must have been observed then, that he went through the back door, that it is asserted by several persons that he was *seen* standing by the side of the Inn for 15 or 20 minutes before the firing, and that Richard Lewis was not in the front street consequently during the struggle; that one of these persons, Nancy Evans, the wife of Evan Evans, a woman far advanced in pregnancy, appears to be an unexceptional evidence *quite in point* —that Abbott declares he did not know Richard Lewis *until* he saw him on that day, that he declares he cannot speak to his dress, that he said in the hearing of William Jones that he was within the passage—that the passage was much crowded— that other persons who knew Richard Lewis, some *equally well placed* for seeing—others, particularly those opposite and above, in the windows, *better*, who saw a man dressed in a drab frock stab a soldier in the thigh did not see Richard Lewis stab him—that no other soldier than Donald Black is represented to have been so stabbed, that a man dressed as he is said to have [?] who was seen to stab a soldier in the thigh *was shot near the spot*; that *Drew's evidence is shown by William Edwards to be ill calculated to support Abbott's*; that many lives have already been taken legally by the soldiers at the command of the Magistrate—and that no soldier or peaceable subject lost his life by the hand of the rioters—It is

submitted that there are grounds on which Mercy towards the
condemned prisoner Richard Lewis may availingly be asked.
I do therefore *humbly and respectfully*—and *earnestly* ask for
the extension of *that* benign prerogative of the British Throne
MERCY for this condemned British Subject, fully believing
also that its extension in this case will contribute to allay a
feeling of irritation, to restore order and maintain tranquility
—objects of the sincere desire and prayer of the Petitioner—
the King's loyal and affectionate subject,
Dated at Brecon the 5th day
of the 8th Mo (Aug') 1831

> Joseph T. Price of Neath Abbey,
> Glamorganshire

To this document Joseph Price received but Melbourne's
official acknowledgment. A now weakened Mr. Justice Bosanquet, however, received the following:

Mr. Justice Bosanquet   Whitehall
                                          9th August 1831
My Lord,
    I am directed by Viscount Melbourne to acknowledge re-
ceipt of your Lordship's letter of the 6th Inst. upon the case of
Richard Lewis, and to inform your Lordship that Lord Melbourne does not feel warranted in taking any course for further
suspending the Execution of the Law.

PS. I have to acknowledge the   I am Etc.
receipt of your letter of the 7th   (Signed) S. M. Phillipps
Inst, the Prisoner Lewis Lewis has
been removed.
(To transportation—*Au.*)

Author's note
The discovery of the lost Bosanquet letters, the Transcript of
Evidence, the three Petitions, the Morgan Petition and the
prison chaplain's refutation of it are no less important than
Tregelles Price's letters to 'Esteemed friends' in high places.
The find makes an important contribution to the personality

and character of Dic Penderyn who has lived in the history
and hearts of his countrymen for a century and a half. A little
more of the legend has now been stripped away and the bones
of irreducible truth exposed, and one fact is stronger now:
when the people of Merthyr ran James Abbott out of the town
they did it in the name of justice that has weathered the inter-
vening years. Was Ieuan Parker, who forty years later confessed to the crime, the man in the grey frock coat who was
seen to stab and run away? Certainly Richard Lewis and
Lewis Lewis were not related, this theory has been quite dis-
proved. The legend that Lewis Lewis was of noble birth now
seems much less likely; the claim that Dic was an unimportant
hostage who hid on Aberdare mountain is now rejected. Perhaps the finding of the trial record which, even as late as a
fortnight before Dic's execution the Lord Chancellor himself
had not seen—may throw further light ... unless it has been
conveniently lost ...? But one thing is sure: as Professor
Gwyn A. Williams said in his Cecil-Williams Memorial Lec-
ture in 1965, Dic Penderyn's last words—'O Arglwydd dyma
gamwedd!' (O Lord, what an iniquity!) have echoed louder
and longer than all the muskets of the Highlanders who mas-
sacred the Merthyr workers before the Castle Inn in June
1831.

Alexander Cordell

The newly found papers may be inspected at the Public
Record Office, Chancery Lane, London, W.C.2.

The permission of H.M. Controller of the Stationery Office
to reproduce the above Home Office material is acknowledged
with thanks.

ALEXANDER CORDELL

RAPE OF THE FAIR COUNTRY

Set in the grim valleys of the Welsh iron country, this turbulent, unforgettable novel begins the saga of the Mortymer family. A family of hard men and beautiful women, all forced into a bitter struggle with their harsh environment, as they slave and starve for the cruel English ironmasters.

But adversity could never still the free spirit of Wales, or quiet its soaring voice, and the Mortymers fight and sing and make love even as the iron foundries ravish their homeland and cripple their people.

'A tremendously lusty story . . . a splendid novel.'
Sunday Express

ALEXANDER CORDELL

THIS SWEET AND BITTER EARTH

The men of the North Wales slate quarries lived dangerous, unhealthy and underpaid lives; as a boy Toby Davies joined them. The quarries taught him precious truths about poverty and exploitation, but Toby also learned of love from the two beautiful women in his life – Bron and Nanwen O'Hara.

Toby came south, to work with coal, but found no easier future. He was there at the notorious Tonypandy riots of 1910 and the police occupation of the Rhondda, and would never forget the savagery of the battles between the men and the bosses.

HODDER AND STOUGHTON PAPERBACKS

MORE TITLES AVAILABLE FROM
HODDER AND STOUGHTON PAPERBACKS

ALEXANDER CORDELL

☐	20515 6	Rape of the Fair Country	£2.95
☐	23224 2	This Sweet and Bitter Earth	£4.50
☐	36650 8	Land of My Fathers	£4.50

R. F. DELDERFIELD

☐	25820 9	To Serve Them All My days	£4.50

MALCOLM MACDONALD

☐	42846 5	The Silver Highways	£3.50
☐	46749 1	The Sky with Diamonds	£4.50

NIGEL TRANTER

☐	49485 9	Rough Wooing	£3.50

All these books are available at your local bookshop or newsagent, or can be ordered direct from the publisher. Just tick the titles you want and fill in the form below.

Prices and availability subject to change without notice.

Hodder and Stoughton Paperbacks, P.O. Box 11, Falmouth, Cornwall.

Please send cheque or postal order, and allow the following for postage and packing:

U.K. – 55p for one book, plus 22p for the second book, and 14p for each additional book ordered up to a £1.75 maximum.

B.F.P.O. and EIRE – 55p for the first book, plus 22p for the second book, and 14p per copy for the next 7 books, 8p per book thereafter.

OTHER OVERSEAS CUSTOMERS – £1.00 for the first book, plus 25p per copy for each additional book.

Name ....

Address..

....